I0572775

This book is a sequel to "You Should've Kept Driving." If you haven't read the first book, please start there.

YOU SHOULD'VE STAYED HOME

by

M. A. Savino

Cover

by

Frina Art

You know what to expect if you read
You Should've Kept Driving.
You Should've Stayed Home will be equally
disturbing, taboo, trigger-filled and
unapologetically grotesque.
There will be teens and preteens mentioned in
this story with possible triggering content.
Reader discretion advised.

This is an NC-17 (formerly X) rated novel.
Reader discretion is advised.

Chapter One
Winter Wonderland

What the fuck have I done?

As if there weren't enough monsters in the world, I went ahead and created another one.

Technically, we are the heroes of this story—righting the wrongs of the sick and twisted fucks of society.

Although the recidivism rate for sex offenders is less than twenty percent overall, my tolerance for their existence is zero, and today is no different.

Ari's nails fold over, her jaw clenched with rage as we watch Eric Wallace pull a little blonde girl, wearing only a nightgown and pink bunny slippers, from his rust-riddled Chevy. This isn't his typical victim. He prefers teens—boys and girls.

A small amount of bile rises into my throat infuriating me.

"Odie, we—"

"I know." I cut Ari off.

We can't wait.

Our original plan was to sneak in, kill him, and leave, but this changes everything.

She changes everything.

"I'm going to rip that fucker's cock off and shove it up his ass." Ari stands and takes a step forward, nearly revealing our position.

I yank her down by her ivory puffer jacket and push her against the fallen oak concealing us. "What did I say?" My eyes pierce through hers making her recoil.

She scuffs the snow with her fur-lined boot, refusing to look at me. "To be patient."

I lift her chin, forcing her to make eye contact. A hint of disappointment shines in her glossy eyes, and frozen snot coats the inner rim of her nostrils. "To be patient and what?"

She flubs her lips and sighs. "Invisible."

"That's right." I release her and smile. "I told you I would let you have the lead, but first, we have to get Wallace away from her."

Her eyes light up as she sees the truth of my words. Until now, I've run the show, forcing Ari to stand by and watch—teaching her how to control her overwhelming urge for attention.

Undoing years of attention-seeking behavior will not be easy, but if she is to take over my legacy one day, I have to follow through.

Mr. Wallace has been out of jail for less than two weeks—out on a technicality and has already grabbed another victim.

My phone vibrates in my snow pants. I remove the disposable device and flip it open as Wallace half drags and half lifts the little girl up the steps.

"Who is it?" Ari peers over the phone as I flip it closed.

"Eve. She wanted to make sure we found the place." I tuck the phone back in my pocket and zip it closed.

Eve is one of us. A victim once tortured beneath the ground in a bunker run by two sex-trafficking brothers, Benny and Griffin.

They're gone now. I made sure of it. The remnants of their bodies reduced to nothing more than a few bones and teeth—barely enough to identify them thanks to the concoction Ari mixed up and tossed in the bunker oven.

Leah, Eve's twin sister, never recovered from her time in the bunker. Despite putting on a strong face and appearing to be doing well, she took her own life, devastating not just Eve, but all of us—leaving an unfillable hole in our hearts.

I know that feeling all too well.

Leah's funeral fell on the first official day of summer, less than a month after we escaped from the bunker. Ari and I watched from afar, not wanting anyone to see us, not wanting the plain-clothed FBI agents to see us.

They never talked. None of the girls did. We all had an unspoken agreement—a pact of sorts.

The authorities never knew how many captive women were in the bunker, and they never will. The only reason they knew about Eve and Leah is because Leah left a suicide note, citing her time in the bunker as the reason, but not revealing names. A neighbor found the note and Leah when she stopped by to drop off misdelivered mail.

Eve gave them just enough information for them to stop asking her questions, but not enough to stop them from continuing their investigation. So, they linger— outside her house, at the funeral, and wherever Eve goes, waiting for the answers to fall into their laps.

A few months later, Eve contacted Ari using a disposable phone that Ari had dropped in her open tote bag with a note at a nearby coffee shop.

A risky move I reprimanded her for.

Not wanting her sister's death to be in vain, Eve began working at a courthouse part-time in the records department. The job is beneath her, but she did it for us…all of us. The actions of Benny and Griffin changed who we are and what we allowed.

Well, not me, I've always been different—always been a killer.

But the women held captive in the bunker, tortured and broken down by those despicable brothers, are mere shells of their former selves—drained of who they once were, and now filled with hatred, feminine rage, and the overwhelming urge for payback. No longer following the expectations of society, we have created our own set of rules, and rule number one is the most important of them all.

Don't fuck with children.

Ari flops sideways beside me and rubs her backside. "I can't feel my ass."

I roll my eyes. "I told you to put long johns under your pants."

Her lips part to respond, but a blood-curdling scream interrupts her.

Our eyes widen and dart to the sound.

Wallace is rolling across the floor of the porch holding his balls. The little girl takes a few steps away unsure of what to do next. Her face twists, uncertain and confused by the unfamiliar surroundings. Trees and snow blanket the landscape camouflaging the trails and driveway—landmarks for escape. She leaps from the porch and sprints between two trees spaced far apart, running for her life.

Running from him.

Wallace grabs the porch railing and pulls himself to a stand. He takes a few shallow breaths and steps forward.

His leg disappears through a rotten spot on his dilapidated porch. "Mother fucker."

I smile.

Karma's a bitch.

He grunts and wrenches his trapped limb, breaking it free with a violent yank, and limps after the girl.

Ari glances at me. "Now?"

A sinister smile spreads across my face. I remove the hunting knife from my hip and place it in her hand, handle first. "Now."

She leaps over the fallen trunk without hesitation and takes off after Wallace.

I hustle to the cabin to check for accomplices. My snow pants swoosh with every stride I take. When I reach the stairs, the little girl's screaming stops my heart.

Something's wrong.

Large heavy flakes drop gracefully from the sky, obscuring my view as I quickly track Ari, the little girl, and Wallace's footprints in the snow.

Audible growling, undiscernible words, and crying lead me to a clearing.

I creep slowly toward the edge of what appears to be a drop-off, pinching my eyes closed—listening intently.

"Fucking bastard!" Ari shrieks.

My eyes spring open at the sound of her voice, and I peer over the edge.

What I thought could be a cliff is nothing more than a steep hill with a small platform at its top. Ari and Wallace are on the edge.

Wallace's eyes widen with every strike from Ari's blade. The fight in him is gone, and he can no longer lift his arms. Blood gurgles from his partial mouth, a previous strike tearing it open. It drains from his right shoulder, knee, and bootless foot.

Head, shoulders, knees and toes, knees and toes.

The song filters into my head like an annoying white noise.

Wallace's boot is nowhere to be found—the snow camouflaging it beneath its rising depth.

She stabs Wallace's eyes, then slices off each of his ears and chucks them over her shoulder.

Blood spatters here, there, and everywhere like a morbid Dr. Seuss book.

Eyes and ears and...

Fuck.

She grips his already torn lips and nose between her fingers, pulls them slightly away from his face, and slices them off in one swipe—peeling them away like the skin of a potato with an annoying and hideous flaw too unsightly to consume while hollering at his immobile frame.

I stand before her—her eyes empty and unaware of my presence.

Mouth and nose…

God dammit.

I approach her slowly. The little girl holds her knees in the wet landscape a few feet away, flinching with every downward strike of the blade into Wallace's body. I gesture for her to get behind me with my hand, but she shakes her head.

Afraid to move.

Afraid of Ari.

Interesting.

With every stab of the knife, I thought Ari would stop, realizing Wallace is dead.

But she doesn't stop.

She can't.

I know that feeling. Rage flows through you like water recently released from a dam.

Before my sister's murder, she was always there to stop me; now I need to be that person for Ari.

Blood soaks the entire ground around them, staining the snow with its warm crimson, and melting it to the grass. It dangles and freezes on multiple locks of Ari's hair. I place my hand on her shoulder right as the blade slices off Wallace's big toe.

She won't look at me. Tears cascade over her lids and freeze on her face within seconds.

"Ari?" I shake her delicately, just enough for her to detach her eyes from Wallace's non-existent and pulverized face. She snarls at me, and I can tell she doesn't *see* me.

She sees him.

Her arm raises, knife still in hand, ready to plunge it into Wallace's hole-riddled body.

I bend forward, grab her wrist, slam it into Wallace's torso, and speak sharply. "Ari, that's enough."

She blinks several times and her bottom lip quivers, her eyes finally seeing into mine. "I…I…I'm sorry. I saw red."

I nod my head and state the obvious. "Well, we are kind of surrounded by it now, aren't we?"

She grimaces. "That's not what I meant."

I laugh and stand taller. "I know what you meant."

The snow crunches to our left, and Ari and I snap our heads in that direction.

My body tenses as the little girl wraps her arms around my waist and hugs me.

I don't hug her back.

I can't.

So, I do the only thing I can and pat her back like a mother burping her child. "You're safe now."

Ari picks up the big toe and sticks it in her jacket pocket before standing. The little girl lets go of me and hides behind my back as she approaches us.

What a strange twist of events.

I don't think she would be so trusting if she knew who I was—what I was.

The snow's falling faster, and the howling wind blows additional flakes into the air around us, cutting visibility in half.

I reach behind me, grab the little girl's nightgown, and pull her to my side. "Stay close."

We climb up to the clearing, and Ari stops moving, her face going as blank as the snow.

Here we go again.

I asked her once what she sees inside her head when her mind goes blank. She shrugged her shoulders and said, '*Nothing.*'

Dark and empty, just like I imagined it would be.

Ari's eyes flicker and stare at the little girl. "I won't hurt you."

Her brain finally catching up to the dire situation.

The girl shivers and squeezes my waist. I hold my hands, palms down out to my sides, not wanting to engage. A smile creeps across Ari's face.

She's enjoying my discomfort.

Ari dives face-first in front of us, flops on her back, and proceeds to make a snow angel. The little girl giggles as Ari starts singing about how *everybody farts* and proceeds to let one loose.

Jesus Christ.

The girl doesn't let me go, unsure of what to make of Ari.

Don't worry kid, no one knows what to make of her.

I roll my eyes and tower over her—my shadow darkening her face—the little girl still attached to me like a relentless parasite. "Are you about done?"

Ari glances at the little girl and then at me. "Wallace's mine to dispose of, right?" She sits up on her elbows and shields the setting sun that shines over my shoulder.

"I gave you my word. Although I have a feeling I am going to regret it." I cross my arms and gaze down at the snow-covered road at the bottom of the hill. "We'll meet you at the bottom."

I peel the girl's arms off me and pat her shoulder. "Time to go."

We leave Ari to dispose of Wallace's remains. The snow bites into the girl's bare arms, reddening it more with every step we take. She trembles at my side, holding herself as she plods through the freezing snow—slippers white with sticky flakes.

At this rate, we'll freeze to death before we get to the fucking SUV.

I stop and stare at her. *I'm not doing this for her*, I tell myself. *I'm doing this for me.*

I remove my mittens and kneel before the little girl. "Lift your foot."

She lifts it slightly. I remove her worthless slippers and slide my mittens onto her feet, one, then the other.

Her voice comes out barely above a whisper, meek and soft. "Thank you."

I unzip my coat, wrap it around her, zip it up to her neck, and cover her head with the hood.

It's way too big—her hands stopping about eight inches before the end of the sleeves. She flops her hands up and down and gazes up at me with a smile, her face barely visible beneath the oversized hood.

Wallace never had a chance to hurt her. Her eyes still hold their innocence, and her heart remains intact.

"Won't you be cold?" Her head moves up and down as she scans my barely covered frame with a wrinkled face and grabs my hand.

"No." I slide my hand out of hers and push a pine branch out of our way. "My vehicle is this way."

The girl stops abruptly and furrows her brow. "What about the others?" she asks firmly after several seconds of silence.

I tilt my head at her. "What others?"

Chapter Two
Under the Floor

I step hesitantly on the cabin porch—the soft, rotting wood bending under my feet.

The girl won't follow.

Ari stops beside me and swallows hard. "How many did she say were inside?"

"She's not sure. Wallace just said she would be, 'easier to handle' than the older girls in his *collection beneath the floor*." I glance over my shoulder at the girl. "Did you find out her name?"

"Yes." Ari puts her hand on the door handle and pushes it open.

She takes a step inside the cool and smoky-scented space, and I follow. "Are you going to fucking tell me or is it a surprise?" I furrow my brow and stand beside her, glaring at her polka-dotted, blood-splattered face.

Her lip curls at something on the floor by the wall. A pair of white briefs lie beside a hamper, a brown stain discoloring the ass of them. "Fucking disgusting." Ari covers her mouth.

The large amount of clutter makes the cabin feel smaller. Flies move from one open can of food on the counter to another and partially eaten meals crust to the surface of every plate in the sink. Maggots wiggle around the rim of an overloaded trash can near the back exit. To our left, a full-size bed, with no sheets or blankets on it, sits in the center of the bedroom. Handcuffs dangle from the four corners of the iron head and footboards.

My stomach tenses as the memory of being held captive spread eagle on the gas chamber room bed, right before Griffin pulled the pin on the tear gas canister, comes flooding back. And for a moment, though brief, I can't breathe.

Ari elbows me. "You, okay?"

I nod, but don't reply—pushing the past back where it belongs, buried in the dark side of my mind.

The old wood boards creak beneath my foot when I take a step forward.

Ari swings her arm across my chest, stopping me from moving, and nods to the floor.

Hinges peek under an oval multicolored braided rug sitting at the base of a crooked, mauve recliner with a stained and worn seat. To the left of the chair, a vintage two-knob radio sits on a small stand, holding a partial glass of water smudged with fingerprints. I approach the crawlspace door slowly. My knees crack as I crouch and toss the tattered floor covering away.

Two trap doors, side by side, hide beneath the dated rug. Heavy breathing and whimpering come from inside, but no one speaks.

More victims.

Old newspapers and pornographic magazines litter nearly every surface. The small television on the counter is missing one of its two dials, and a set of vice grips dangle in its place. A piece of aluminum shines at the top of one of its antennas. In the center of the room, wood sits beside a cast iron potbelly stove providing minimal warmth.

Ari picks up a piece of timber and tosses it inside. Hot embers float into the room and fall silently to the floor.

The floor doors each have a padlock on them.

I flick them upward with my fingers and look at Ari. "We need to find the keys or something to break the locks with."

"The man has them in his pocket," a little voice says behind us, causing Ari and I to jump. "When we got out of the truck, he almost forgot them. He shook them in my face and said, 'I can't forget these, and stuck them in his pocket." She holds her hands in front of her and wiggles imaginary keys.

I glance at Ari. "Go get the keys."

She nods and heads for the door. The little girl follows her outside.

The girl talks like she's older than her size. To me, she looks like a kindergartener, but I am willing to bet she's in at least second or third grade, making her around seven or eight.

Perhaps her parents are short.

Coughing draws my attention to the underground enclosures.

I lean my head forward, closer to the floor. "We're going to get you out."

No one answers.

I get it. I wouldn't answer either. Who knows what they've been through?

Rescuing kids isn't our usual job. We go after and eliminate traffickers of women. But when Eve shared Wallace's case file with us, my stomach knotted, and the images made my heart pound.

When the police raided Wallace's house after a local teenage girl went missing, what they found inside nearly destroyed them. In each of his bedrooms, Wallace had a teenager shackled, spread eagle to the bed. There were two girls and one boy, all emaciated and naked. Their punishment for lack of compliance was holding back food. And judging by the state of the teens when found, they defied him many, many times. The local teen was not inside the home and is still missing.

What the captive teens told the detective on the case from their hospital beds had him vomiting in the garbage can outside their rooms.

Blood-coated keys land on the floor by my hand. "It took me a minute to get them out of his pocket. He's one of those weird people who use the tiny front pocket of their jeans to store things," Ari says rolling her eyes.

I scoop up the keyring holding only two keys, one for Wallace's truck and one for the padlocks, both sticky with drying blood. I insert the padlock key and heave the hatch open.

The foul odor overwhelms my sinuses, and I leap away from the hole, landing on my ass. Ari covers her nose and heads for the exit, taking the little girl outside with her. The stench, putrid and familiar, fills the room quickly.

Dead body.

A rotting corpse has a very distinct scent to it. One that, once you get a whiff of it, you will never forget.

I wait nearly a minute for someone to emerge from the crawlspace beneath the cabin, but it doesn't happen.

I crawl to the opening and peer into the darkness. "Hello?"

Whimpering comes from the orifice, but no one dares to leave the floor.

"Why won't they come out?" Ari asks, standing in the doorway, hand still covering her nose.

"Wallace. He must have tested them." I shake my head and sigh heavily. "He likely opened the hatch, much like we just did, and when one of them tried to escape, he hurt them."

"Well, they can't just stay down there." Ari crosses the room and paces back and forth in front of the hole.

"Hello, down there." She leans over the opening. "My name is Ari, and this is Odie. We came to rescue you."

There is no movement or response.

I shake my head. "That's not going to work."

She frowns and tries again. "Wallace is dead. He can't hurt you anymore. I killed that motherfucker."

"Ari!" I say abruptly, making her take a step back.

"What?" She raises her hands and shrugs her shoulders. "I thought it would make them more comfortable with leaving if they knew Wallace couldn't hurt them anymore."

"So, you thought telling them you murdered him would be more convincing?" I tilt my head and give her a death stare.

She places her hands on her hips, twisting her waist from side to side, and grimaces. "Well, I guess not when you say it like that."

I stand, bring an old wooden chair with a woven seat in front of the hole, and sit down. Ari grabs the second one by the table and drags it over. It bounces off the uneven flooring and drops noisily beside me.

"No. Go get water from the trunk and any snacks you didn't eat on our way here."

She furrows her brow. "But the water will be frozen."

I point to the stove and the empty pot hanging beside it. "I'll start boiling some water to set them in so they can melt faster."

Busy work. That's all this is. I need her to do something besides stand beside me and say the wrong things.

"Take the little girl with you," I say over my shoulder as Ari heads for the door.

"I'm not a little girl. I'm going to be eight." The kid crosses her arms in the doorway and crinkles her face.

I smile and nod. "Well, not a little girl who's almost eight, I'm going to need you to go with Ari and help her bring some stuff back for the kids under the floor. Can you do that?"

"Of course I can. I'm not a baby." She turns on her heels, tosses her hair aside, and stomps confidently off the porch.

"Boy, someone has certainly gained some confidence and vigor since we got here." Ari chuckles and steps towards the door.

"It's a facade, Ari. She's dissociating to protect herself."

Ari's face drops. "Like trauma blocking?"

"Something like that. Now go."

She steps into the doorway of the cabin and glances back at me. "My dad locked me in the basement once for an entire day. I thought I was going to starve to death. I can't imagine how they are feeling."

"What did you do?" I stand, place the pot of water on the stove, and sit back down.

Ari smiles broadly. "I stuck a firecracker in his gas tank—almost blew myself up. Thank God, I had a long fuse."

A stifled laugh comes from beneath the floor, and I smile at Ari. "Get going." I shoo her away with my hands.

After she is out of sight, I focus on the task. How do I get them to trust me?

The only thing I come up with is to tell them something true just like Ari did.

"I can't feel pain," I blurt. "It's my superpower. You probably think it's cool, but not feeling physical pain isn't all it's cracked up to be. People with my condition usually don't live longer than a few years. There are a few rare cases, such as mine, when people live into their twenties, where I am now. I could die tomorrow or ten years from now, who knows? But with the time I do have, I've vowed to save people like you. That's how Ari, the other woman with me, and I met. You see, the man who kidnapped her and held her and many others captive is the same man who dated and murdered my sister several years ago."

Quiet crying starts inside the left hole.

"Amelia was my everything. I still remember the day she realized I wasn't afraid to hurt anyone for her, and not just myself, regardless of the consequences." I smile to myself thinking back on the memory.

"I was only nine years old when we heard the ice cream man's distinctive bell coming down the street. We skipped across the road, and each got the same thing, a chocolate twist with rainbow sprinkles. On our way back across the street, a car sped right towards us. I could see the person monkeying around with his phone behind the wheel. He slammed on his brakes at the last second and screamed at us—screamed at my sister. He startled her so badly that her ice cream flew up in the air and landed on the man's luxury hood. And instead of getting out of the car and asking if she was okay—if we were okay, he gets out of the car with a cloth, stuffs it in my sister's hand, and orders that she clean his hood."

Two distinct voices whisper inside the right hole and one of them speaks. "What did you do?" A shaky teen boy's voice asks from the still-locked right hatch.

I grin broadly. "I kicked the guy in the balls."

Grunting comes from the boy below, feeling the man's pain without experiencing it.

"And after he was down on the ground writhing in pain, I kept kicking him anywhere he was vulnerable— chest, head, face. I couldn't stop. The thought of what could have happened to my sister was all that I could think about. Amelia grabbed me around the waist and pulled me away from the man. He was no longer moving, and blood coated his face. I had kicked him so hard and so many times he was placed on a ventilator until the swelling in his brain went down. After that day, my sister made me swear, forced me to swear that I would never do that again—never hurt anyone like that again, regardless of the situation. So, I kept my promise to her. Held back for her. Didn't react for her." I wipe a tear off my cheek.

"And because I promised her, I didn't react when I saw the signs her boyfriend was abusing her years later. I didn't stop him—couldn't stop him without breaking my word to her. She died because I didn't save her. My promise to her was too important."

I'm suddenly at a loss for words. The memory of the day I lost my sister fills me with rage. Griffin pulled the trigger, but he wasn't the only one at fault. Like many bystanders who stand by and allow someone to die for fear of being sued or becoming a victim themselves, I am just as guilty of watching without acting—waiting for someone else to save her, but no one did.

My ears ring louder and louder until I hear nothing else.

The water boils noisily behind me, pulling me away from my dark thoughts and back into the room. It overflows onto the top of the stove and sizzles.

"So, why did I tell you this story?" I stand and remove the pot from the stove and set it on a trivet in the center of the table.

I didn't notice before, but Ari and the kid had returned and were standing by the door leaning against its frame. Both of their eyes are wet with tears. Ari wipes her face, brings four bottles of water to the table, and sets two inside the pot.

I return to the opening and let my legs fall over the edge of the left side, preparing to drop into the pit of darkness.

"Don't go down there," Ari says, crossing the room and gripping my shoulder.

I slide her hand off me. "I have to."

My feet crunch into the partially frozen soil when I drop into the space. I thought the hole would be deeper, but my breasts up to my head are still above the floor.

I drop to my knees and peer through the darkness. "I'm telling you this, so you know that what I am about to tell you is the truth." I wait for my eyes to adjust to the darkness. A small amount of moonlight seeps through the wooden slats surrounding the perimeter beneath the cabin allowing me to see nothing more than a few shifting silhouettes. A wooden divider on my right separates one side of the confined space from the other. I move forward. My knees slowly sink into the mud as the earth becomes warmer beneath them. A shadowy figure sniffles in the dark only a few feet in front of me. A tiny orange light shines on the ground and the blades of a space heater flick with every rotation like the joker card in the spokes of a bicycle wheel. Behind the person in front of me, I see at least two more moving shadows. One of them is whimpering.

I shuffle a little closer, my hands in front of me, and sit back on my heels.

They have no reason to trust me. I am a stranger, and a stranger is who did this to them. But I need to get them out of the floor.

"I know you don't know me, and have no reason to believe what I'm about to say, but I need you to. If you go up there..." I point to the underside of the cabin floor. "...I promise you; no one will hurt you. I promise you;

we are here to help, and I promise you, tonight you will see your families again."

A dirt-covered pale teen steps into the enlightened space I'm crouching in. I rest my hands on my thighs, not wanting to make any sudden movements that may scare her back into the darkness. The scent of unwashed armpits and urine stale the air between us.

She flinches when I slowly lift my hand. "It's okay." I smile softly at her, grasp a lock of tangled hair dangling in front of her blue eyes, and curl it around her ear. "What's your name?"

"Erika," she murmurs.

Her weak and shaking arm is barely strong enough to accept my hand when I offer it to her. I have her come up beside me, and we crawl together to the space beneath the hole in the floor, burping trapped air from the mud as we go.

I stand up and scan the room for Ari.

She comes out of a small room off to the side, blood still dotting her face. "I had to pee."

I look behind her. "Where's the kid?"

Ari points over her shoulder with her thumb. "She's going now."

"When she's done, go back in and clean the blood from your face."

I lift my body with my arms, sit on the floor at the edge of the opening, and reach my hand to the teen inside. "Come on."

She peeks above the floor and looks around the room. Her fingers whiten as she grips the wood in front of her face. "Who's that?" The teen points to the kid standing in the bathroom doorway.

"That is someone Wallace never had a chance to hurt—never had a chance to put under the floor."

I place the strap of her torn cami back on her shoulder, and she shifts her body away from me. The underwear she's wearing is torn at the seam.

"Is he really dead?" she asks without looking at me.

"Very."

Ari slides around the kid and moves closer to us. "I'm Ari. Odie helped save me once like we are saving you now. It's what we do." She puts her hands on her hips, stands tall, and stares off into the unknown. "We are heroes," she announces with a serious, unsmiling face.

The girl stares at the stains on Ari's jacket.

Ari pulls it away from her body. "Oh, don't worry. It's not mine." She unzips the jacket and tosses it onto an old, overloaded, freestanding bookshelf that immediately crashes to the floor.

I cover my eyes, shake my head, and hoist myself to a stand. "For the love of God Ari, be careful."

"It wasn't on purpose," she says reaching around me and offering her hand to the teen in the floor. "It's safe out here. I promise."

The teen struggles to gain enough strength to pull herself out of the floor. Her dirt-smudged arms shake with every attempt. We grab her under each of her armpits and lift her frail, thin frame together. She collapses on the braided rug, closes her sunken eyes, and tightens her arms around her brush-burned knees— curling her body into a protective ball.

The kid brings partially melted water to the teen and sets it down while Ari unlocks the second hatch.

A head pops up at once and Ari jumps back. "Holy shit. You sprung from that hole like a game of whack-a-mole—scared the shit right out of me."

The teenage boy climbs to the surface and helps the next boy out. They aren't as hesitant and scared as the girls are to come to the surface, but none of them are smiling. They wear even fewer clothes than the girl I just pulled out of the floor and mud covers nearly every inch of them. Black circles darken the perimeter of their eyes and sink deep inside their skulls. Each boy wears only the underwear they were most likely kidnapped in. Cuts and bruises dot their arms and legs.

There are three of them—two with brown hair, one with blonde. They accept a bottle of water from Ari and stay huddled together.

Safety in numbers.

I turn to the teen lying on the rug. "How many more of you are down there?"

The teen sips some of the water and wipes her dry, shriveled lips. "Three." A tear glimmers in the corner of her eye. "I mean two. Tara is dead. That man starved her to death. He said we needed a lesson. We tried to sneak her food, but when he caught us, he didn't feed us for days."

"It's not your fault." Ari opens a box of apple breakfast bars and passes one to each of the boys and the girl on the rug.

The others haven't come out yet.

I glance at the only framed photo on the wall.

It's a picture of a little boy holding a shotgun. His father with a tight grip on the back of the boy's neck, and his mother holds the hem of her sleeve beside them. On the ground by their feet lies a fawn.

Wallace's first kill?

Wallace lives in Winchester, Virginia, but the cabin his family has owned for years is in the southern region of the Poconos. Wallace's case made national news, and he couldn't go home. So, he hid here, three hours north, where he thought he was safe.

But no one is safe from us.

I drop back inside the confined space on the left, where the remaining girls still hide. Ari passes me a bottle of water and two breakfast bars. I place them on the moist ground in front of me. "I'm going to leave these here. Come out when you're ready."

The girls don't reply. I stand when I reach the opening in the floor. Ari extends her hand to me and helps me back to the surface.

One of the boys steps away from the others. "Are the police on their way?"

When I reach into my pants pocket, the boy takes several quick steps back.

I remove the spare disposable phone we keep for emergencies and place it on the table behind me. "There are minutes on it already. Out the door to the right, you'll see a large fallen tree with a massive trunk. There is service there. All we ask for is a head start."

"You're not staying with us?" The teenage girl glances at Ari and lifts herself to a shaky stand.

"We don't have enough room in the car. Plus, we can't be here when the police arrive. They'll wonder how we found you." Ari scoops her winter coat from the floor.

The teenage boy steps forward. "And how did you find us?" He looks from Ari to me.

"We know people who work in the justice system. I told you; this is what we do." I walk to the cabin door and turn around. "It's your job now to keep them safe until help arrives. We will wait by the bottom of the hill until the police drive by." I nod to the wall clock. "The time is wrong, but it still works. In fifteen minutes, make the call."

The boys stare at the girl and eat their food quietly as we exit the cabin.

Ari stomps through the snow behind me as we make our way down the steep, long driveway back to the SUV.

"But what about Wallace? You said you'd wait for me at the bottom of the hill, and I could do what I want with him."

I stop abruptly, and she slides into me. "So, what are you following me for?"

She smiles broadly and heads in the direction of the cabin.

I call to her. "Where are you going? Wallace is that way." I point through the forest to her right.

"To get something from behind the cabin," she shouts over her shoulder.

I roll my eyes and continue down the hill. The trees crack and squeak under the weight of the wet snow coating their limbs.

The SUV has a layer of fresh snow on the windshield and windows when I reach it. I brush it off with my arm. The door handle cracks, dropping fragments of ice on the ground when I open it. Snow floats through the door when it creaks open and drops silently on my seat.

Fantastic. Now when it melts my ass will be wet.

I steer the SUV down the road until I see the steep hill with Ari standing at the top.

"Odie," she screams from the top, shaking a sled over her head. "We're coming down."

We? I must have misheard her. My window groans but doesn't budge. I crank the heater on high and direct the vent towards the window, pounding the top and bottom edges gently before trying again. It scrapes down slowly, crackling and moaning as it goes. I squint through the flakes and the kid waves at me from Ari's side.

God dammit.

They disappear, and I stare through the windshield, grinding my teeth. My heavy breaths fog the glass as I wait impatiently. Several minutes go by, and I consider leaving them both.

For the love of God, what is taking so long?

Movement in the corner of my eye catches my attention. The tip of a sled peeks over the edge of the hilltop.

Finally.

Ari slides over the edge, with the kid sitting between her legs, and waves at me with Wallace's severed arm as they barrel down the hill heading straight for me.

I chuckle to myself.

It's clear to me now that Ari was born with this dark humor inside her all along, drawn out into the open after Griffin and Benny tortured her in the bowels of the bunker.

Perhaps this is why I allowed her to come with me the day I left without her, and she ran me off the road.

Not only because she makes me laugh, but because her knowledge of explosives far exceeds mine, much like my ability to filet a quadricep and cook it to tender perfection with vegetables and olive oil exceeds hers.

"Oh, shit!" Ari shouts when she realizes they are seconds away from slamming into the side of the SUV.

She cranks the sled to the left, tipping it over, and she, the kid, and multiple body parts tumble into the snow.

I storm over to her. "Ari, what the fuck are you doing? We can't bring her and these body parts with us."

She spits out a mouthful of snow and smacks a wayward lock of hair away from her face. "But I thought we could take an order to go?"

"An order of what? Aged skin? Wallace barely had any muscle on his body." I pick up the severed arm and strike her in her dumb head with it. "Look at his bicep. It's skin and bone. There's no meat on it."

The kid sits beside Ari, her face twisted with a confused look. "Meat for what?"

"Just get in." I open the SUV's back passenger door, flicking Wallace's arm into the snow behind me like a baseball player who just struck out.

The kid hesitates and then climbs inside beside my red igloo cooler. I stiff-arm Ari in the chest when she reaches for the front passenger door handle. "When we get to the next town, we are dropping her off. Got it?"

She fiddles with something in her blood-stained jacket pocket. "Fine, you don't have to get so angry about it."

"Angry?" I ball my fists and gaze up at the blackening sky. "What have I told you about picking up strays?"

"Not to." She yanks her hand out of her pocket and rolls Wallace's big toe between her fingers. "But I was a stray once, and besides, she wanted to come. She said she feels safer with you."

Safer with me.

Sirens blare in the distance.

The police are coming so there's no more time to argue with her.

I sear a hole in her face with my eyes. "Get rid of that fucking toe and get in. It's not a rabbit's foot for God's sake."

She throws it over the SUV and slides in her seat. I sigh heavily and flop behind the wheel.

The kid clears her gritty throat behind Ari. "I'm thirsty."

Ari passes a partially frozen, half-full, bottle of water back to her as I shift into drive.

"Got any food?" She places her hand on the cooler.

Ari stares through the windshield and doesn't answer. Her mind floating away with the drifting snow, leaving me to answer the kid's question. "Not in there. I'll drop you off at a gas station when I find one and give you money for food."

The uneven road bounces us back and forth as we trudge through the heavy snow and make our way back to the highway. The kid leans her head against the window, staying silent for most of the ride.

She hasn't asked where we are going or mentioned wanting to go home.

How odd.

"What's your name?" I ask her reflection in the rearview mirror.

She glances at me, then looks away from my inquiring green eyes and stares out her window. "Amelia," she whispers.

Chapter Three
Twitch

I slam on the brakes, locking them up. We fishtail and slide sideways into a used car lot at the intersection of the highway and the road we were just on. A fluorescent bulb flickers inside an old phone booth to the right of the dealership's front door.

Ari doesn't move. She hasn't taken a single breath in the last thirty seconds.

The pounding in my head quickly escalates into a hammering rage.

I clench my jaw. "Out," I growl at Ari.

She pivots her head slowly and swallows hard. "Why?"

"I said, get out!" I scream at her. "Both of you."

Ari's face drains of color and her eyes widen with fear. "But, Odie, I thought it was a sign like she was meant to come with us."

I fumble with my door handle and whip it open.

Amelia leaps from the SUV and backs away from it quickly. The eyes of the devil have taken the place of mine and rage boils through my veins like hot lava rushing to my head and prickling its way across my scalp.

I yank Ari's door open. "What you have done has led us here to this place." I point behind me at the dealership. "What you have done, has given me a reason—a sign of my own."

"A reason for what?" Ari's voice barely carries above a whisper.

I point to the flashing message sign at the edge of the road pointing to the car lot.

Ari's mouth moves as she reads without speaking.

'Need a vacation from your life? Is the family getting on your nerves? We offer car rentals for cheap.'

I grab her by the jacket and pull her from the vehicle. She stumbles over her own two feet, slips, and lands harshly on the icy gravel. "Ouch."

"She's not a sign." I slide my fingers behind the flexible letters on the roadside advertisement and flick them out of their channels, striking Ari in the leg with one. "That's a fucking *sign*." I lean into the SUV and rummage around the center console.

Amelia backs further away from us, unsure of what is happening. Ari sits on her butt and crosses her legs. "You consider me family?" She smiles sheepishly.

I toss quarters in the air above her. She doesn't attempt to shield her head from the falling coins.

Family.

She's crazy. I have no family. They're all dead.

What the fuck was she thinking? Allowing the kid to come along because her name is the same as my sister's?

Not only that, but part of our agreement was there would be no secrets, no half-truths, and no holding back information that may be relevant.

Allowing a kid with the same name as my sister to come with us is not only irrelevant, it's irresponsible.

I already lost one Amelia, and that was enough for me.

Ari's mouth drops open—the sudden realization of what's happening finally catching up to her.

She leaps to her feet. "You're leaving me here?"

"Not just you." I back away from her and slam the passenger doors, front and back, closed.

She follows me around to the driver's side. "Odie, I'm sorry."

"Are you?" I climb into the driver's seat, shut the door, and lock myself in.

The snow starts falling again, lighter, and fluffier this time. I put the SUV in drive and Ari pounds on the window. "Odie, please don't leave me. I don't want to be alone."

The window crackles and groans down, fighting against the cold like we all are. I nod to the kid. "You're not alone."

Ari sets her glossy and watering eyes on mine. "But you're my best friend."

I look away from her and glare through the windshield. "I have no friends—no family. I am alone, and I like it that way."

Her grip releases from the window frame and her face drops at my harsh words. The wheels spin when I slam my foot on the gas, then grab the frozen lot, and I turn onto the highway, leaving them behind.

* * *

Silence can be so loud. I still hear her chattering in the seat beside me, despite it being empty.

The disposable phone vibrates in my pocket.

I flip it open. "*Hello?*"

"*I'm cold.*" Ari's teeth chatter on the other end of the line.

For a moment, I feel bad.

A very brief moment.

"Call someone who cares." I roll the window down and chuck the phone over the railing of the Morea Road Bridge.

Winter is my favorite season—beautiful, quiet, and an opportunity to use the great outdoors as extra space for meat that won't fit in my freezer. How I wish I could be home now. It's the perfect day for a delicious, slow-cooked stew.

Mmm…stew.

I've been through this tiny town in Pennsylvania many times in my back-and-forth commute from New York City to Roanoke. Just off Interstate 81, Frackville is home to one of my favorite bars. It's the only place that makes a rare burger the right way.

Still mooing.

The town is just over three thousand people, and the bartender and I are on a first-name basis.

I steer into the parking lot, shift into park, and climb over the seats to the back of the SUV. Going into a bar muddy and half-dressed is not how the people who frequent here usually see me.

Thank God for tinted back windows or someone would have just got a view of a whole lot of ass. After using disposable wipes to clean the mud from the crawlspace off me, I shimmy into my black knee-length, long-sleeved pencil skirt and suit jacket set, brush my hair, and twist it up into a bun. I spray a floral perfume onto my neck and slip my bare, pale feet into my heels, ignoring the light blisters of my cold-damaged toes that dot the surface of my skin. I step out of the vehicle and immediately notice my shoes feel tighter than usual. They squeeze the sides of my feet, creating an annoying pressure with every step I take.

Frostbite.

The negative part of my favorite season.

I step inside the bar and as usual, everyone turns their head and stares at me. A lot of the bar patrons are travelers commuting from one major city to the next.

Strangers.

Locals give me a passing nod as I head for my favorite table in the corner close to the back exit. They've seen me many times before. But the businessmen, truckers, and vacationers gawk as though they've never seen a black-haired beauty with green eyes, and a body to die for, out in the wild.

One traveler, a tall, well-built man, in a blue dress shirt, eyes me from his place at the bar. A few locks of his strawberry blonde hair that aren't tied back in a tight bun, hang around his face drawing attention to his pale grey eyes. A cream-colored jacket rests on the back of the chair beside him.

Rusty, the bartender, smirks at him when he sees the businessman watching me. "I wouldn't. She's meaner than she looks." The man smiles and Rusty finishes drying a glass before asking me, "Your usual?"

I rest my elbows on the laminated table, press my fingers together in front of my face, and give him a subtle nod.

He shouts my order through the passthrough window leading to the kitchen, grabs bourbon from the top shelf, drops one ice cube into a balloon glass, and pours the amber fluid over it.

The businessman grabs Rusty's arm. "I'll take it to her. No need to come out from behind the bar."

Rusty glances in my direction, and I nod, permitting him to let the man deliver my drink.

He keeps his eyes on mine as he waltzes confidently to my table. "I see you're sitting alone. I am as well. May I join you?"

I half expected him to sit down without asking—invite himself regardless of what I thought. But he used his manners, so I reward him with a smile and gesture for him to sit across from me.

He slides my beverage slowly across the table to me with one finger, keeping his eyes locked with mine. I bring my hands against my mouth, brush my fingers lightly across my lips, and lick them seductively from top to bottom, before slowly dropping my hands on either side of my glass.

I lift the bourbon to my mouth, fogging the inside of the glass with my breath, and toss the contents down my throat. The glass clanks hard against the table surface. The man didn't startle like I thought he would.

He stands and adjusts the front of his pants. "Excuse me."

His ass reminds me of Griffin's, and so does his walk—confident and cocky.

The bartender sets another drink in front of me and removes the empty glass. "Careful, with that one. I've heard he gets rough with women."

I smile up at him and wink. "I like them rough."

He cackles and strolls away, taking his place behind the bar.

The man returns from the restroom, pulls his jacket he left at the bar off the chair, and rests it on the back of the seat across from me. "I didn't catch your name." The chair scrapes across the floor as he scoots closer to the table.

"Because I didn't give it to you," I say, turning my attention to the plate the bartender slides between us.

Crimson juices drip from the edges of the burger. I pull the two halves apart, examining the inside for the right amount of red.

Gagging comes from across the table. "That's not cooked enough. You should send it back."

I smile, pick up the first half, and smell its bloody rawness. "It's perfect."

He balls his fist in front of his lips. "I think you should reconsider your diet."

"I think you should consider yourself lucky. You could be the meat between these buns." I take a massive bite of the nearly raw burger. Red juices dribble down my bottom lip onto my chin. I dab it with a napkin.

The comment takes him by surprise, and he peers around the crowded room. "What did you just say to me?" he whispers, leaning across the table.

I savor the meat in my mouth, coated deliciously with provolone cheese, hints of butter, caramelized onions, lettuce, and tomato, close my eyes, and moan. "You heard me."

He shifts closer to the table and wipes his face with his palm. "I'll put my meat between your buns any time you want, sweetheart. All you need to do is ask."

Gotcha.

My eyes flick open, and my pussy flutters between my legs. I haven't had a good fuck since Femi rammed his cock into me beside Benny's dickless corpse months ago. I could go to his mansion in Virginia Beach and allow him to ravish my body—letting him fuck me for days.

But with Femi, there are strings attached—an expectation for me to stay a while.

I'm not ready for that.

"What is your name?" I ask, taking another bite of burger.

He smiles and sits back in his seat. "Joe."

Joe?

How boring.

I toss my drink into my mouth and gulp it down. "Well, Joe, it's time for me to go."

When I stand, Joe grabs my arm. "I have a hotel down the road a few miles." He stands and closes the distance between us. "Why don't you come and have a drink with me in my room?"

I stare down at the hand holding a tight grip on my forearm and slowly bring my eyes to meet his. "Joe, you're playing a dangerous game. I suggest you remove your hand from my arm and sit back down."

He yanks my body, bouncing my breasts against his chest. "I like to play games, Miss…?"

I slap my palm hard between his legs, crushing his balls in my grasp. He lets out a high-pitched squeal and releases my arm. I study the lines of his face and the shadow of a beard growing back while flashing him a sinister grin. "Doe…Jane Doe."

Rusty shakes his head in my peripheral vision and smiles broadly.

I release Joe, strut confidently to the bar, and drop a one-hundred-dollar bill on its top. "Keep the change." I wink at him.

He's all too familiar with how vicious I can be. During a visit last summer, a drunk patron spat anti-gay nonsense at Rusty after his boyfriend came in to see him. I sat beside the drunken dirtbag, listening to his yammering for what felt like hours.

I never intended to fracture the man's skull, but when he grabbed Rusty and spit in his face, I lost my cool.

The man's forehead bounced effortlessly against the bar top before I launched him backward out of his seat. The heavy antique whiskey decanter has sat on its display shelf near the bar for years collecting dust. It was time someone made good use of it, so that's what I did, cracking the drunk's skull like a walnut. Thankfully, Rusty, his boyfriend, and I were the only ones in the bar.

Rusty and his boyfriend reported the incident as a freak accident.

Freak indeed.

The wind tosses my hair across my eyes when I step outside the bar. I cross the lot and unlock the SUV door. My body launches sideways against the driver's seat as Joe leans against me.

"Leaving so soon? I thought we had a connection—an understanding." He stares at my lips.

I trace his jawline with my fingernail, and he closes his eyes. My other hand smooths the front of his jacket as it slides down and checks the status of his manhood. It springs to life beneath my touch and is an acceptable size.

If I'm going to fuck someone or let them fuck me, it needs to be worth it.

I tilt my head, brush his neck with my nose, and whisper, "Get in."

* * *

He remains silent beside me. The abandoned dirt road I turned onto is not only pitch black, but also miles from civilization.

A perfect place to be.

I smirk at Joe sitting confidently beside me. "Are you sure you want to do this? I can turn around and take you home to your hotel."

"And miss the opportunity to fuck that perfectly shaped ass; I think not." He unbuttons his pants, and his zipper slowly clicks down. "Pull over."

I hit the brakes in a moonlit clearing, and Joe hops out before the SUV makes it to a full stop. He moves swiftly to the driver's side door, and my breath catches in my lungs as he whips the door open.

Things are about to get rough.

"Fuck me, Joe," I say in a low, breathy voice.

He snatches me quickly by the hair, lifts me from my seat, and leads me to the front of the SUV. The ground disappears beneath my feet as he slams my body, stomach first, onto the hood of the Jeep. He grips the side of my skirt and tears it up the side, pushing it onto my back.

"No underwear. How convenient," he murmurs in my ear.

His cock makes a quick and aggressive entry between my swollen and neglected pussy lips. He rams into me, pushing me further up the hood with every thrust from his hips.

Not bad, not bad. But Joe, you're capable of so much more.

A broad toothy grin spreads across my face. "Is that all you got?"

Joe grabs my throat from behind and squeezes. His violent thrusts slam into me deeper and harder. The hood pops and bends beneath us. My throat moans against his crushing palm.

He squeezes my throat tighter and spots dance over my eyes.

I grab his wrist and pull his hand off my neck.

He takes my arms and pulls them behind my back, pressing my bound wrists against my spine with one hand and twisting my hair around his fingers with the other.

My thighs tingle, and my orgasm races to the surface, exploding from my body soaking his cock. I pant heavily. It's been too long and despite just dropping a soaker on this mother fucker, I need more.

"That's a good girl." He turns me around to face him.

I open my mouth to speak, and he covers it. "If you think we are finished, because you got yours, you are mistaken." His hand drops away from my face, and my body lifts into the air. I land hard beside the SUV as he slams my back against the ground knocking the wind out of me. He slides my legs over each of his shoulders and stuffs his cock into me once more. The grinding depth builds pressure inside my stomach. It feels like his cock is so far inside me it may push its way through my flesh and pierce my abdomen.

His teeth clench, and he growls with every forward thrust—trying to be an animal.

I've got news for you, Joe. I'm the animal.

I grip his hair and pull him up to face me. "Fuck me harder, you weak bitch."

He furrows his brow and glares at me. "You want it harder? Fine…" His cock yanks out of me and he forces me onto my stomach. "…I'll give you harder."

His cock slides in slowly, and I moan.

A squeal escapes my lips when he suddenly grips my ass cheeks, pulls me slightly away from him, and slams me with everything he's got. He drops his ass back onto his heels, grabs me around the waist, and forces me down onto his lap.

There is no passion here—just straight-up fucking. At least with Femi, I can feel the heat of his desire for me.

Joe is merely a one-night stand.

His last one-night stand.

He pushes me forward, stands, turns me around, and lifts me from the ground. My inner thighs tighten around his waist as he grips my ass and bounces me up and down on his cock.

He stares at my soundless face. "You like that baby?"

"I can do better," I say with a devilish grin.

Joe's face goes blank, and he furrows his brow. "Prove it."

His cock slides out of me as he lets me go and lays on the ground at my feet like a loyal dog.

Good boy.

He grins at my fierce gaze and interlaces his fingers on the snow-covered gravel behind his head. "The ground's kind of cold. Maybe we should go finish inside the vehicle." He sits up and puts his hands around my waist when I straddle him.

"Don't be a pussy." I shove him back down, grip his cock in my palm, and yank it a few times to harden it back up, before lowering myself onto it.

"Oh, fuck that feels good." Joe's eyes roll back into his head.

I grind my pussy into him, harder, deeper, and faster. It's coming.

More pent-up fluids race their way to the outside world. I rotate my pussy lips around and around until I burst fluids over his cock. "Oh, God," I cry out.

Joe grabs my hips and presses my sensitive pussy harder against his cock. "Don't fucking stop." His eyes are glossy with desire.

He closes them, ready to blow his load into me.

I need this to be worth it. I need to be one hundred percent satisfied with this encounter.

I need to see his thighs.

I yank my pussy off his cock and his eyes spring open. "Where are you going?"

He reaches for me, but I slap his hand and yank his pants down, revealing his thighs. "Just checking out what's on the menu."

My mouth waters at the sight of them—thick and muscular.

They're perfect.

He grabs my hair and shoves my lips against the tip of his cock. "My cum is what's on the menu. Now open your mouth, bitch."

Bitch?

How rude.

I grab his balls and give them a forceful squeeze. He lets out a yelp and untwists my hair from his fingers.

"I'm in charge." I leap onto his cock, nearly folding it in half.

He grabs my legs. "Fuck, be careful. You'll fucking break it."

I lean down and whisper in his ear. "You mean like you tried to break me?"

His eyes close as I lick his ear, sit up and rotate my pussy like a cowgirl riding a mechanical bull. I need another one.

Not because it's necessary, but because two is satisfactory, but three times is the mother fucking charm.

I reach between my legs and touch my pussy lips. Joe grabs my hands, moves them away, and takes over, twirling his thumbs in a circular motion.

"Close your eyes, baby. This is going to hurt." I bounce hard up and down on his cock. With every downward drop, air launches from his lungs.

I slide my hand into my suit jacket, grip the pearl handle of my knife, and pull it from its protective sheath.

The moonlight shimmers off its razor-sharp blade. I gingerly place the tip over his heart, grind my pussy one last time, and plunge it into his chest.

Joe's blood-curdling scream echoes around us as his eyes spring open, and his cock softens inside me.

Shit. My orgasm builds up like water pushing against a breached hull on a sinking ship. His dying cock didn't finish the job.

I yank the blade from his pierced heart and push the knife handle inside me. Blood pools around my ass cheeks, warming my pussy and lubricating my hole as I fuck the handle on his chest.

Breach.

Liquid mixed with blood squirts from between my legs landing on his face and left eye. "Oh, yes, baby. That's it. Fuck me with that stone-cold knife." I slide it in and out of me a few more times ensuring another orgasm isn't waiting behind the last.

I sit up on Joe's chest and grin. "That was amazing." The knife handle makes a squishing nose as I remove it from my body and stare at the blood dripping off its blade. I drip a little onto my fingertips and paint a red smiley face on Joe's forehead.

"What did you do?" The words are barely audible from his dying lips.

His left hand grips my right loosely, and we hold the knife together. The life in his eyes slowly fades, along with his strength—blood runs freely from the hole I created. I sit on his useless cock, watching his eyes until they no longer see me—dilating into black holes with nothing but emptiness inside them.

I smear the blood from his chest onto my thighs like lotion. There's something about the feel of it. The way it slides across my skin, painting my legs red like the backdrop of a Gothic canvas ready for its first stroke of black paint.

I rest my head against Joe's bloody and soundless chest, waiting for my heart rate and panting to return to normal. Snow floats down from the trees around us and lands silently on my face. The heavy flakes weigh my lashes down, and I blink repeatedly to flick them off.

My fingers twirl in his sparse chest hair. "I told you this game you're playing is dangerous." I sit up and rub my cum into his flesh. "And I just won the top prize."

Fucking him ignites a spark inside me. A spark I'd been trying to keep from lighting. A spark that starts a fire that only one person can extinguish.

Femi.

I shake off my thoughts of him and slide down Joe's corpse, stopping just below his quads. My blade slices horizontally across his upper thigh, removing the skin like scales from a fish. I toss the useless flesh in the bushes and cut away a perfectly oval-shaped hunk of meat. I wiggle it over Joe's dead eyes. "Thanks for playing."

I sit cross-legged beside him, examining the thick fresh cutlet. It's of high quality and will make an excellent bacon-wrapped filet with a side of lemon pepper asparagus and an ample amount of mashed potatoes.

I fucking love mashed potatoes.

The bush beside us rustles, and I freeze. I can't see anything out of the corner of my eye, but I can hear breathing.

Something or someone is watching us.

Watching me.

Fuck.

Chapter Four
Don't Run

I hold my breath and turn my head slowly.

Air staggers from my lungs. Running from a black bear or any bear is never a good idea, especially one so close I can smell its rancid breath. I keep my focus on the body beside me, and the bear keeps its focus on me.

After placing Joe's meat inside my bra, I place my hands slowly on either side of my body, lift my butt, and move away from Joe's corpse, careful not to move too quickly. The bear takes a step forward. My heart thumps against my chest, and I dare not take a breath, but staying here is not an option.

I move my legs under me and crawl backward on my hands and knees toward the SUV.

The bear emerges completely from its hiding place and circles Joe's body, sniffing it as he goes.

When my toe bumps the rubber of the tire, I sit back on my heels and patiently wait for an opportunity to stand.

Judging by the narrow shoulders and smaller size, the bear must be a female. She takes a few steps in my direction, glances back at Joe's body, and then stares at me.

She knows.

I don't know how, but she does.

Somehow, she senses what I am—a predator hunting for food like the rest of the wild creatures of the forest—predator recognizing predator.

Her eyes peer over her shoulder, lingering on something I can't see in the darkness.

I pull myself upright and lean against the corner of the front bumper.

She looks back at me one last time, turns her back, and saunters away, disappearing between two pines.

A burst of air blasts through my lips, releasing my held breath. I place my hands on my knees.

"Jesus Christ."

My hand fumbles with the handle of the SUV. I open the door and press the trunk button. It groans open, but not all the way. It always does this when it's cold.

So annoying.

I duck under, pull out my duffle bag, and toss it in the snow next to Joe. "What a fucking night, huh?"

Snowflakes drift inside his open mouth.

I work quickly, rummaging through his pockets, taking the money from inside his wallet, and removing his knock-off Rolex.

Cheapskate.

After shedding my clothing, I use snow to remove most of the blood from my flesh and my last wet wipe to remove the rest. I scan the forest frequently, waiting for the bear to return with a friend. My legs disappear into a pair of fleece-lined sweatpants. I hike them up, tie them, pull a matching sweatshirt over my head, and stick my feet in a pair of green and ivory wool socks.

I force my boots on, drop my dinner in the cooler with a few handfuls of snow, and hop back into the SUV.

When I turn on the headlights, multiple sets of glowing eyes shine back at me.

I guess the bear wasn't the only one watching.

Waiting.

My mind wanders to Ari and the kid.

I'm not calling her Amelia. She's just a kid we rescued, so to me, she will always be known as *the kid*.

I turn onto the main road and continue heading south.

The ride home takes forever. At least when Ari is with me, her talking makes the time go faster. My gas light blinks at me, and the infotainment system shows me a list of stations nearby.

The first one I encounter has two patrol cars sitting in the lot. Two officers lean against their vehicles sipping coffee and laughing. The next one is too large, has too many cameras, and is way too crowded.

The third one I approach will have to do.

I've passed by the tiny station several times but never stopped—always opted for the average-sized places that have more food and drink options.

I pull alongside the pump and hop out. A taped-on note flaps up and down, and I press the tattered tape against the pump screen.

'Prepay cash inside.'

Cash only? Huh.

I yank the barred front door open and step inside. The four men to my left stop talking at once. They sit behind a bulletproof transparent wall with a small rectangular hole about waist high where you slide your money onto the counter.

Everyone's hair is the same.

Dreadlocks.

Reggae plays quietly on a table with four sets of playing cards.

I continue walking to one of two cold drink coolers. One has different selections of beer and wine coolers and the other has water, juice, and soda. I grab a four-pack of wine coolers, turn, and bump right into the chest of a six-foot Jamaican.

He doesn't move and neither do I. Most women would back away and apologize.

But I'm not like most women.

I gaze up at him and study his curious face. "Hello."

"What's going on." His accent is subtle.

I shake my drinks beside us without looking away from him.

His brow furrows, and he tilts his head. "Is that blood?"

Shit. I missed a spot.

I reach up to wipe it, and he grabs my wrist.

Don't react. Don't react. Don't react.

He licks his thumb, traces my jawline with his spit, and wipes the dried blood from my face. "There, all better."

"Thanks," I say with a tight smile.

I fight the urge to wipe his bodily fluids off me and step around him. The wine coolers rattle against each other as I drop them on the small counter and slide a hundred-dollar bill through the opening.

The man stands uncomfortably close behind me. I feel his eyes scanning me up and down. His breath warms the space between my shoulder and neck.

"I need fifty dollars on the right pump."

The man behind the partition glances at the man behind me, who gives him a nod of approval.

Two twenties slide towards me, and the man behind me slaps his hand on top of them. "Who's blood?"

I squint my eyes and flash him a Cheshire Cat smile. "What blood?"

His laugh starts as a low chuckle and quickly grows loud. The others join him. He takes the forty dollars, places it in my palm, and squeezes, crumpling the bills. "What blood indeed."

I ball the money when he lets my hands go, slip it slowly, and seductively into his front pocket. "Keep the change."

He smiles broadly as I grab my four-pack of coolers, turn on my heels, and stroll out the door.

I twist off the gas cap and stick the nozzle in the hole. No gas.

They're fucking with me.

I glance at them through the front window, and they are all watching me with pearly white smiles—trying to lure me back in.

Not today, gentleman. I have shit to do.

Outside the store are stacks of firewood. I reach into the door of the SUV and remove the bloody knife I used on Joe from its sheath. I walk to the front of my vehicle, lock eyes with the men, and flick the knife. It stabs into the wood pile just beneath the window, and they all flinch away, gawking at each other. The man who I tipped nods to one of the others and the pump springs to life.

The gas pumps slowly, stopping repeatedly, and takes forever. My new friend shoves the front door open, wiggles my knife free from the wood pile, and strolls in my direction.

Here we go. I may have to kill him.

Of course, that would mean killing them all. I don't like killing without a good reason.

He stops a few feet from me and rotates the blade.

I never cleaned it. Blood still stains all parts of the knife. He shakes his head, stops beside the windshield wiper bin, dunks the knife in, and dries the knife with a paper towel from the cracked dispenser beside the pump.

He passes it to me, handle first, and nods. "What blood?"

I keep my eyes locked on him as he backs away from me until he reaches the store and ducks inside. The others lean with their heads and arms against the window, watching me. The pump groans to a stop one penny shy of fifty.

How annoying.

Tapping draws my eye to the store—the man who gave me my knife back, waves frantically for me to come back inside. I smile and open the door to my vehicle.

Sorry, boys. No time to play today.

The minute my ass hits the driver's seat something seems off, and I freeze. A cold breath blows fog between the seats beside me. Someone's here with me.

Behind me.

I glance in the rearview and see the needle before I have a chance to react—before I can stop it from plunging into the side of my neck.

Chapter Five
Where the Heart Is

My head thumps with a relentless headache, and it takes several minutes for my eyes to focus. Next to me on a nightstand is a towel, washcloth, and a fresh set of clothes.

When I sit up to glance at my surroundings, the blanket drops below my naked breasts. That's when I realize that not only am I naked, but I'm in a familiar house.

Mine.

Fucking Ari.

I toss my crisp white comforter aside and stagger to the bathroom. On the sink sits a bottle of Tylenol and a glass of orange juice. I take four, turn on the dual shower heads, climb under the steaming water, and close my eyes.

How I missed home. Although I'm not sure how the fuck Ari found me or how she got me here.

The glass shower door slides open and closes behind me, and my eyes spring open.

"It's too hot," Femi says, reaching around me and turning the gold faucet handle. The Eye of Horace tattoo on his wrist stares up at me—judging me for leaving him.

He nuzzles my neck, lips parting slightly as he kisses me from behind. "I missed you." His concrete cock presses against my ass and rocks back and forth.

I reach behind me and grab it. "I missed you too, Pussycat."

My body slams against the transparent door, crushing my breasts against it. Femi presses his cock between my already swollen and recently used lips, skipping our normal foreplay.

He fucks me hard against the glass, making it rattle with every thrust. His hand tightens around my throat as he speaks. "You didn't miss me." He yanks my body away from the shower door. His grip tightens and his breaths become more desperate and rapid as he throws the partition aside.

My body leaves the floor, and he carries me to bed—keeping his brown sultry eyes fixed on me. His face wears a well-trimmed beard. Quite a change from the goatee I've enjoyed for so long. A single gray hair sticks out just to the left of his perfect lips, and I am likely the cause of it.

I bounce hard onto the mattress—my ass teetering on the edge.

He spreads my legs apart. "If you missed me…" He leans forward, placing his muscular abs against mine, and slides the tip of his cock back and forth over my clit without entering. "…you would have come back sooner."

An orgasm builds inside me, longing for him—waiting for him.

Needing him.

I run my fingers through his black, dripping-wet hair, grab his head with both hands and force him between my legs. "Eat my pussy."

He holds his mouth just outside my opening. "Tell me you're sorry?" A warm breath flows over my pussy lips making them quiver and swell.

I moan and reach for him, but he grabs my hands and pins them to the bed.

"Femi, please," I beg, rotating my pubis closer to his face, grazing the hair covering it.

His tongue glides gingerly over my pussy lips, one side, then the other. "Say the words." He raises his left brow and flashes me a playful smile. "Say them."

I can't take it anymore. Even though I don't mean it, the words flutter from my mouth. "I'm sorry, Pussycat."

My body slides back inadvertently as he plunges his tongue inside me. He grabs my thighs and pulls me back to him. His mouth takes everything between my legs into it, and I orgasm violently, coating his palate.

"Oh my God," I scream to the ceiling and grip the hair on his head—stuffing him further into me, suffocating him without guilt. "More," I order.

He disengages from me, flips me onto my stomach, and yanks my head back by my hair.

She's here with us. Doc sits in front of me in the chair by the bed, her legs crossed, a sinister smile on her face. "I think she missed you as much as you missed her." Her eyes lock on Femi's, then onto mine. "And I missed you too."

I smile and close my eyes. Femi lifts my body from the mattress so I'm on my hands and knees. His cock enters violently, shoving me forward, and with every thrust inside me, Doc removes more and more of her clothes.

When Femi and I met, Doc was already his employee—taking care of his men, their medical needs, injuries, and prescriptions. I could see there was something between them—something they tried to deny. Both became distracted by my presence, and their efforts to remain professional became awkward and uncomfortable. But the day I realized her lust wasn't just for him but for me as well, I came up with a solution to satisfy everyone.

Well, almost everyone.

She can't have him unless I give them the okay. And she can never have me. I will never indulge in that fantasy. But I let her watch—watch him fuck me, watch him make love to me, watch him eat the pussy she longs to taste.

She hasn't had him for even longer than me and six months is a long time.

I could stop now and let her have some fun, but right now I'm feeling greedy and possessive of what's rightfully mine.

"More," I shout, staring directly at her disappointed face.

Femi grabs my arms, folds them behind my back, and rocks into me while he whispers in my ear. "Not sharing today?"

I smile over my shoulder at him. "Not this time. I want it all."

The thrusting is faster, harder, and more violent than before. With every ram into me, he growls noisily, releasing the pent-up desire inside of him.

I was gone too long. He's lost control of himself and the strength he possesses. He pulls my arm back hard and something in my shoulder pops. Fluids fill my insides as he pants heavily and grinds to a satisfied halt.

Doc's eyes widen. She stands and places her hand on Femi's shoulder. "Get off her."

He doesn't move, still panting heavily against my back, rocking his forehead against my upper spine. "I'll get up when I'm ready."

She shoves him hard away from me, knocking him to the floor. "I said get up!"

I've never heard her speak to him or anyone else like this. No one speaks to him like that. No one except me.

Femi is not a tolerant man when it comes to disrespect, especially when physical aggression is involved. He wipes his face with his hand, storms to the side of the bed she's on, and glares at her. I push myself upright with both hands, but my left arm fails, and my face smacks against the mattress.

"What the fuck?" I say to Doc using my right arm to slide backward off the bed and stand.

"What the fuck, is right," Femi says, not taking his eyes off Doc.

She takes a step away from him, but he grabs her arms. "You better have a good reason for putting your fucking hands on me like that," he sneers.

His eyes pierce through hers. The skin on her arms depresses as he tightens his grip. She opens her mouth to speak, but fear closes her throat.

"Femi," I say when I realize why she did what she did.

"Say something," he whispers to Doc, stroking the side of her face with glazed-over eyes and a blank expression, ignoring me.

It doesn't happen very often. Most of the time he's cool, calm, and collected. But on occasion, like when someone puts their hands on him in a disrespectful manner, he has been known to strike.

I grab a pillow off the bed and launch it at him, striking him in the face. His head pivots towards me very slowly. The rage in his eyes rapidly disappears when he sees my left shoulder.

"Oh, fuck." He lets Doc go, climbs over the bed, and reaches for me. "What did I do?"

I slap his hand away from me, walk around him, and close the now-open door, stopping Doc from leaving the room. "Stay."

A tear shimmers in the corner of her eye. I lift her downward chin and smile. "I'm not mad at you for shoving him. You were trying to keep me from getting hurt worse."

Femi stops beside me. "I'm so fucking sorry. I didn't mean to hurt you."

"Doc, do you accept his apology?" I ask glaring at him.

"I was talking to you." He huffs at me.

I turn my body to face him and jam my pointer into his sternum. "I know you were talking to me, but you should be saying those words to Doc." I point at her. "She never does anything without good reason. You should know that by now."

He places his hands on his hips and frowns. "Doc, I'm sorry."

"It's fine. I shouldn't have shoved you." She kisses the side of his face, the side of mine, and leaves the room.

I'm still mad. I know I shouldn't be, but I am. How dare he frighten her? I grab the clean clothes from the stand and stop abruptly. I can't use my fucking left arm. Someone needs to help me dress. Femi stops in front of me and reaches for the clothes. "Let me help you."

Doc reenters and sets her medical bag at the foot of the bed.

I step around Femi and hand Doc my clothes. "She can help me."

He sighs heavily. "I deserve that."

We say nothing until he's finished dressing and leaves the room.

Doc has me sit on the bed with my dislocated arm facing her. "I'd say get ready, this is going to hurt, but I'd be lying."

I chuckle, and she shifts my humerus back into the shoulder joint where it belongs creating an enormous amount of pressure relief. She takes a sling from her bag and sets it on the bed between us. "You're going to have to wear it for a few weeks, but in a couple of days we will do some little exercises to keep it from stiffening up on you."

"A few weeks?" I stand and huff.

Doc places my underwear by my feet, and I stick them in the holes. She shimmies them over my ass and hesitates, staring at my lower abdomen before covering it the rest of the way. My blush linen pants drop in front of me, and she pulls them up to my waist. "Well, you are going to have to delegate some work to Ari. She's eager to do more."

I roll my eyes. "Yeah, a little too eager."

Doc feeds my injured arm through the sleeve of a button-up linen shirt, and I slide my hand through the other. I try buttoning it up myself but doing it one-handed isn't easy. Doc takes my hand and moves it away. As she buttons my shirt for me, I stare at her face, studying her perfect features—high cheekbones, flawless skin, beautiful lashes batting over her gorgeous blue eyes.

She fumbles with the adjustment clip on the sling and tightens it against my chest. Our eyes lock on each other, lingering far too long. I feel a twitch where I shouldn't and step away from her.

She puts her head down and sighs. "Why do you deny what's between us?"

I stuff my feet in slippers and walk towards the door. "There is nothing between us."

I continue through the door and down the pictureless hallway. Ari keeps telling me I need to put up photos, but I never saw the point in putting holes in my perfect white walls and hanging up meaningless images.

Ari's standing by the stove, shoving vegetables around my favorite diamond-coated frying pan. "About time you came out of your room," she says over her shoulder.

I cross my arms and stare at her, waiting for her to explain. She glances back at me and smiles. "Oh, don't be like that. You're the one who taught me to take someone by any means necessary if there is no other way. Well…" She opens the fridge, removes a wine cooler, and sets it in front of me. "…you weren't going to come back willingly so; I saw no other way."

I drop my ass onto a stool on the other side of the snow-white quartz island and frown at her. "I didn't mean drug and kidnap me, you ass."

She whips her head to face me. "Hey, to be fair, you never said taking someone by any means necessary excluded you. Maybe, next time you'll be more specific."

I glare at her. "I guess so."

Ari slides a plate of food in front of me. "Do you want to know how I found you?"

"Yeah, that'd be fucking nice, so I don't make the same mistake again."

"Well…" She smiles proudly. "…When you tossed your phone over the bridge, it landed next to a homeless guy in his pile of clothing. He told me he didn't even know it was there until I tried calling you again."

I rub my forehead, irritated by my carelessness. "Where's the kid?"

Femi reaches around me, twists off the top of my wine cooler, and sets it back down. "After you abandoned Ari and Amelia…"

He pauses after saying her name, and it pisses me off.

"…she tried calling you, and the homeless guy answered and let her know where he found your phone. She then called me. And since I know your route home…" He pulls up a stool beside me. "…I had Chicken Wing pick Ari up and told them what route to take to look for you."

Ari drops a plate in front of Femi and slides an omelet on it. "Thank you." He smiles at her. "After you were subdued, they paid the Jamaicans a significant sum for their silence and to tell the police an amazing story of how they found and rescued Amelia." He shakes a large amount of hot sauce onto his eggs.

"But why? Why drug me, bring me home, and go through this whole fiasco? You could've just let me be and gone on your merry way." I stab my eggs, frustrated with their antics.

Femi slams the hot sauce down on the counter. His stool squeaks as he turns to face me. "Because you told Ari to call someone who cares." Femi looks around the room. His eyes land on Ari and Doc. "We care. Don't you get it?"

I rotate the stool, hop off it, and walk away from them. A cold breeze casts goosebumps all over my body when I step out onto the balcony.

They drugged me, kidnapped me, brought me home, and have the nerve to say it's because they *care*? I am weak because of them. I let my guard down because of them—vulnerable because of them.

The door slides open behind me. Femi places a blanket over my shoulders and sits in the chair to my right. I ignore him and continue staring at the mountains in the distance.

After several minutes of silence, I turn to him. "Did you do it on purpose?"

"Do what?" He leans forward in his seat.

I stand and let the blanket fall off me. "This." I point to my left shoulder he dislocated during sex.

He stands abruptly and pins me against the balcony railing. "I can't believe you would even think that of me."

His arm pulls me closer when I lean away from him and stare over the railing. "I don't know what you want from me."

We stand there, neither speaking, for several minutes. I feel his eyes on me, but I won't look at him. This is why I didn't want to come back here—get roped in. Things are less messy when I'm alone. There are no feelings to worry about hurting, no expectations, and certainly no love. My focus needs to be on finding and killing the people responsible for taking women from their homes and children from their beds.

Femi turns my head to face him, and I gaze over his shoulder, watching Ari laugh hysterically at Femi's driver. He scrunches his face and talks with his hands like he's telling her a funny story. Doc sits on the couch with her arms crossed. I wish they would just let me go.

"Look at me," Femi says tilting my chin. "I love you."

I shrug away from him and reach for the door. He grabs my hand and pulls it to his chest. "Don't do that. Don't fucking shut me out. You know I want you to be my wife."

An uncomfortable queasiness builds in my stomach. Marrying him would lock me into his life for the rest of mine and that's not what I want.

But it's not just that. There's an air of unsaid words swirling around him. It's not like usual where he's speaking and stops short of saying something he knows will piss me off—that I can figure out or guess what he was going to say. This is more like; he wants to tell me something but won't or can't. It's infuriating.

He leans against the railing and stares off in the distance. His face frowns and his brow furrows. A long sigh flows through his lips, blowing steam into the space before them. His grip tightens on the railing. "I hate when you go away for such long periods. Every time you come back; you feel more distant than before."

Well, duh. People say that distance strengthens the heart, but that's not what I say. I say distance is safe, being alone is safe, and relying on only yourself is safe. Right now, it's more important to me to teach Ari how to do this. She needs to learn to work alone.

Femi's still talking, but I can't hear him. My mind blocks out the noise around me, so I can think.

I need some peace—some mindless activity to relax. The blanket drops off the chair and Femi bends down to retrieve it. I slip inside and close the patio door, locking him out so he can't follow me.

Chapter Six
Losing Control

Femi taps on the glass behind me as I approach Ari. She turns away from Femi's driver and walks towards me. "Why did you lock him out?" She points to Femi's grimacing face behind the glass.

"Because he's being clingy, emotional, and secretive." I enter my bedroom and swipe my comforter off the floor. "You and Chicken Wing seem to be getting awful close lately."

Ari flops onto my bed and sighs heavily at the ceiling. "I think I'm going to fuck him."

I drop the comforter and gawk at her. "Ari."

"What?" She sits up cross-legged and grins at me. "He's cute."

"Chicken Wing is not that cute. He's a meatless, scrawny being. The only thing going for him is his fighting skills."

Her eyes light up. She stands abruptly, picks up the comforter from the floor, and quickly folds it. "I know. He has a red belt in Jiu-Jitsu. And he's not meatless. He's just very lean."

I giggle. "If he were any leaner, he'd be a fucking rabbit."

She gasps and rotates her hips around and around. "Oh, I hope he fucks like one. I'm a girl in need."

"Good grief." I shake my head and rummage through my dresser. "Just remember what I told you about trusting people and getting too close."

"Yeah, yeah. I know. I'm not looking to marry him; I just want a little booty."

I sit at the foot of my bed. "That's all I wanted in the beginning too, but now…"

"Now what?" Ari asks, sitting beside me.

The mattress sinks and my body leans against hers. I move over a couple of feet, fold my hands on my lap, and gaze up at the ceiling. "…now I'm suffocating and just want to be alone."

Ari moves closer to me and turns her body, so our knees are touching. "Listen to me. I know you want nothing more than to run out that door and rid the world of evil all on your own..." She grabs my hand and squeezes. "…but for now, you need us, and we need you. Once I am ready to go off on my own, you'll have your chance. Just do me a favor and stay in touch with me. I don't care about them." She nods towards the living room.

I smile and bump her with my shoulder. She's right. The only one I truly trust out of everyone is her. She will always tell me the truth and in detail. And even though she keeps things from me on occasion, which pisses me off, she's slowly learning to trust that I won't ever hurt her. She says what's on her mind and in her heart no matter how uncomfortable and annoying it can be.

Doc strolls into the room, and my eyes lock on her freshly painted neon green toenails. Her feet are long, lean, and worthy of photographing.

We need to get her an Only Fans page like me.

I haven't done any painting in a while. My fingers twitch and long for a quality brush, blank canvas, and plenty of blood.

For now, I'll just have to settle on inventorying my chest freezer on the basement level.

"Did you tell her?" Doc asks Ari, crossing her arms over her chest.

She does this when she's upset or irritated.

I glance at Ari. "Tell me what?"

Ari smiles, takes a deep breath, and blurts. "We are going to Miami for Christmas." She keeps her mouth stretched in a horizontal grin. "You're meeting my family."

I storm around her and head for the kitchen. "The fuck I am."

Doc grabs a shot glass from the cupboard, overpours tequila, and hands it to me.

She always knows what I need to stop me from exploding.

"But Odie, my brothers and sisters will all be there too. I want to introduce them to my best friend before…" Her voice trails off, and she focuses on the kitchen tile.

"Before what?" I toss the liquor down my throat and pass it to Doc with a nod. "Before I'm dead?"

Her eyes dart to mine. "You're not going to die. I won't let you."

Not going to let me?

I accept a second shot from Doc and gulp it down.

Meeting Ari's parents, or anyone's parents, is not something I'm interested in. I have a hard enough time being around the few people in my life now, and they even make me feel claustrophobic.

Six brothers and sisters. And her mom?

"No," I say firmly.

"But Odie, everyone will be there, not just my family and us."

Us.

"What do you mean by everyone?" I step into her space and glare down at her. She keeps her focus on the floor, refusing to look at me or elaborate.

Femi taps on the balcony glass door. Snow coats the top of his head. He tightens the blanket around his neck and gestures for me to let him in.

Ari doesn't have the money to buy tickets for all of us to go, let alone pay for a beachfront home for so many people. He had to have helped her.

Chicken Wing walks towards the balcony, and I step in front of him. "Don't."

He raises his hands, shrugs his shoulders at Femi, and walks away.

I ignore Femi's incessant waving and clench my jaw at Ari. "What did you do?"

She walks and talks as she heads for the balcony. "Don't worry, Femi and I planned the whole thing out. No one is coming into town the same way, we are staying at separate places, and it will only be you coming with me to my mom's house, not the others."

I slam the door shut and drop the wooded rod in the track, keeping Femi outside. "For the last time Ari, who is everyone?"

Ari steps around me, pulls the rod from the track, and yanks the door open, letting Femi inside. "Audrey, Gina, Eve, you, me, Doc, and of course Femi and his men."

I grab my hair and squeeze it. "Are you fucking crazy? You can't bring all of us together to the same place, in the same town, and expect no one to follow. Detectives, FBI, and Homeland are still investigating what happened in the bunker."

Femi stands between us. "Odie don't get upset with her. She just thought we could all use a vacation together."

"Yeah, a little family time." Ari chimes in.

I'm going to lose it. I can feel the rage boiling through my veins. If I don't get away from them, I may toss them all over the fucking balcony. I back away from them with my hands up and close my eyes. "We are not family."

Ari frowns and opens her mouth, but Femi shakes his head, silencing her. My nails dig into my palm, leaving imprints on them and drawing blood beneath my middle fingers.

Doc takes my uninjured arm and leads me towards the bedroom. "Give us a minute," she says over her shoulder.

The door clicks quietly behind us. Doc watches me pace back and forth, her head pivoting like she's at a tennis match. I yank the sling off my arm and open and close my hands several times.

I stop pacing and storm towards Doc.

Her eyes widen and she quickly backs away, putting her hands up. "What are you doing?"

I stop abruptly, jerk my head back, and tilt it in confusion. "What?"

The door opens beside us and Femi peers around the door. He quickly shuffles inside with his hands up and steps towards me cautiously. "Give it to me."

His face isn't angry. No, that's not what I see. This is something else, something I've never seen.

Fear.

He's afraid, but of what? Me?

Sure, we've had some banter back and forth about me one day deciding to kill him in his sleep. I'd cut a bunch of chunks out of his very defined and muscular thighs for stew and eat a whipped serving of mashed potatoes off his perfect ass cheeks. We'd laugh about it, and he'd say he's not scared of me.

But right now, he is.

I try and think about the last several minutes, but I can only remember bits and pieces. Fuck, I'm so angry. The pulse in my neck throbs hard and fast and the tips of my fingers tingle. My hands want to hurt someone.

They want to kill. It's like being on steroids and you have an overwhelming urge to crush everything in your path.

Femi steps towards me and takes a deep breath, holding it.

I furrow my brows. "What?"

The air from his lungs staggers out, and the smell of bourbon floats into my nostrils. He takes another step towards me and wraps his hand around the knife in my grasp.

My eyes widen. I don't remember grabbing it. I don't even remember the last few seconds.

Femi nods for Doc to leave, handing her the knife on her way out.

Fuck. What the fuck is wrong with me?

Sometimes my brain does things mindlessly, and I lash out, but it's usually against the person who pisses me off or I'm about to kill.

But this time the lines between friend and foe cross and blur, becoming the same.

Doc is not my enemy. She never has been.

I'm losing control. There's too much going on, too many people around me and in my life. My throat tightens, and I can't swallow. I stare at my shaking hands.

I'm not afraid, I'm not afraid, I'm not afraid.

I say it to myself repeatedly, but it's not working.

Why can't I stop shaking?

Femi hugs me, and my body stiffens. "It's okay. It's just a little anxiety. It will pass." He strokes my head.

No. It's not. I want to kill—need to kill. Right fucking now. My fingers dig into Femi's spine, and I bury my face in his chest, smelling his perfect skin.

I need to get away from them—get away from him before I hurt him.

He forces me in front of him, creating space between us and dislodging my claws from his back, sensing my shift in demeanor to that of a predator. His eyes dart between both of mine. He yanks me towards him, kissing me hard on the lips, driving my teeth into them. I push him back, lick the metallic liquid from inside my bottom lip, and glare at him.

My body backs up against the wall as he turns the tables—becoming the aggressor and trying to take control. But no one controls me.

"You're having naughty thoughts, aren't you, my love?" His low deep voice sends chills of desire between my legs making my pussy quiver.

I feel my body relaxing—the anxiety subsiding, and my need to taste him shifts to an overwhelming urge to fuck him.

Dammit.

He's like a leech sucking the life out of me—drinking the poisonous venom from my mind.

That's my job.

I'm the fucking leech.

I'm the goddamn poison!

I twist away from him and head for the stairs. "I need some time alone."

The basement level lights up with a flick of a switch. One of the many reasons I purchased this place was for the basement and its in-ground drain and plumbing. I had a massive tub installed in the center of the room—plenty of room to hold a body and process its meat.

The freezer squeaks open. I grab two legs and toss them in the tub to thaw. Waiting until the meat thaws just enough to still be frozen but not rock solid is the best time to cut. I remove all my clothes.

The wall phone rings, and I roll my eyes.

It's like being a parent and trying to have alone time with children. It never fucking lasts.

"What?" I huff into the receiver.

"Check the refrigerator," Femi says then hangs up.

Refrigerator? The only thing I put in there is extra alcohol and occasionally overstock cases of water.

I yank the door open. Inside is a leg with a tourniquet around its upper thigh and a note.

Freshly cut this morning.

The tourniquet throws me off a bit. I never use them. Most people don't unless they are planning to keep the person who the limb belonged to alive. I sit on the tub ledge, rotate the leg in my hand, and sniff it gingerly.

Mmm…the clean smell of fresh flesh arouses me. I remove the tourniquet and set the limb next to the frozen ones. It's funny how many different colors of skin there are. The three before me are unique in their own way.

I roll my utility cart closer to me and select a carbon steel knife. My thumb slides over its edge, feeling its sharpness.

Feeling its power.

Carbon is much stronger than stainless steel, cutting through hide and flesh like butter. I rest the sharp edge parallel to the fresh leg Femi provided on my lap and peel off the first layer of skin like a wood bench plane across a piece of oak.

Chapter Seven
A Bloody Good Time

I sense Femi is behind me but say nothing. He likes to watch me work, lurking in the shadows like a stalker waiting for his victim to be vulnerable.

Only I'm no victim.

If he gets close to me it's because I let him.

"Come here," I say over my shoulder.

He strolls over, removing his attire and dropping it on the cement. His cock touches the back of my right arm when he stops beside me and lifts my chin. "I love when you wear red."

His finger smears a droplet of blood across my cheek and over my mouth. I exhale and swipe my tongue left to right, seductively lapping up the crimson lipstick he's applied to my lips.

He sits on the tub ledge, leans to the side, his eyes not leaving mine, and digs his fingers into the fresh bloody body part beside us. His hands slide against each other, smearing blood and evenly coating them. He grasps my breasts simultaneously rotating his bloody palms, painting them red. I close my eyes and let him cover me in blood.

This is the Femi I know. This is the only Femi I want. Not the one desperate to fuck me in the shower. I want the version of him who seduces me with the blood of our enemies.

The one who takes his time to touch every inch of me, using the blood to ensure he misses not a single part of me.

His fingers slide between my legs, coating my pussy lips with crimson before entering. "Oh, how I've missed you."

I turn my body and rest my feet on the floor in front of him. "Show me how much."

He removes his fingers from inside me and kneels. His palms each grab a knee, and he opens my legs slowly, kissing each one before licking my pussy, left lip, then right, cleaning them of foreign fluids.

"Do you want me to be nice?" His tongue dips in and out of me, then twirls around my clit. "Or do you want me to be mean?"

I grip the tub edge on either side of me tight. "Mea—"

The word didn't make it through my lips. My head launches backwards and my eyes pinch closed as I scream. Femi's mouth sucks my entire pussy inside of it and his fluttering tongue plunges deep inside me. His tight grip on my ass cheeks making escape impossible. We moan together, me enjoying his attention and him my flavor.

I want him to fuck me.

I need him to fuck me.

A shadow catches my eye.

She's watching us.

I grip Femi's head hard and force him further inside me. He pushes his head against my palm, trying to catch air, but I won't let him. My eyes are on her.

Picturing her.

Wishing it were her.

She enters the room and swipes a tacky blood-coated piece of hair away from my face. Her touch is soft, tender, and inviting.

I nod, allowing her to get what she's so desperate for. Permission to fuck him.

Femi's head cranks backward, her fingers twisted tightly in his hair. She leans down to his ear and whispers, "fuck her."

She tosses his head forward, his eyes locking on mine with an eager smile.

A broad smile stretches across his face. "Not yet. Go get our friend from the closet."

Doc nods and walks backward away from us. She stops at one of my storage closets, opens it, and rolls a man out into the open. He's naked and bound to an armless desk chair. I stand and walk over to him. His eyes are wild and wide. He scans my red-painted body up and down and screams muffle through his taped mouth. One of his legs is missing, and so is his hand.

I trace the outline of his wrist where his hand used to be. "What happened here?"

Femi kisses the back of my shoulder. "There was some information we needed from him. He gave it up after I took his hand."

The man's words muffle through his bound mouth. He shakes his head back and forth.

"We?" I raise my brow.

Femi walks around me and removes a piece of fabric from the man's lap. "Look what we have here."

Doc grabs the man's cock and strokes it several times.

It's beautiful. A large, curved, and veiny cock, just as hard as the cement beneath my feet.

"Do you like it?" Femi asks. "Doc gave him a little something to keep it nice and hard for you."

Is he kidding?

Femi's cock is hard enough and does an amazing job, but there's something about a curved dick.

Those fuckers hit differently.

They scrape parts of your insides you didn't even know existed.

My eyes get stuck, locked on its perfection and fuckability.

Femi walks me forward from behind. "Take a seat, my love."

Doc pulls a pillowcase over the man's head, and I straddle myself over his lap. Femi grips my hips and guides me onto the curved cock.

It scrapes the entire right side of my vagina, putting pressure on that side of my stomach. I close my eyes and ride the stranger beneath me. The chair rolls back and forth. Doc stands behind it, steadying it with her hands on the back of it. Femi walks behind her, reaches under her dress, and slides her panties down. He waits for me to give him the okay.

I nod, and he pushes her forward, folding her at the waist. The man's covered head blocks my view. I place my head against the side of the man's and stare at Doc's twisting expression as Femi guides his cock inside her. Her eyes pinch closed as he thrusts hard into her, hesitates, and thrusts again. I can't feel pain, but I can see the pain he causes her. Every time he rams her, her brows furrow, and her face tightens, trying not to cry out. I rock on the curved cock beneath me, an orgasm racing to the surface. My thighs tingle, and I close my eyes. Our breathy moans echo around the room as we fuck for several minutes, no one wanting it to end.

Something metallic touches my fingers. I open my eyes and glance at Doc. She passes me a scalpel and removes the pillowcase from the man's head. They may be finished fucking, but I'm not. My orgasm has trapped itself somewhere inside me. Femi pulls my head back and kisses my blood-coated ear before whispering. "You're not letting his cock get deep enough my love." He grabs both of my hips. "Let me help you."

He pushes me down onto the man's lap, allowing his cock to reach deep inside the depths of my body.

I stare into the horrified face of the man in front of me, barely holding on to life after all the torturous things that they have done to him.

Who am I to stand between him and death?

I grip the back of the hair on his head. My body bounces rapidly up and down with Femi's help.

"It's coming," I say in a throaty moan.

Femi grinds my hips around and around. My orgasm ruptures violently from me as I slice the man's throat. "Oh fuck, Daddy, yes."

Arterial spray splatters across my face, warming it. Femi lets me go, but I continue to rock long after I'm finished—long after the man's dead. His blood drains down my breasts and abdomen.

I slow down and interlace my fingers behind the head of the corpse I'm sitting on. Blood pools around my feet, and I slide them around in it. Femi combs my hair away from my face from behind. "Did you enjoy my gift, my love?"

I moan, remove the tape from the corpse's mouth, and kiss his lips. "You did fantastic."

"So, you'll stay home?" He takes my hand and helps me off the dead man's lap.

Here comes the strings.

"Who said anything about leaving?" I walk away from him and step into the shower in the next room.

"I know you, Odie. When things get uncomfortable, you need to be alone."

"Son of a bitch," Ari shouts from the next room before I have a chance to respond to him.

She hobbles into the shower room, one side of her covered in blood and holding a manila envelope. "I slipped in your mess."

Femi takes the envelope from her. "It's from Eve. Your next job."

Ari climbs in the shower, fully clothed, and turns the shower head to herself. "Whelp might as well kill two birds with one stone."

I shake my head and stare at the tile by our feet. Blood swirls down the drain in a vortex. Ari shakes her head, splattering me in the face with her wet hair. I wipe my face with my palm. Although the shower is big enough for both of us and at least two other people, I feel crowded. Femi passes me a towel and grimaces, sensing my irritation with Ari's intrusion.

"Have the guys clean up this mess, would you?" I ask Femi, wrapping a towel around myself and taking the manilla envelope from him.

I stop on the second step leading upstairs and stare at the upward-bent clasp securing the envelope's contents. Normal people push the metal clasps to the left and the right of the hole, but Femi always pushes both clasps straight up.

I've asked him many times not to open and review our cases. Does he think if one is too dangerous, and he tells me not to take it I'm going to listen?

Not.

I decide.

I toss the envelope on the kitchen island and storm to my room to take a thorough and private shower.

After pulling on jeans, a T-shirt, and tennis shoes, I head for the kitchen to retrieve the envelope. Chicken Wing is watching television and the envelope from Eve sits on the coffee table open in front of him.

Now someone else has read it. If people see something already open, they think it permits them to read it—mail, Christmas cards, bills, etc.

I'm sorry but if you pick up my bill and read it, it's yours now. You better fucking pay for it. You nosey ass mother fucker.

I'll look at the case file later. Right now, I need to get out of the house.

I reach for the Mercedes fob and Femi grabs them first. "We need to talk about the next job." He takes the sling off the counter and puts it on for me. "And you need to keep this on."

"Sure. When I get back, I'll read the case. Right now, I need some air." I hold my hand out, waiting for the key.

He holds it away from me. "I don't think we should take it. You need a break and a vacation. A real vacation. Not saying you're on vacation then going off and doing a small job. Not only that, with your shoulder like it is, you're not up for it."

Seriously? This is why I like working alone.

"Femi, give me the keys. I'll look at the job when I get back and then decide."

He pulls me against his bare chest. His body wash fills my nostrils, intoxicating me. "Don't leave."

I hesitate, then snatch the key fob from his palm without looking at him. "I'll be back."

"Promise?"

I grab my jacket from the back of the chair, glare into his glossy, insistent eyes, and answer, clenching my teeth. "I promise."

His eyes undress me as I back away.

How dare he make me promise?

He knows me well, and so do the others. The longer I am around them, the more predictable I become. I need to get the fuck out of here.

My word is my motherfucking bond, so I plan to keep my promise to him.

Eventually.

My foot slips sideways when I step outside. I grab the five-gallon bucket beside the house, pop its top, and toss a cupful of salt across the walkway. Tennis shoes aren't the best option for snow, but my boots are still damp. I walk the shoveled path to the car and wipe the windshield and driver's side door with my sleeve, clearing it of a fluffy layer of flakes.

I whip the Mercedes door open and flop in the driver's seat. The passenger side door springs open, and Ari slides in beside me.

"No," I say firmly.

She frowns and crosses her arms. "Why? Because you want to take off without me?"

"I promised Femi I would come back." I roll my eyes at her.

"But you didn't say when." She yanks the seatbelt and quickly clicks it. "I'm not letting you out of my sight. Besides, you shouldn't be driving with that arm."

Fuck. She's right.

Not just about the driving part, but about me not coming back right away. They are getting smarter, figuring out my plans without me telling them.

I climb out of the car and knock on Ari's window. She ignores me and stares through the glass ahead of her. "I'm not getting out of this car."

"I know, and you're right. I shouldn't be driving."

A smile spreads across her face. "Did you just say I'm right?" She pushes the door open, striking me in the knee. "About which part? I want to hear you say it."

I take her place in the passenger seat and ignore the question. She leans on the door frame, unwilling to move or close the door until she gets her answer. The wind blows snow sideways across her face.

"You'll freeze to death if you don't get in the fucking car," I say in a huffy voice.

She leans in and smiles at me devilishly. "As long as I die knowing I was right, that's all I care about."

"Goddammit, Ari just get in!" I yell at her.

She crosses her arms. "Say it."

I close my eyes, take a deep breath, and give in. "Fine. You were right. Now get in the fucking car before I change my mind and leave."

She skips behind the vehicle and disappears. I turn the rearview mirror, looking for her. After several seconds, her face appears in the mirror partly covered in snow.

Snow falls into the car with her when she flops behind the wheel. "Fucking slippery out there."

The entire left side of her has a layer of snow from slipping sideways. That's two falls today. She's clumsy as fuck.

She presses the start button and twists the dial shifter into four-wheel-drive. "Where to?"

The touchscreen mounted below the dash brightens under my fingertips as I punch in an address. "Mill Mountain."

Ari shifts into drive and plows through the snow-covered driveway. Mill Mountain is less than ten minutes away, and I like to go there to clear my head and people-watch. This time of year, they have a lot of indoor activities and educational programs for children. My parents took my sister and I once when we were younger, and I will never forget it. It was the only time I remember all of us being happy simultaneously.

And right now, I need to feel happiness.

Ari babbles on about the weather and her and Chicken Wing's conversations of late. I try and listen but eventually, her voice fades into the background like white noise. The snow coats the trees outside, and I long to stand amongst the trees at this very moment listening to them crackle and bend beneath the weight of the snow blanketing their limbs.

We steer into the parking lot, and Ari's eyes light up when she sees the sign. "They have a zoo?"

I push the door open. "Yes."

She puts the fob in her pocket and whips the door closed. "I love zoos."

Shocker. I think to myself.

Ari skips ahead of me and opens the door for a boy and his mom. She continues holding the door open, waiting for me, her eyes glossy and full of joy.

I step through the doorway into the warm space and immediately want to leave. Children on a class field trip before the start of winter break clutter the lobby, and quickly swallow the space around me. My stomach tightens and my throat closes.

They're touching me. My heart pounds inside my head. If my body could sweat, it would be dripping already. I don't mind a child or two around, but this many makes me want to scream. The noise grows with every minute they have to wait—shouting their excitement to each other. I try to speak, but grunting is all that escapes my lips.

Ari pulls me from between two giggling girls and directs me into the gift shop. "Let's start here before you implode."

Oh, thank God. I was seconds away from plowing through the children and running out the door.

Ari fits a raccoon hat on her head and places her fists on her hips. "I'm Davy… Davy Crockett.

I laugh through my nose. "You look more like a deranged mountain woman."

She takes the hat off and tosses it back on its shelf. "Odie, what do you want for Christmas?"

That's a loaded question.

I move closer to her. "Well, I'm itching to paint again. It's been a while."

"I asked you what you wanted, not what you want to do."

My fingers glide over a magnet with an image of the mountain, feeling its smooth texture. "There is nothing anyone can give me that I don't already have." I peer over her shoulder.

The children are filing out of the lobby and heading into the learning center. I pick up a brochure about predators local to the area and thumb through it—snakes, coyotes, black bears. Huh, no images of me.

How disappointing.

"Do you want to know what I want more than anything in this world?" Ari asks, distracting me from my thoughts.

No. Not really.

I grab a souvenir pen and write 'Willow' in cursive at the top of the list of predators on the brochure, slide it and the pen back into their displays, and walk around her, entering the now-empty lobby. "We can go to the Lizard Meet and Greet. It's starting in just a minute."

Ari flubs her lips. "Listen, I know you don't consider me family, but I consider us at least friends. It would be the greatest gift in the world to me if you met my mom and siblings."

Her eyes shimmer with pending tears. I'm hurting her feelings by not wanting to meet her family.

I'm such an asshole.

But what does she expect? She's not even supposed to be here. I'm not supposed to be here. I should be off dismembering a body somewhere and painting a masterpiece.

She tilts her head down and stares at her left boot, scuffing it against the marble floor. "I'm sorry I drugged you," she says louder than she should have.

I take her by the arm and direct her to the lady's room. "Ari, pay attention to your surroundings before you say such things."

Her body shifts side to side, and she rolls the fabric of her jacket between her fingers. A sign she's seconds away from emotionally dumping on me.

She sucks in a few shallow breaths and unloads. "I'm sorry. I'm sorry I'm so hyper. I'm sorry I'm not a good friend. I'm sorry to be such a disappointment. If you want to leave me and the others for good, I will help. All I want is for us to have one last reunion with everyone, then I will never bother you again."

And here comes the tears.

Fuck. Now I feel even worse.

Perhaps all the people eating has softened me a bit— made me more like them.

Domesticated.

Normal.

"Fine."

Her brows raise so high I thought they might shoot off her face. "Really?"

My body relaxes as I let go and give in to her wishes, letting her have her way.

"Yes." I close my eyes, anticipating what comes next.

She bear-hugs me, crushing my body in her grasp, and bounces up and down. "You won't regret it. I promise."

Somehow, I doubt it.

I open the door. "Come on. Let's go touch some snakes and lizards."

"I've never touched a snake before." She smiles broadly and walks through the entranceway.

Yes, you have Ari.

I am a serpent. My venom spreads inside her more every day.

Poisoning her.

Making her like me and less like them—turning her into something else. Someone else.

A monster.

Chapter Eight
Henry

Ari's unusually quiet as we head to the car. The hands-on Lizard Meet and Greet was a hit with everyone who attended, especially Ari. I wanted to stay longer and study endangered red pandas. They are solitary creatures that prefer to be alone except during mating season.

It would be my spirit animal if it weren't technically an herbivore. They do occasionally eat rodents, so I guess it is still in the running. As for Ari, if I had to guess, her spirit animal is a squirrel—vocal, runs in a zig-zag pattern when being chased, intelligent.

She half dragged me through the rest of the zoo, not even stopping at the gift shop to buy the raccoon hat she mentioned going back for.

Maybe she needs to poop. I never understood why she can pee in public or even shit on the side of the road, but she can't do it in a public restroom. I had to pull over once so she could take a crap behind an empty house for sale. Thankfully, I had napkins in my glove box. After she relieved herself, she tells me that they were like little marbles shooting out of her butthole, and they rolled down the sloped property.

I wish she would stop oversharing. Just thank me and take the hand sanitizer I'm handing to you. That's all.

She zips her jacket up higher beside me and shifts the car into drive.

"Did you have any animals growing up?" she asks, turning onto the main road and heading back to the house.

I flip through a zoo donation pamphlet. "No."

"Did you know that sixty-nine percent of people report that having a pet reduces anxiety and stress?" She clutches her chest and grimaces.

"No." I continue reading the pamphlet.

Ari presses the gas, speeding excessively. The car slips sideways and then regains traction.

"Slow down," I say to her, tossing the brochure into Femi's glovebox.

I hold it open, my eyes stuck on the contents inside. The little black box has a red bow around it with a tiny note.

Anything for you.

Ari glances inside the glovebox. "Is that what I think it is?"

"Probably." I slam the compartment shut.

"Are you going to go through with it?" She grabs her jacket and pulls it away from her body. "Ouch."

I slap my hand down on the dashboard. "Ari, stop the car."

She comes to a slow and calculated stop less than a mile from the house. "Do you have to use the bathroom?" she asks sheepishly.

"What did you do?" I squint at her as she shifts her jacket uncomfortably with her fingers.

Her face stretches with an ingenuine smile. "Nothing."

The head of a red and green lizard pops out the top of her jacket and smiles at me.

This fucking thing literally smiled at me.

"God dammit, Ari."

She pulls it from her coat and rests it on her shoulder. "Someone relinquished him to the zoo. I couldn't just leave him there unwanted and sad."

Its mouth parts slightly and licks the side of Ari's cheek.

Her eyes light up, and her head pivots slowly to face me. "See. He loves me, and I love him. When I looked at him and he smiled at me, I knew I had to be his mom."

"Ari, turn the car around and take him back," I say softly, trying not to scream at her.

She holds it tight against her chest. "I can't take Henry back now. We have bonded."

"Henry? Seriously, Ari. Do you know how big iguanas get?" I twist my body and sigh.

"I don't know, a foot or two." She pets Henry's head, and he bobs it up and down.

I rub my forehead hard with my fingers. "Ari, iguanas can grow to five feet. But you already know that don't you?"

"Yes," she says quietly.

Lying to me isn't allowed, and she knows it. It sits high on my list of rules, right next to withholding critical information.

Henry climbs off Ari and onto my sling. He creeps down my arm, sits in my lap, and closes his eyes.

"Aww. He likes you." Ari smiles and pulls back onto the road.

Breathe. Just breathe.

It's not the end of the world, but a missing iguana will not go unnoticed.

"Ari, we can't keep him. The zoo likely has cameras and will call the police." I stroke Henry's textured head.

She turns into the driveway. "No, they won't because I technically didn't steal him. One of the kids from the tour did. I saw him with it by the boy's bathroom. I yelled at him to drop it, and he did, then ran. I picked it up and stuck him in my jacket."

"And let me guess, there are no cameras in the hall by the bathrooms," I say without looking at her.

"Bingo." She reaches for Henry to take him off my lap, and he whips his tail at her, drawing blood from her hand.

"Hey. I'm your mama. Now, stop that."

I chuckle as she tries again with the same result.

"Ouch." She smears the blood on the side of her finger. "Bad Henry." She points at him like a child.

Henry may only be a foot and a half long, but he's a feisty little thing.

"We can take him with us to Miami, then we are letting him go," I say unzipping my jacket, picking him up, and placing him inside to shield him from the cold.

Ari frowns. "But he's mine." She follows me into the house where most everyone watches television and eats leftover stir fry I had defrosted from the freezer earlier.

My stir fry.

Most of Femi's men know what meat I use in my stir fry and are smart enough to avoid it. But a couple of new recruits have no idea, and no one can tell them. I don't care for one recruit, so watching him devouring a huge bowl of man-meat and vegetables makes me smile. Femi says he just takes his job seriously and that's why Manuel's always lingering and watching me.

I think Manuel is too quiet and needs a knife through his gawking eyes.

As soon as I unzip my jacket, Henry leaps off my chest and lands on the back of the couch. Femi's mouth drops open, and Doc quickly moves away from it.

Femi smiles at me. "Did we get our first pet?"

Our.

I shake my head. "No. Ari stole it. And no, we didn't get a new pet. We're taking him with us on our next job and letting him go."

"Not if it's this cold. He'll freeze to death." Ari unzips her jacket and tosses it over a chair. "His name's Henry."

Doc gasps. "Oh my God. Did you have him inside your shirt?"

"Yeah. Why?" Ari furrows her brow.

I point to the blood soaking through her top. "I think he scratched you a few times."

Ari pulls the shirt away from her skin with two fingers. "I thought I felt something warm. I figured he just peed on me."

Doc picks up her medical bag from the counter and ushers Ari to the bathroom. Chicken Wing pulls open the fridge door and removes the spring mix meant for dinner and the mango and blueberries meant for smoothies. He makes a bowl of food for Henry and sets it on the floor.

Henry climbs quickly off the couch, strolls over to the dish, and snatches a large piece of greens.

"Henry, huh?" Chicken Wing smiles at me.

I shake my head. "Not a word, or I will chop off your fucking arm and feed it to Henry."

He laughs at the ceiling. "He's an herbivore. I'm not on the menu."

"You will be if I coat your meat in a nice fruit paste." I grin sadistically and lock eyes with Manuel.

Chicken Wing stops laughing. "I'm just messing around."

I stand so close to him that my breast touches his chest. "I'm not."

He steps away from me, sweat beading at his temple. "I'm sorry."

Femi stands from the couch, wipes the stir fry from his lips, and steps between us. "Can you excuse us?"

Chicken Wing nods and leaves the room. Femi gestures to Manuel with his hand to leave as well. Manuel crosses his arms and leans against the bookcase, refusing to go.

Femi strolls over to Manuel and speaks to him quietly. Manuel's face reddens. His fists ball by his sides, and his face twists with irritation.

He's arguing with Femi.

Oh, hell no.

I storm towards them. Femi turns and rests his hand on my shoulder. "No."

"No?" I raise my brows. "This is my house, and he's not going to be disrespectful."

Manuel smirks and backs out of the room, disappearing down the hallway.

"Odie, he was just expressing his feelings about leaving us unprotected. That's all." His hand drops away from my shoulder.

I glare at him. "I don't need protection. And if I'm around, you don't either."

He places his hands pressed together in front of his face and sighs heavily into them. "I don't need you to protect me, Odie. That's what they are for." He points down the hallway.

Femi's eyes land on the envelope sitting on the counter, open. He slides it across the counter with his palm and passes it to me. On the outside, written in permanent marker reads:

Family photos. Do Not Bend.

It's from Eve. I recognize her handwriting anywhere. It's very elegant, like calligraphy. She always marks the outside with inconspicuous content descriptions to make people less likely to open them before they get to me. The last one read, 'household manuals.'

Who the hell would want to open and read them?

But this time, the thought of checking out family photos must have been too much temptation for Femi's men or anyone else who saw the envelope.

I'll decide whether to take the job or not. But knowing Eve, I will. She always finds the worst of the worst.

The images slide from the envelope onto the granite. The first one is of a man, wearing all white, smoking a cigar. Beside him, sitting in a short red dress is a young girl. A mini post-it note says, 'missing' with an arrow pointing at the girl's face. I flip the image and move on to the next one.

It's a woman with pencil-drawn eyebrows.

I fucking hate that.

It makes me want to shave the beautiful long brown hair she has flowing over her shoulder off and draw the hair back on to match her penciled-on brows.

Another note reads, 'Girl last seen with this woman, along with five others.'

Six young girls are missing, all last seen with her.

The next photo is of the woman and the man in the white suit. She's much taller than him—at least a foot taller. He's resting his hand on her ass, smiling as he speaks. In the final image, she is crushing his hand in her left hand and holding a gun to his head with her right. Her teeth are white and perfect. Next to his shocked face reads, 'Missing, presumed dead.'

I drop the folder onto the coffee table and sink into the seat beside Femi. "She's in charge?"

"Looks that way." He leans forward, picks up a paper that fell to the floor, and hands it to me.

Henry walks across the photos on the coffee table, scratching the face of the woman in the image. I smile and read the notes Eve sent to me with a summary of what she found out.

Woman in photo: Luisa Mercardo, age 40.
Occupation: Real Estate Mogul
Estimated worth: $75,000,000.
Estimated number of employees: 1,000

"Huh." I glance at Femi. "Why would a woman with so much power and money have so few employees?"

He shifts a lock of hair away from my face. "My guess would be she doesn't trust anyone. She probably pays her tight group of employees a handsome sum, and they have their employees separate from her."

"Like having a thousand bosses under your control," I say more to myself.

"More like soldiers." He removes a folded piece of paper from his pocket. "I was saving the best for last."

I open the paper and smooth the creases. Luisa has ten primary employees who deal directly with her and her alone—her Generals. Those ten generals each have one hundred soldiers under their command, each with different jobs and responsibilities. The generals are of different ages and races. The youngest general is twenty-three and the oldest is eighty and resembles the Crypt Keeper.

My fingers flex against the file, partly wrinkling the page. Beneath each of the general's names are their last known addresses, photos, ages, and suspected crimes. Listed amongst the long list of criminal activities is trafficking and it's not just of women. It's men, women, children, and worst of all, babies. The Crypt Keeper's preference is to take children and babies and place them with families he employs, who raise them to be compliant vessels.

They are innocent. Never knowing what the right way is to live. Only believing what their alleged mothers and fathers tell them and teach them.

Their bodies are not their own and belong to others once they reach a certain age.

My stomach churns.

Fucking disgusting.

The page crushes in my hand. "We can't go to Miami. This is too important."

Femi removes the balled-up paper and chucks it across the room. He unbuttons the top of my shirt and grins. "Oh, we are going to Miami, my love. His hand slides in and grips my breast. "Because that's where she is." He nods to the scratched image beneath Henry's tail. "It's where they all are."

My heart races as he leans in front of me and takes my nipple into his mouth, sucking it gently. I gasp and stroke his silky black hair, pressing him further against me. He shifts to my other breast and circles the nipple with his tongue, flicking it several times like a hunting serpent. I smile as he moves slowly to the floor, grips the sides of my pants, and shimmies them down to the floor, taking my underwear with them.

"When do we leave?" I ask in a breathy voice rotating my hips towards his face.

His thumb strokes my pussy lips. "Tomorrow."

I grab his hands and push them against my clit. "Quit teasing."

He removes his hands from beneath mine and kisses me, starting at the inside of my knee until he makes his way to my inner thigh, stopping with his mouth between my legs, but not touching. "All this talk of work is making you wet my love." He blows a breath across my pussy, cooling my moist lips.

I moan and squeeze my inner thighs. "Oh, Pussycat. She needs you." His tongue slides inside me, and I close my eyes. "That's it. Right there. Deeper." I grip his hair and push him into me. His tongue strokes my sweet spot, and I explode on his face.

He lifts his head away from me, his mouth glistening, and licks my liquids off his lips. "I fucking love how you taste."

"I have more for you." I grab his head and shove his body backward onto the floor. His head disappears beneath me as I sit on his face and rock my tingling pussy lips against his mouth. He grips each of my ass cheeks, applying a gentle upward pressure on occasion to catch his breath.

"Fuck, Femi. It's coming." I gasp a breath and scream.

He pulls my body against his face, slurping and sucking at the same time. I hyperventilate as the juices keep coming—keep releasing.

His palms grip my legs and force my body towards his cock. I reach inside his pants, yank it out of its hiding place, grip it tight and feed it into my pussy, my eyes never leaving his.

He rolls me onto my spine, holding my frame tight against his and keeping his cock inside. His pace is deliberately slow.

Annoyingly slow.

He's making love to me. I'm not in the mood. I want to fuck.

"Fuck me harder," I whisper.

He closes his eyes and maintains the same pace. "No. I want to enjoy you."

I dig my nails into his ass cheeks.

"Fuck, Odie!" Femi shouts.

"Do as I say," I growl at him refusing to release his skin from beneath my claws.

His cock rams me hard, and I let his butt go. He pulls out of me, flips me onto my stomach, and lifts me onto the couch. I place my palms on the back of the couch, bracing myself for the pounding he's about to deliver. He pushes my knees forward from behind, presses his body against mine and his cock inside me, wraps my hair up in his fist, and whispers. "You asked for it."

The first thrust almost pushes me up and over the back of the couch. The second succeeds. I'm dangling over it like a folded blanket waiting for use. He holds my hips firmly in his grasp and propels his cock into me.

Hard.

Too hard.

My stomach churns, and my mouth starts to water. I raise my body but a hand against my upper back presses me back down.

Bare neon toes appear beneath me on the floor, and Femi's pace slows. Doc stands beside me and smiles when I crank my neck to look at her.

I nod, granting her permission to join.

Femi jumps away from me, stands on the couch cushion, and grabs her by the shirt. "Open your mouth."

She kneels to the floor, raises her head, and opens wide.

His cum shoots from the tip of his cock and sprays across her face, missing her mouth entirely. I unfold myself, climb over the couch, and squat in front of her. She closes her eyes when I touch her face, smearing Femi's semen into her skin like lotion. Her mouth parts slightly, and I stare at it. Her glossy lips shimmer under the lights, calling me to them.

Femi rubs the back of my head and pushes my face gently closer to hers, wanting me to kiss her—wanting me to fuck her.

I can't do it. I push back against his hand, but he holds it firmly. My face prickles and my body trembles as Doc caresses my cheek with her fingers and leans toward me. Our lips are so close, I feel them on mine without touching them.

"No." I stand abruptly, bumping Doc with my chest and knocking her to the floor. She stares at me. Her face twisted in a disappointed frown as I once again reject her.

I keep my face stern and uncaring.

This is not a three-way relationship.

This is an understanding.

It's him and I or her and him with permission, and only with me in the room.

Nothing more.

He knows this, and so does she. Yet here they are working together to try and change my mind.

"Odie, I—"

"No," I say raising my hand and covering Femi's mouth. "Don't you tell me you're sorry. We both know that would be a fucking lie." My eyes fill with rage. I let my hand fall away from his mouth. "You will not dictate or change the terms of our agreement. The only one that can do that, is me."

He sighs through his nose, and the air shifts the air on my cheek. "I wasn't going to apologize." His eyes drift to Doc, and she shakes her head. He looks back at me, closes his eyes, and blurts, "I want you two to have a closer relationship, not just for me, but for yourselves. It's clear to me you're holding back your feelings for her. Can't you see how much your rejection upsets her? I don't mean we have to have a three-way relationship, what I mean is, when I'm not here you are free to do as you please together, and when I am if you want her to join, she can, and if not, she won't. It's that simple."

Oh, he thinks he can tell me it's okay to fuck Doc if I want just as long as he's not around to see it. Fuck him. He doesn't dictate what I do when he's not around. I'd rather fuck her in front of him and give him blue balls than allow him to think he runs this fucking relationship.

"Nothing about this arrangement is simple. But you know what is?" I glance at Doc and glare at him. "I can walk out that fucking door, leave my house, my belongings, and everything I have behind and never come back. You, her, Ari, and everyone else, none of you would ever find me again. I would just, poof, disappear like Houdini. Now that, that is fucking simple."

Henry leaps on the back of the couch and licks the cushion several times. He looks at Femi and then at me and rubs some loose shed on his face against the cushion. The floor creaks behind us. Someone is in the room, but I maintain eye contact with Femi, refusing to allow a distraction to keep me from getting my point across for the umpteenth time.

Ari reaches between our half-naked bodies and removes Henry. "He's too young to see all this."

Femi stifles a laugh, and I unlock my fierce eyes from him. I catch a glimpse of us in the floor-length wall mirror. My hair is a tangled mess resting on top of my head and the sling is wrapped partly around my neck. Leftover fluids dribble down Femi's leg. I glance at Doc. The partially dried cum on her face crusts on one corner of her lashes holding it shut.

"We need a shower."

I walk away from them, leaving them to process the words that just mindlessly floated from my mouth.

We.

Chapter Nine
Taking Control

I've never invited Doc to shower with us. I have always made her shower alone. Showers between couples are intimate and not to be shared. But it's time for me to let go a little. Besides, Christmas is coming, and everyone is in the spirit of giving.

I'll call it an early gift, but it won't be without strings. Which she doesn't know or care about at this very moment as I turn on the water and wash the semen from her face.

Femi leans against the shower wall, watching me intently. I'm sure he expected something more than me just cleaning his cum from her lips, but they're not getting it.

This is my only present.

For now.

The washcloth glides down her cheek and around her breasts. Doc closes her eyes and moans, her fingers drifting between her legs. Femi's cock hardens when they disappear inside her pussy.

He raises his eyebrows requesting permission.

I shake my head, telling him no.

I'm leading this shower adventure. Not him.

I place my hand on his shoulder and press him down so his eyes are level with her pussy. "Open your mouth," I order.

Doc's eyes spring open as Femi yanks her fingers from her pussy and stuffs his tongue in their place. She rocks into his face, and her eyes pinch closed as she moans.

His hands spread her lips farther apart, and he licks them one, then the other, and dives back in.

I grip the hair on the back of her head. "Open your eyes."

She gazes deep into my eyes and breathes heavily, her brows furrowing—an orgasm imminent.

I yank Femi's head away. The only fluids he's allowed to drink are mine.

Doc grabs her pussy. "Please. It hurts." She pleads with her eyes, desperate for me to grant her permission to let her pussy juices fill Femi's mouth.

"No." I smile at her and leave the shower.

I grab my flesh-colored dildo from under the sink and place it in her hand. "Get it yourself."

She stares at the size of it and frowns. "I can't."

I look at Femi's cock and then at the dildo, switching it to vibrate mode. "If you won't, he will." I place the shaking sex toy in his hand.

He places the tip of it against her opening and nuzzles her neck. "Say yes."

A breathy and barely audible 'yes' filters from her tremoring lips, and he slides the oversize faux cock into her swollen pussy. I grab her throat and squeeze it. "Look at me."

Her top teeth bite down on her bottom lip as Femi moves the toy in and out of her seductively.

Partly giving in to her is a way for me to try and be more like them—giving in to desire. Doing this gives me leverage—power over her.

She may be his employee and under his orders, but when it comes to the bedroom, I run the show.

I decide how far things go. And if everything goes as planned, Femi won't be her boss for much longer. She will be under me, with my girls, and doing my bidding.

With me.

"It's coming," she says in a shaky voice.

"Take it out," I say to Femi.

He looks at me but doesn't comply.

I yank it out of her body violently, grab her hand and press her fingers into her pussy, keeping my hand on hers and rotating it until she explodes.

"Oh my God." She sinks to the floor, holding my wrist and taking me down with her.

I remove her hand from my wrist and hold my hand out to Femi to help me. "Merry early Christmas," I say as I stand and step out of the shower, pulling Femi behind me.

I pass him a towel. He wraps it around his waist and follows me to the bedroom. His cock acts like a pole against the terry cloth material, pitching a tent and holding it away from his body.

He puts his hands on his hips. "That wasn't very nice."

I frown and pull on a pair of stretch waist shorts. "I'm not a *nice* person." I stop beside him and glare at him. "She got off, isn't that all that matters?"

"You're making this hard for her. You know how she feels about you." Femi follows me to the kitchen still wearing a towel.

Henry passes us, crawling across the floor towards my room.

"Feels about who?" Ari asks over her shoulder without taking her eyes off the show she's watching.

I open my mouth to reply when Doc's screams echo down the hallway.

She runs into the hallway, half-dressed, hair dripping all over the floor. "Get your fucking pet a cage."

Ari rounds the couch and picks up Henry. "He's not a pet. He's family."

I shake my head. If Ari considers Henry family, then what am I?

Doc balls her fists and yells at her. "He's not family. He's a fucking reptile, you idiot."

"Hey!" I shout and step between them.

I grab Doc's arms, pull her against my chest, and brush a damp piece of hair away from her face. "Don't call her an idiot. Not now, not ever again. Understand?" I say in a stern voice, my eyes piercing through hers.

She opens her mouth to speak, but Femi answers. "She understands." He grabs Doc's hand and pulls her sideways away from me. "Go pack your things," he orders.

I stare at her defined calves as she saunters away and disappears into the guest bedroom.

Ari stands beside me, holding Henry against her chest. "Thank you."

"Go pack," I say, walking around her and ignoring her insistent stare.

I defended her like a mother or friend would. I know that's what she wanted to say to me, but she's learning not to point out things that make me seem more like a person instead of the monster I am.

Before I met Femi, things were so much easier. I didn't have to worry about hurting anyone's feelings or defending anyone.

Caring.

I could move about my environment and care less about strangers' judgmental words and eyes. One fierce stare from me is all it would take for them to retreat and mind their business. But now I have people who care for me, and they aren't afraid to stand firm and voice their opinions and concerns. They aren't afraid of me. I allowed myself to become soft thanks to Ari. Teaching her not to draw attention to herself has backfired on me. Every time I do or say something not perceived as normal by the masses; she lets me know that I too, have a problem with drawing too much attention. Even the clothes on my back have changed. It's better to dress like a bum in sweatpants and no makeup than to wear a mini skirt and brush my hair.

Being normal is hard, but acting normal is even harder.

A hand waves in front of my face. "Are you stuck?" Chicken Wing asks, smiling at me.

I unlock my eyes from the floor and shake the fog from my head. I'm so distracted. I swear the longer I'm around Ari, the more her random visits to the blank space inside her mind rub off on me.

Chicken Wing holds a bourbon out to me. "You need this more than I do."

His real name is Evan, but after seeing him without a shirt for the first time, I changed it.

I accept his offering and gulp it down. "I'm going to need you to stay close to Ari."

He leans against the counter and crosses his arms. "Are you worried about the mission?"

"Men are strong, but women can be ruthless." I rotate the empty glass in my hand.

He nods and pours more bourbon into my glass. "Like you?"

I don't answer. I polish off the glass of liquor and head to my bedroom.

Luisa Mercado isn't going to fall for an alluring woman stranded on the side of the road like Griffin and Benny did. She's not going to just invite us into her home or yacht willingly. I think about when Femi and I met. We hit it off at once. It started with honesty. Telling each other something disturbing and true. That similar frame of mind and way of thinking pulled us together like a magnetic force making it easier to trust each other.

We need to find a common interest to rope her in and make her want to bring us into her world. If she's anything like me, it won't be an easy task.

I slide my closet door open, grab the handle of my rolling luggage from the top shelf, and pull it to the floor. Let's see—unusually warm summer, beach, clubs, crazy psycho bitch that needs her throat cut. I remove a few fitted knee-length sun dresses, a couple of sweatpants sets, and slutty nightclub attire, leaving them on their hangers, and fold them into the luggage. Red lingerie, with white fur trim, brushes my cheek and lands on top of my pile of clothing.

I peer over my shoulder. "What do I need that for?"

Femi smirks in the doorway. "I thought it would be a nice Christmas morning outfit." He reaches behind his back and tosses red silk boxers at me, hitting me in the face with them. "And I'll wear these."

"I prefer to wear nothing at all."

He squats beside me, resting his elbows on his knees and interlacing his fingers. "Thank you for agreeing to this." His tongue glides across his bottom lip before he bites it gently.

I want to bite it too. My eyes flick to the bulge between his legs but settle on his thighs hidden beneath a pair of gray sweatpants and my mouth waters.

Fuck.

He lets me lick them, kiss them, and even nibble them, but he won't let me taste them. Not the way I want to.

"Odie." He lifts my chin with his pointer finger, forcing my eyes away from his meaty legs. "When we get to the beach, I'm going to need you to control yourself."

His comment confuses me. "What are you talking about?" I grab my Fast Box gun safe, slide it out from under my bed, and toss it on top of the lingerie.

He sighs heavily and sits beside me. "There are going to be a lot of people there."

"And?" I furrow my brow, add six V40 grenades to my luggage, and zip it closed. "I've been to a beach before, Femi. You have one behind your mansion."

He drops his head between his knees and sighs. "Miami is different. My mansion was only us and my men—people you know and trust." His eyes race up my body from toes to tits before locking on mine. He stands and stretches his arms over his head. "It's going to be crowded, and we all know you hate crowds."

I close my suitcase, zip it, and stand. "You're being ridiculous. A beach is a beach. Besides, if it gets to be too busy, I can just leave, or Doc can give me a Xanax or something."

He smiles and drops his head, staring at my plush vanilla carpet. "I need you to let me know if it becomes too much."

Letting him or anyone else know I am having a hard time shows weakness—vulnerability. The only person who recognizes when I'm about to lose my shit besides him and Doc, sometimes before I even do, is Ari.

"I'll be fine." I stand, grab my suitcase handle, and roll it out to the living room.

Chicken Wing and Ari are assembling the two-foot square portable travel cage for Henry she bought from the pet store on the kitchen island. We can't travel for several hours with a lizard crawling around the vehicle.

Ari grins when Chicken Wing nudges her shoulder with his elbow. They like each other, and I approve.

For now.

He seems to help her focus and relax. When they talk, she hangs on to his every word, keeping her from rambling and fidgeting, a few of her annoying habits. Relationships are about balance, and they seem to be teetering in the center of a level. Their bubble floating between the lines exactly where it should be.

Doc pads into the room and drops a carry-on bag and two rolling suitcases beside mine. Femi moseys in behind her and sets his bag down.

Our relationship is anything but level. We float from one side of the line to the other, occasionally meeting in the middle. The problem is me.

When leveling two things, you adjust one side or the other until you find the middle—the balance.

But when a third source is involved, finding balance and common ground can be difficult if not impossible.

The problem with us is that I'm the third source. Doc has worked with Femi for years without a problem, always professional, and always in balance, never crossing the line.

I brought her into our sexual relationship. Seeing her desire for him, and how much she loved him but was too afraid to cross that line. The only problem is by bringing her in, feelings developed unexpectedly. It wasn't my intention, but here we are—him loving me, her loving him, both desiring my attention and acceptance.

Both want me to take our relationship a step further, but that wasn't a part of my original plan. Part of my original plan was to use her to keep his mind off me when I left him. I've never stayed with one person this long, so he should be happy I haven't left sooner. And when he presented that diamond to me, I thought I was going to vomit.

Vow to stay with the same person for the rest of my life? Is he fucking crazy?

No.
Hell motherfucking no.

Chapter Ten
Life's a Beach

Oh, fuck. This is a bad idea. Having me come to the beach is like dropping a recently recovered addict into a room full of their drug of choice.

Now I know why Femi was concerned.

So…many…legs.

A buffet of tan, pale, hairy, and hairless limbs waiting for me to slice them into filets.

My mouth waters excessively.

Nom, nom.

I guess Ari and I are both working on our self-control today.

Femi's wearing linen pants. He's a smart man, prepared for the situation we are now in, and keeping my appetite in check.

I carry my chair to the edge of the water, keeping a minimum number of people in front of me, but it doesn't matter. Within minutes of sitting down, a God-like, muscular, and lean man, in a pair of red, white, and blue well-fitting boxers, stalks towards me, tossing his shoulder-length dirty blonde hair back and forth. My legs clamp shut, and my knuckles whiten against the chair's arms.

God fucking bless America.

My stomach tenses as the distance between us grows smaller. He's walking directly to me.

What sweet fucking hell is this?

God Dammit. Someone give me a fucking blade.

A body appears before me blocking my view. I try and look around it, but it shifts back in my way.

"No," Doc says. "Focus on me."

Grrrr.

She kneels before me once the man has walked past me and out of danger. "You didn't put on sunblock, did you?"

"My legs are pale. I'm trying to give them a little sun." I won't look her in the eye, despite her intense gaze, keeping my focus on a stray hair on my leg, flapping in the ocean breeze.

"You should be wearing your sling." Sunblock splatters into Doc's palm.

She rubs her hands together and wraps them around my calf.

I jerk my leg away. "What are you doing?"

"If you won't put it on, I will." She smears it around my calves and works her way down to my feet.

She fills her palm with more lotion, rubs her hands together, and places a hand on each of my thighs.

Air catches in my lungs, and I hold it there as her hands glide down my naked legs and skirt dangerously close to my pussy, making it twitch.

"Breathe," she whispers seductively.

Her bright yellow suit barely holds her breasts at bay, and a tan line develops along the edge of a strap. She grabs each of my arms and spreads the lotion up and down my biceps and forearms.

"I'll take over," Femi says in a firm voice appearing beside us.

Doc hands the lotion up to him and grimaces before standing, disappointed she didn't get to finish. She gazes down at me and sighs. "You need to have more put on in a few hours, or you'll burn."

As she walks away, my eyes lock on the string disappearing between her ass cheeks. Her bottoms cover next to nothing, making them useless.

"Lie down and turn over," Femi says, kneeling beside me.

I recline my seat and roll onto my stomach. He squirts the lotion onto my back and kneads it into my skin aggressively. "Watching her rub your skin made me jealous."

Jealous?

Femi has never been jealous before.

His hands slide from the back of my knees up to the bottom of my butt cheeks and stop. "It made me horny."

Pressure enters my pussy as his thumbs slide between my legs and move in and out. He kisses my left cheek. "I need you."

Tingling creeps up my thighs but suddenly vanishes as he removes his fingers, leaving me wanting.

"What are you doing?" I sit up on my elbows and look back at him.

"She's here." He stands and offers me his hand.

"Who?" I take his hand, and he pulls me up against his chest.

"Luisa," he whispers.

I try and turn, and he grabs my face, crushing it between his fingers, and kisses me hard.

This isn't him. He's never been aggressive or forceful with me, at least not in public. It must have to do with her proximity or something he sees.

"What are you doing?" I push him hard away from me.

He falls backward over the chair, landing hard on his ass. His eyes widen. "Sorry."

A small part of me felt guilty for pushing him so hard, but I wanted to be sure our interaction was enough to draw Luisa's attention. I need her to think either we are a fighting love triangle, or Femi is a third party who recently came into the picture and wants our relationship to go a step further.

I storm away from him and almost run into Luisa.

Mission accomplished.

"Excuse me," I say to her and continue walking to Doc who's lying on her stomach with the back of her top untied. I run my fingers gently from her spine down to her sides and grab the straps. "Come on, babe." I cross the strings and tie them. "Let's go in the water."

She shields the sun from her eyes when she turns over. "Everything okay?"

I take her hand and pull her to her feet, not letting her hand go and keeping her body close, her backside facing Luisa who's facing us.

Luisa's dark eyes fixate on Doc's bare ass. I can't tell if they are so dark brown, they appear black, or if she's so evil her eyes no longer have color and have blackened over time. She licks her bottom lip and rubs her upper thigh with three fingers.

Gotcha.

Luisa prefers the company of women. And that is our way in. Tempting her desire using Doc is a dangerous but necessary game to complete our mission. She will bring Doc into her world, and Doc can then leak critical information on Luisa's habits, frequent locations, and any vulnerabilities that she may have.

I pull Doc behind me, stepping around Femi, still lying in the sand where I pushed him down. He turns on his side with a sinister smile and winks at me when I glance down at him. His thumb hooks the spandex top of his linen pants and pulls them down slightly, revealing an untanned patch on his hip bone—white meat.

Fucking tease.

He must have seen Luisa ignoring all the barely dressed men around her but paying attention to the beautiful women, especially Doc.

Luisa stands at the water's edge, watching us and letting the waves float over her feet. Guards dressed in inappropriate beach attire, stand slightly behind her, keeping their feet dry from the incoming tide. More men linger about, maintaining their distance, but unable to hide their purpose. They look ridiculous and stand out like a bunch of women wearing bikinis while modeling in a foot of snow. It makes me wish for a rogue wave to come ashore, soak their black attire, and flood the chambers of their weapons. Perhaps one or two would float out to sea and be unable to swim. I would grab their heads and force them beneath the waves, fucking their drowning and dying faces between my legs with my pussy.

For being forty, Luisa has a rocking body—muscular and lean abs, well-cared-for and unwrinkled skin. Her brown bikini rests perfectly on her curvy hips.

"Is she watching us?" I ask Doc, moving in front of her and putting my back to the beach.

Doc nods and dips beneath the surface of the water. She emerges and smooths her long blonde hair, turning her face to the sun like she's at a photo shoot for a swimsuit magazine. Perfectly timed for Luisa to witness her glorious and sexy emergence from the water.

Even I can't keep my eyes off the droplets of water glistening on her skin. I wrap my arms around her and pull her against me.

She needs to believe we are together—believe we are a couple.

"Kiss me when she's looking," I say to Doc.

Doc moves away from me, the ocean waves helping her. "What?"

I swim closer to her, keeping my mouth close to the surface of the water. "She needs to believe we are a couple, so later we can break up when I cheat on you with Femi." I wink at her.

She laughs aloud as though I said something funny when I didn't.

Playing her part.

I swim to her like a shark stalking its prey and slowly stand. A wave pushes us closer to the shore, the water now coming up to our hips. She nods, indicating we have our target audience. I drag my tongue against her salty abdomen, stop just before her lips, and plunge it inside. Her mouth tastes like strawberry taffy, and the shape of her tongue curves around mine, holding it tight against her lips.

The fire between us ignites at once like a slow-burning relationship finally coming to a head. We walk into deeper waters exploring each other's mouths. The skin on her face smells of coconut and passion fruit, and her lotion-coated flesh glides like smooth silk beneath my palms. She shoves her hand between my legs, grabs the fabric covering my pussy, and moves it aside. My eyes spring open, and my stomach tenses, sensing the impending invasion of her fingers. I can't do it. It's too much—too far. I yank her hand from between my legs and shove her away from me.

Kissing passionately to sell a relationship is one thing, trying to take advantage of the situation is another.

I fight against the waves and exit the ocean. Doc stays in the water staring out at the open ocean. Even though I can't see her face, I can feel the pain of my rejection emanating from her.

She turns towards me. Her face is red from anger or embarrassment. Perhaps both. Opening our relationship will only create more problems. I like the way things are.

The current arrangement we have satisfies what I want, and that's all that matters to me. I don't have room in my life for two lovers, one is work enough.

Fuck. Here she comes—fists tight at her sides and jaw set. This isn't part of the show for Luisa, this is Doc ready to hurt someone—ready to fight.

I half expected her to try and hit me. Instead, she storms by me, bumping into me on her way by, and stops to talk to Ari who just returned from purchasing two lemonade slushes. She shoves the drinks into her folding chair's cup holder and Chicken Wing's empty seat beside her. Her face frowns, and her head nods as Doc speaks in her ear. I roll my eyes when she glares at me.

Ari's becoming more like the disciplinary parent on this little trip of ours. She wouldn't have let us fight, staying in the middle like a mom scolding her two children for being petty.

Part of me was up for a good throwdown. I'd deserve it for all the times I've rejected her or kept her from fucking Femi. It wouldn't be an epic battle. I would allow her to punch and hit me as much as she wants, knowing I couldn't feel a thing, nor would I strike back. In the end, she would still be mad, and I would have a bunch of bruises for her to look at for a week or two and feel guilty about.

Luisa eyes me from several feet away. I take a step in her direction, and a hand grabs me.

"Odie, now is not the time," Ari says to me. "Come sit down."

Her partially sunken lounge chair takes two of us to pull from the sand. We move the seats back several feet, keeping the incoming tide from washing them away. Femi is speaking with Chicken Wing in the distance.

"You need to be careful with this one," Ari says, rubbing sunblock into her skin. "She's not an idiot.

Chicken Wing told me nothing is as it seems with her, and we need to be careful."

"I know what I am doing." I lie back on the lounger and throw my arm over my forehead.

She abruptly turns sideways in her seat. "Odie, even from the few minutes I've been sitting on this beach watching you, I can see your personal feelings are clouding your judgment. Whatever is going on with you three, you need to figure it out before it gets one of you killed."

I sit up and glare at her. "I have personal feelings for no one."

She grimaces at me. "Fine. Call it what you want. Call it puppy love or desire. I don't care. I care about you and everyone else on this beach who would die for you and what we all believe." She lays down. "Don't shut us out and pretend not to care because you're afraid."

I roll off my lounger and walk away from her.

Afraid?

I'm not afraid of anyone or anything.

I walk along the edge of the water with my head high. In the corner of my eye, a pair of fantastic-looking legs stop me from going forward. I trace them up to their owner.

My, oh my. This silver fox has certainly taken care of his body over the years.

"Can I help you with something, young lady?" Silver Fox asks.

Ari grabs my arm and pulls me away before I have a chance to engage. "No, sir. She thought you were her dad."

"My dad?" I furrow my brows at her.

She keeps pulling me along without saying anything and doesn't stop until we reach the pier. "Odie, we have a couple of things to discuss." Henry pokes his head out of her beach bag, and she tucks him back in. "First off, why are you checking out that slab of aged meat?"

"Did you see his legs? Sometimes, aged is fantastic."

Ari closes her eyes and sighs. "Yeah, well he looks contaminated, and his dick is probably riddled with herpes."

I curl my lip. "That's disgusting."

"Glad I could help." She clears her throat and focuses on the sand. "My brothers are here."

"I know. You told me they and your sisters would be in Florida for Christmas."

She grins and nods. "Yeah, I did. But when I say here, I mean at the beach. Right now."

I look around. "Really? Where?"

She grabs my hands and shakes her head. "Odie, before you meet them, you should know something."

"Why do you keep shaking your head? I told you I would behave," I say, glaring at her.

"I'm not shaking my head at you." Her eyes peer over my shoulder.

I turn around and the hot and sexy fuck in the red, white, and blue shorts smiles at me. "Hi, I'm Bryce..."

Oh, no.

He narrows the distance between us and stretches his hand out to me. "...Ari's oldest brother."

God dammit.

I stare at his hand for so long, that he rescinds his greeting.

Ari bumps my shoulder with hers. "This is my best friend, Odie."

"Nice to meet you, Odie," he says in a gritty voice.

A flirty laugh escapes my throat, catching me by surprise. I can't move. I'm stuck trying to control the overwhelming urge to shove him under the pier and fuck his brains out.

A younger version of Bryce stops beside him wearing blood-red shorts. "Is this her?" he asks Ari.

My teeth grind against each other as I stare between his legs. There are two of them. I feel like I'm in a Wrigley's Gum Double Your Pleasure commercial. I'd put both their sticks in my mouth, just saying.

I want to scream at her. It's not her fault that her brothers are sexy beasts, but she could have warned me before we left Roanoke.

She smiles at my discomfort of knowing I want them, but can't have them, testing my self-control once more. "Yep. Odie, this is my brother, Tyson."

It takes everything in me to bring my eyes level with his. "Hello."

Tyson's hair is darker than Bryce and his skin is much paler, but his legs are equally muscular.

"Ari, can I speak to you in private?" I say with a tight smile and walk backward into the ocean.

She passes her bag to Tyson and follows me. "Everything okay?"

I wait until we are several feet in before I speak. "Ari, your brothers are sexy and—"

"Stop." She puts her hand in front of my face, cutting me off, and frowns. "No. You're not using them as an excuse to get out of dinner. You will keep your hypersexual, cannibalistic thoughts in check, and we will enjoy a nice dinner on Christmas Eve and then open gifts."

I glance at the brothers watching us with shielded eyes and smile at her. "Are they included in my Christmas presents?"

She wrinkles her face, and the water beside me gets warm. "Their presence is all the presents you'll get if you don't behave yourself."

I move several feet away from her. "Did you just pee beside me?"

She grins broadly. "Did it make you stop thinking about my brothers inappropriately?"

"That's disgusting." I move further away from her.

"Good." She swims towards me when I stop moving. "Every time you think about something inappropriate during dinner, think about my warm pee encapsulating your right thigh underwater."

I swallow hard and gag inadvertently. "Gross."

Bryce enters the water and walks towards us. "Everything okay?"

"Yeah. Everything is great." Ari smiles and waves him away from us. "Remember the pee."

I roll my lips into my mouth, hold back the bile rising in my throat, and nod. "I'll try my best."

"Good." She gives two thumbs up to her two brothers who are now speaking with two other guys watching us with their hands on their hips. "Because if you don't, I'll shit in my hand and throw it at you across the table like an angry fucking ape."

Jesus.

"You've changed." I frown at her.

She smiles at me. "You have no one to blame but yourself." Her head disappears beneath a wave and reappears a few feet closer to shore.

I ride a wave up beside her. "Ari, who are the other two people with Bryce and Tyson?"

She turns her attention to the shore and swims away without answering.

I swim behind her and yank her back to me by her bikini bottoms, nearly ripping them off. "Who are they?" I point to the newcomers on shore.

A wave rips us apart and rolls us in separate directions. My head scrapes against the crushed shells embedded in the sand, and I roll several times before landing on my feet, still in waist-deep water. Ari lands on her ass in foot-deep water with her back facing the beach. I wade toward her.

When I get to ankle-deep water, I stop walking. "Stay down," I yell to her, but I'm too late. Another wave pushes her onto the sand and retreats.

She rolls onto her side and staggers to her feet. Multiple beachgoers cover their mouths and point. I stifle a laugh and shake my head. She gazes down at her naked half. Instead of trying to cover herself like most people, she rocks her hips side to side rapidly, jiggling her butt cheeks at the audience behind her. "Get a load of this bitches."

Her bottoms float by me and stop beside her, and attention-seeking Ari reappears, drawing more than just a crowd of onlookers' attention.

Chapter Eleven
Exposed

"Is she with you?" Luisa asks, standing beside me in ankle-deep water.

Her sudden presence surprises me. I was so focused on Ari's brothers and now Ari, that I didn't notice that she and her men were moving dangerously close to us.

Close to me.

"Unfortunately," I answer honestly as Ari feeds one leg into her bottoms while her brothers partially shield her body with a towel.

Luisa chuckles and studies the side of my face. "What is your business in Miami?"

"Who said I was here on business?" I say, watching Doc approach and scan the shore; no doubt looking for me.

We remain quiet for several seconds. Both of our eyes lock on Doc's perfect ass when she turns around. Doc spots us and enters the water.

Luisa can't look away, drawn in by Doc's perfection and sex appeal. Like a fish taking the bait, Luisa opens wide for her worm.

She nods at Doc. "Is she yours?"

Doc exits the water. The sun glistens off her tanning skin. I follow a large droplet of salty liquid as it races down her throat and disappears between her breasts.

"Sometimes." I smile as Doc stops in front of us.

Doc looks Luisa up and down. "Nice suit."

Luisa swings her hands behind her back, puffing her chest to enhance the presence of her breasts, and holds them there. "Thank you, Miss…"

Doc scans Luisa's face. "Ivy."

She lies so easily.

It makes me wonder what other lies she tells or secrets she hides.

They smile at each other, flirting without words, just body language.

Anger builds inside me, but I'm not mad.

It's jealousy.

But I'm not the jealous type, never have been.

Inserting Doc into Luisa's life is a dangerous plan, but it's the only way to get eyes on the inside. Find out her routine—her schedule.

Femi walks alongside a hotel building, slides open a patio door and disappears inside.

That's my cue.

"Excuse me. I'll be right back." I wade away from them, walk under and around the pier, and come back near the hotel, ensuring everyone sees me.

I tap on the glass sliding door.

Femi pulls the door open, and I step inside. He closes the curtains but leaves a gap. "Do you think this will work?"

"We are about to find out." I remove my top and bottom and sit on the bed with my legs gapped open.

Femi peeks through the opening. "Here they come."

"Luisa's with her?" I touch my pussy, warming it up for him.

He walks towards me and removes his pants. "More like following Doc from a distance."

My breath quickens as he drops to his knees between my legs. "It might be a bit sandy." I smile at him.

He licks his lips. "I don't fucking care."

I pinch my eyes closed and moan. His tongue floats in and out of me, making my pussy lips swell.

A shadow appears in the curtain gap.

She's watching us.

I grab Femi's hair and yank him on top of me. "Fuck me."

He lifts me from the bed and throws my body onto the table closer to the window. The table bangs against the wall with every violent thrust he delivers.

"Harder, Daddy," I shout loud enough for our watchers to hear me.

Femi grabs me around the waist, lifts me to my feet, and shoves me against the wall face first, inches from the patio door. He spreads my cheeks with his hands and buries his face between them, licking my pussy, taint, and asshole, making it pucker.

His body pins against mine, crushing my breasts into the wallpaper. The tip of his cock tracing around my hole without entering. "Are you ready, my love?"

I reach behind me and grip his hair. "Give it to me, Pussycat."

My body slides up the wall as he pushes his cock inside me, tearing a piece of wallpaper at a seam. I grab the torn paper and rip it away, pushing the curtain further to the side and dropping it on the ground. My mouth drops open, and I smile seductively at Doc's face twisting in false agony at my betrayal only a few feet away from the glass. Luisa's behind her, her fake eyebrows arched to the sky.

I press my forehead against the wall. "Fuck me deeper. Make me cum."

Femi grabs my wrists, holding them above my head, and rolls his hips upward, grinding his dick deep inside me. "Tell me when it's coming," he growls and grunts in a breathy voice.

He releases my hands and grabs an ass cheek in each hand, thrusting into me rhythmically. I push back with my body, disengaging his cock, and turn to him, panting heavily. "Now."

He hoists my entire body up, places my thighs on his shoulders, and takes my entire pussy into his mouth.

I pump myself into his face. "Taste my cum."

The shadow in the window vanishes, and I reach for the curtain to shift it further. Doc is covering her face, and Luisa has her hand on her shoulder. They are walking away from the window.

"Oh, fuck." My toes curl, and I explode into his mouth.

He sucks my clit into his mouth, draining my pussy of its juices. My head nearly strikes a dangly light fixture as he pulls me away from the wall and drops me on the bed, entering me quickly.

I push him off me. "Lay down."

He rolls onto his spine and puts his hands behind his head. "Ride that cock like a good girl."

I turn around so my back is to him, and sit on his cock, riding it backwards. His thighs tense as I grip them tight, holding them for leverage, and bounce up and down.

"Fuck, Odie. That feels good." He places his hands on my waist and presses me down on his lap.

I grip his deliciously tan thighs and grind deeper into him. "Oh, Pussycat."

His cock flops out of me as I slide my legs backward towards his face and rest my abdomen against his, my ass in his face. I lick his thighs, one at a time, and pause. His cock pokes me in the throat, begging for me to take it in my mouth.

But that's not what I want.

I crush his thigh in my hand and latch on to it with my lips, sucking the blood to the surface.

Femi pushes me off him, forces me onto my stomach, and whispers in my ear in a breathy voice. "What do you think you're doing?"

I nuzzle his head with mine and moan. "Come on baby. I just want a little taste."

Warm air enters my ear as he speaks. "Let me fuck your ass."

My ass cheeks instantly tighten. The thought of him putting his sizeable cock in my asshole scares the shit out of me.

It's something we've never done before, and I never planned on doing.

"No," I say and shift uncomfortably beneath him.

He rests his forehead against my spine and rocks it back and forth. "Come on, Odie, we've done everything else. I promise I'll be gentle."

"You must give me something in return." I smile knowing he'll never agree.

His cock glides along my anus. "Anything. I'll give you anything."

"Are you sure about that?" I glare at him over my shoulder with a devilish grin.

"Anything." He moans and bounces around the outside of my hole a few times.

"I want a piece of your thigh."

He recoils away from me and his cock softens slightly. "I was afraid you were going to say that."

His cock hardens against my ass, and he pulls the drawer beside us open, removing a lubricant. "I'll do it."

Fuck. I never expected him to say yes.

I try and shift away from him, but he holds me still with a palm on my lower back. "Shhh, just relax. I promise to go very slowly."

Warms liquid fills my ass crack, and he lays his chest against my back.

"Femi, I don't think I can." I move my cheeks back and forth, keeping him from inserting his cock inside me.

His right-hand wraps around my throat and his left directs his cock to my asshole and pushes. "Shhh…just the tip to start."

I recoil away from him, and he pulls me back to him by my neck. "Be a good girl and hold still."

The pressure is too much. I buck him off me, and he lands on the floor. "No," I say firmly.

He sits up on his elbows, glances at his thighs, and rocks them back and forth with a smile. "I guess you didn't want these thighs as bad as you thought."

I grab my bikini and quickly cover my breasts. "I shouldn't have to allow such a traumatic act to get what I want."

He covers his face to hide his outward laughter. "You want to take a piece of me and grill it with some vegetables. Don't you think that would be traumatic for me, my love?"

"Oh, Pussycat, don't be a pussy." I enter the bathroom and turn on the shower.

Sand rinses from my hair and covers the tile by my feet. I curl my toes and swish it to the drain.

"Oooodieee." Femi draws my name out and slaps the shower curtain aside. "I think you forgot something." He points at his neglected cock.

I smile and turn my back on him. "Do it yourself."

He grabs my hair and yanks it back. "Not going to happen."

My body flattens against the shower wall, and he raises my right leg, resting my foot on the soap shelf. I yelp as he shoves his cock into me, ramming my body up and down the shower wall, fucking me hard from behind.

How I've missed this. All the fucking and pussy eating he does makes it hard to stay away.

But not impossible.

He flips me around, stuffs his cock into me, and grabs my throat, crushing it in his grasp. His eyes are set on mine, dark and determined to get what he wants. His cock in my ass. "Give me your ass," he orders, tightening his grip further and pressing a finger inside my anus.

"No." The word barely passes through my lips, his grip strangling me and cutting off any further objection.

His finger leaves my anus and enters his mouth. "Just as tasty as the rest of you," he moans, sucking his finger and placing a second hand around my throat. He tightens his grip with every upward thrust, grunting through gritted teeth as he struggles to finish.

It's too tight. Spots dance around my widening eyes and a flashback of Griffin choking me in the gas chamber floats into my head. I slap Femi's shoulder several times, trying to tap out, but he doesn't stop thrusting into me—choking me.

Killing me.

I dig my nails into the back of his hands, drawing blood, but he doesn't slow, caught up in the moment, the feeling of fucking and killing me at the same time. His head launches back, and his cum fills my insides as I land a punch to the side of his face.

He lets my throat go, covers the side of his face where I struck him, and pins me to the wall with his body. "Did you just punch me?" His eyes darken.

"Let me go, or I'm going to do more than just punch you." I rest my knee against his cock.

His face relaxes and his eyes soften. "If I went too far, I'm sorry." He steps back, freeing me.

I step around him, yank a towel from its bar, and dry off quickly. "If you ever do that to me again, I will fucking kill you."

"Ouch. That's a bit harsh." He grabs a towel.

I snatch it away from him, throw it behind me, and point in his face. "No, harsh is what comes after I kill you. Harsh is when I slice away all the usable meat from your bones, stuff it in a grinder, and make ground meat out of it. Harsh is when I take your bones, bleach them fuckers and turn you into a skeleton model on wheels. Harsh is when I roll your hinged bones into a God damn room full of your men and teach them about anatomy. That's fucking harsh, Femi!" I scream and storm away from him.

I pace the room and take several cleansing breaths. *Calm down. Just calm down. It wasn't on purpose. It wasn't...*

"Odie?" Femi's voice comes out soft and quiet. "I'm so fucking sorry." His hands wrap around my waist from behind, squeezing my stomach gently. He rests his chin on my shoulder. "Please forgive me."

I rest my palm on his hand and remove it from my stomach. "Don't ever do that to me again."

He sighs heavily. "I didn't mean to go so far."

I lie back on the bed and close my eyes. "I know."

* * *

The phone rings in my dream, and I ignore it until it stops. Light slowly filters through my lids, and the hotel room comes into focus.

The phone chimes noisily but this time I'm not dreaming.

"That's the third time. Maybe you should answer," Femi groans beside me.

I didn't intend to fall asleep. Too much sunshine can drop anyone into a coma unintendedly, so I'm not surprised.

The ringing phone pierces my ears. I snatch it from its base. "What?'

My face drops at the sound of Doc's crying voice, and I sit up at once. I couldn't understand what she was saying, her words slurring intermittently.

"Where are you?" I ask, pulling on my bikini bottoms.

Femi stands and rests his ear against my head, trying to listen. "Did she say boarded building?"

I push him away from me. "Stop crying, and tell me where?"

This is my fault. Whatever has happened is because I pushed her into this—made her the bait. Femi wanted to come, but I wanted to bring her home on my own. Whatever happened, she wouldn't say over the phone.

After weaving in and out of traffic for several miles, I arrive at the vacant lot of the abandoned restaurant on the outskirts of the city. The boarded-up windows and graffiti covering the walls tell many tales to commuters and vacationers passing by—whose territory the building falls in, names of past hurricanes, water level marks, and multiple real estate advertisers who've unsuccessfully tried to sell the hopeless property. I use my hip to move the partially broken door aside and walk cautiously toward the kitchen.

Crying and music comes from a walk-in freezer. I push the door open, and my blood boils. One of Luisa's guards is on top of Doc, his hand covering her mouth— his cock thrusting into her. I yank my knife from its sheath on my thigh. Doc's eyes widen, seeing my blade rise and fall behind the man's back, stabbing him in the spinal cord, and paralyzing him from the waist down. His body drops beside her. I straddle his midsection. He raises his hands, trying to grab my blade and keep it from coming down on his face. But he moves too slowly, and it plunges through his right eye socket. He screams and reaches for me, but I stab his hairy chest. He grunts and holds my bloody hands wrapped tightly around the handle of my knife. His mouth moves, but no words come out, just blood.

A lot of it.

I lift my right hand slowly, pulling the blade from his chest. Blood bubbles through the opening and drains onto the floor to my right, warming my knee as it pools beside us.

Doc crawls away, retreating to the closest corner. Bruises and blood dot her visible flesh. Condoms litter the ground around us.

"Mother fucker!" I scream at the dying man beneath me.

I can't stop stabbing him. Flashbacks of what happened to me and the other women flood my head like poison. With every rise and fall of the blade, blood splatters across my barely covered flesh until he no longer moves.

He's dead, but it doesn't stop me. I gouge his left eye out and throw it over my shoulder. His cock sheers off with a quick flick of my wrist, and I stuff it in his dead, open mouth.

"Please, stop," Doc pleads.

She's never seen me in action—only after the fact or just before.

Her voice fades into the background, and I pretend I'm alone. My heart rate slows and my breathing steadies.

Work mode.

Although the man's thighs are scrawny and worthless, I cut away a large piece of meat.

I stand, slide my bloody blade back inside its holder, and reach for Doc.

She won't come to me. Her empty eyes stare at the bloody slab of meat dripping in my grasp.

I back away, giving her some space, and step into the kitchen area. Femi rounds the corner and walks into me.

He holds my blood-soaked body by the arms, away from his suit. "Jesus, Odie. What happened?" His body leans sideways, looking behind me. "Where is she?"

"They hurt her." I glare at him, rage burning through my eyes. "I'm going to kill them all."

He releases my arms, and I lift my right hand, holding the man's thigh meat in my palm. "This is just the beginning. I'm going to bring them all back here..." My eyes wander to the meat grinder and sausage stuffer on the counter. "...and make homemade sausage out of them."

Femi cups his hand over mine, closing his eyes to the chunk of muscle that one day may be his. "Who hurt her? What are you talking about?"

I ignore him and turn towards the door. "They are all mine. You stay the fuck out of this."

He grabs my arm and spins me around to face him. "I'm not staying out of this. I'm knee-deep in it, Odie. Now, tell me what the fuck you are talking about. Who are *they*?"

"Luisa's men!" I shout in his face, spitting on it at the same time.

He wipes his cheeks and cups my face in his hands. "I will take care of this. You need to stand down."

I curl my fingers around his and throw his hands away from me. "You are not going to stop me from getting my revenge."

Ari appears wearing a knee-length red cocktail dress with Chicken Wing, who has his gun drawn. He's wearing dress pants and a black button-up shirt. She removes a plastic bag from her wristlet and shakes it open between Femi and me. "I'll take that."

I drop the hunk of meat in the Ziploc, and Femi grabs the back of my head, pulling me to him and kissing my forehead. "I won't stop you, but you aren't doing this alone. Whatever happens is on all of us, just not you. Now, where is Doc?"

"In the freezer," I whisper, wiping his moist kiss from my head.

He steps around me and immediately returns from the walk-in. Pots and pans fly off their shelves and crash to the floor. "Son of a bitch."

His fingers wrap around a metal shelving unit, and he shakes it violently while growling.

"Boss." Chicken Wing places his hand on Femi's shoulder.

Femi's head pivots like the kid from The Exorcist, and his eyes turn into black orbs. "Don't touch me," he snarls.

Chicken Wing raises his hands. Femi charges around him and back into the freezer. He emerges carrying Doc and stops beside me. "Clean up before you come outside."

I look down at my body, almost completely covered in blood, and walk slowly towards the restroom sign.

Ari glances at Chicken Wing. "Grab my bag from the trunk and bring it to me, and then leave with Femi. We will meet up at the club later."

He nods and disappears through the two-way doors leading to the dining area of the restaurant. I push the ladies' room door open, and the strong odor of urine and feces contaminates the air.

Ari enters behind me, carrying her bag, and covers her nose. "Oh, gross." She passes her bag to me, and I let it fall to the floor. "There is a change of clothes inside and some of those wipe things you like. I'm going to grab some water for you to clean up with."

I remove my bathing suit and stuff it inside the toilet tank. Ari's bag sticks to the floor when I try and lift it.

Fucking nasty.

Inside the bag is a black halter dress covered in lace, a pair of matching spiked heels, and an emerald green, sequin-covered designer handbag.

'*Meet us at the club later,*' is what Ari had said. How could they think about drinking and dancing after what happened to Doc?

I must have missed something either when I was sleeping or in the short period since I left the hotel.

The door beside me flies open and slams against the wall. Ari drops two kids-sized sand buckets on the contaminated ground. "It's ocean water, but it should help rinse some of the blood from your hair."

After cleaning all the visible blood off, I shimmy into the tight but flexible dress, slide my feet into the heels, and pick up the small handbag. It's larger than I usually carry when going out. I unzip it and peek inside.

A small low-profile thigh knife with a sheath, a disposable phone, lipstick, a pack of gum, a lighter, and a travel bottle of perfume are stuffed inside.

I wrap the sheath around my upper thigh, tuck the knife in, and glance at my reflection in the smudged bathroom mirror.

"Fuck."

My hair's a fucking tangled mess thanks to the ocean water drying it out and making it frizzy.

Ari grimaces at my reflection and frowns. "I'm going to have to fix that mop on your head."

She pulls a folding hairbrush out of her purse and rakes it through my hair. Broken pieces of hair float in front of my eyes and onto the front of my dress when she gets to my bangs. I grab her wrist. "Ari, why the weapons?"

She continues brushing my locks and sighs. "Because they're going to be there."

"Who?" I swat her hand away from my head.

"Luisa's men, the generals, Luisa. All of them." She removes a black hair tie from her wrist, twists my hair into a messy bun, and secures it. "While you were out in the ocean, Chicken Wing and I were doing some eavesdropping. Luisa has a big meeting with her generals tonight. It's a closed-door session, so while she's upstairs in the penthouse meeting with her generals, her guards will all be downstairs in the club, drinking and partying."

I move a few feet away, turn, and gaze at her reflection in the mirror. She tucks her brush back into her wristlet and stares back at me. "What?"

"Where's my sample of meat?" I ask with a devious smile.

Chapter Twelve
Sweetheart

The number of eyes on us at the grocery store was ridiculous. We can't be the only women who have ever shopped in cocktail dresses at five in the afternoon before.

We stop in the baking aisle, pick up some gourmet dark chocolate baking squares, and browse the cookie cutters.

Ari pulls a heart off the peg and smiles broadly at me. "It's perfect."

I grab a gourmet display box complete with a transparent window and toss it in the cart. "It sure is."

We stroll down the greeting card aisle and pick out a roll of red ribbon, a pair of scissors, and a package of scotch tape.

Ari slaps her hands together and rubs them aggressively. "This is going to be so awesome."

The cashier scans the heart-shaped cookie cutter. "Are we making cookies for Christmas?"

"No," Ari giggles. "Just one chocolate-covered treat."

The parchment paper and chocolate beep across the scanner. "What are you using for filling?"

I hand the cashier a one-hundred-dollar bill and smile. "Meat."

Ari bursts out laughing, and the cashier blinks several times. "Alrighty, then."

The cashier purses her lips in a tight smile and raises her eyebrows. "Here's your change. You ladies be careful."

I push the money back to her. "You keep it."

Ari pushes the shopping cart to Femi's Mercedes and pops the trunk. "Are we making this here, or do you want to go to my mom's?"

"Are you crazy? We can't do this at your mom's house. Besides, I told you I agreed to dinner on Christmas Eve only." I slam the trunk down and stroll to the driver's side.

"Oh, no you don't. Doc's orders. No driving." Ari takes the keys from me.

The mere mention of her name bothers me. I knew Luisa would be ruthless and unpredictable, but I never thought she would do that to Doc when she seemed so smitten with her.

I lean my head against the passenger side window and gaze at the setting sun. Our rental is beachfront and separate from Eve, Audrey, and Gina's. Ari handled all the lodging arrangements but has yet to tell me where the others are staying. She claims it's for our protection. She's right. The less we know, the better if this mission is going to work, and we plan on staying after for Christmas.

Femi is standing with his hands in his pockets beneath the beach house when we arrive. He's flanked by four other men, two on each side.

I hand Ari the grocery bag. "I'll meet you inside."

His men walk away from him when I approach. "What's going on?"

"We are moving Doc to the other house. Audrey can help her with whatever she may need."

He doesn't look at me when he speaks. Upset over what happened, and in work mode, there is nothing I can say to make the situation any better or make him less angry. I walk away from him and head inside.

Screaming comes from Doc's room, making me cringe. I move swiftly to her bedroom and shove the door open. Two of Femi's men are grabbing her arms and pulling, trying to get her out of bed for transport. Her head bounces around as she screams and thrashes about, her legs tangled in the sheets. She feels trapped. What they are doing to her is making her relive her nightmare all over again—dragged away, held down, and tortured. Violated.

"Out," I order them.

They let her arms go and stare at me, making no motion to leave. Who am I to them? I'm not their boss, just their boss's lover, so they think they don't have to listen to me when I bark an order.

They think wrong.

I storm up to the closest one to me and crush his balls in my grasp. He yelps and stands on his tiptoes, refusing to look down at me. "I'll eat these fuckers later with a side of spaghetti if you don't take your ass out of here."

He gasps and locks eyes with me. "Yes, ma'am."

I smile at his high-pitched voice and release him. He hobbles away holding his balls. My head snaps to the other guard who immediately covers his cock, puts his head down, and steps into the hallway. I close the door behind them.

Words will never fully describe how she looks. She's always overseen aftercare—taking care of the abused and beaten. Now she lies cowering in her bed, blankets covering her up to her neck in a secure ball, protecting herself from them.

From me.

I slide out of my heels and step silently towards her. Her knuckles grip the blanket around her tightly, whitening them.

"Let it go," I say softly tugging the covers.

Tears cascade over her cheek, land on her pillow, and spread out, soaking it thoroughly.

I gently take the blanket from her fist. When the covers slide down her thighs, she tightens them, wrinkling the small amount of skin on her bruised and scraped-up knees.

"I'm sorry. This is my fault, and only I can fix it."

She won't look at me. Her eyes stare somewhere into space, seeking solace in the darkness of her mind. I crawl next to her, slide my left arm under her head and my right arm around her waist, spooning her. Her body trembles before me like a person with an unsteady hand trying to hold soup on a spoon without spilling it. I squeeze her gently, and her body tenses, but I don't let go. She cries softly beside me for several minutes then goes quiet. Her breathing slows and her body relaxes as she falls into a deep slumber.

Femi enters the room, and I nod. He pushes his arms beneath her and lifts her slowly off the mattress. She nuzzles her head into him but does not wake. I follow them to the Mercedes, and Femi climbs inside without letting Doc go.

Chicken Wing glances at me in the side mirror from the driver's seat and nods. I comb Doc's hair away from her face with my fingers, kiss her forehead, and close the door. They back down the driveway away from me, but I don't move until the SUV is down the road and out of sight.

Ari stands in the doorway, watching me. "Ready?"

I pass her without a word and head for the kitchen. "Where's the meat?"

She opens the fridge and hands me the thigh muscle. "What do you need me to do?"

I stare at the red slab, bleeding on the granite counter. "All of it."

Ari's eyes light up, and a massive grin spreads across her face. "Really?"

The kitchen chair scrapes against the tile when I sit. "Find something to beat it with until it's of equal thickness all the way around."

The drawers clank open as Ari rummages through them one at a time. She locates a wooden vintage meat mallet with a textured head and slaps the meat repeatedly, splattering its juices all over herself, the counter, and the floor in front of her.

"It's kind of big," she says when the pummeling finally stops.

I stand and peer over her shoulder. "I guess we are making two."

She turns and grimaces. "Well, what are we doing with the second one?"

"We can save it for someone special."

I hand her the cookie cutter. "Set it on and press."

The meat easily cuts into two red hearts. Ari takes the unused portion and wiggles it. "Should we save this for stir-fry?"

I grab it with two fingers and throw it in the trash. "No, it's not enough, and I don't like mixing meat from different sources."

"Now what?" Ari asks, thoroughly examining the hearts with a kiddish grin.

"Now you set them on Parchment paper and freeze them." I slide the roll of paper to her. "Then when they come out, we dip them in melted chocolate several times so there are multiple coats, decorate if we choose, and then put them back in until the chocolate hardens."

Ari places the meat hearts neatly on the paper, plops them on a frozen pizza in the freezer, and sighs. "Do you think they'll be done in time for us to take them with us to the club?"

I look at the wall clock behind her. "Yes."

Chicken Wing enters the room alone.

"Where's Femi?" I ask him.

He opens the fridge and grabs a bottle of beer. "Staying with Doc."

Hearing him say that shouldn't have bothered me, but it did. Perhaps his feelings for her are stronger than I thought.

"What's with the red hearts in the freezer?" he asks, holding the freezer door open.

Ari closes the door and smiles. "They are for Luisa. Well, at least one of them is."

Chicken Wing raises his eyebrows. "Okay, I won't be eating any of that then."

"Want to watch a movie?" Ari asks him.

He looks her up and down. "Sure. I have to show you something first in my room."

Ari smiles broadly. "Oh, is it something for me?"

"Maybe." He smiles and strolls away.

She follows him like a lost puppy looking for a treat. I sink into the couch cushion and flip on the news.

Nothing exciting is going on with the weather. News stations sprinkle information in bits and pieces about how the investigation into the now-connected bunker killings is going. Initially, the FBI thought the first bunker explosion was rival traffickers fighting over business and territory. But now that there are three linked incidents, they are leaning more towards vigilante justice, and most people aren't complaining.

We are doing the job the authorities won't—killing them all.

Screaming startles me to a stand.

I race to Chicken Wing's room and whip the door open, slamming it into the wall.

My eyes turn to orbs then squeeze shut. I quickly back out of the room, closing the door behind me. Seeing the back side of Chicken Wing's narrow and bony ass slamming into Ari while she holds her ankles, I may never unsee.

I glance at the bleach on the washing machine and think about using it. No amount of it could rinse the filth from my eyes, or the memory from my mind. I flop back onto the couch, and Henry crawls on my lap. I picture Chicken Wing and Ari getting a big house together and giving Henry a room of his own.

Then I remember that this is real life, and it can be nasty.

She likes him, and I hope he feels the same. Because if he hurts her, I will fucking kill him.

Chapter Thirteen
Preparation is Key

Ari emerges from the bedroom, her hair a tangled mess. A broad smile stretches across her face from ear to ear. "Yep. He's a fucking rabbit."

I drop my head. "Ari, please don't share any details."

She flops beside me on the couch. "That man had me flexing in positions I didn't know my body was capable of."

"Ari, please stop talking." I stand and walk away from her.

She follows me to the kitchen, "Well, you saw how he had me. Good lord, I thought he was going to dislocate my hip."

Fuck my life right now.

I grab a glass, fill it halfway with bourbon, and head to the balcony.

You'd think walking away and closing the balcony would be a hint I want to be alone, but nope, here she comes.

"Want me to tell you the plan for this evening?" She scuffs her chair against the balcony floor until it's facing me.

I usually do the planning but judging by the items she loaded in my purse; she is already a step ahead of me.

This ought to be interesting.

I swallow the last gulp of my liquor hard. "Spill it."

She slaps her hands together and smiles. "Okay so, Luisa and her generals will be having a meeting in the penthouse of the hotel above the club. While they are busy with that, almost all her guards and some assigned to each of the generals will be downstairs. They'll be a few guarding the meeting and the elevators too, but our focus will be on taking out as many of the men in the club as possible, weakening her army."

"Wait now. Hold on. Why not just take the few men out by the elevators and go straight up to the meeting?"

Ari frowns at me. "Because the minute we kill the guards at the elevator to the penthouse, all the men in the club will converge on our position."

This doesn't sound like Ari talking. This sounds like Femi. Ari doesn't think this far ahead.

I ask an obvious question. "Where is Femi going to be in all of this?"

"Oh, that's the best part. Once shit inside starts hitting the fan, the generals and Luisa will likely vacate the premises. Then Femi and his men are going after the generals and Luisa directly when they drive away from the hotel."

"No." I stand and lean against the railing, staring out into the ocean. "Going after Luisa is on me. What happened to Doc is my fault. Luisa is mine for the taking, not his."

Ari stands and rests her butt against the rail beside me. "Odie, this job is no different than any other. In the end, every one of them will die for their crimes."

"No different. Seriously, Ari?" My voice rises. "This woman ordered God only knows how many men to rape Doc. That makes this job not just a job. It's fucking personal."

"He doesn't want you near this woman. Not after what happened to Doc." She hands me her glass of bourbon. "I don't either."

"I don't give a fat rats ass what Femi wants." I toss the drink into my throat. "I'm killing Luisa."

Ari sighs and looks out to the ocean. "How about I send a package with our chocolate heart?"

I shake my head. "They will check the food cart before they roll it anywhere near the penthouse."

"I can hide the explosives in champagne bottles tucked in an ice bucket. The trigger will be under the bucket, and I can run a wire into each wine bottle from the bottom and silicone it, so it doesn't leak. Add a little C4 in there somewhere, and boom we kill them all. Or at least, most of them."

I glance at her from the corner of my eye. "You're kind of nuts. Do you know that?"

She smiles, grabs my hand, and pulls me inside. "Let's go call Femi and tell him the new plan."

"No." I stop walking. "If you do that, he may change the plan entirely. "I'd rather let us do all the work without him knowing. He'll thank us later."

"Good point." She swings her arms at her sides on her way to the kitchen, grabs the emerald bag she filled for me, and dumps it on the kitchen island. "Let me show you something."

I pick up the perfume and remove the cap.

Ari snatches it away. "Don't spray this on yourself." She removes a piece of paper from the magnetic notepad on the fridge, squirts the page once with the perfume, and lights it with the lighter.

Whoosh.

Flames incinerate the page at once and smoke billows from the edge of Ari's eyebrow. I pat her brow with my fingers. The scent of singed hair fills the room.

"Jesus, Ari. What the fuck is that?"

"It's Benzene. And the best part is, even if you spray it toward someone's face but miss, you can ignite the vapors." She sniffs the end of the perfume sprayer. "It even smells sweet."

She pushes it under my nose, and I push it away. "I am not sniffing flammable liquid anywhere near my nose." I pick up the lipstick. "And this?"

I pop the lid and rotate the lipstick up. It's a red color with glitter.

"That is called ruby slipper." Ari smiles and takes it from my hand. She glances at Chicken Wing who has just emerged from a shower. "Come here my little white rabbit."

Oh, Christ. She gave him a pet name. I have one for Femi and usually, it wouldn't bother me, but the fact that I saw this rabbit in action nauseates me.

"What's up Bomb Pop?" He sits beside her.

She giggles and looks at me. "He calls me that now on account of me liking to make bombs and my hip popping when we were—."

"No. Stop talking. Don't finish the sentence." I roll my eyes. "Just get on with the demonstration."

Ari grabs Chicken Wing's hand and draws a smiley face on it with bright red lipstick. "I apologize in advance, White Rabbit, but you need your vaccine."

She presses the base of the lipstick with her pointer. A button in its center depresses, sending a spring-loaded needle through the angled lip color, and into the top of Chicken Wing's hand.

"Ouch. What the fuck was that?" Chicken Wing asks rubbing the back of his lipstick-smeared hand.

His eyes narrow and roll back inside his head. He falls sideways in slow motion, landing unconscious on the floor in a heap.

"Doc helped me find the right dose of Propofol to knock someone out. Now the only downfall is…" She tosses the lipstick into the open trash can. "…you can only use it once. So, choose when to use it wisely."

"And the gum?" I hold the pack up.

"Laced with fentanyl. Don't eat or touch it or you'll overdose."

I flub my lips and raise my eyebrows. "Sounds like you've thought of everything."

She repacks everything in my bag and passes it to me. "Sure did. Right down to those spiked heels of yours. You could stab someone right through the throat with those fuckers."

Femi's newest bodyguard, Manuel, enters the room and steps over Chicken Wing. "What the fuck happened?" He kneels and presses his fingers to his throat.

Ari spins in her chair and looks down at him with a straight face. "I fucked him into a coma." She hops off the seat. "Come on, Odie. We've got work to do."

I smile at Manuel's frowning face. "Go ahead, Ari. I'm going to coat the hearts."

"Cool. I'm going to play with champagne bottles on the lower level."

After Ari disappears, I melt some chocolate in the microwave to save time, pull the partially frozen hearts from the freezer, and coat them evenly. I thought about decorating them, but I think it would take away from the perfection of their shape. I set one gingerly inside its box, tie a red bow neatly around it, and place it in the freezer to let the chocolate harden back up.

Manuel eyes the second one. "What is the inside made of? Some kind of fancy gelato?"

Gelato? Does he know nothing?

This is the most he's ever spoken to me. He usually just lurks in the shadows or watches me from afar, invading my privacy. Perhaps it's time he knows what I'm all about—who he's really dealing with.

I place the second heart in the freezer, walk around the counter, and stroll up to him, bumping his chest with mine. He does not step back or move to create distance. His eyes lock onto my lips as I speak and his mouth parts—his teeth biting his tongue.

"What do you know about me, Manuel?" I cock my head to the side and scan his face.

He smells delicious. And despite his lingering and stalkerish presence, I find him intriguing upon closer inspection. His hair is short with a hairline on one side and his perfectly trimmed goatee has not a single hair out of place.

A well-manicured, nice-looking guy. I wonder what his legs look like. My eyes drift from his face, between his legs, and down to his hidden quadriceps.

He pushes my body against the wall, knocking the air from my lungs, and lifts my chin. "You are a seductress. A woman who when she wants something, takes it. A woman who is exceptionally beautiful, but extremely dangerous to anyone who crosses her." His thumb drifts over my bottom lip. "My job is to protect Femi. Not only from people meant to harm him outside these walls…" He eyes the room surrounding us and then glares at me. "…but from you."

Me?

Well, I guess that makes sense. I have been having a harder time controlling my desire to eat him.

I slide my palm up the front of his shirt and hold his neck gently. "If you are supposed to be protecting him, then why are you here?"

He takes my hand and brings it down to his crotch with a sideways smile. "Because you're here, and my boss told me to."

"And if he told you to fuck me and I agreed, would you?"

A throaty laugh escapes his mouth. He stares down at Chicken Wing who shifts on the floor, then grins at me. His canine teeth sit forward compared to the rest of his teeth.

A little bit of vampire in the bloodlines, I see.

"I wouldn't fuck you into a coma." He presses my palm against his cock and grinds it. "Princess, I would fuck you to death."

It hardens in my hand, curving to the left.

Interesting.

I wonder if he and the curved-cocked corpse in the basement are related. Either way, I have a plan for this cock in the future if he proves to be too much trouble.

"Am I interrupting something?" Ari asks, entering the room with a cardboard box and staring at our hands both touching the space between his legs.

"No." I step away from Manuel, grab the remote, and sink into the couch cushion. "He was just curious about what was in the center of our chocolate hearts."

Ari snorts. "It's the heart-shaped piece of a very bad man's thigh." She sets the box on the counter and drops into the seat beside me. "What are we watching?"

Manuel tilts his head. "Man thigh, huh?" He stops in front of us, blocking the television. "We should go."

"Go? You're not coming with us." I shake my head. "This is an all-girls mission and last I checked…" My eyes lock on the bulge between his legs. "…you aren't a girl. Now move."

He shifts out of the way, sits in the accent chair across from us, and rests his elbows on his knees, folding his hands in front of his mouth. "We are supposed to be on our way to the club by now."

Ari rolls her head backward. "For the love of God, don't you know anything? We have to wait for the chocolate to harden first. Why don't you take a walk or a shower, something, anything besides sitting here with us making us feel like your prisoners?"

He sits back in his seat and strokes his bottom lip with his pointer finger, eyes flitting between Ari and me. "Twenty minutes. Then we are leaving." He takes his phone from his front pocket.

"We need at least an hour," I say, not taking my eyes off the weatherman.

His fingers type quickly across his phone, and a few seconds later, the screen lights up his face and pings with an incoming message.

"The most I can give you is thirty minutes." He stuffs his phone back in his pocket and leans back in his seat.

"It's not enough time for the chocolate to harden."

Manuel leans forward, glaring at us over furrowed brows. "Then you'll have to leave your little meat dessert out of this mission then, won't you?"

Ari grabs her bag from the stand beside the couch, unzips it, and nudges my side with her elbow. "Thirty minutes will be fine." She points to the three lipsticks in her pouch.

"I guess we could make it work or put it in the cooler." I press a button on the remote. "This weather documentary is over in thirty-two minutes. We will leave then."

His long lashes bat at me a couple of times before he sighs. "Fine."

I smile at him with my eyes and turn my attention back to the Hurricane Katrina documentary. The season this year has been underwhelming so far which isn't a bad thing. But it could also be a sign of what's to come—

Mother Nature saving her energy for a massive storm meant to swallow Florida whole.

Manuel pushes off the arms of the chair and stands. He sets his phone on a side table and heads to the kitchen. A timer counts down across his screen. Seriously? He's timing our agreement. I nudge Ari and point to Manuel's phone.

She rolls her eyes, gets up, grabs the phone, and deletes the timer.

A glass of bourbon appears between us a minute later. I gaze over my shoulder at Manuel. "No thanks."

Ari takes the glass and sets it on the table beside her. "I'll take that."

Manuel picks up his phone and sighs through his nose. "Who canceled the timer?"

"What timer?" Ari and I answer simultaneously.

He grabs the remote, presses pause and resets the countdown to when the show ends. "Fifteen minutes."

Ari and I smile at the television.

She pulls a stick of gum from her bag and holds it out to Manuel. "Gum?"

Ari's trying to overdose him, maybe even kill him depending on how much fentanyl she laced the gum with.

He shakes his head and glances at his phone screen. "Fourteen minutes."

His play-by-play is irritating.

We continue watching the documentary for what feels like forever, occasionally stealing a glance at each other.

I'm tired of waiting—tired of being watched like a fucking criminal incarcerated in maximum security on a twenty-four-seven lockdown. I lean to Ari and whisper in her ear. "How long does that last?" I point to the lipstick in her bag.

She pulls it out. "I'd say it's pretty long-lasting."

Manuel snatches the lipstick from Ari's hand. "What are you two whispering about?"

"We were talking about how long my lipstick lasts. Why? You want to borrow it?"

He pops the lid and rotates the lipstick up, staring at the end of it. "I'll pass."

Ari grins. "Not your color?"

Manuel sits back down, closes the lipstick, and curls it in his palm. "I'll hang on to this until we get to the club."

Ari springs from her seat, still holding her bag. "You better give it back when we get there." She storms away from us, heading to the balcony doors behind Manuel.

"You can't go with us to the club. We have a plan, and it doesn't include you," I say to him.

He drums the arms of the chair. "Look, Princess, you don't have a fucking choice. I'm assigned to you, and until Femi changes my assignment, I'm going to be right by your si—." Manuel grabs Ari's hand as she plunges her backup lipstick into his neck from behind. He stands abruptly, his eyes rolling back, and falls to the floor.

Ari peers down at him holding the lipstick from her purse. "Shut the fuck up and take a nap."

A loud and airy bout of gas staggers from Manuel. We erupt in laughter. Tears cascade over our cheeks smearing our makeup and blackening the undersides of our eyes.

We step over his body and head to the kitchen still laughing.

Chicken wing grabs Ari's ankle. "What's going on, Bomb Pop?" Words slur out of his mouth with a bit of drool.

She kneels beside him and wipes the saliva from his lips. "Take a nap, White Rabbit. We'll be back later."

The timer on Manuel's phone rings from the floor in the living room. Ari crawls on her hands and knees and presses the stop button on the alarm, silencing it. I grab the box on the counter. "Let's load the car now, come back in, and clean up. That will give the hearts more time to solidify before we go."

After we clean our faces and reapply a fresh coat of makeup, we head for the Mercedes. My phone rings in my bag.

"Who is it?" Ari asks, opening the trunk.

"Femi." I add the chocolate-covered heart to the box inside. "I'm not answering."

Ari raises her eyebrows. "Because he's trying to steal your thunder?"

I shoot her a sideways glance. "That and he hired a babysitter to watch me."

"Manuels, your bodyguard?" Ari chuckles.

I shake my head and climb into the passenger seat. "His job is to keep me safe and keep Femi safe from me."

"From you? That's comical."

My phone rings again.

Ari picks it up. "Bomb Pop catering, how may I direct your call?"

I giggle but stop at once when Ari's face drops. She holds her pointer finger to her lips, silencing me.

"I have her phone, Femi. I don't know where she is." She winks at me, chucks her phone underneath a palm tree in the front yard, and starts driving away from the house. "I lost mine."

The car stops suddenly. "What do you mean, where am I going? To the club, as planned," she says into the receiver and frowns. "I don't know why Manuel isn't answering his phone. Maybe he and Odie are busy." She grimaces and takes a pen from the center console.

I place a piece of paper between us, and she writes:

He's tracking the phones.

That is exactly why I always say no phones. After what happened to Doc, I shouldn't be surprised that he's taking these extra precautions, but I don't like someone monitoring me without my knowledge.

Ari closes the phone. "He hung up. I don't think he liked the fact that I said you were with Manuel and busy." She makes air quotes with her fingers.

I take the phone from her and throw it out the window. "Drive."

The car barrels backward down the driveway. Chicken Wing opens the doors on his hands and knees, trying to function. "Wait," he says weakly.

Ari steers the vehicle onto the road and blows him a kiss. "Ladies only. Sorry."

She speeds down the road and the infotainment system lights up.

Femi's calling...

I stare at the screen and hit the end button. "We need a different car. Something old and hard to track."

Ari pulls the car to the curb in front of a laundromat. "So we can be invisible?"

"Yes." I peer through the window at the wash, dry, and dry clean advertisement in front of the building. "What are we doing here?"

She pushes the door open. "Stay here. If we are going to be invisible, I need some supplies."

The toe of her shoe catches on the curb. She trips into the building as someone leaves, holding the door open for her as she half falls, and half walks into the establishment. I shake my head. I've never been around someone so clumsy before. Perhaps she's just too anxious and high-strung to pay attention.

She whips the door open and tosses a metal wire on my lap. "Hold that."

"Where the hell did you find a metal hanger? No one uses these damn things anymore." I pick up the thin, flimsy metal, a hint of rust texturing its surface.

"Dry cleaners do. But they leave them in bins for free when they start showing signs of rust." She leans away from me, picks her wedgie, and starts the car. "These fucking underwear always ride up my ass on the right side. I swear that butt cheek is bigger than the other. It just sucks my drawers right into my butthole. So, annoying."

I chuckle. She's oversharing, but this time it's funny because I've thought the same thing about my left buttock. Sometimes I feel like it's not worth it to wear underwear at all.

Ari slaps the turn signal down and steers into a senior living home. She stops the Mercedes behind a powder blue, two-door Buick. "My grandma had one of those."

"Ari, we can't just steal some old man's Buick." I frown at her.

"Sure, we can. We will just leave the Mercedes with the keys inside and a note saying, 'Congratulations you won a new car, and we towed away the old one,' and leave the keys in it for them."

"But how are we getting the keys for the Buick?" I turn sideways and furrow my brows.

"I know how to hotwire a car. I'm not an idiot." She puts the Mercedes in park beside the Buick, climbs out, and pops the trunk.

I stand beside the Buick. "Well shit, last time I checked I wasn't an idiot either, but I don't know how to hotwire a fucking car."

"Ari rolls her eyes at me. "It all starts with getting the door open." She takes a metal ice scraper, wedges it between the window and door frame, and gently pulls, creating a slim gap. "Grab that folded handkerchief and wedge it in the space when I move the window away from the frame."

I stare at the handkerchief she left on the hood of the car. "Ari, I bought this for Femi for his birthday."

She wrinkles her face and frowns. "So? Christmas is a few days away, you can buy him a new one."

I stuff the material in between the crack she created. "Now what?"

"Now, I grab the hanger, straighten it, and make a hook at the end to grab the lock with so I can pull it." She sticks her tongue between her teeth and quickly untwists and straightens the hanger, leaving a small V-shaped hook at one end. The hanger scrapes through the tiny opening, and she grabs the lock, pulls it up, and opens the door to the vintage eighty's car within seconds like a pro.

"Why am I not surprised?" I sink into the passenger seat after she unlocks the door for me.

She moves the seat forward, sets the box in the back, and flops behind the steering wheel, holding a flathead screwdriver. "Don't worry, I'll show you how to hotwire another day. Right now, we are in a hurry."

The end of the screwdriver disappears inside the keyhole and with a quick slam of her palm against the handle, she breaks the locking pins and starts the car.

I glance at the cigarette burn in the seat and ceiling by the visor above her head. "Ari, how many cars have you stolen?"

The car growls noisily as she pumps the gas a few times then cranks the shifter down. "Seven..." She smiles, backs out of the parking space, and shifts into drive. "...including my grandmas."

Chapter Fourteen
Crispy Criminals

Ari pulls up to the curb outside Carlos' Hotel, Club, and Lounge, a newer beachfront hotel and club in Miami. Part of their dance floor is inside the building, and the other half is just steps away from the sand. When the weather is bad, they close a massive window-filled garage-like door.

Across the street is Femi's black Range Rover. I tap Ari's arm and point. "We can't let him see us go in."

She puts the Buick in reverse. "We will park on the side and walk around to the oceanside of the dancefloor."

"But how are we getting this stuff to the penthouse?" I point into the back seat with my thumb.

Ari bumps the curb and cranks the shifter to park. "You'll see."

I don't like the sound of this. Nor do I like surprises.

We exit the vehicle, and Ari takes the box from the back seat. The packed dance floor is full of holiday vacationers and locals enjoying the unusually warm December.

A bouncer stands by the entrance to the dance floor. Velvet burgundy ropes attached to gold stands run along the edge of the outdoor space, directing the foot traffic to him. I recognize those tattooed biceps and ass immediately. If he were the center on a football team, I'd pay billions to be his quarterback to see that fine ass bent over in front of me for days.

Ari told me while we were at the beach that her brothers moonlighted at clubs and bars on the weekends as bouncers. I didn't realize they would be working at this one. Bryce takes my hand and slowly rolls a mint green, glow-in-the-dark stamp across the back of it.

"Is this the delivery for the penthouse?" Tyson asks, coming up beside us.

This is a bad idea. Having her brothers here puts them at risk.

Ari unhooks one of the ropes and walks away with Tyson, leaving me standing there with Bryce still holding my hand. Someone behind me clears their throat. I look back at Bryce, and he pulls me off to the side to stand next to him before taking care of the next person in line. "Don't worry," he shouts over the music. "You'll be safe beside me until she gets back."

I chuckle to myself. He's the one who isn't safe. I've been daydreaming about his thighs since I drooled over them at the beach. They scream from beneath the fabric of his faded jeans, begging for me to latch on to them.

"Hey." Bryce's voice draws my eyes away from his legs.

I lock onto his bicep and stroke it with my fingers. "You have nice muscles."

He curls his arm, tightening the skin and expanding the size of it. A vein runs across the top and disappears into the crook of his elbow. "Here, feel it." He takes my palm and slaps it on his arm. "Nice and hard, right?"

My pussy twitches, and my mouth waters. "Very." The lump in my throat makes it hard to swallow.

It takes everything in me not to gouge out a chunk. My body inadvertently leans forward to get a closer look. Thoughts of what I want to do to him take over my mind.

"You have a strong grip." Bryce's hand pulls at my wrist, fingertips still tightly depressed in his bicep.

I can't let go. I don't fucking want to. I want to take him into the bathroom and ride his cock while taking some samples of that grade-A meat of his.

Ari's face appears in my field of vision. Her eyes are wide, and she shakes her head at me. "Let go, Odie."

I frown at her.

"Don't you give me that face. They'll be plenty of time to play." She peels my fingers from her brother's arm, detaching my claws from his flesh. "Just not with him."

Bryce smiles out of the side of his mouth as Ari pulls me away from him.

"Ari, we can't blow shit up with your brothers here," I say to her back.

"They work short shifts tonight, so they are leaving by ten." She glances at her watch. "That's only five more minutes."

Pressure builds in my left arm as she continues pulling me until we reach the lady's room, where a long line of women wait to go in.

Ari pouts and shoves the men's room door across the hall. "I'm not fucking waiting."

Two men stand at the urinals, pissing. They look at each other and smile. Ari slams the handicap stall open and yanks me inside.

"What are you doing?" I ask.

"I have to pee." She takes several strips of toilet paper off the roll and lines the seat before sitting down. "I set everything up on the serving cart to be taken to the penthouse," she whispers.

"When is it being delivered?" I peer through the crack in the door as the two men leave without washing their hands.

Gross.

"About fifteen minutes." She wipes and pulls up her red bikini bottoms.

The door to the men's room bounces off the wall and one of Luisa's men I recognize from the beach enters. I nod my head to Ari.

She flushes and peeks through the crack. "Can I do the first one?"

I smile and twist the lock to open. "Abso-fucking-lutely."

As soon as the man unzips his fly and the stream begins, Ari steps out of the stall. "Hello."

The man, dressed in all black attire, looks her up and down. "This is the men's room."

She pulls a lipstick container from her bag, removes its lid, and leans towards the mirror beside the urinal, preparing to apply it to her lips.

He shakes his head, shifting his long black bangs away from his eyes, and continues peeing. When he uses one hand to grip his pants and the other to zip his zipper, Ari presses the lipstick into the side of his neck. He swings wildly at her. Ari ducks and crawls away from him. He reaches for her and his body falls straight down nearly landing on top of her.

I lock the bathroom door. "What's your plan?"

"Help me get him in the stall." She grabs his right arm.

I grab the other, and we drag his lightweight frame into the confined space. She takes the lipstick and draws on the wall above the toilet.

I like to be fucked in the ass.

"Umm, what are you doing?" I furrow my brow at her.

She chucks the used lipstick in the toilet, flushes, and pulls a knife from under her dress. "Having some fun."

I cock my head at her. "Where did you just pull that from?"

"Not my vagina if that's what you're thinking." She pulls off his shoes and throws them against the tile wall behind her. "Help me take off his pants and underwear and sit him on the toilet."

We remove his clothes, push them across the floor behind us, and hoist him onto the seat. His eyes roll back into his head. Ari places her hand on my chest and walks me back against the wall. "Just stay back in case this doesn't go as planned."

"In case what doesn't go as planned?"

She pulls a tampon and lighter out of her handbag. "I'm going to give this asshole, a new asshole."

Oh, my God. She's going to blow his ass up. Literally.

"Won't that be too loud?"

"No. His body will muffle the explosion." She reaches between his legs. "Man, his legs are hairy." Her face scrunches as she shoves the exploding tampon up the guy's bony ass.

He makes a grunting noise, and his head drops onto Ari's upper back. "Eww, get him off me, his breath smells like old beer."

I lean my palms against his shoulders, pushing him back against the toilet tank, making it rock. His head flops back and his mouth drops open, revealing a top row of mostly yellow teeth.

"How long does it take for the fuse to burn?" I ask.

She drapes the wick between his legs, leaving it dangling over the porcelain throne. "I don't know. Could be seconds. Maybe a minute or two. I've never done this before."

Jesus Christ, she's going to kill us.

I unlock the stall, leave it open, and unlock the bathroom door, keeping my hand on its handle for a quick escape. Ari steps outside the stall, reaches in, and flicks the lighter several times.

"Go!" she shouts, pushing me into the hallway, and closing the door behind us.

The hallway still has a few women waiting to use the bathroom. Ari smirks at them. "I wouldn't recommend going in there, some guy is blowing it up."

They crinkle their noses as if the thought never crossed their mind. I don't care what gender the bathroom is, if I need to go, I'm going regardless.

A hollow, echoing noise comes from the men's room as we exit the hallway. The women stare at the men's bathroom door but say nothing. From where we were standing, it sounded like muffled fireworks set off in an enclosed space. We continue walking across the dance floor and head for the bar area. Off to the sides are stairs that go up to the paid tables. A group of Luisa's men sit on a massive couch with their arms around a couple of familiar women. We each have our own assignments and missions, but our goals are all the same—kill as many of Luisa's men as possible, in any way we see fit. Audrey and Gina work as a team often, and it's highly effective.

I lock eyes with them and keep walking.

Ari bumps my elbow. "Don't worry. They have the same package in their bags as we do."

Two men sit across from each other in a private corner booth having a conversation. One of them has scratches up and down his arms. I grit my teeth. He must be one of the men who hurt Doc.

"Ari." I stop walking.

"I know. I see it. Let's go sit with them, shall we?" She smiles and pulls me behind her.

"Hi," she says cheerfully and uses her ass to scoot the man over. "Mind if we sit."

"We do." The one with the scratches huffs at me. "You ladies need to sit elsewhere. Someone's sitting here." He stares at the side of my face as I sit beside him and rest my palm on his knee.

"I don't see anyone." I look around the room and glare at him. "Do you?" I ask Ari without looking at her.

"Nope. Must be taking a shit." She laughs obnoxiously loud and slaps the table.

From where we are sitting, only the bartender has a direct line of sight.

"What happened here?" I slide my fingers over the man's fresh scratch marks. "Get in a fight with a cat?"

He crushes my left hand in his grasp. "No. A non-compliant cunt who wouldn't do as she's told. Now get the fuck out of here before I do the same to you."

I shake my hand when he frees it and nod to Ari. No one calls Doc a cunt and gets away with it.

No one.

Our hands disappear beneath the table, both of us grabbing our knives safely tucked inside the sheaths attached to our thighs, and slowly scoot away from the men. Once our butts reach the end, we grab the edge of the table and swing at their necks. My blade disappears to the side of the man's Adam's apple, and Ari's strikes just under the guy's ear, hitting the carotid artery.

They grab their necks and gawk wide-eyed at each other. We yank the blades out, roll them in the table napkins, and drop them back in our handbags. Blood drips from our fingers as we return to the paid table section searching for Luisa's men, Audrey and Gina.

They're gone. I pan the room looking for them and spot Gina and Audrey ushering the men into a room with double doors off to the side. Once the men clear the entrance, Audrey removes a champagne bottle from an ice bucket sitting on a rolling cart, lights its wick, and tosses it inside. Gina slams the doors closed, uses a steel cable seal, like truckers have to secure their cargo, and casually walks away. Flames filter through the cracks in the doors. Blood-curdling screams draw the crowd of people on the dance floor's eyes to the sealed room. Multiple people run to the doors and try prying them open.

Ari, Audrey, Gina, and I quickly step onto the dance floor on the ocean side and speed walk our way to the exit.

"Is there a way out?" I ask Audrey.

"Nope. There are no windows." She smiles and spins Ari in a circle when she grabs her hand.

The fire alarm sounds overhead as the club employees realize there's a fire.

"How did you get them to go inside?" Ari asks, letting go of Gina and unhooking the rope keeping us from walking on the beach.

"I told them Audrey and I would let them run a train on us. Men are such pigs." Gina removes her heels and her bare foot sinks in the sand. "How many did you two get?"

"Three." Ari removes her heels and throws them in the garbage can.

"Ha. We got you beat." Audrey grins and kicks off her stilettos. "Me and Gina got eight."

An explosion rocks the building behind us. We spin around and stare at the penthouse level of the hotel where Luisa is meeting with her generals. Flaming particles of wood, paper, and other debris rush to the ground and crash onto the outdoor dance floor.

Something hits the side of my arm and lands in the sand. I chuckle at the burned and bloody jaw. A single gold tooth dangles from its singed gums.

"I bet that's real gold." Ari bends over and picks it up. "Ouch. That fucker is still hot."

I roll my eyes at her. "You don't need it."

"It would make a cool necklace though," she pouts.

The bottom of my foot covers it and pushes it into the sand. "No trophies."

She crosses her arms. "Fine."

Firetrucks and police cars barrel down the street, heading towards Carlos' Hotel, Club, and Lounge. Ari and I walk straight into the ocean, remove our dresses, and clean the blood from our bodies, the cool evening air chilling our moist skin. Audrey and Gina take off their dresses and stuff them in an oversized purse.

We stroll along the water's edge in our bikinis. To anyone who sees us, we would just look like a group of girls out for a late-night swim.

"Do you think Femi will be mad about us going rogue?" Ari asks, rubbing the goosebumps on her upper arm.

"I don't care. He doesn't dictate how our missions go, we do." We cut towards the side street where we parked the Buick. "You girls be safe." Audrey and Gina grin and keep walking.

Ari climbs behind the driver's seat, and I slide in beside her.

She wiggles her nose and shifts the car into drive. "What's that smell?"

I roll the window down, inhale a long, deep breath and moan. "Scorched flesh."

Chapter Fifteen
Parting is Such Sweet Serenity.

After wiping down the Buick and leaving it a few blocks away, we jog back to the beach house to shower. Although I didn't get to witness Luisa being blown to bits, just picturing her body parts scattered around the room, painting the walls of the hotel with her flesh like a long-lost Picasso, is satisfactory enough.

The high-pressure shower head massages my tired muscles and weak shoulder. Not wearing my sling doesn't do me any favors. I rest my hands against the shower wall and sigh. Taking lives has always been easy for me, but there is an uneasiness about this mission I can't seem to shake. Perhaps it's because so many people are involved. Learning to rely on others to do their part and not fuck it up takes faith and trust, neither of which I have much of. I twist the water off and shouting carries down the hallway.

My wet footprints follow me into the living room.

Chicken Wing, Manuel, and Ari stop yelling and stare at me. I didn't think to put on a towel before I jogged into the room.

Manuel scans my body. "Damn." He yanks a blanket off the back of the couch, wraps it around me, and holds it together with one hand against my chest. "You shouldn't have left."

"I don't answer to you or anyone else." I pull away from him.

His grip tightens on the blanket, and he yanks me against him. "You may not answer to anyone, but I'm assigned to you." He leans in and whispers in my ear. "That means, where you go, I go."

I place my palm over his hand that still grips my blanket and slowly back up, taking him with me. "Then I guess we are going to the bedroom."

He sighs. "Guess so."

We walk to my bedroom, where I shove him away from me and let the blanket fall silently to the carpet.

I turn my back, letting him get a good look at what he can't have, and pull a red, silk nightie from the closet. "Can you help me?" I ask throwing it and striking him in the face.

He picks the lingerie up by its thin straps and throws it back. I see the silhouette of someone in my peripheral, but my eyes are on Manuel.

Femi catches the nightie mid-air, surprising us both. "Out."

A fresh white bandage covers his forearm.

"What happened?" I ask.

His eyes stay locked on Manuel. "You're fired."

Manuel's fists ball at his sides. "Sir, I—."

"No." He holds his hand up in Manuel's face. "I didn't ask for your excuse. I asked for your absence."

Somebody's in a bad mood.

Femi holds the door open, waiting for Manuel to leave before closing it. He throws the nightie on the bed and glares at me. "I hope you're happy."

"And you're not?" I sit on the bed and gap my legs open.

He slams my legs closed and purses his lips. "Ari's explosion killed one of my men, I got burned, and Luisa got away."

I stand abruptly. "What do you mean she got away? You had one fucking job."

Femi paces in front of me, swipes his face, and points. "I just told you one of my men is dead, and I got burned because of you and Ari's little side plan, and you're worried about Luisa?"

"Which guy?"

I mean it's like a legitimate question in my opinion. Perhaps, I didn't like the guy anyway.

A burst of air from his nose strikes me in the face as he closes his eyes. "God, woman. You drive me crazy. You're so…so…"

"Loveable?"

"No. Hell no. Infuriating. That's the word I'm looking for." He rests his hands on his hips and stares between my legs.

"She misses you." I grab my pussy lips and open and close them, making them talk. "Eat me, Pussycat."

He laughs in his throat. "You know what? No. I'm walking away."

"But we have more to talk about." I smile and wiggle my pussy lips at him.

He points at me and then to my pussy. "Talk to her since she has so much to say."

His hand hesitates on the door handle.

I imagine he's having an internal debate about staying, with the angel and devil commentators on his shoulder shouting reasons to stay and not stay back and forth.

That's right, come back and talk to my pussy.

He parts his lips and turns his head slightly in my direction. "No," he says to himself. His mind finally made up. The door bounces off the wall as he whips it open, creating a hole. "Stay home." The door slams closed, vibrating its casing, and leaving me alone.

Stay home?

How dare he tell me what to do?

I rifle through my beach bag, searching for my disposable phone to call Eve.

Fuck.

Ari has it.

Knowing Femi, he has an army surrounding us to keep me from leaving. I pull a black, strapless body-con dress with a built-in bra from its hanger, pull it over my breasts, and scoop up my crimson heels.

My balcony faces the pool, ocean, and patio area. Ari's room is on the same side as mine. I drop my shoes over the railing, and they land on the lounger by the pool. When my bare foot touches the palm-etched patio stones, a set of red heels lands beside me.

"Psst." Ari waves at me from her balcony. "I knew it. You and I think alike." Her leg flops over the edge.

No, not really. I planned to go alone.

I stand beneath her, preparing to let myself get crushed if she falls.

The patio door in front of me slides open and one of Femi's men, a former Ranger, steps outside. "Where do you think you're going?"

A milky substance, with a snot-like consistency, splatters on his cheek.

I stare above his head. Ari isn't wearing any underwear, and her whole ass is hanging out of her tight nude mini-skirt.

The ranger wipes his cheek and smears the substance between two fingers. "Hey, what the fuck was that?"

Ari drops beside him and smiles. "Sorry about that. It was just a little bit of White Rabbit cum. He wanted to give me a good fucking before he got in the shower."

Gagging and retching come from the Ranger. "That was some dude's semen?" He wipes his hands on his Army fatigues, his face paling.

Ari slaps him on the shoulder. "Not just his. There's a little bit of me too." She sniffs the side of his face. "Yep. You smell like our love juices now. You're welcome."

He gags, and Ari and I take a couple of steps back. His hand grips the railing beside him and his body bends forward—clear liquid dribbling from his watering mouth. He heaves massive chunks onto the patio. It splatters upward and releases a vile scent into the air. He backs up to the edge of the pool and rests his palms on his knees. "Fucking nasty." A groan filters from his throat. "You two can't…" More undigested food tumbles to the ground. "…can't leave."

I smile at Ari. She tilts her head at the Ranger, places her bare foot on his hunched-over frame, and kicks him backward into the pool. He flails his arms and yells in the direction of the patio door for help.

We snatch our heels and run towards the ocean. Our bare feet sink deep into the loose and soft sand. The mostly deserted beach offers a wide-open escape route. A few stray couples and shell collectors mill about, minding their own business. A wave rolls warm salty water over my feet. I splash through the next one and peek over my shoulder.

No one follows.

"Where are we going?" Ari asks in a breathy voice, jogging beside me.

"Anywhere but here." I glance behind us a second time and stop running. "Huh?"

Ari stops just ahead of me and walks back. "What?"

"They aren't following us." I pant and swipe stray hair behind my ear.

"Probably because they know Femi's going to fucking kill them for letting us get away." Ari squints and wrinkles her face, focusing on the street. "Is that the Buick?"

I didn't think we ran that far, but there she sits in the parking lot of a condominium. "It is. Do you have my phone so we can call Eve?"

"No. I didn't have any pockets." She pats her hips and shrugs. "I already tried calling her when I noticed she wasn't at the club with Audrey and Gina."

"She's probably keeping an eye on Doc." I lift the passenger side door handle of the Buick. "We need to drive to their beach house."

She shakes her head and sinks into the driver's seat. "But I thought we weren't supposed to be in the same place together. It's one of your rules."

"I know my rules, Ari." I roll my eyes and buckle my seatbelt. "But this is important. We need to find out where Luisa's keeping her yacht."

Plus, I want to check on Doc and see how she's doing.

Ari backs the Buick out of its parking space and turns onto the main road. She drives by four towering condominiums and two beach houses, then pulls to the curb. "We're here." She shifts the Buick into park and climbs out.

I exit the car slowly and furrow my brow. "You booked our places less than a mile apart? What were you thinking?"

She pushes the Buick door quietly closed. "First of all, it's a mile and a half, and second…" She gazes up at the six-story luxury resort. "…none of the rooms are in any of our names. If you ask me, they got the better of the two places."

We step into the elevator. Ari removes a key from somewhere in the depths of her cleavage, inserts it in the keyhole beside P6, and turns it. That must be one of the reasons she picked this place. Most of the hotel rooms are on the first few floors, but to get to the penthouse, you have to have a special key or keycard for the elevator to go up to those floors. It keeps vacationers from accidentally arriving on the wrong level.

"They're in a penthouse, and we are in a beach house?" I tilt my head at her.

"Well, yeah. You don't think we could have had room to sleep all of Femi's men in a three-bedroom penthouse, do you? It made more sense to rent an eight-bedroom beach house for us and his band of merry men."

I snort through my nose. "There is nothing *merry* about those men."

When the elevator door opens, a sign on the wall has two arrows. One pointing to P6 to our left and P5 to our right. The entire top floor has only two rooms. We turn left and stop. The door to the girl's rental is ajar. I place my pointer over my lips, and Ari nods. We creep along the wall, moving silently toward the room. I push the entrance open with one finger, and it creaks noisily. I take off my heels, and Ari does the same before stepping on the marble floors. A small gun appears in my peripheral vision.

My head snaps at Ari. "Where the hell did that come from?" I ask, barely above a whisper.

"My bra."

It falls to the floor in front of me, landing loudly, and she puts her hands up.

I move to the front of her and do the same. "Put the gun down," I say to Manuel who has the barrel pressed against Ari's temple.

"What the fuck are you two doing here?" He tucks the handgun into the small of his back. "You're supposed to be at the house."

"You were fired, so I could ask you the same thing." I put my hands down and scan the living room and dining room. "Where is everyone?"

"That's a good question." He walks into the kitchen and

opens the fridge. "Empty. The place is clean. It's like no one was ever here."

I storm past him and check every room. "Impossible. This is where Femi brought Doc—where Eve, Gina, and Audrey should be."

Ari picks up her gun and points it at him. "Why are you here? More importantly…" She takes a step towards him. "…why are you here with a fucking gun, Manny?"

"First of all, don't call me fucking Manny. And second, I came here looking for Eve, same as you." He stands in front of Ari, letting the barrel of the gun touch his chest. "You wouldn't dare pull that trigger."

Ari tilts her head—a sinister smile spreading across her face. Her finger rests on the trigger. I quickly push Manuel sideways, and the bullet shatters a vase on the coffee table.

He drops to the floor and covers his head. "Jesus. Are you fucking crazy?"

I grab him by the bicep, pull him to his feet, and furrow my brow. "Never, ever, tell Ari she doesn't dare do anything. Because I can assure you, she will, every fucking time."

"You ladies are out of control." He yanks his arm away from me and storms out of the penthouse.

He has no idea.

Ari's eyes fixate on the blank wall to her right. I wave my hand in front of her eyes, and she blinks several times.

She wipes a stray tear from her cheek. "Why was he looking for Eve?"

"Maybe he wants to find Luisa and kill her to get back in Femi's good graces," I say walking towards the door.

The elevator doors close as we approach, taking Manuel down before we have a chance to get to them. We stand and watch the numbers slowly go down until they stop on the first floor. The door to P5 slowly opens to our right and Ari and I glance at each other before stepping onto the elevator that has arrived to pick us up. We press the down button, not wanting the P5 tenants to join us.

The doors groan towards each other, and a set of manicured hands grab them, stopping them from closing.

Chapter Sixteen
Who we are.

Audrey's makeup blackens the space beneath her eyes—vertical lines of mascara streak her cheeks on both sides. She grabs Ari by the shoulders and hugs her firmly.

"Audrey, you're crushing me," Ari grunts.

She releases Ari. "I'm sorry. I'm just so happy you're alive."

"What do you mean?" I ask, putting my hand up to block her embrace.

She wipes her runny nose on her wrist and waves us out of the elevator. We follow her quick steps into P5. Gina sits on a massive half-circle, ivory-colored leather couch.

Her knee stops bouncing when she sees us. "Oh, thank God." She crosses the room and hugs Ari. "We thought you were dead."

I put my hand up, stopping her from hugging me. "What do you mean, you *thought* we were dead? Where's Eve and Doc?"

Gina points at the couch with a shaking hand, but I decline, preferring to stand.

Audrey grabs four crystal whiskey glasses from the sideboard and drops a round ice cube in each. Her pouring hand trembles as she fills them to the top and passes them out to us. "We haven't seen Eve." She sits beside Gina. "She never showed up."

My ass sinks deep into a pumpkin-colored club chair across from them. "What do you mean? She had a courier deliver the case to me and knew we needed her for this one." I kick off my shoes.

Audrey gulps down the whiskey and coughs. "I thought it was weird too. Then came the break-in."

I raise my eyebrow and glance at Ari, who's holding the round ice ball in her palm and rolling it across its surface, making circles. "What break-in?"

Gina sits forward on the couch. "Audrey and I left to buy our dresses for the club, and when we came back…" She rotates her whiskey glass in her hand. "…the entire room was trashed—suitcases dumped, cushions on the floor, mattress flipped over, papers everywhere. They took the folder containing the file she sent by courier."

"Wait…" I stand and pace back and forth. "…Eve doesn't make copies of our files. Why did you have one?"

Audrey's eyes follow me. "I don't know. After we found the room a mess, we cleaned up, asked the front desk to move us discreetly across the hall, and registered the room under an old friend who lives in town."

The ice ball rolls across the tiled floor, drops into the groove between the tiles and continues rolling in a straight line toward the balcony door.

"Whoops." Ari stares into her empty glass. "So, why would someone break in, destroy the place, and steal the file that shouldn't exist to begin with?"

"That's a good question," Gina says, taking Ari's empty glass from her. "Maybe because it shouldn't have existed?" She takes the whiskey bottle, tops off each of our glasses, and sets it on the glass coffee table. "I think the more important question we should be asking is why? Why did Eve make two copies of the file?"

The room falls silent. The ice in my glass cracks when I take a sip, splitting the sphere in half. I examine the two sides. The ice is still the ice, it just has two sides now. Perhaps the same applies to the files.

"Maybe they aren't copies," I say aloud instead of in my head. "What if they are two parts of the same file? What was inside yours?"

"We don't know," Gina says. "We planned to read it thoroughly after we went dress shopping. Yours?"

"Photos of the target, Luisa. Her yacht, missing girls, her generals, and their duties. Have you tried calling Eve again?"

"No." Audrey stands and takes my empty glass from me. "As for Doc, we saw Femi try and bring her right after the room was ransacked, but we didn't let him know we were here."

How dare she not render aid to one of us.

I storm towards her. "Why? Doc needed your help."

Audrey puts the drink in my hand. "I was this close to opening the door." She holds her thumb and pointer finger an inch from each other. "But then, I heard Femi say, 'We need to find Audrey and Gina and stop them from going to the club,' so I didn't. The only people we trust are you and Ari. And if you didn't want us at the club, you would've called us."

"And since we didn't hear from you, we went to the club as planned." Gina crosses the room and stretches her empty glass out to Audrey who promptly fills it. "What happened to Doc?"

My teeth grind together, thinking about how I found her and what Luisa's guy was doing to her. I close my eyes and try picturing something else, anything else, but her. "Luisa's men raped her," I blurt it out and turn my back on them—not wanting them to see the rage boiling beneath the surface of my skin.

"That must be why Femi didn't want us there. He's worried it will happen to us too, right?" Gina's voice comes out shaky at the end.

She's afraid.

I turn around and everyone looks at me.

What we do next is on me, and I don't want them to get involved if they are scared or unsure. Finding Eve is our number one priority. Killing Luisa must come second.

"Something about all this seems deliberate," Ari says, sitting back on the couch. "The split case file, Eve's disappearance, and the break-in."

When Ari senses something I listen. Sometimes her brain catches things that no one else does. When it works that is. It's like bits and pieces of a puzzle floating around inside her head, occasionally coming together and completing a picture.

I sit beside her. "Talk it out to us. It doesn't matter how stupid or irrelevant, say it."

She scrunches her face and sighs. "Well, it all started after White Rabbit and I had sex."

"No, Ari skip ahead. We don't need to hear those details." I roll my eyes and shake my head at the others.

Gina raises her hand. "I have a question right away. Who the hell is White Rabbit?"

"Chicken Wing," I say frowning at her.

Her head recoils, and she grimaces. "You fucked Chicken Wing?"

Audrey pinches her eyes closed and scrunches her face—images of Ari and White Rabbit fucking, flashing through her mind.

"We are getting off-topic. Ari, please continue, sparing us the irrelevant details." I rub my forehead.

She sits forward and rests her glass on the coffee table. "So, after we did the deed for the first time, he became clingier—always nearby, watching me, asking where I'm going. You know, kind of stalkerish."

"Probably because you're his first real girlfriend," Gina chuckles over her glass before taking a sip.

Ari waves her off. "At first I thought maybe I could've been the best pussy he ever had..."

I cringe and squeeze my glass tighter. "Ari…"

"I know, I know. Relevant information only. So, anyway, it wasn't until after we fucked for the second time, that I thought his motives were something more. That's why I was climbing over the balcony to leave when you caught me." Ari points at me.

"What did he say?" I ask.

"It wasn't about what he said." She looks at me. "Remember when you taught me to listen to what people aren't saying? You know, the weird sense you get when someone wants to ask you more or say more but doesn't? Well, I sensed it, not just once, but multiple times. He's hiding something, and it was enough to give me a bad feeling. So, I asked him flat out what he was hiding."

"And what did he say?" Audrey asks.

"Nothing. Just ignored the question and walked away from me."

Silence is an answer. That is what I always say. If you're hiding something and someone asks you directly what it is, and you know you can't say a thing for fear of the consequences or worse, death, that gives away more information than making up some lie or turning the question back on the original inquirer.

"Because he's been ordered not to talk." I walk over to the door and peer through the peephole. The hallway is empty.

"The thing that made me want to leave is what happened after." She widens her eyes and rolls them.

Gina, Audrey, and I exchange glances. Ari stands by the balcony door, peering out at the ocean. She hums an unknown tune, her eyes locked on a boat in the distance.

"Ari?" I place my hand on her shoulder. "What happened?"

She shakes her head and frowns, trying to remember what the hell she was talking about. Her eyes light up. "Oh, yeah. So, I walked away from him, you know, well more like, stormed away pissed off and grabbed my purse to leave. He grabbed my wrist, hard and told me I *need* to stay."

Oh, this motherfucker wants me to kill him.

"Ari, did he hurt you?" I take a deep breath, shoving my rage deep inside. I know she likes him but manhandling her doesn't fly with me.

"I took a move from your playbook and snatched him by the balls."

That's my girl.

"He apologized at once and just told me to wait for him until he got out of the shower. He said his orders are to keep his eye on me for my safety."

Oh, fuck. It's my fault. I told him to stay close to her. He was following my orders, not Femi's.

"So, I told him I'd wait but as soon as he was in the shower, I scaled the balcony and left."

"What about you?" Audrey says to me. "What made you want to leave?"

I smile at her. "Because Femi told me to stay home."

The girls erupt in laughter.

"That's the funniest thing I've heard all day." Gina slaps her knee. "Did he really think you were going to listen?"

"No, he didn't." Manuel's voice booms over our cackling.

Our faces drop. The gun in his hand has a silencer, so he could take us all out and no one would hear a fucking thing.

I slam my glass on the table, cracking it, and launch my body to a stand. "God dammit, Manuel. What the fuck are you doing, following me? Femi fired you. Why are you even here?"

He takes a step away from me. "Sit the fuck down."

"Sit the fuck down?" I take a step closer, stalking him like a lioness ready to pounce on her prey.

His phone rings in his pocket, and he removes it to answer. "Got them. All of them. Same hotel, just the penthouse across the hall." Garbled words filter through the receiver. "Don't worry, they aren't going anywhere."

He shoves the phone back into his pocket as I approach him. "I said, sit the fuck down." His voice elevates.

Ari, Audrey, and Gina gather behind the couch, using it to shield their bodies from the imminent fight.

"Why are you here?" I stare at the barrel of the silencer. "And why do you have a silencer on that gun? Are you planning to assassinate us?"

My bare feet step silently closer and closer to him and my scalp prickles—rage racing through my veins.

Who does he think he is, holding a gun on us?

"Move back," he orders flipping off the gun safety. "My orders are to keep you here. Femi will be here shortly, and I don't want to shoot you, but I will if you don't back the fuck up."

I raise my hands and grin. "Oh, I see. You're doing this to get back in Femi's good graces."

He looks from me to the girls. "Not just his."

I laugh outwardly. "Do you think you'll be back in ours after holding a gun on us? On me? There's still time to get out of this alive, Manuel. All you have to do is walk out that door."

He shifts his weight from one foot to the other and glances at the door. "Time for me to get out of this alive? Femi warned you to stay home, but you didn't listen. Now you have to face the consequences of your actions."

"What consequences?" Ari steps around the couch and approaches us.

Manuel thrust the gun forward, pointing it at her face. "Move back."

Ari takes another fearless step forward. "Or what?"

She stands firm, refusing to listen. Gina and Audrey lift their heads and hustle to Ari's side. It's us against him.

"You can't shoot us all, Manuel." I grin devilishly and put my hands down. "Give me the gun and go."

He turns the barrel of the gun from Ari to me. "No. I only need to shoot you. Because without you, they aren't as brave or bold. You are the head of the snake…" His grip tightens on the gun handle. "…and without the head, the rest of your body dies."

"Femi wouldn't allow it," Gina announces.

Manny chuckles and shakes his head. "Femi permitted me to defend myself if necessary. So, if you don't sit the fuck down and shut the fuck up, I will shoot you—all of you."

Either Manny is lying, or Femi has lost his fucking mind. It's time to test the water and call his bluff. "Take your shot, Manny."

"Don't test me, Odie." He steps backward and holds the gun with both hands, prepared to fire. "Not another fucking step."

I take another step and the barrel of the gun flashes. My arm jerks backward and blood drains down my arm, dripping onto the floor. Ari covers her mouth and so does Gina and Audrey. I glance at the slice of missing flesh, the bullet grazing my bicep, and glare at Manuel with darkening eyes.

His eyes widen at my lack of painful response.

He lowers his weapon, and I take another step towards him. "You missed." I smile broadly.

Audrey runs to the kitchen area and yanks a towel off the stove handle. She wraps it around my arm and ties it. "You need stitches."

I lock eyes with her. "Later. Right now…" I turn away from her and glare at Manny. "…Manny and I have unfinished business."

He takes another step closer to the door. "You didn't even flinch." His eyes dart around the room landing on each of our smiling faces, not understanding.

Gina steps in front of me. "You can shoot, cut, punch even stab Odie, she will never feel it—never feel the pain."

"Bullshit." He scans my body.

"It's not bullshit. Watch this." Ari moves Gina aside and stomps my left foot. "See."

I stare at the red mark on my bare foot and glare at her. "Really, Ari?"

"What? If you could feel pain, you would know that someone stepping on your bare foot hurts like a motherfucker, but stomping is debilitating. It was the only way to prove we are telling the truth."

I rest my hand on the silencer and remove the gun from Manny's shaking hand. "Femi assigned you to me to protect me and him from me, but did he tell you why? Did Femi tell you why he needed protection from me?" I toss the gun over my shoulder. It strikes the tile and skids across the floor.

Ari picks it up and points it at him. "Because she's a maneater."

Manuel's eyes furrow and dart from me to Ari. "Maneater. Is that a metaphor for an assassin?"

A throaty laugh starts in my throat and bursts from my mouth into a hysterical laugh. The girls stand beside me, and we laugh together.

Ari points at him. "You think Odie's an assassin." She wipes hysterical tears from her cheeks. "Odie's a cannibalistic serial killer." She slaps her knee and crosses her legs. "Oh my God, I'm going to pee. That leftover stir fry you ate at her house, had meat from a previous victim in it."

Manuel gags. "It's not true." He covers his mouth. "You're lying."

Ari snorts and collapses to the floor slapping the tile with her palm. "This is funnier than when you fed Benny the Jenny stew."

I tilt my head at him. "I never lie when it comes to food. Now let me see those thighs."

He grabs his waistline, holding his pants tight against his body. "You all are lying. You're just trying to scare me into talking."

Ari pokes the towel tied to my arm and stares at her bloody finger. "You should let Audrey stitch you up before slicing and dicing him."

I sigh heavily. "You're right. I wouldn't want to contaminate anything. We need to secure him first."

Gina opens a bag beside the couch and spins a set of cuffs on her finger. "Let me see your hands."

"No." He takes a few steps away from us. "You're all crazy. Just a band of fucking lunatics."

"I bet he knows more about what's going on," Ari says, pointing the gun at his cock. "Start talking."

His back hits the door, and his palm rests on its curved handle. "I ain't saying shit."

I swing my hand between his legs, grip his cock, and slam him into the door. "Where do you think you're going?"

He stands on his tiptoes and screams. "Let go, let go, let go." His hands claw madly at mine, digging his nails in.

Ari rests the barrel against his temple, and he stops moving. "How does it feel?"

He looks at the gun in her hand without turning his head and hyperventilates. "Look, just let me go, and I'll disappear. You'll never see me again."

I lean in, studying the side of his face, and neck, and whisper. "Oh, you're going to disappear, but not because we let you leave." I release his cock and back away from him. "But first, I want to know what you know. Everything."

He lifts his chin and snaps his shirt down straightening it. "Fuck you."

Well, aren't we being defiant? He's awful brave for someone with a gun pointed at his head. I nod to Ari. She points the gun at his foot and pulls the trigger.

"Agh, God dammit." Manny hollers falling to the floor and holding the tip of his shoe. "You shot my big toe off."

She points the gun at his forehead, and his eyes cross. "You have another one."

He pinches his eyes closed and pants heavily, rocking his body forward and backward. "I can't fucking tell you. My boss will fucking kill me."

I take the gun from Ari's hands and crouch down in front of him, making our eyes level. "What do you think I'm going to do?" I rest the barrel of the silencer under his chin. "Femi is the least of your worries."

"I'm not talking about Femi." He swallows hard. "I'm talking about Luisa."

Chapter Seventeen
Cocky

My face drops. "What the fuck did you just say?"

He uses one leg to push himself backward to lean against the wall. "The job was to work for Femi as his bodyguard so I could spy on you—all of you. She wanted me to learn your behaviors, habits, and weaknesses. She's going to kill all of you."

I stand and look down at him. "Not if we kill her first."

Gina appears beside us. "Hold out your hands." The cuffs dangle in her grasp.

His eyes widen. "Fuck no. Y'all aren't holding me hostage."

Gina and Ari grab his arms and pull him away from the wall. He flails his limbs wildly, twisting his body and thrashing about like a toddler throwing a temper tantrum at a toy store. Ari reaches for his kicking leg, and he strikes her in the chest knocking the wind from her lungs. She takes several gasping breaths and drops to the floor on her hands and knees. He crawls towards the door, dragging Gina with him, her hands still wrapped around his arm trying to pull him back. I dive on his spine and wrap my arm around his throat, choking him. He slaps my arm and bucks up and down, bouncing me. His head launches backward, and he screams, his body suddenly going limp.

I peer over my shoulder. Audrey pulls a needle from Manuel's thigh. "He's making too much noise."

Gina secures his wrists in cuffs. I stand, and we each take an arm, pulling his flaccid body into the bedroom.

"Ari, get the plastic drop cloth and prepare the bed. Audrey, help me with his bottoms."

Audrey puts her hand on her chest. "His bottoms?"

"Yes, take off his shoes, pants, and underwear."

She takes his shoes off and drops them beside us. "You want him naked?"

I take her hand and squeeze it. "Audrey, you don't carve and cook a chicken with its feathers still on, do you?"

Her face twists. "No, of course not."

"This is no different." I let her hand go. "Let's defeather this mother fucker."

She yanks his pants and underwear off. "Oh, my."

We stare down at his curved cock.

Ari grabs his dick and shakes it. "That's a G-spot stroker for sure."

Audrey raises one eyebrow. "He probably has Peyronie's disease."

She lets his dick go and wipes it on her top. "Is it contagious?"

"No," Audrey shakes her head and laughs not taking her eyes off his cock.

"Want to take it for a spin?" I grab it and point it at her.

"Oh, no. That's your thing, not mine. You go ahead." Her face reddens.

Ari shakes the plastic over the mattress after removing its sheets. She tucks the sides and ends under the mattress and sighs. "There, that ought to catch most of the blood." She leaves the room and returns with a white porcelain plate. "Here."

"Is that for, that?" Gina asks, pointing at his cock.

I remove the plate from Ari's hand and set it on the nightstand. "Yes. I don't have much time. Femi will be here soon."

Gina unravels twine from the kitchen and ties his legs together. She grabs his foot and stares at the bloody space his toe used to be. "I can't believe he works for Luisa. It just pisses me off." She crushes his foot in her hand. Manuel makes loud groaning noises, still too out of it to scream.

I want to fuck him—ride his cock until my loins rupture so hard I levitate away from his body. But I need him to wake up first. "Help me get him on the bed."

We hoist him onto the bed and Gina uncuffs his hands and cuffs them around the metal headboard post.

My knees sink into the mattress as I straddle his chest and slap him across the face. "Manuel."

He moans and his lashes flicker but don't open.

"Leave us," I say sliding my pointer up and down his toned pectorals.

Audrey sets a scalpel and suture kit on the nightstand. "Let me know if you need any help."

The door closes softly behind her and heavy metal music vibrates the walls. They don't want to hear what comes next.

I stand on the bed and remove all my clothes. "Manuel, wake up." I nudge his ribs with the side of my foot.

His eyes are barely open, and he glances up at me through the slits. "Fuck you," he murmurs.

I drop down onto his thighs and grab his cock. "Oh, no, Manuel. I'm going to fuck you." I fill my mouth with mucous, spit on the tip of his dick, and smear my fluids up and down his shaft. He closes his eyes—enjoying my touch. He must think he's getting a bonus.

"Do you know if you die suddenly with a stiff cock, it stays that way after death?"

His eyes spring open. He stares at the scalpel now placed against his throat. "Don't. I'll tell you whatever you want."

I tighten my grip on his cock, and he squeals. "Wait, I know the name of Luisa's yacht."

"Where does Luisa keep her yacht?"

"I don't know. The only thing I can tell you is the name, *Mother of Seaduction*." His body presses into the plastic, moving further away from the blade as I press down. "Please, don't. She docks usually at a marina near her meetings then moves it elsewhere. She never stays in the same place for long. That's all I know, I swear."

I curl my fingers around the tip of his cock. He gasps and stares at the ceiling as I jerk him off until his cock is as hard as stone. "Thank you for the useless information, Manuel." I release his cock and plunge the blade into his throat. "But it's not going to save you." It makes squishing noises as I remove it and his throat gargles blood from its new hole. I always wanted to know if it was true—if someone's cock really does stay hard after death sometimes.

I'm pleased to report that the rumors are true.

I've never fucked a corpse before. I usually kill my victims while I'm actively fucking them. My hands glide up and down his rippled abdomen. I rub his cock back and forth across my clitoris. "Oh, God Manny don't be a tease. Put that cock inside of me." I lift my body and lower my pussy onto his cock, rotating forward and back, pressing his shaft deep inside me. "Fuck baby you feel so good." I smile at his open empty eyes. His cock glides back and forth over my pleasure zone. My thighs tingle, and a prickling sensation races from my inner thighs straight to my clitoris and ruptures on his cock. "Oh, yes

Daddy. I want you to taste me." I yank his dick out of me and sit on his open mouth, bouncing my pussy on his dead face. I grab the headboard and thrust my pussy lips against his mouth over and over. "I'm going to cum again. Here it comes." I scream as an orgasm sprays from my pussy onto his tongue.

I'm not done. I want more. What the fuck is wrong with me? He has me feeling insatiable. If I knew dead men could make me feel this way all the time, I'd only fuck corpses from now on.

I need more, I need more, I need more.

I flip my body around and bounce back onto his cock, riding it backward.

The door to the bedroom opens halfway. Ari's eyes widen, her mouth falling open and I make no effort to slow down, caught up in my fantasy. "Ummm…I'll come back later." She closes the door.

My hands clench his thighs tight as another orgasm spills out of me, emptying my body of everything it has. "My God." I let his cock slide out of me, turn around, and lay on top of Manuel's chest, snuggling my head up to his blood-soaked neck, panting like a thirsty dog. "I'm going to have to keep you."

My finger swirls the blood around the hole in his throat. I draw a smiley face on his tan chest and give it x-shaped eyes. If I wasn't in such a time crunch, I would take a nap. I sit up, grab the scalpel from the bed and rest it against the base of Manuel's cock. The blade disappears into his skin. I press and saw through it like a sausage with that gross meat sleeve they slide over it to hold it together. The blade pops out the other side, freeing the appendage from his body.

He is no longer of use to me, but this I can save for future use.

I place the severed, softening cock on the plate. I know Ari was expecting more, like Filet of Manuel broiled and wrapped in bacon, but we have too much going on right now.

The edge of the bed lowers as I sit beside him. The pooled blood beneath his neck rolls across the plastic and spreads across my left butt cheek. I stand and untuck the edges of the plastic, folding them over him on both sides. I lean down, kiss his forehead, and whisper, "Thanks for the ride."

Chapter Eighteen
A Sour Mood

Ari stares down at Manuel's wrinkled and curved cock. "Huh. It's neat how it maintains its curve when it's dead."

I nod. "Put it in the freezer for me, would you?"

"Sure." She rotates the plate in her hand, examining the appendage. "So, how was it?"

"Best I ever had." I grin and duct tape the plastic sheeting around Manuel's body.

She wrinkles her nose. "Even though it was all one-sided?"

"Yes."

"Huh. I'm going to have to try it sometime." She walks away, talking to herself on her way to the kitchen.

Gina strolls in carrying another roll of sheeting. "Thought you might need this." She sets it on the bedside table. "Did he give you anything?"

"Not much. Just the name of the yacht." I tear off a long piece of duct tape and wrap it around Manuel's head and neck several times.

"That's it?" She shakes out the plastic sheeting, helps me tip the body on its side, and tucks the fresh one beneath him. "Maybe he's the reason for Eve's message."

I stop wrapping the body. "What message?"

She smooths the plastic over Manuel and tucks it on the opposite side. "The one on the envelope."

"Family photos? What the fuck would that have to do with Manuel?" I unravel a large piece of tape and wrap it around the corpse several times.

"*Family photos*? That's not what our envelope said. Ours said, *trust no one*."

A phone vibrates beneath the plastic. I glance at Gina and close my eyes.

Fucking rookie mistake.

There's too many distractions and people involved in this case. Only Ari and I work most of the jobs. Everyone else usually keeps their distance.

Gina passes me the scalpel. I cut a hole in the plastic big enough to slide my hand through and dig Manuel's ringing phone from the pile of his clothes we wrapped up with his body. It stops ringing and rings again.

"Who is it?" Audrey asks, entering the room with a fresh change of clothes for me.

"It says, *Boss*." I hand the phone to Gina for disposal.

"Do you think it's Luisa?" Audrey tapes up the hole in the plastic.

I shrug my shoulders. "There's no way of knowing. *Boss* could mean Femi or Luisa at this point. The only way to find out is to answer."

A set of keys lands on the corpse and falls to the floor. "Well, no matter which one of them it is, if they didn't know where we were before, they will soon." Ari points to the keychain. "That's an Air Tag. If Luisa, Femi, or any of their men drives by this place, they might be close enough to pick up on its signal."

I swipe the keys from the floor, open the window, and chuck them towards the ocean. They land quietly in the sand.

Audrey wipes all the surfaces with gloved hands. She grabs the stick vacuum and runs it over the area rugs, cleaning as much of our existence as she can. The cleaner the room, the less housekeeping will do when we leave.

"We should go," I say plucking a blonde hair dangling from the dresser drawer.

"I'll grab the beach wagon," Audrey says leaving the room.

The whiskey calls to me from the next room. Alcohol is the only thing that calms me down when I'm frustrated or pissed.

Right now, I'm both.

Eve was trying to get a message to us by sending different notes on each folder and splitting the file. But without the second file, we may never know what it was.

Ari lifts a calendar from beneath a heavy magnet on the fridge when I enter and carries it toward me. "Fuck. Dinner with my mom is the day after tomorrow." Her eyes shimmer and lock on mine. "We're still going, aren't we?"

We shouldn't. But I know if I don't get this dinner over with, Ari will plan another family get-together another time.

"Yes, we are still going," I sigh.

Ari grabs me and hugs my neck. "Thank you. I promise you won't regret it."

Oh, sure. Sitting me at a dining room table surrounded by her tasty ass brothers is a fantastic idea.

What could go wrong?

I tap her shoulder and gently push her away from me. Violating my personal space is something Ari will never stop doing. She just doesn't have it in her.

Audrey rolls the beach wagon into the bedroom. I stand and follow her. We each grab an end of Manuel's corpse and drop it in the wagon.

I step on his midsection, pushing him deeper into it. "We need to dump him somewhere before he gets too stiff to move him."

"How about the ocean? We can roll him to the end of the pier and drop him in. The sharks will do the rest," Ari says, grabbing the wagon handle and pulling. Her body recoils back. "Man, he's a heavy fucker."

I shake my head. "No. The pier won't work. The waves could push him back to shore."

We need to find Luisa. "We'll rent a boat. That way we can check a few marinas for Luisa's yacht and take him out into the open ocean."

"Now?" Gina's voice raises an octave. "It's dark out."

She's right. We can't rent any boats after sunset or before sunrise.

Fucking laws always getting in the way.

"We need to do something with him soon, or he'll start to smell," Audrey says, tucking the flat sheet under the mattress, and remaking the bed.

Ari's eyes light up. "My mom has a chest freezer in her garage."

"Are you nuts? You can't put a dead body in your mom's freezer." I shake my head at her.

Sometimes she doesn't think before blurting things from her mouth.

"Why not? She never goes in there, parks in the driveway, and it's been empty for a long time." Ari huffs and crosses her arms.

"I guess we could dump him in the tub for now and cover him with ice." I shrug. "Tomorrow, we'll take him to your mom's while the girls rent a boat or yacht for a few days. After we eat, we'll meet you at the marina and take him out to sea," I say to Gina and Audrey.

Ari and I lift Manuel's body and drop it in the tub while Gina and Audrey get bags of ice from the corner store. After the girls return and put Manuel on ice, I head to the other bathroom. Thankfully, the penthouse has three full bathrooms so I could still take a shower. I scrub Manuel's bodily fluids off me and watch them circle the drain. I pull my arm towards me, examining the missing skin where Manuel shot me. It's stopped bleeding for now, but I need to have Audrey wrap it.

The shower curtain launches to the side.

Femi's face is red, and his brows furrowed with rage.

I roll my eyes and smile. "Hello, Pussycat."

"Don't Pussycat me. Where's Manuel?"

"In the other bathroom, didn't Ari tell you?" I peer over his shoulder. A group of his men crowds the living room. "What the fuck is going on?"

He storms from the room, leaving the door and curtain open. My naked body is visible to his men. A few divert their eyes, but the rest just stare.

Perverts.

I slide my hand down my abdomen, heading for my pussy, and yank the curtain aside.

If they want to see more, they'll have to come to me, which they won't do, fearing Femi's wrath.

The entire shower curtain, rod, and all, crash to the floor outside the tub. "What did you do?" Femi's eyes are nearly black with anger as he tries to take deep breaths to calm himself. He pinches the bridge of his nose and closes his eyes before exhaling.

He opens his eyes and places a hand on each wall, blocking me in. There's an anger inside them I don't care for or appreciate. He doesn't deserve a reply from me. I grab my towel from the sink.

He snatches it from my hand and throws it behind him. "Answer me."

One of his men runs into the room, slams the toilet seat open, and vomits violently.

Another appears in the doorway, his face pale as the wall beside him. "Sir, there's something you need to see."

Femi's head twists to face me. "What is he going to show me, my love?"

I tug another towel from the towel bar and pat myself dry. "Dessert for Luisa."

He pinches his lips together, wiggles his pointer finger at me, and walks away. I finish drying, pull on a pair of shorts and a white tank top, and stroll barefoot into the living room.

Ari flops onto the couch beside Audrey and nudges her shoulder with a smile. "We should've made some popcorn."

Audrey studies Ari's face, her fingers fidgeting in her lap. "Why?"

Femi stands with his back to me and his eyes on his men. "Odie, is that a cock in the freezer?"

Ari's head recoils and then points at Femi and me. "Because this is about to be the greatest show on earth. We got front-row seats to this fucking circus." She sits back and gulps down a glass of bourbon.

"Of course it is. Why wouldn't it be?" I roll my eyes and walk away from him.

"We are making a chocolate-covered banana out of it," Ari chimes in from the couch.

Chicken Wing sits beside her, speaking quietly in her ear. I can tell she's not listening to him. Her eyes are focused on Femi and me. She winks, and I wink back.

Femi grabs my bicep tight. "Hey, are you listening to me?"

I glance at his tight grip, and he removes his hand slowly, fresh blood coating his palm.

"I told you; you should've let me put a stitch in that," Audrey says coming up beside me. She slaps a white piece of gauze on my arm and secures it with two pieces of medical tape. "Keep it covered so it doesn't get infected."

"What happened?" Femi asks, his eyes softening.

"What happened?" Ari stands from the couch abruptly and stomps towards Femi. One of Femi's men steps between her and him, and she shoves him away from her, knocking him over the coffee table. "Get the fuck out of my way." She points in Femi's face. "What happened is Manuel, who you hired, came in here with a fucking gun, pointed it at my head and shot Odie. That's what fucking happened." Femi reaches for the hand she's pointing at him with, and she slaps it away. "Don't touch me."

Femi steps away from us both, places his hands behind his back, and stares out the window. "I only wanted him to keep you here—make sure you were all safe," he says over his shoulder.

"You knew?" I ask speed-walking to his side. "Femi, what the fuck? Did you know he works for Luisa?"

His head snaps in my direction. "What? Who told you that?"

"He did," Gina says from behind us, pointing through the bathroom doorway.

He reaches inside his jacket pocket, removes an envelope, and hands it to me. "That explains how she found Eve," he says without looking at me.

I snatch the envelope from him and open it quickly. My heart stops and the room spins. Ari walks towards me, reaching for me as I fall to my knees. The image of Eve floats to the floor, landing face up for all to see.

Her eyes stuck open in a state of horror, and her tongue plunging through a jagged hole in her throat. Multiple knife wounds plaster different parts of her body. Rings around both of her wrists bleed from fighting bindings wrapped too tightly around them. Sharp lines spell out a carved message across her abdomen.

Ari collapses on the floor beside me. "I'm going to fucking kill that cunt."

Chicken Wing kneels on the floor beside her and rests his hand on her back. "We are going to take care of her."

Ari's head whips to face him. "Get your fucking hand off me before I chop it off and stuff it up your ass." She points at Femi and stands. "This is your fault. If you wouldn't have hired Manuel and just let Odie and I do this job alone like we always have, Eve would still be alive."

"No." He steps closer to her and their faces nearly touch. "You would all be dead if I weren't involved."

Femi snaps his fingers, and one of his men carries over a manilla envelope. He takes the envelope and shoves it into Ari's chest. "Here, see for yourself."

Ari lets the folder fall to the floor. I grab it by its corner and dump the contents onto the carpet.

It's us—all of us.

I fan the images across the floor. Audrey, Gina, and Ari sit in front of me, examining the photos one by one. The pictures are from our first day on the beach, at the abandoned restaurant, and in the parking lot of the store Ari and I shopped in.

Femi's knees crack when he squats beside me. "I warned you not to underestimate Luisa. I told you to let me handle her and the generals, and you girls were to take care of the general's men." He scans each of our solemn faces. "But when you decided to blow up her meeting, we lost the one opportunity to take her out." He points to his men around the room and stands. "This mission is over. The element of surprise is gone. Luisa has doubled her guard and has men searching for you."

"How the fuck does she know about us?" Audrey picks her photo up from the pile.

"Me." Doc steps into the room, her arms wrapped around herself. Multiple bruises of various shades and stages dot her forearms and wrists. A green and purple bruise discolors her cheekbone. "It's my fault." Tears tumble over her chin and drip in her shirt "Before Luisa's men…" She wipes her face and turns her head, refusing to look at me as I come to a stand. "…before they did what they did, Luisa put a gun to my head—a revolver. She took all the bullets out except one. Every time she spun the barrel and pulled that trigger, I thought I was taking my last breath. And every time it would just click. She said she felt something was wrong with our presence but couldn't quite put her finger on it."

I stop in front of her and lift her chin. She keeps her eyes closed. "Look at me," I say sternly.

Her eyes flutter open. "I'm sorry. I only told her we were hired to do surveillance on her operation by a rival competitor, that's all."

"What competitor?" I ask.

"Me," Femi says. "She told her it was me. Said she only knew my first name and that I paid a large sum to find out what I could about her operation."

I push Doc's face away from me with my palm. "You got Eve killed and put a target on all of our backs!" I shout.

She raises her shoulders and tightens her grip on her stomach. "Please, Odie. I'm so sorry." Her knees buckle and she collapses on the floor. "Please, forgive me." Her hands wrap around my calf.

I snatch her hand and twist it off me. "I will never forgive you."

Doc drops her head and sobs.

Ari sticks the picture of Doc's battered body in the abandoned restaurant under my face, blocking my raging eyes from seeing Doc. "Odie, look."

I take the photo from her and study it. "Shit."

"What?" Audrey and Gina say simultaneously.

I dive on the floor beside Doc. She covers her face. I ignore her and dig through the pockets of her trousers until I find her phone.

Ari puts her hand out to Chicken Wing. "Give me your knife."

He pulls it from its sheath and passes it to her. "What are you doing?"

"In the picture, Doc's phone is neatly placed within arm's reach where she could see it and call us." Ari places the edge of the blade between the seams of the phone.

"Meaning?" Audrey tilts her head.

"Meaning, they took it out of her pocket for a reason—left it for a reason." The phone parts separate.

"And she wouldn't have done that for no reason," Gina says more to herself than us.

"Exactly." Ari drops the two sides on the carpet, and a tracker falls out. "Fuck."

The lights go out, darkening the penthouse.

Fuck indeed.

Chapter Nineteen
Run

The door to the penthouse slams open. Emergency lighting allows a small amount of light to filter into the room. Gunfire erupts immediately, and everyone scatters.

Femi yells to us and points down the hall. "Get to the bedroom."

We crawl across the floor. Gunfire sprays over our heads and fragments of furniture, walls, and blood showers our backs. Audrey reaches the hallway first and disappears around the corner. I glance behind me and stop moving. Ari reaches for Chicken Wing, and his eyes widen. Blood spreads across his chest—a bullet striking him in the back and exiting the front. A cannister lands beside him and smoke spins out of it.

"No!" she screams and crawls towards him, disappearing in a cloud.

"Ari, no!" I grab her ankle and pull, but it's quickly yanked from my grasp.

I pound the floor with my fist, stand, and run through the cloudy space, down the hall, and into the bedroom. Audrey shuts the door and stuffs a rolled-up towel beneath it. Gina yanks the sliding door open, allowing the contaminated air to escape.

"Where's Ari?" Audrey asks.

I shake my head. "They took her."

The door rattles behind me. I stand beside the dresser and push it with my hip, barricading the entrance. "To the right of the balcony is the fire escape to the roof and ground. Get the fuck out of here. I'll hold the door."

Someone rams the door, and my body bounces forward. I press my feet into the floor and lean all my weight against the dresser, holding them at bay. Audrey climbs over the side of the balcony.

Gina watches Audrey climb down, slowly backs into the room, and flattens her spine against the wall. "I can't do this."

My feet slide forward, and I push the dresser back with all my strength. "Yes, you fucking can. Just go."

"I'm afraid of heights." She jogs to me, places her shaking palms on the dresser, and leans. "You, go. Besides, if anyone can save us, it's you." A tear slides down her face, and the wrinkle in her forehead deepens. Snot rolls from her nostril onto her lip as she sobs. "Go," she cries out with glossy eyes.

She's right. I am the only one who can save them if Luisa doesn't fucking kill them first. My eyes lock on the balcony chairs. It will buy her more time. I race away from Gina, grab one of the iron chairs, and slam it at an angle under one of the drawers.

"Listen to me." I place my hands on her shoulders. "When you can't see me through that balcony window anymore, I need you to try. Shut the patio door and lay the chair down so the top and leg are in the track. It will buy you more time."

An axe blade breaches the door, creating a hole. Someone pulls it out and peers through the slit. "Let us in. We promise we won't hurt you."

I snatch the hotel pen from its notepad and plunge it through the opening. Screaming filters through the door, and Gina's body jars forward. "Odie, I can't hold it much longer."

I wipe a tear from her cheek. "I'll come for you and Ari."

"I know you will." She sniffs snot up her nose.

The dresser slides towards us and an arm reaches through the opening. Gina's eyes widen. "Run!"

I sprint across the carpet and dive for the fire escape. My right arm catches me, but the left fails, and I nearly fall.

Fucking shoulder.

Below me, Audrey waves for me to hurry.

"Don't wait for me," I yell down to her.

She nods and runs down the alley between our building and the next.

My feet slide in something slimy when I reach the bottom, nauseating me. I shouldn't have looked down, but I couldn't help it. A partially eaten cheeseburger smushes under my heel. Mold covers half of the bread.

"Are you going to eat that?"

I turn to face the voice behind me, curling my lip. "No."

The homeless man pulls up his tattered brown sleeve and grabs the side of the burger that I didn't step on. He pulls off the moldy part and shoves it in his yap.

Bile races to my mouth, and I cover it with my fist. "Oh, God."

I back away from him.

The patio door shatters above us. The chair holding the dresser against the door lands on the ground, breaking one of its legs.

"I will give you a thousand dollars if you hide me in your cart and roll away," I say, pinning my body against the wall so Luisa's men can't see me.

"No." He huffs and grabs the handle of his cart. "Don't touch my things."

His bloodshot blue eyes grow smaller as he squints. "You're one of them, aren't you?"

A heavy boot steps on the fire escape.

God dammit. I don't have time for this.

He grabs my arm with his filth-covered hand and shakes me. "Who sent you? The government?" His greasy grey and white bangs dangle before his furrowing brow. "I got her." He looks up at the man climbing down the fire escape and pulls me away from the building.

Jesus. I'll never live it down if I'm caught and turned over to Luisa by a homeless lunatic.

I yank myself away from him and run towards the ocean.

He screams after me. "You can't get away. They're always watching."

My head disappears beneath the dark waves. I stay underwater, swimming sideways, letting the current push me down the beach, away from the penthouse. Pressure builds in my lungs. My face breaches the surface of the waves, and I gulp a quick breath. The moonlight illuminates my face. I stare at it for a brief second before retreating beneath the wake.

Fatigue slows me down, so I push off the ocean floor and swim towards the pier. I swim between the pilings and stomp through the thick sand, pulling up my heavy saltwater-soaked shorts.

"Jesus, lady. Are you nuts?" Someone yells at me from the pier. "There are sharks all over."

I wave him off and continue across the sand, heading for a pair of high-rise condominiums.

A woman slaps her flip-flops together and sets them on her railing beside a drying bathing suit and cover-up. Once the door closes behind her, I swipe the sandals, slide them on my feet, and wrap the dry cover up around me.

My toes stop a full inch from the end of the flip-flops. They are way too big for me. I stroll down the sidewalk, the toes of the sandals catching intermittently.

So fucking annoying.

I need dry clothes. Along the main strip, a few tourist shops stay open late. I duck inside one. The bald sales associate looks up briefly from his book and then continues to ignore me. He deserves to lose merchandise at this point. I don't like stealing but desperate times call for desperate measures. I pluck a pair of coral sweats and a black half-shirt with a coral palm tree off their hangers. The salesman continues to ignore me, so I squat on the floor behind a rack and quickly change my clothes. I stand and casually walk right out the door. The salesman must be reading a really good book because he didn't even notice.

Multiple motorcycles line parking spaces a few storefronts down. Loud music blares from a bar door as a couple exits. They hold the door for me, and I shuffle inside.

Keeping secrets from the girls and Femi isn't something I do regularly. However, due to the gravity of this job and the number of players involved, I called a couple of my Army buddies. I advised them I wouldn't contact them unless necessary and after the events that just transpired, it's necessary.

I flop on an empty bar stool, and the bartender drops a black square napkin in front of me. "You look like shit."

"Thanks." I glare up at him, smile, and scan the room. "Nice place."

"I know." He winks.

His eyes are green like mine, but his hair is the same color as the sand trapped between my toes. A sleeve of tattoos flows down his arm, stopping at his Garmin Descent diving watch.

I take his arm in both hands and examine the colorful mermaid tattoo. "Nice work."

"Got it done locally." He rests both hands on the bar top and scans the bare parts of me. "You have any ink?"

"Not yet." I smile and lick my bottom lip. "But I thought about it."

He slides two crystal glasses in front of me, drops an ice cube in each, and pours in Apple Crown Royal. "What would you get?"

Someone taps their empty beer bottle. The bartender nods at him. "I'll be right back. The drinks on me."

Oh, how I wish the drink was on him. Glistening on his rippled abs he's hiding beneath his fitted t-shirt that reads, 'Ladies, if you can't ride waves, I'll let you ride me.'

I may take him up on that offer.

He returns from helping the bar patron and grabs a dollar sitting on the bar top beside me. His hand shakes up and down, trying to let the bill go, but it sticks to his hand. "Fucking gross."

I seize his wrist, pinch the dollar between two fingers, peel it off his palm, and drop it on the floor behind me. No one wants a sticky bartender dollar, no matter how financially strapped you may be.

"Thanks." He stares at my hand still holding his wrist. "You can let go now."

"Are you a diver?" I ask, reading the time on his watch.

I already know the answer, but this is part of our game.

He covers the dial. "Yes."

I let his hand go and tilt my head. "And what about your shirt? Is that an open offer?"

"Under certain circumstances." He leans down so he's at eye level with me. "You never answered my question."

"And which question is that?" I trace his jaw with my pointer.

"What ink would you get?" He stares deep into my eyes.

I crook my finger at him, calling him closer to me, and whisper in his ear, "Maneater."

His head tilts toward mine, his cheek touching mine. "Because you eat men literally or because you chew them up and spit them out like they mean nothing to you?"

I lick the edge of his ear and breathe one word into his canal, warming it. "Both."

His head recoils and stares at me, trying to read my face—checking for the lie he will never find.

Another bartender appears beside him. "Wes, I finished the dishes, so I can take over the bar."

"Follow me," he says without taking his eyes off me.

We walk to the end of the bar, where he steps off a platform and joins me at floor level. I remember Wes being short as fuck, I just didn't remember him being this short. My mouth is level with his forehead.

He smiles up at me when I stop walking. "Don't let my height fool you."

"Oh, I know better." I grin broadly.

A door beside him opens slowly, revealing an office inside. I walk around the dimly lit room. A sophisticated stereo system and surveillance monitors cover an entire wall. He sits in a rolling plush chair and pulls me in front of him.

I stare down at him and grin as he grips my sweats and pulls them to the floor. "Don't be afraid," he murmurs.

Afraid? We've been out of contact too long.

He picks up a remote and presses a button. The lights go out, plunging us into darkness. I gasp as he grabs my hips suddenly and yanks me forward. His breath, heating my pussy lips. "Once the music starts, I won't stop until

I'm finished. I'm going to only ask you once, do you want me to fuck your brains out, here and now in this office?"

Well, damn. Wes appears to have stepped up his game. How exciting.

I reach between his legs, and he grabs both my wrists, slamming them onto the desktop. "No, touching. Only I get to touch. Now, I need your consent."

I've never not been able to touch before. I like having some sort of control. But if I'm going to ask him for his help, I need to let go and play along.

"I thought your shirt said I was to ride you?" I ask.

Hot air strikes my pussy lips making them flicker. "It's a lie. Now, give me your answer."

Fuck it.

"I consent."

"Good girl."

Heavy metal music blares overhead. My body lifts into the air and drops stomach first onto the desk. His tongue glides from between my pussy lips, across my taint, and into my asshole making it pucker. He continues licking it—plunging his tongue in and out. I tighten my cheeks, and he grabs them with both hands spreading them apart.

I've never had a tongue in my asshole before, and I must say, it feels better than expected. He continues eating my ass for several seconds before pressure enters it slowly. I reach behind my back and grab his hand to stop him, but he slaps it away. His thumbs glide in and out of my hole and his cock plunges into my pussy.

Holy fuck.

He thrusts into me, using his thumbs in my ass to hold me still, and thrusts again.

I smile in the dark. This feels fucking fantastic. I don't want it to ever end.

My pussy ejects out an orgasm, and he yanks his cock out at once. His mouth encapsulates my pussy, and he sucks my juices. He flips me onto my back, seizes me by the shirt, and lifts me at the same time. My head whips forward as he pushes me backward, and I bounce off the couch cushions.

He drops on top of me, the weight of his body on my chest making it hard to breathe. His face forces its way between my ear and shoulder. He licks my lobe and growls, "You may be a Maneater, but I'm a Womaneater."

His hands slap against my bare knees, grips them tight, and yanks them apart. He dives back between my legs and devours my pussy. I grab his hair and shove his head further inside me. He grips my wrists and pins them to my sides.

No touching.

I squeeze the cushions, folding my nails over, and rock my pelvis towards him. His lips suck my inner thighs, one then the other. He makes his way up my abdomen, lifting my shirt and licking the salt from my tan skin. My nipples tighten when they enter his mouth, and he sucks the life out of them. His hand encapsulates my throat, and he rams his cock inside me without warning, making me cry out.

"Scream for me," he shouts over the music, relaxing his grip on my neck.

I open my mouth, prepared to do anything he asks, not wanting this experience to end. My pussy erupts violently, coating his cock as I scream at him. "Don't stop."

He lifts his body slightly away from me, grinding his hips into me, rolling my pussy lips against my body.

"Oh, fuck, Wes."

The music lowers, and he leans down to me. "I'm almost finished, but it doesn't have to be over."

My eyes dart to the sound of a door closing behind me. Wes climbs between my legs and sucks my pussy lips. "You see, this shirt isn't mine." His tongue flutters across my anus. He sits up and presses his fingers in and out of me, before gripping my pussy lips and pinching them. "It's my best friend's."

He releases my pussy lips and pokes them with just the tip of his cock.

"Oh, my God. I don't care who's fucking shirt it is at this point. Just fuck me." I grab his waist.

"No touching." His friend's hands grab mine and pull them over my head.

Kinky.

The music quiets as he pushes his full length into me. "Holy fuck, I've missed you." He pulls out a little and waits. "I don't want it to end."

Ditto.

In the dim light, I see him staring at his friend. He nods and looks down at me. Sweat drips from his forehead, landing on my cheek. "Fuck him while I watch."

Here comes the fun.

"What are you going to do for me?" I roll my hips towards him.

His cock pushes inside and moves in and out slowly as I rock beneath him.

"Anything you want, beautiful." He tucks his hands beneath my spine, matching my pace. "I could fuck you for days."

"And I will let you." I grip his friend's arms and stroke them. "You too," I say to the man hiding in the shadows behind me.

"Consent," the best friend says, stroking my face.

"I will ride you like Sea Biscuit's jockey."

Wes pulls out of me, hoists me to my feet, and shoves me over the side of the couch. He fucks me hard from behind. With every violent thrust, the arm of the couch cracks. The rolling desk chair rolls beside us. His friend is preparing for his turn. His massive cock hardens in his grasp as he strokes it up and down. Dick has always been blessed with a cock no ordinary woman could ever handle. Even his name makes sense. Lucky for me, I am no ordinary woman.

"Oh, fuck. Fuck, fuck, fuck," Wes hollers over the music, his semen flooding my insides.

'I've never felt so good before.
This empty place inside of me is filling up.
I simply cannot get enough.
Oh, I want it. Oh, I want it…'

—Jack Skellington, The Nightmare Before Christmas.

Wes's cock slides out of me, and he leans against the desk in front of us panting heavily. A broad smile stretches across his face. My feet leave the floor as Dick snatches me in a bear hug from behind and flops into the chair, rolling it away from Wes. He separates my ass cheeks and guides my pussy above his cock with one hand.

He holds it just outside the opening and swipes it back and forth, coating the tip of it with his friend's and my combined juices. "This is going to hurt," he whispers and presses me down.

"No, it won't," I say in a breathy voice with a smile.

My pussy stretches open, beyond its normal capacity. Dick has what I call a pussy splitter attached to his body. Ever since our first encounter years ago, I have never seen one any larger, and I want every inch of his historical cock inside me. My stomach churns as I rock on his lap, my crowded organs have no room to move compliments of the invader raiding their space.

I leap away from him. "Turn on the fucking light."

The room slowly brightens, and I gawk at the burly muffin man sitting in the chair. His beard is trimmed nicely, but his body resembles the guy from the Hangover movies who carries the man purse. He's gained some serious weight since our last encounter.

The funny thing is, I don't give a fuck if he looks like someone's dad. I want all that dad dick inside me.

I shove him onto the couch and climb on his lap. "Get ready for the best ride of your fucking life." I grab his cock tight and shove it in my pussy.

His mouth flies open. "Jesus Christ." He grips my hips as I bounce up and down.

I ignore the bile rising in my throat, needing this unapologetic three-way fuck with familiar and trustworthy faces—something worthy of my life and time. I grip the back of the couch, crushing its material in my grasp. It's too pliable. The couch takes away from the full experience. I climb off from him and his head snaps down. "Where are you going?"

"You'll do anything for me, right?" I grab his thighs and slowly tug him towards the floor. "No matter what I ask." His back hits the floor, and I turn to Wes. "Get over here."

He walks slowly toward me as I straddle Dick's cock and sink it deep inside me. Wes's cock hardens the closer he comes to us. It's average at best, but what I like about him most is his gold-metal-worthy ability to eat the shit out of my pussy. If there was ever a time to try the one thing I could never do with Femi, it's now.

"Get behind me," I say to Wes.

He kneels behind my back, and I whisper over my shoulder. "Fuck my ass." I remove my shirt, lean my body forward, drop my breasts on burley dad's face, and relax my anus.

Wes licks my ass with his tongue startling me, and I shift slightly away from him. He grabs my cheeks and guides his cock inside, entering me slowly. The pressure of Wes in my ass and Dick's massive cock in my pussy squeezes the divider inside my body that keeps the two holes separate.

And I fucking love it.

Wes slides his cock out of my ass and cums on my lower back. I sit up and bounce up and down on Dick, fucking him like our first time all over again. The mission I'm about to embark on may be my last so I'm going to go out in style, making sure I enjoy every fantasy I've ever had but never dared do. No one has to know what happened between us, and they will keep our encounter top secret.

Always have.

Big man grunts beneath me and shouts. "Oh, God damn. Oh, baby, it's coming."

"Me too, Daddy. Don't stop. Make mama cum," I holler at him.

He grabs my hips and helps me bounce harder and faster on his lap. My thighs are usually the only thing that prickles, but not this time. This time, my stomach tags in, and everything from my waist down ignites in a fiery fit of fucking passion, exploding onto his cock while he ruptures inside of me.

I drop onto his chest and pant. He strokes my spine with his rough hands, and I twirl his chest hair with my fingers. "Did you enjoy that?" I sit up and smile at him.

"Fuck yes, I enjoyed it." He combs my hair away from my face. "I missed you."

Wes pulls on his pants. "We missed you. You know that, Sergeant Parks."

It's been a few years since someone has called me that. It sounds foreign. Sergeant Odeya Willamina Parks no longer exists. All that's left of her is Odie—sex addict, seductress, vigilante, killer.

Maneater.

I smile. "Dick, you've got some dick-do going on." I smack the sides of his stomach with both hands, and it jiggles.

He moves me off his lap. "What the hell is dick-do?"

I grin broadly and stand. "Your belly sticks out further than your dick-do."

Wes launches the water he just sipped from his mouth, showering Dick and me. "You ass."

Dick rolls onto his hands and knees, grabs my hips, and pulls me close to him, burying his face into my stomach as he talks. "I may have dick-do, or whatever you called it, but it certainly doesn't affect my performance."

I place my finger under his chin and lift it slightly. He rises to a stand, and I grip his cock, hardening it back up. "It sure hasn't."

He moves me away from him and points at my pussy. "I think she's had enough for today."

I glance down and blood dots the floor beneath me. It streaks the inside of my thighs like an unexpected period.

How inconvenient.

Wes passes me a roll of toilet paper. "So, what did you need from us?"

I wipe the blood from my body. It smears into my skin, staining it. I'll have to take a shower or dip in the ocean.

Wes steadies me with his hand when I stumble to the side. "Whoa, there. Maybe you should sit for a minute. That was quite a ride you took."

I let the dizziness in my head pass. When the spots before my eyes clear, I grab my sweats and pull them on. "It's dangerous."

Wes crosses his arms, and Dick leans against the desk beside him, still naked. "Do we look scared?" Dick asks grinning.

"They'll be men with guns who aren't afraid to shoot you." I slip my feet in the oversized flip-flops.

Dick lifts his ass from the desk, strolls to a closet beside me, opens the door, and flicks on the light. Inside is a gun safe. He turns the dial one way then the other and back and it opens, revealing an assortment of automatic weapons.

"We like to hunt," Wes says, kissing my neck from behind. "And I'm eager to kill."

Chapter Twenty
Don't Speak

The beach house appears abandoned from afar, but I didn't want to take any chances. Wes and Dick wait in the Hummer a few blocks away. I enter the house from the oceanside sliding glass door, tiptoeing silently toward my room. The front entrance handle jiggles, and I flatten my body against the wall, hiding in the shadows.

Audrey flicks on the light.

I cross the room quickly and slap the switch. "Leave it off."

She jumps and grabs her chest. "Jesus, Odie. You scared the piss out of me. Where's Ari and Gina?"

"Luisa has them," Femi's voice booms from the next room.

I round the corner, and Femi sits in a chair in the corner of our bedroom, flanked by multiple men, five on each side. He stands and sighs heavily, strolling toward Audrey and me, rubbing his chin.

Fuck.

He does this when he has something sinister planned in the bedroom that usually involves tying me up and him touching every inch of my body, teasing me for hours without fucking me. It's pure fucking torture.

We need to get out of here now, or we won't be leaving at all.

"Where's Doc?" I ask, grabbing Audrey's arm and pulling her behind me, backing us away from him.

His hand falls away from his face. He raises his eyebrow and glares at me. "Don't worry about where Doc is. Your fucking side plan got my driver killed."

"You have another one," I say with a sideways smile. "Besides, you didn't like Chicken Wing that much anyway."

He widens his eyes. "But your fucking friend did. Does that matter to you at all?"

"Why should it? He's not the one for her. Besides, relationships only complicate things. You know that."

"Where have you been?" Femi asks, changing the subject and stepping towards us.

I reach behind my back and guide Audrey closer to the exit. "It doesn't matter where I've been, what matters is what comes next."

"Well, you two aren't going anywhere until I get some answers." Femi nods and two of his men stand behind us, stopping us from leaving.

I lift my head and smile at him. "Lying low."

There bitch, now you have your fucking answer.

"Move," I say to his men.

Ludacris plays inside my head. *Move bitch, get out the way...*

Femi steps within inches of me. "Judging by the state of your hair and the blood spot on your sweats, I'd say you've been doing more than *lying low*." He nods to the two men behind us. "Everyone out." He glances at me from the corner of his eye. "We need to talk." He gestures towards the doorway with an open palm to Audrey, indicating he'd like her to leave as well.

Once the room is empty, he closes the door quietly. At first, he won't turn around. His eyes focus on a cobweb floating back and forth a foot away from the ceiling. A tremor rises in my stomach, feeling his anger radiating outward from his body like heat from a paved road on a hot summer day.

"Femi, we don't have time for this bullshit. We have to get Ari and Gina before it's too late." I reach around him and place my hand on the door handle.

He seizes my hand, crushing my fingers together, and pulls me in front of him. His fingers glide down my bare bicep. He turns my arm, examining the fresh dressings covering my wound. I push him away and frantically grab at the door handle.

He shoves me face-first into the wall beside the door frame. "I told you to stay home." His fingers hook into the elastic of my sweatpants on both sides and yank them to the floor. "Who were you with?"

I push back against him. "You don't control me, and I don't answer to you."

His body drops to the floor behind me. He grips my inner thighs, violently pries my legs apart, and shoves his face between my legs, smelling me. "Oh, my love. Fucking someone before killing them, or in front of me is one thing, but fucking someone else just for fun is another story, especially when lives are on the line."

I throw my ass against his face, knocking him backward to the floor. He lands on his back. "I did what I did because lives are on the line. Now excuse me, I need to go save my friends."

He grabs my leg as I step over him, trying to get to the door. "What do you mean you fucked someone because lives were on the line?"

"Not just someone…" I peel his tight fingers off my leg. "Two someone's."

I almost made it to the door. I got it open and everything. It slams shut, nearly chopping off my fingers. Femi spins me around, grabs my throat, and throws me on the bed. "You're not going anywhere until you tell me who you fucked and where they are."

"No." I cackle at him.

The weight of his body knocks the wind out of me. I gasp a quick breath as he readjusts his position. My midsection sinks further into the mattress as he sits on me, raises my arms above my head, and brings his face within an inch of mine. "This isn't a game, Odie. Tell me where they are." His voice barely clears a whisper. "Tell me."

I peck his frustrated lips and smile. "No."

His hands tighten around my face, crushing my cheekbones, and forcing my mouth open. "Tell me!" Femi screams a familiar scream—one of frustration, one of anger, one of someone fed up with trying to break me and force me to talk. I pinch my eyes closed, and when I open them, Femi is gone and the only face that remains is one of a ghost. The ghost of my enemy.

Something in my head snaps. If I didn't know any better, I would say it was my last fucking nerve, but that's not what this is. A soldier's memories can be haunting, debilitating, and even dangerous. Some will cower, ducking to the sound of a backfiring vehicle or a firecracker. But others, others respond differently. We must protect ourselves from all enemies, foreign and abroad. We must not let them win, let them break us, let them control us. One thing an enemy can't do is force you to speak. They can torture you, cut you, play loud music, and do the same to your fellow soldiers. But if you are strong, unafraid to die, numb to the pain, and indifferent to the death of your fellow man, they will have no choice but to kill you or continue to contain you. In this case, this situation, all I know is what my enemies of the past have tried to do, and confining me isn't it.

I close my eyes, take a deep breath, and change into the soldier I once was, screaming my name, rank, and birthday in his face. "Sergeant Odeya Willamina Parks 13-5-1-20 born November 4th, 1999."

His shoulders raise, and his eyes squint as I scream it a second time, my spit glistening on his face.

He throws his hand over my mouth, and I buck my middle sending his body a foot in the air. "Oh, no. Don't start that bullshit with me. I am not your enemy, and you are not a prisoner of war."

I ignore him, staring at the ceiling. He removes his palm from my mouth to wipe his face. A metallic taste trickles into my palate.

One of his men enters, drawn to the room by the sudden silence.

"Get out," Femi yells over his shoulder.

I lock eyes with Audrey, standing in the hall behind Femi's guard as the door slowly swings shut and shout, "I am Sergeant Odeya Willamina Parks 13-5-1-20 born November 4th, 1999."

"Stop it." He stares deep into my eyes and shakes my shoulders gently. "Look at me, Odie. See me."

I pretend not to see him—pretend I'm somewhere else standing in a white room with a cup of crimson liquid filling my hand, waiting for me to begin my masterpiece.

The bed rises as Femi launches to a stand, freeing me from his forced confinement.

Most people would take this opportunity to run.

But I'm not like most people.

I swing my legs over the side of the bed, grab Femi's shirt with my left hand, and swing my right fist, landing a harsh cross punch to his cheekbone.

His head jerks right, and he steps back, crouching. "I won't fight you, Odie, so just stop."

He grabs my jabbing fist, forces my arm over my left shoulder, twists my body away from him, and secures me in a rear naked chokehold.

My eyes blur, and my energy and fight slowly vanish as the room starts to blacken. Femi's voice is so far away.

He repeats the same thing, over and over. "Listen to my voice. Can you hear me? I am not your enemy." His arm loosens from my throat long enough for me to catch a single breath before he tightens it around me again. "I want to let you go—let you breathe, but I need to know that you're you and you know I'm me."

My face tingles and spots dance around the blank space before me as he slowly lowers us to the floor.

"Say my name," he whispers and relaxes his hold on my neck, letting me breathe.

"Femi." I choke.

"No, beautiful…" he murmurs squeezing my neck tighter than before. "…when we are together, flesh against flesh, alone in our bed, with your head against my chest and your fingertips grazing my thighs, who am I?"

I close my eyes and picture the last time we had an intimate evening at his mansion. We talked about our day, how we felt, like a real couple—a moment of normalcy. My body relaxes, and I breathe his name. "Pussycat."

His arms immediately release me, and I collapse sideways, sucking the ample air.

Femi strokes the hair on my head and sighs. "I'm sorry, beautiful." He curls his body against my spine, and we remain on the floor, silent and cuddling as though what just happened was normal.

I've only had one previous incident where I had what I call an out-of-body experience. One of Femi's men made a mistake, and he was screaming his defense at Femi. The louder he screamed and pointed, the less he seemed like himself. Femi tried to remain calm, speaking his replies in a soft voice, explaining to him that his gambling problem was his own, and his pay was his pay, but when the guard put his finger in his face when Femi refused to fund a lump sum to get him out of debt, Femi responded. I tried to stay out of it and let them tussle on the floor like a couple of high schoolers, and I would have, but the guard wouldn't stop screaming, and I just wanted silence.

Peace.

I took the paperweight from Femi's desk and struck the guard in the head with it, but I didn't stop there—not after he fell to the floor, not after I struck him a second time, not when his body stopped moving. Femi grabbed me, and I struck him in the shoulder with the paperweight, leaving a bruise that lasted for weeks. It wasn't until he put me in the same hold he just released me from, and talked to me, made me see the room, smell the blood, hear his voice, did I stop wanting to strike the man.

He redirected me.

What he doesn't realize is, that he just became the man whose face no longer exists on the floor—the one with demands, the one who refuses to shut up until he gets what he wants.

The one who screamed in my face.

"When you're ready, we can pick up your men and save Ari and Gina together." He hugs my waist.

My body stiffens and my heart rate rises, thumping relentlessly in my chest. He thinks I'm going to tell him. It doesn't matter who it is, enemy, friend, lover, Femi, Pussycat, I will never answer. My solemn oath as a soldier is to protect Dick and Wes from all enemies, including potentially jealous lovers.

It's unbreakable.

"No."

He rolls away from me, stands, and runs his fingers through his hair. "Fine. Don't talk. Play your little games. I'll bring Ari and Gina back myself. If your people get in my way, then they'll die too. Either way, you're not going." He yanks the door open, bouncing it off the wall, and nods to his men. "Tie her up."

This motherfucker.

I flip onto my hands and knees and dart towards the door, turning my body sideways to wedge between Femi, who is standing in the doorway, and the wall. Femi's hand grazes my spine as I sprint down the hall. His arms clothesline my midsection as they grab me, launching my head and feet forward and taking my breath away. I plant my feet and launch my head backward connecting with his face.

The cartilage of his nose crunches on impact, forcing him to let me go.

"Fuck, Odie. You broke my nose." He covers his nose and blood drains between his fingers.

I walk around him and stop short in the living room. Henry hangs on the curtain by the patio door peering outside. I'm with him. We both need to get the fuck out of here. I crook my finger at Audrey who is sliding chopped fruits and vegetables off a cutting board and into Henry's bowl. "We are leaving. Now."

Henry's feet shuffle rapidly across the floor heading for his now full dish. He takes a massive piece of melon and bites down, squeezing the fruit of its juices. Femi stops beside me, dripping crimson on the floor between us. My eyes fixate on the pattern, a half circle—a smiley face in the making.

"This is childish, Odie. We should be working together not apart." He sniffs the blood in his nostrils and Audrey passes him a paper towel.

"You should have Doc look at that," I say stepping around him, heading for the door, then stop abruptly. "Where is Doc?"

Femi places his hands on his hips, a crinkled white paper towel sticking out of his nose. "Safe."

Safe. A one-word answer. It's not surprising. He's playing games, and I am not in the mood for a quid pro quo.

He rests his palm against the front door, leaving a smudge of blood on its clean white surface. "Where's your men?"

"Safe." I turn the handle and the door opens slightly.

Femi slams it closed. "My men and I are going; you and Audrey stay home."

Stay home. Here he goes with that bullshit again. What does he want us to do? Stay home and have a girl's night? Eat popcorn and watch movies?

I need an alternate exit. Audrey peers over Femi's shoulder and gestures towards the balcony. There's a long awkward pause where no one speaks, and the room falls completely silent except for the sound of Henry's chewing. Audrey and I preparing to run, Femi and his men preparing to stop us.

We didn't stand a chance.

Femi's men surround us quickly like linebackers the moment our feet shift in the direction of the balcony. They converge on us like an efficient enemy, forcing us apart and directing me to my room and into a chair in the corner.

There's no sense fighting them, we won't be here long. I wink at Femi as his men bind my ankles to the chair legs and wrap rope multiple times around my wrists. One of the men removes duct tape from a bag and Femi snatches it from him. "I'll do that."

Another guard puts a fresh paper towel in front of his face. Femi pulls the blood-soaked one out and twists a new one in. Blood races up the thin paper. He kneels to the floor in front of me and rubs the bridge of his nose. "Last chance to work together."

"Fuck you." I focus on the wall behind him.

Tape presses hard against my lips.

Femi stands and exhales a stale breath carrying hints of red wine into my face. "I don't want to lose you. You're too valuable to us—to me. It's better this way."

He nods to the guard to his left and walks away from me, leaving the man behind to babysit.

Us.

There is no us.

Audrey hollers from the other room. "You can't keep us here."

A door slams and after a few minutes, the beach house falls silent except for an occasional cough from the next room and a sniffle from the skinhead standing to my right.

I smile as a red dot appears on my guard's back. He continues pacing to the opposite side of the room, unaware of the shaking target on his spine. When he turns around, he stops abruptly. "Fuck."

The bullet shatters the balcony door and strikes his vest, knocking him to the floor and taking the wind from his lungs. He writhes back and forth, rolling on the ground and covering his head, protecting it from a second shot that strikes the floor beside him. "Jesus Christ. Who the fuck is that?"

Audrey's guard rushes into the room, and a third bullet zings over his shoulder, piercing a hole in the wall beside his head. He raises his hands at once, surrendering like a coward.

Heavy boots land on the balcony, and the door slides quietly open. Dick stands beside me, reaches over, and peels the tape from my lips. "Hello, beautiful. Need some help?" He cuts the rope from my wrists and hands me his blade.

The guard who just entered advances towards us, pointing a handgun at Dick's face, and suddenly stops. His eyes cross and blood drains from the hole in his forehead before he collapses in a heap on the floor.

I make the final cut on the bindings surrounding my feet and stand. "I had everything under control, Corporal."

The bald guard sits up on his knees with his butt resting on his heels. "You killed him." He glances at Dick, and then at me, removing his cell phone from his pocket. "Femi's going to be so fucking pissed when I tell him."

Dick passes me his sidearm.

"No, he won't." I stop beside him. "Because you're not going to tell him." I point the gun at his temple, and he drops the phone.

"Please, Odie. Just let me go." His eyes gloss over and tears shimmer on his cheek. "I'll do anything you want—work for you, tell you whatever you want to know. Just don't fucking eat me."

"Fucking pussy." Dick shakes his head. "I'll go get your friend and call Wes to let him know we are clear." Bits of glass drop intermittently from the tread of his boots as he walks away, leaving a path to the next room.

Once he's out of sight, I push the barrel of the gun against the bald guy's head. "You aren't good enough to eat…" I drag the gun across his forehead and stop in front of him. "But I need paint, and I'm itching to create a masterpiece on that wall beside you."

His head turns to the blank wall, and I pull the trigger.

Wes enters and steps over Baldie's body. "You good?"

"I need to paint."

He inhales a quick breath and exhales, flubbing his lips. "Well, I thought you may have left that little hobby behind overseas. Using it to scare away our enemies is one thing, but we are on American soil now. You need to be careful."

I curl my palms over both of his shoulders and grin. "Baby, I never let a perfectly good wall go to waste."

"You're crazy." He kisses my neck and walks away. "Don't be long," he says over his shoulder.

Oh, how I missed this—the feel of my fingers against the texture of a blank canvas, the first stroke of color, the metallic smell of my victims. Femi will regret taking control of this case. I don't care how much he thinks he's trying to keep me safe, all he's doing is putting himself in more danger.

From me.

Our relationship when started was based on necessity—my need for a favor from him to help me find Benny and Griffin and avenge my sister's death. But that need is over.

I plunge my blade into the bald man's chest and wrench it open. My hand disappears inside and reappears coated in blood. I follow the crimson paint as it races down my arm. The wall sucks the color into it, accepting its message like the gospel of Jesus Christ himself—a warning, a prediction.

Femi chose the path that led us here—me tied to a chair and Audrey guarded in the next room, leaving a bad taste in my mouth like a bitter glass of cranberry juice. Sure, you drink it despite it drying your mouth and puckering your lips because you know it's good for you in the long run but drinking it every day just isn't realistic. That is why I prefer not to have a serious relationship with anyone.

My fingertips tingle as I create a shadow, shading the side of the moon high above a skull sitting on a blood-painted yacht engulfed in fire, burning above a blackened ocean.

I sense there's something in the wind that feels like tragedy's at hand...

—Sally, The Nightmare Before Christmas.

Chapter Twenty-One
Overboard

No one speaks—the silent ride to the marina resembles the calm before a storm. We know what's at risk but say nothing of our concerns. We, as soldiers, have a job to do. Fear and weakness are not an option. Luisa outnumbers us twenty to one, but we are not afraid.

We are soldiers. I glance in the rearview and lock eyes with Wes. His unblinking eyes and emotionless face meet mine. In the Army, we were the only Delta Force team with three members—a trifecta of the top three most deadly and efficient soldiers. The military tried to separate us and spread out our keen and natural abilities. They offered Wes and Dick promotions to lead their own people, but in the end, we stayed together—them under my command, right where they belong.

I decided it was best to have Audrey stay in another hotel until this was all over. We already lost track of Ari and Gina; I need to know she's somewhere safe where no one will find her.

Dick stares straight ahead in the passenger seat. His army green tactical pants have more pockets than I ever would know what to do with when not on a mission. He smiles at me when he catches me side-eyeing him repeatedly while driving.

"What?" He looks down at his T-shirt. "It matches."

Wes leans forward in his seat. "I tried to get him to pick a different shirt, Sarge, but you know how he gets."

Dick holds his Marvin the Martian shirt away from his body. "First of all, Marvin is a classic, second, I'm on overwatch so no one is going to see it, and third his quote, '*Where's the Kaboom,*' is fitting for this operation, don't you think?" He glances back at Wes.

"Whatever." Wes flops back in his seat.

I pull to the curb a quarter mile away from the marina, and Dick hops out of the Hummer in front of a high-rise hotel. He pulls his hat down low, shielding his eyes, and peers into the vehicle. "See you later."

"See you later." I wink at him.

Wes sinks into the seat beside me and pushes the trunk button on the keychain. "Don't miss." He shuts the door.

Dick leans his palms on the window frame. "I never miss."

He pushes off, rocking the vehicle slightly, and disappears behind it. The trunk closes and he nods to us both before strolling toward the entrance. His legs tilt outward and his steps are wider apart than they should be. The massive cock dangling between his bowlegged limbs affecting his walk. It has to be uncomfortable in the summer. I imagine wearing the cooling boxer briefs I mailed him from Duluth Trading last Christmas has helped him significantly. Men don't like buying underwear until they have more holes than material. They might as well wear them as shirts at that point like the retro fishnet tank tops people still wear.

They'll always be stupid and ugly in my opinion. Either wear a fucking shirt or don't. It's like fishnet stockings—pointless fucking things. The only thing either article of clothing is good for is snagging on every motherfucking thing or catching a fish when you have no pole.

I drive a few blocks closer to the marina and turn into a parking garage. Wes places his hand on the back of mine. "Things haven't been the same since you left us years ago. I still remember the day. Do you?"

Of course, I remember. How could I ever forget? That was the day I let them both know I was leaving, preferring to be on my own as a civilian instead of having a polyamorous relationship with them. I know they wanted to help me with finding Benny and Griffin, but I needed to get revenge my way. There could be no initial personal attachments. That's why when I met Femi, it worked. He got me what I needed, and I got a man willing to fuck the shit out of me in a tub of our enemy's blood. That's Femi's nature as a feared and ruthless criminal.

Dick and Wes aren't criminals. They are decorated soldiers who have vowed to protect me. We share a deeper connection than Femi and me in a different way. But I know without a doubt they'd do anything to be with me, including kill.

Wes squeezes my hand, bringing me back to the present. "You said you needed to be alone. After this is over, Dick and I don't want to be shut out again. We miss you."

Good Lord. Did they not go off and find anyone else in the two-plus years since my absence?

"Don't you two have wives or girlfriends and kids by now?" I remove his hand from mine, turn sideways, and lean against the door.

He stares blankly through the windshield, reaches between his legs, and retrieves his bag from the floor before looking at me. "Odeya, there is no one out there like you, that we trust like you, that makes us feel the way we feel. When you left, we didn't fucking know what to do with ourselves. It's like a piece of us was missing. Sure, we fucked women here and there, but it wasn't the same. The chemistry just wasn't there. You weren't there."

"Wes, you know what I am, who I am, what I like to do. You two are part of a handful of people who truly know everything about me."

"Exactly. So, why not embrace that? Embrace us? Let us stay a part of your life for Christ's sake."

I know the answer to his question—the reason behind my distance and refusal to make them permanent fixtures in my life. The fear of losing them for good. The one and only person I attached myself to fully, loved unconditionally, and confided in was my sister, and I let her down. I can't make the same mistake twice. It's bad enough we lost Eve. Now Luisa holds Ari and Gina captive.

"You know why." I unlock the door, dropping a hint for him to get out.

He steps into the lot and peers into the vehicle with gleaming eyes. "There's been no one else since you, and we are willing to wait as long as it takes for you to change your mind."

I tilt my head and smile. "I won't."

Being harsh has always been part of my nature. They know this. They also know I will likely never change my mind, but it won't stop them from trying.

"We'll see." He sighs through his nose, shuts the door, and jogs to the stairs leading down.

I glide to the bottom of the parking garage ramp, stop, and slap the turn signal down. A familiar vehicle speeds by, followed by two more, heading in the direction of the marina. Doc sits in the passenger seat with her eyes facing forward.

Why the hell would Femi take Doc with him to rescue the girls? She should be recovering from her ordeal. Perhaps he's anticipating the carnage and wants to have her on hand to triage in case shit goes sideways. Instead of turning, I drive straight, taking a different route to the docks.

I park in the corner of the lot and exit the vehicle, straightening my mini skirt. Wearing a minimum amount of clothing will not only intrigue Luisa, but it will also make me appear less dangerous to her men. I adjust my breasts, lifting them higher in my black halter top, deepening my cleavage. My feet slide into a pair of black closed-toed spiked heels with red trim. Heels are my only weapon. Entering armed will only escalate things. Casually stepping onto her yacht as though I'm arriving at a party will draw less attention.

As soon as the yacht comes into view, I stop walking. Multiple limousines, SUVs, and fancy cars line the private dock. It's the generals. She brought the generals not killed in the blast at the hotel here for the show. Two men in suits wait on the walkway, one with a German Shepherd at his side, waiting to sniff out weapons someone may be concealing.

A mirror reflects in my eyes from afar. Dick signals that he's in position and ready. I move closer to the yacht, and that's when I see Ari and Gina, both tied to rolling chairs. Ari's swollen face smiles at me as I stop before a tall, bearded guard in a white suit with a dog at his side.

Causing trouble as usual. I shake my head at her and frown.

The man slaps my arms and orders me to raise them. I do as he instructs. The dog smells my pussy under my skirt, backs away from me, and growls.

"Lift your skirt," the guard orders.

I smile at him. A few men on the yacht approach slowly, their weapons drawn, as the dog alerts its handler that I'm hiding something dangerous.

My hands slide down to my side, and slowly lift the hem, revealing my naked backside. The dog circles me and barks multiple times before sitting down.

The guard squats before me. "Spread your legs and turn around."

I separate them, turn, and back into his face. "Eat me, Daddy." I cackle.

He pushes me away from him, falls backward, and wipes his cheek. "Nasty. What do you have hanging between your legs?"

I frown at him, trying not to laugh at Ari howling with laughter in the background. "It's a tampon. You do know what a tampon is, don't you?"

The guard stumbles to a stand. "Take it out."

"Enough," Luisa yells from the sundeck. "Let her through."

I smile at the guard and shimmy my dress back over my ass. "Don't call my pussy nasty. What you meant to say is it smells like teen spirit."

He shoves me towards the yacht. "Fucking move, slut."

And there it is. I am no longer a killer to them, just a slut looking to get my freak on. The final guard to pass before boarding raises his hand. "Wait."

He swings his rifle behind his back and steps towards me. His rough hands glide slowly into the front of my halter and sweep the space under my breasts, checking for hidden weapons. When he steps back, he licks his bottom lip and nods. "She's unarmed."

I slide my hands between my legs. "This is all the weapon I need."

His eyes lock on my hands, waiting for me to show him more. I grab his shoulders and push him sideways into the ocean. "Pervert."

Water splashes on my leg as he flails about in the water, screaming. "I can't swim." His head disappears beneath the yacht suddenly, and no one makes any attempt to save him. Luisa shakes her head, not allowing it.

"Welcome aboard." She extends her hand to me.

I ignore it, and she relaxes her arms to her sides. "So, what should I call you? Willow? Odie? Odeya? Jane Doe?" She turns her back on me and accepts two glasses of wine from a waiter dressed all in white.

"Don't drink it, it's probably poison," Ari chimes in from behind her. She's only wearing her bra and underwear. Her dress sits neatly folded over the railing.

Luisa turns to one of her men and nods.

He slaps Ari across the mouth. Blood drools from her bottom lip onto her bare leg.

I remain emotionless, not wanting to give Luisa a reason to use Ari and Gina against me.

Luisa keeps her focus on my face, waiting for a reaction as the guard slaps her a second time.

Ari chuckles at him. "You hit like a girl."

She nods to the guard. He balls his fist, and Ari closes her eyes and bunches her shoulders, bracing for the inevitable strike. The hit lands on the side of her head, knocking her and her chair sideways onto the deck.

Luisa sighs at my lack of response. "You know, I know your reputation is one of a killer, but I don't doubt your feelings for these girls, especially this one." She pushes Ari's moaning body with her ivory pumps. "This one's your protégé, is she not?"

I take the glass of wine from her, sip it, and rest the glass on a small round table. "I have concluded that working with you as opposed to against you may be more beneficial to both of us." I smile sinisterly at Luisa.

Luisa rests her fingers on both my shoulders and slides her hands down my arms seductively, stopping at the wrists. "A partnership? Hmm. Yes. There has been so much death already. Why not agree on something that will satisfy us both?"

I stare at her right hand still holding my left wrist as the other hand lets me go. "But the loss of my men has repercussions and will require an appropriate punishment and response." Her eyes leave mine and lock on Ari. "This one is responsible for the explosion at the club, correct?"

"I'd say the majority of your losses are a direct result of her actions." I remove her hand from mine and take a step back.

"So, we agree…" Luisa's eyes snap in my direction. "…tossing them overboard is our only option?"

I walk over to Ari. "Yes. Tossing them overboard will suffice."

Ari's face pales and she recoils her neck, confused by my comments.

Luisa's men sit Ari upright and lift her chair, so it teeters on the edge of the railing.

I lean beside her and sweep a lock of her hair away from her face. "It's nothing personal. It's just business. And in this business, you have to adjust your position according to the environment. You are nothing more than collateral damage." I darken my eyes, pull her head back by her hair, and whisper in her ear, "Don't be afraid." The back of her chair dislodges from the guard's hands with a quick yank of mine, dropping Ari into the ocean.

She quickly disappears beneath the wake, sinking to the bottom like a rock.

Luisa grins, raises her eyebrows, and snaps her fingers. Her men grab Gina's chair. She screams and throws herself side to side as they lift her and toss her over the yacht railing.

Twenty-Two
Keep Your Distance

I scan the docks looking for Femi but he's nowhere to be found. Where the fuck did he go?

Luisa sighs heavily and gestures for me to sit in one of the two chairs on the deck. I turn my seat so it's facing Luisa's men and relax my legs open, revealing my pussy to them. They try to ignore me, but let's face it when a pussy is in full view of most men, they can't keep their eyes off it, and neither can Luisa.

"You're a very sexual woman, aren't you?" Luisa asks, raising her empty glass to the waiter who fills it.

"I have certain needs I fulfill regularly." I gaze up at the generals, watching me intently from above.

"Then you should understand why I am in the business I am in. You see, you aren't much different than the men and women I conduct business with. They have needs and desires, like you. It's my job to find them what they desire and deliver it. For a price of course."

Fuck this bitch. Finding people, children and teenagers is nothing like me. I go after the scum of the earth. The people she services are my victims.

The waiter fills my glass and stares at my legs. I slide my dress higher. "Do you want to taste me?" I ask him.

His eyes dart to Luisa's, and she dismisses him with a stern glare. "I'm not sure how seducing the help will get you anywhere. They won't be able to save you, not from me—from us." She waves her hands up and in the direction of the generals. "The way I see it, your only option is to join us." Her fingers stroke the top of my hand lightly. "You'd be a lovely addition to my collection."

Collection.

Does she speak of killers, women, or victims? If there are kidnapped victims on this yacht, I need to get them off and safely away.

"Perhaps, if you showed me your *collection*…" I make air quotes. "…perhaps then I'll be persuaded."

Her eyes brighten. "Well, then. Let's take a walk."

I shouldn't go with her. Right now, Dick has me covered. Once I'm down below, I'm out of sight, but I need to know.

Luisa gestures for me to walk in front of her. I don't bother lowering my skirt, exposing my partial left cheek. I sense her eyes on me. She wants me but knows I'll never agree. There's something about longing and desire that filters into the air, emanating from people's bodies like perfume. I can always feel it—sense it. It makes people do things out of character for them—taking without asking, stalking their victims, collecting trophies. Perhaps it's only the twisted and sick fucks like us that have this intuition. Luisa and I may be different in our beliefs and businesses, but something we do share is the desire to fuck anyone we want when we want—me, men, and her, women.

Unfortunately for her, I am not into her type of fantasy, but she doesn't care as her hand slides up my skirt and strokes my backside when we stop before a set of double doors.

"Joining me comes with conditions." She yanks my body against her and moves her hands up and down my thighs slowly. Her breathy words warm my neck. "You come on to my yacht, offer a partnership, and throw your girls into the sea. To me, that can only mean one thing." She spins me around and shoves me against the doors, making them rattle. "You crave power—long for resources like mine, and the ability to live out whatever your desires may be, to satisfy the itch you can't seem to fully scratch in your current situation." Her fingers glide closer to my pussy gently grazing my clit. "Perhaps you're afraid to make that leap and allow yourself to let go and live out your true fantasy without a second thought of how you were brought up or what others may think of you." Her finger slides inside my pussy. "I can show you what it's like to be me—what it's like to be free."

I close my eyes and breathe heavily against the door as her fingers push deeper inside me. How does she know how I feel? Can she sense my longing? My reluctance? I can't let her seduce me.

My ass thrusts backwards knocking her against the opposing wall. She raises her hand to her guard who points his gun at me. I grab her pussy and stroke her cheek with one finger. "Is this what you want?" I rock my forehead against hers and shove my tongue down her throat. Tinging spreads across my clit and into my thighs. "You want to fuck me, don't you?" I unbutton her pants and walk my fingers to her pussy, but don't make entry.

"Yeeeeess," she whispers, pushing my fingertips inside her and holding them there.

"Make him go away, and I'll fuck you right here in this hallway." I flick my fingers rapidly over her clit.

She snatches my wrist, yanking it violently away from her, and narrows her eyes as she shoves me back. "Do you think I am stupid?" She straightens her crips ivory suit jacket, buttons up her pants, and frowns. "I know what you are doing, trying to seduce me—get me alone. It will never happen." She takes a deep breath and removes a key from a long chain dangling between her breasts. Her hand grips my forearm and squeezes. "Join or die. Those are your two options."

I nod, agreeing only for a moment to get a glimpse behind the partition before me. She inserts the key, turns it without taking her eyes off me, and pushes the door open. Inside are the six missing girls from the photos. Each one has ropes around their wrists and are attached to metal rings on the walls. They scream when they see me, pleading with mumbling words through their taped mouths. All the windows have blackout curtains preventing anyone from seeing in. My blood boils at the sight of the bruises on their backsides and faces.

Don't react. Don't react. Don't react.

It's what Luisa wants. She hasn't taken her eyes off my face since the door revealed her prizes inside.

"So, now you know. How does seeing these girls, tied up, battered, helpless make you feel?" She crosses her arms and stands in front of me.

"I feel nothing."

I'm lying of course. I want to rip her fucking face off and nail it to the wall behind her like tribal art.

She moans inside her throat and calls to her guard in the hallway. "Have Torrence come down."

The guard nods and radios to the surface.

Torrence is the youngest of her generals. An overeager young buck with a hungry desire to rise above the others and be Luisa's right hand. Right now, the Crypt Keeper holds that title.

Luisa smiles when Torrence enters the room. "Pick one," she orders.

He grins broadly and unbuckles his belt.

"If seeing them doesn't disturb you, perhaps a little demonstration is at hand. You see, I don't just take girls

to sell off to the highest bidder. I also take care of my
people."

She grabs Torrence and yanks his pants down,
revealing his rock-hard cock. "This room is his room.
These are his girls. She points to each one. "You can have
a room full of whatever you desire. Men, women, boys,
girls…" Her voice trails off and she releases Torrence.
"All you have to do is say yes to being my one and only
female general."

Oh, that is not going to happen. Although the thought
of having a room full of hot, sexy, and well-equipped
men is ever so tempting, I can get them without
kidnapping them. My people fuck me because they want
to. Only my enemies and people like her and Torrence are
treated the way these innocent girls are.

I close the double doors, locking us inside with the
girls and keeping the guard in the hallway from seeing
what comes next.

"What are you doing?" Luisa asks, crossing her arms.

I stroll around Torrence, rubbing his now bare
shoulders as I walk behind him. "Well, he has had
everyone in this room…" I stroll to the windows and
open all of them. "But he hasn't had me, and I prefer
fucking under the light of the moon and candlelight." I
step over to a scented candle and smell it. "Do you have a
lighter?"

Luisa's hand disappears inside her pocket and pulls out
a gold Zippo. She lights the wick, and I set it on a small
dresser. Her hand slides up the wall and dims the lights.
She sits in a chair by the door and unbuttons her trousers,
ready to watch the show while pleasuring herself.

Torrence shifts his weight from one foot to the other,
tightening his fist at his sides, ready to pounce when his
boss gives the order. I unzip the front of my dress,
dragging the zipper slowly down from my breasts to the

hem by my thighs, letting the material fall silently to the floor.

Luisa stands, circles my naked frame, and plucks the string of my tampon, dropping it on the floor before locking eyes with Torrence. "Take your time. I want to enjoy this smoke show."

My chest slams into the wall beside the hull windows. I turn my head and peer through the tinted glass. A reflective light flickers about a block away from Dick's hotel. Wes is now in position as well.

Torrence's cock drills into me, and my body glides up and down the walls rhythmically, taking his time, following his boss's orders. But she can't see me. I want her to see what's about to happen. I want to see Torrence's eyes when he dies. I push back against him, dislodging his cock from my pussy. "Pick me up and fuck me." I push his back against the glass.

Luisa leans against the wall beside us as Torrence picks me up and guides his cock inside me, fucking me up in the air. I smile at her as I pant and scream. "Fuck me harder." My palm slaps the glass once with five fingers and the second time with one, letting Wes and Dick know we have six civilians needing rescue. Light reflects in my eyes, signaling for me to get out of the way. I wiggle away from Torrence, dislodging his cock from me, and stop in front of Luisa. "Join us," I say seductively, my fingers tugging at the button of her pants. She parts her lips to respond but doesn't get the opportunity. Torrence grunts and drops suddenly.

I back away from her, a tiny smile twitching in the corner of my mouth. Luisa's eyes lock on the hole in the window and her head slowly pivots from the hole in the window to the hole in Torrance's back as he lands face-first on the carpet. She turns slowly to face me, but not in time to stop me. I grab my stiletto heel and swing. The sharp edge pierces her throat, silencing her when she attempts to shout for help from the guard in the hallway. I wrench it out and blood spurts like a fountain onto the floor. Her knees buckle and she drops to the floor still holding the hole in her neck. She can't scream, she can't run. All she has to do now is die while I watch. I grab a wineglass from the small table, claw her hands from her throat, and let her artery fill the glass with her vital fluids. With the last bit of energy she has, she reaches for the door handle, trying to open it.

I take her hand, coated in blood, drag it over my breasts and stop at my pussy. "This is the last pussy you will ever see before you die." I grit my teeth at her. "The one that killed you."

Luisa tips sideways and rolls on her back staring up at me, blood gurgling from her open mouth.

I kneel beside her. "I told you it was the only weapon I needed. You should have listened."

Her last breath bubbles out a small amount of blood and her eyes fall empty. I rifle through Torrence's pockets and remove a small pocketknife.

The girls cry as I approach them. "I'm going to get you out of here, but you have to be very quiet."

They each nod, tears glistening off their cheeks. I saw through their bindings, releasing them one at a time from the walls they'd been chained to for an unknown amount of time. Some of them collapse, shaking violently with anxiety, disbelieving they are finally free. They take turns hugging and huddling together, crying quietly when they see Luisa dead on the floor, eyes open, and silenced for good.

I pick up my tampon from the floor and pass it to the tallest girl. "Hold this."

She takes it by the string and frowns. "Why?"

"It's a bomb," I whisper, opening the door quietly, and peering through a small crack.

The girl gasps and passes it to a petite blonde beside her.

The guard has his back to me, making his normal laps up and down the hallway. I tiptoe across the carpet, leaving bloody footsteps in my wake, cup my hand tight over his mouth from behind, and slice his throat. One of the girls stifles a whimper, and I press my pointer to my lips. At the top of the stairs, two guards pace back and forth. I take the tampon from the girl's grasp, light the end, and toss it between the men.

The men glance down at the burning tampon, tilt their heads, and glance at each other, hesitating to act. A fatal mistake. I push the girls to either side of the stairs as the feminine product blows and launches the men in opposite directions. Gunfire erupts on the deck as Wes and Dick open fire from afar, riddling the generals on the upper deck with bullets. I ascend the stairs and peer over the edge, staying low to the ground. Luisa's men fire their guns widely trying unsuccessfully to reach the source of the gunfire. When only a few men remain, I stand on the deck and wave the girls up to the surface.

Femi and his men leap from blacked-out SUVs and cars, revealing their positions in the far corner of the lot only a couple of spaces from where I parked.

It's about time he showed up. He missed all the fun.

I grab the hand of the closest girl to me, pulling her to the surface for the first time in who knows how long. "Keep your head down, and go that way." I point to the back of the yacht. "Get to the parking lot where that man in the steel gray suit is." I point through the smoke at Femi who's frowning at me from afar.

The girl shakes her head and clings to me. "I don't want to go."

A bullet zings by my ear. I snatch the girl's forearm and yank her to the ground. "You have to go, or we'll get caught in this crossfire. Now, crawl that way." I point.

She digs her nails into the deck floor gauging it as I try and push her along. "Please, don't leave us." Tears spill over her lids and drip on the deck.

A bullet ricochets off the floor between us. I scream at her. "Fucking go, God dammit."

She springs to her feet and runs towards Femi, covering her head, and protecting it from flying debris. The rest of the girls emerge, and I direct them to follow her.

I smile and wave at Femi as his men help the girls stay low and disembark from the back of the yacht. Guards fall to the left and right of them, Wes, Dick, and Femi's men covering their escape.

Someone grabs me from behind and presses a gun to my temple.

"Enough. It's over. You call off your men," General Crypt Keeper's raspy voice says.

A red dot appears on his chest. I raise my hand indicating to hold the shot. The general releases me and puts his hands up. I need him alive. He is the only one besides Luisa who may know where more victims could be.

"Tell me where all Luisa's victims are," I order.

Sirens blare in the distance. Police will be arriving at any minute.

The Crypt Keeper raises his brows and frowns at the red dot making circles on his chest. He blinks several times. "I have a safe at my house. It has everything about her business inside. The combination is on a scrap of paper in my wallet."

I rifle through his pants, slap open his brown leather wallet, and pluck the items from inside one at a time, tossing them at his chest as I go. A small square piece of paper slides from behind his driver's license. The combination, written in black ink and small print, is blurred on the surface of the paper but still legible. I raise my arm and hand, keeping my palm facing outward, and bring it down sharply.

Fire away.

A bullet sails through the Crypt Keeper's chest, killing the last of the generals and putting an end to the six girls' nightmare.

Ari's dress still sits on the railing. I slide it off and shimmy it over my hips, tucking the safe combination and the general's driver's license under my breast. Femi walks towards me as I step onto the dock, untie the yacht from the dock cleat, and push it with my bare foot. It rocks a smidge away from me and slowly moves away from the docks. The red and blue lights of emergency vehicles bounce off buildings and houses a few blocks away.

Femi stops beside me and grabs my arm. "What the fuck are you doing here? Where are my men? Where's Luisa?"

"Questions, questions, too many questions." I grin broadly at him as a red dot appears on his suit jacket.

He releases me at once. "What the fuck is this?"

I step toward him and bump him back with my chest. "This is me taking control." I bump him again. "This is me being who I am." I shove him hard. "This is me not letting you or anyone else try and tell me to stay home."

I slap him hard across the face. He grabs his chin and rocks it back and forth. "This is me telling you, you should've stayed home."

He glares at me. "I deserved that." He drops his arms to his side and relaxes his stiff posture. "I shouldn't have tied you up. I'm sorry. Please, just come back with me to the house."

"No. I have plans tonight." I walk away from him.

He tries to follow, and a bullet bounces off the dock by his feet, lodging in the wood. "Jesus Christ." He points in the direction of the muzzle flash. "With whoever that is?"

I turn to him and flash him a devilish smile. "Maybe."

His teeth clench. "Odie don't do this. You can't leave me. I want you to be my wife. We are partners."

I drop my head and smile at my blood-stained feet. "I already have partners."

His eyes close and his nostrils flare. "Can you at least tell me what happened to Luisa? To my men?" He glares at me through darkening eyes.

I extend my arm in front of me, raise it, and give a thumbs up. The charges Wes set beneath the yacht detonate and it explodes, sending debris high into the sky. Femi cowers, covering his head and looking behind him. The flames from the yacht burn inside his eyes.

I stop beside him, turn his head to face me, kiss his lips softly, and whisper. "They're dead."

Chapter Twenty-Three
Invited

Femi doesn't move. His eyes stare blankly at me like I just took away his favorite toy, and he wants to cry. Throaty noises filter from his slightly parted lips, but no words escape them.

The Hummer pulls in the lot and beeps. I turn on my heel and stroll towards it. Dick hops out, his sniper rifle still slung over his shoulder and holds the door for me as I climb in beside Ari.

Dick slides into the passenger seat, shuts the door, rolls his window down, and slaps the side of the Hummer. "Hey, Femi…" He smiles broadly when Femi locks eyes with him. "…Kaboom."

Wes chuckles from behind the wheel and shakes his head before pulling away.

Leaving is never hard but keeping the person or people you left from finding you again, now that can be a bitch. Tomorrow is Christmas dinner at Ari's mother's house, and I'm not looking forward to it. How is it possible that all her brothers are hot? You'd think that the more kids someone pops out the more likely you are to get an ugly one. But not Ari's family, their sexy male genes are strong.

"I can't believe you pushed me overboard," Ari says slapping my forearm and bringing my mind back into the SUV. "I could have died."

Wes tilts the rearview mirror and smiles at me with his eyes. "She sank right to the bottom, Sarge."

"I knew you'd save her," I say to his reflection and turn to Ari. "I had to appear like I didn't care so Luisa didn't decide to just torture you for fun." I move a lock of hair away from her face. A slight bruise shades the area below her eye. "It's a good thing that punch hit the side of your head instead of your face. We can still cover this bruise with some makeup."

"It doesn't make the pain on the side of my head hurt any less." She rubs her temple and glares at her wrists. "I'm glad I'll be wearing long sleeves and bracelets too."

I stroke her bruised wrists. "I'm sorry about Chicken Wing."

She looks away from me and stares out the window. "Yeah, well, it kind of ended before it even started."

"I have to admit, I may have shit myself a little when they tossed me over," Gina announces from the third row.

"I'm sorry." I peer over my shoulder at her. "I had to get you both off the boat and out of danger."

Gina made it out virtually unscathed. She was more cooperative than Ari.

Ari leans forward and squeezes the water from her padded bra. "Well, now what? We can't go back to the beach house." She pulls up the single strap holding her bra. The other strap dangles beside her, coming unhooked.

"You are staying with us," Dick says without looking back. "But first, we have to lose this tail."

Ari, Gina, and I all glance through the back window. A few cars behind us, Femi weaves in and out of traffic trying to catch up to us.

"Want me to pull over?" Wes slows the car down and turns right at the intersection.

I shake my head and sigh. "Lose him."

Our heads snap backward as Wes stomps on the gas barreling down the main street swerving around multiple vehicles. Femi does the same and pulls in right on our bumper. Wes cranks the wheel onto the exit and enters the highway going ninety miles per hour. One disadvantage of having such a large vehicle is it doesn't make a great getaway car, especially when the person pursuing you is driving a Bently. Having multiple vehicles has its benefits. Perhaps when this is all over, I'll invest in a second vehicle as well.

We jerk backward as Femi taps our bumper and honks repeatedly.

Persistent bastard.

I'm going to have to disable his car. I tap Dick on his shoulder. "Give me your sidearm and roll down the back windshield when I get back there."

Dick passes me his gun, and I climb over the passenger seat. My body vibrates as Wes purposely drives over the rumble strips on the shoulder of the road. I whip my head around and glare at him. "Knock it off."

"I like the way your ass jiggles." He nudges Dick. "Don't you?"

Dick turns around. "I don't know, I missed it. Hey, Sarge, can you climb back over again so I can see."

"Fuck you, guys." I roll my eyes. "Roll down the window."

I place my hand on Gina's shoulder. "Stay down."

She crouches down in the seat. Femi honks at me when my face comes into view and gestures for us to pull over. Ari drops beside me, one tit hanging out of her bra, and gives Femi the middle finger. He revs the engine and hits the back of the Hummer, bumping us forward. I elbow Ari back and point the barrel of the Glock at Femi's engine. He hits the brakes, but it's too late. The bullet strikes the center of the hood, creating a spark, and smoke billows over his windshield. The distance between us grows, and Femi has no choice but to pull over.

Wes maintains speed, takes the next exit, and head back in the direction of the bar.

"Well, that was exciting," Ari says, tucking her boob back where it belongs and climbing back into her seat behind Wes.

After making several unnecessary turns and driving by the bar a couple of times, Wes backs into his one-car garage behind the building.

Dick opens the door for me and offers me his hand which I accept. "We only need to stay for the night. Tomorrow, Ari and I have a Christmas dinner to go to."

Ari skips around the SUV and stops beside us. "They should come."

Oh, fuck that's the last thing I need to deal with.

"No. I'm sure they have better things to do than hang out at your mom's house for Christmas. Besides, there won't be enough room for everyone to sit and probably not enough food."

"Oh, you don't know my mom. First off, she makes enough food to feed all of us kids for a week. Second, we have a dining room table so big it can seat twelve and a six-foot table for extra company. And third, she would want us all there. Now, before you think of another excuse, it's not up to you." She smiles and turns her attention to Dick. "It's up to them."

Wes slaps Dick's stomach. "We love to eat. Don't we big fella?"

"Fuck yes. I love a good home-cooked meal, especially at the holidays."

I flub my lips and walk away from them. "Whatever. Let's just get through tonight, and we will see about dinner tomorrow."

Dick pulls a key out of one of his many pockets. He inserts it into a gray steel door lock and heaves the heavy partition open, revealing a stairwell. "Third floor. After you," he says to Ari.

Ari stops in front of him. "Why do they call you Dick?"

He grins showing off his nearly perfect teeth. "Because I have a big shlong."

Her eyes grow wide. "Can I see it?"

"Ari!" I slap the back of her head. "Not appropriate."

Dick shakes his head and rests his hand on her low back, guiding her towards the stairs. "Maybe another day." He winks at her. "For now, let's just get you ladies upstairs."

We reach the third floor and Ari places her hands on her knees, panting heavily. "Jesus, why don't you have a fucking elevator?"

"Because they don't work in a storm and aren't safe to ride if there's a fire." Dick inserts the same key into the steel door in front of him and pushes it open.

I glance down the short hallway to an emergency exit with a tiny square window. "What's through there?" I nod to Wes.

"Fire escape stairs. Don't worry. They're counterbalanced so they don't go down unless you step on them. And before you ask, the only way to the roof is through the apartment, unless you're a ninja."

Ari glances at Wes. "I need a shower. Where's the bathroom?"

He points to an open door to his left as I step into the wide-open space. To our right, a black leather sofa sits across from two black low-back accent chairs. On the floor in front of the furniture, rests a zebra-skinned rug. A black brick-painted fireplace with an electric insert provides warmth in the cooler winter months, an unnecessary addition. Above the fireplace hangs a large painting of our three-person unit. I rub my fingers along the gold-textured frame. Dick and Wes stand tall on either side of me as I kneel before my last kill while serving overseas—a tiny smile tugging at the corner of my otherwise serious face. I grin. The original image was an eight-by-ten photograph. They had this special made by an exceptionally talented artist.

Me.

It took me days to get all the details right. The rust coloring in the painting is real blood donated by Wes and Dick themselves to add a touch of uniqueness and authenticity to it as an original work of art. I sign all portraits I sell on Only Fans the same way, a smiley face with the letter 'X' for eyes, keeping my identity a mystery.

Most people wouldn't notice at first glance that the man's head is face down, but his body is face up. We played basketball with the decapitated head that day using another enemy soldier as our hoop. The man cried as he held his arms open, fingers touching, in the bed of their pickup truck. Every time I'd make a free throw, the bloody head would strike the man's face, and he'd cry harder, pleading for us to stop.

Pleading for his life.

Neither of them deserved to live after we caught them dragging children away from their parents fully intent on taking advantage of the young girl's virginity and young age.

We let one live a little longer than the other. Who do you think took the fantastic picture this painting came from? After stuffing the man's pockets with large amounts of American money, he sauntered off, heading toward the desert. Once he was a reasonable distance away, Dick and Wes each took a shot at him, utilizing their sniper skills. The mission was our last, and we wanted to go out in style.

"Hungry?" Wes asks, stopping beside me and gazing up at the portrait.

"What do you have?" I peer over his shoulder at Gina.

She sits on the couch with her arm over her eyes. I feel the same. What a long day.

Wes takes my hand and walks me to the fridge. "Have a look."

I jerk the double-door freezer door open, and the second heart-shaped chocolate-covered thigh we didn't get to deliver sits inside. "You took that from the beach house?"

"I couldn't let it go to waste. I figured you had plans for it." He reaches around me, pulls it out, and sets it on the counter. "While you figure out what to do with that, Dick and I will head to the roof and grill some burgers." He removes raw beef and eggs from the refrigerator. "I have a set of your fatigues in my closet if you want to throw them on for old times' sake."

"I told you to throw them away."

He kisses the side of my face. "I'll never throw anything that's been on your body away."

His ass thrusts forward, and he yelps as I pinch his left butt cheek. "See you upstairs, Corporal."

"Can I come?" Ari enters from Dick's bedroom wearing a Wile E Coyote sitting on an Acme rocket t-shirt, her hair dripping wet from a recent shower. The shirt hangs to her knees and fuzzy brown slippers with claws cover her feet.

I must have been staring at the painting longer than I thought.

"What the hell are you wearing?" I ask.

She looks down at her outfit. "What? I wanted to be comfortable after my near-death experience." Her eyes dart to the counter. "Hey, is that the dessert we made?"

"It is, but I'm going to dismantle it and make a Steak-umms out of it."

Ari wrinkles her nose and covers her chin with one hand. "Huh, a Steak-umm? Hell, I'll try it. Everything else you make is good."

She stops at the large open window leading to the roof ladder, waiting for Dick to finish climbing through it.

He sits on the edge, half inside and half outside, and gawks at Ari. "You eat what she makes?"

"Of course I do. Odie is a fantastic cook, and she's teaching me too."

He takes her hand, kisses it, and says, "Darling, do you know what meat she uses?"

She pulls his hand towards her chest. "Darling, if you don't get going, you'll be the meat she's cooking."

Aww, a girl after my own heart. She's learning. I may not leave her behind for good after all.

Dick continues through the window, pops his head through, and wiggles his pointer at me but says nothing. Ari pushes him back and disappears through the opening. The metal clanks beneath their feet as they ascend the flight up to the roof.

Gina snores softly, moaning intermittently in her sleep. Wes stops at the end of the couch, shakes out a throw blanket, and covers her up. "Should we wake her up for dinner?"

"No. Let her sleep. Just save her a burger. She likes them well-done dressed with cheese."

"Well done? Gross." Wes grimaces, strolls to the window, and heads to the roof.

I take the chocolate heart, grab a wooden meat mallet, and strike it, breaking the layer of chocolate off the outside. It's not a ton of meat but it will be enough to dress at least one sandwich. I strike it multiple times with the mallet until it's so thin, it's nearly translucent. Then I take a knife, cut it into thin strips, and place them on a small plate to carry upstairs. The refrigerator door squeaks open, and I remove a handful of portabella mushrooms, a pack of provolone, and some frozen onions and peppers from the freezer. I can't stick this tiny bit of meat on the grill so I will have to cook it on the side burner in a pan. I drizzle a teaspoon of olive oil into the pan, drop the peppers and onions into it, and carry the rest through the window.

The upper deck has an amazing view of the ocean. The boys keep it simple with four chairs circling a firepit and one massive propane grill. Off to the side, a four-foot by eight-foot elevated garden provides fresh tomatoes.

Dick passes me a glass of bourbon. "I don't know if Wes talked to you already, but I want to make sure I did." He looks at Wes and Ari talking then back to me. "We want you to stay. When all of this is over, stay with us. Your friend can stay too if that's what it takes."

My throat tightens, and despite being outside, it feels like the walls are closing in on me. I'm suffocating, they're suffocating me with their love, attention, and friendship. I should be happy. Normal people would be, but I can't take the lack of space. I need to be free to do what I want, when I want, alone.

Alone, dammit.

"I know what you're thinking, you like to be alone and have your space. I get it. We get it. That's why we are willing to reenlist to give you that space. All we ask is that you be here when we come home on leave."

"Stop." I hold my hand up, silencing him. "You know who I am and what my condition is. I can't guarantee a fucking thing, nor can I let you two enlist and risk your lives to make me more comfortable. I forbid it."

"As our Sergeant, or as our girlfriend?"

"Both," I blurt, surprising myself.

Dick raises his brow, and his face brightens with a massive smile. "Both? Really? Do you mean that or are you just saying what I want to hear to shut me up?"

I gulp down my liquor and hand him the glass. "Get me another. I need to get drunk to deal with you people."

Dick walks away from me and Ari jumps up from her seat. "So…are you going to—"

"Jesus, Ari," I interrupt her. "I don't know what I want. I don't know if after Christmas I'm staying. I don't know if I'm going to be in a relationship again with Dick and Wes. I don't know. I don't know. I don't know." I huff.

She recoils her neck and exhales a burst of air in my face. "Well, that's not what I was going to ask. I just wanted to know if you'll let me cook the Steak-umms or not?" She crosses her arms and taps her bear claw foot at me. "And what relationship?" Her eyes narrow.

I glance at Wes and Dick who are watching me from the grill, smoke floating in the space behind them. I never told her or anyone else about us—about them. It's no one's business but ours. Ari has a relentless need to know everything, and I am not up for talking about it at this moment.

I smile at her and gesture with my hand towards the grill. "Have at it."

She bounces up and down, hugging me and my body stiffens. When she lets me go, a drink appears in front of me. I take the glass from Wes and sigh before sitting by the fire. He sits across from me, flames illuminating his face and eyes drifting up and down my bare legs. I know what he wants. His eyes always tell me when he's in the mood.

Maybe that's what I need. A good hard fucking to straighten me out and get my mind right.

He sits forward and rubs his hands together, staring at the dark space beneath the fabric of my dress. His eyes float to the grill and back to me. We need to eat dinner first and wait for Ari to pass out. At the rate she's tossing back bourbon, it won't be long.

I sit back in my seat and part my legs, teasing him. He sits beside me and puts a fresh drink in my hand. Dick and Ari have their backs to us. Wes slides his palm up my leg, slowly, in a smooth and calculated manner. His fingers disappear inside me as I chug down my liquor and place my hand on his, forcing his appendages deeper inside me. He grazes my clit with his thumb, his eyes darting from me to Ari and Dick who are too busy cooking to notice I'm getting fingered six feet away from them.

"It's coming," I whisper panting softly as he picks up the pace, sliding his fingers over my G-spot faster and harder. I grip his wrist, digging my nails into his flesh as I burst on his fingertips.

He grins at the creamy juices coating his fingers, opens his mouth, and sucks off my fluids. "I love dessert before dinner."

I take the hand in his mouth and redirect it to mine, licking off any excess he may have forgotten. "Don't be greedy."

"What are you weirdo's doing?" Ari staggers into the seat to my right. She leans forward and fills my empty glass with bourbon, spilling it over onto the coffee table. "Drink up bitches. The wicked witch is dead."

I take the glass and clank it against hers and Wes does the same. "To a successful mission."

Dick leans over and bounces his glass off mine. "I'll drink to that."

Chapter Twenty-Four
What the Fuck?

I sit up in bed and rub the crust from my eyes. Wes snores softly beside me, hugging his pillow. His top lip curls upward against the fabric.

Fuck, so much for a wild night.

Sun filters through the curtains warming my arm. I toss the blankets aside, sit on the edge of the bed, and stare at my naked flesh.

The mattress rises as I stand, and a blob of semen drops on the top of my foot.

Fucking Wes.

I take my pillow and smack him hard in the face with it. "Seriously?" I yell at him. "While I was sleeping?"

He covers his head, blocking a second blow from the pillow. "Sarge, you were awake. You don't remember?"

"Don't you Sarge me. And no, I don't fucking remember." I strike him a third time.

"I do." Ari shuffles into the room wearing a green t-shirt and gray sweatpants. "You know next time you two get trashed and decide to fuck on the roof, maybe make sure the next roof over isn't having a party. You two are nasty."

My face prickles as it reddens. I grab a throw blanket from the chair beside the bed and wrap it around myself like a towel. "I don't even remember eating." I rub my forehead trying to rid my brain of the hangover fog.

"You didn't." Ari places her hands on her hips. "But he did." She points at Wes. "You sick mother fucker."

I turn and gawk at Wes. "You ate my Steak-umms?"

He scoots to the edge of the bed and stands. Ari gasps as he saunters naked to the bathroom. "No, beautiful; I ate you," he says over his shoulder. "Taking a quick shower."

Ari shakes her head. "I just don't get it. The Steak-umms have to taste way better than pussy does, but he wouldn't even taste it. At least I got Dick to try it."

"What?" I raise my brows.

I've tried to get both of them to try man-meat for years. But despite many attempts and their comments about how good it smells, they always declined.

I cross my arms as Dick enters the room wearing the t-shirt and slippers Ari had on last night. His massive cock sticks to his leg.

"Ari, why is Dick wearing the clothes you were wearing yesterday?"

She smiles broadly. "Because we came downstairs after you and Wes started fucking on the roof and played strip poker. I lost, but he still showed me his cock."

I glare at Dick. "Did you fuck Ari when she was incapacitated?"

"He would never," Ari says, cranking her neck at me. "You came downstairs and climbed through that window…" She points to the still-open window. "…saw his ding-a-ling dangling, stumbled up to him, and pulled him to his room by the dick."

What the fuck is wrong with me? I know I needed a good fucking, but it would have been nice if I didn't get so drunk I don't remember.

I stare at the floor, still trying to pull the memory of last night from my head, but it's lost somewhere in the darkness.

Ari's purple-painted toes appear beneath me. "You know, I've never seen you so relaxed as I do right now. I think being around these two makes you less uptight and more comfortable. You should do it more often."

I lift my head and lock eyes with her. "After dinner tonight, I'm leaving."

"You mean we?" She reaches for me as I storm around her and head for the kitchen.

I know what this is. They must have talked to her about encouraging me to stay.

Wes leans against the counter by the fridge dripping water on the floor from his hair. "Listen, don't be upset. I'm sorry you don't remember last night, but if it makes you feel any better, you had a fantastic time."

I slam the fridge closed and walk quickly away from him.

"Where are you going?" He jogs behind me.

I toss the double doors of his closet open. "Where are my fatigues?"

"I gave them to Gina this morning when she woke up. She's going to get bagels for breakfast." He stares down at the blanket still wrapped around me. "And buy you three clothes. You can't go to dinner wearing a blanket."

"Want to bet?" I storm by him, bumping his shoulder as I pass. "I can't believe you let her go alone. What if Femi sees her?"

Dick stands in front of me, blocking the passage to his room. "Where are you going?"

"Move, Dick. I know you have something in that massive closet of yours I can throw on. I need to find Gina."

He puts his large hands on my shoulders. "Turn around, beautiful."

I let him spin me around to face Ari who's wearing my army green t-shirt and grey 'Go Army' sweats.

Fuck. I didn't even notice before. Great, so everyone has clothes except for me. I am sure that was part of their diabolical plan.

Keys rattle and clank against the front door. I cross the room quickly and pull a knife from the butcher block. Wes folds his palm over my hand. "Relax, it's Gina." He shows me his phone screen revealing Gina at the door fighting to hold multiple bags and balancing a cup holder with five coffees.

Dick opens the door and takes the coffee from her. I have to admit, my green camouflage fatigues look good on her. They rest on her bony hips in a sexy supermodel way. She tied the bottom of the T-shirt showing off her bruised abdomen and has my hat pulled down to shield her eyes, making herself less identifiable from afar.

She walks towards me and passes me a clothing store bag. "Here, I went by the size of this outfit. I hope you like it."

I grab the material of her shirt and tug it, untying the knot. "I can see your bruises. You should keep them hidden."

My hand vanishes inside the bag. I lift out a gold and red striped tunic sweater with silver tassels hanging from the hem. On the back reads 'Heart of Coal.' At the bottom of the bag is a red Santa hat, green elf slippers, and black leggings. "What the fuck is this?"

Ari pulls her sweater over her head with a massive smile. The front of her shirt reads, *'No presents for you'* with a photo of the Soup Nazi from Seinfeld wearing a Santa hat. Multiple soup bowls with black circles with a line through them cover almost every inch of the sweater. Instead of tassels, felt soup spoons dangling from the hem.

"What? She didn't tell you?" Dick asks smoothing his, *'Want to see my chestnuts?'* sweater over his stomach. "It's a themed dinner."

I'm boiling inside. Dinner is going to be insufferable enough, now I have to be humiliated as well.

Wes picks lint off the front of his sweater and smiles, holding his arms out to me as he reads the front of it aloud. *"Come sit on my lap?"*

In the photo on his sweater, Santa has a massive boner and is waving over a hot blonde in a mini skirt.

"What does yours look like?" I ask Gina who has her back to us. The back of her red sweater reads, *'OH, SANTA'* in all caps.

She doesn't turn around when she replies. "Well, I thought I was picking a safe one, but..." She slowly turns around. "I didn't realize Dasher and Dancer's noses were so strategically placed."

The room erupts in laughter. Gina's breasts each have massive reindeer noses right where her nipples are. It looks like someone pasted brown pom poms to her tits. Ari and I lean against each other trying not to fall over, tears cascading down our faces.

"You win. Hands down," Ari says pointing at her.

Gina purses her lips, trying not to laugh, and places her hands on her hips. "Very funny."

Wes and Dick help Ari and I off the floor.

Gina takes me by the elbow and walks me away from them. "We need to talk."

I don't like her tone. It sounds like a mom about to scold her child.

We step out onto the platform where the stairs to the roof are, and she closes the window.

She glances inside at the others and then frowns at me. "Did you buy Ari anything for Christmas?"

The question catches me off guard. I never buy presents—haven't in a long time. The last person I purchased a present for was my sister.

"No," I reply barely above a whisper. "Honestly, we didn't talk about gifts, so I assumed we weren't doing them. Fuck."

She reaches into one of the pants many pockets. "Well, don't worry. I bought something while I was out. It suits Ari, but I already bought her something so, I thought you could give it to her."

I take a red box from her and open it. Inside is a necklace with a solid gold bomb charm with a twisted gold fuse.

It's gaudy, flashy, and perfect for Ari. I tip the box up and read the gold cursive inscription. '*Your friendship is the bomb.*'

"Where did you find this?" I chuckle and snap the box closed.

"Pawn shop on the corner." She grins broadly. "It suits her, doesn't it?"

I nod. "It sure does."

Wes knocks on the glass, rattling it beside us. He waves for us to come inside. Gina turns away from me, and I grab the window frame, keeping her from opening it. "Thank you."

"Don't thank me yet. Wait until you see what she bought you." She giggles, moves my hand, opens the window, and climbs inside.

Does this mean I have to buy presents for everyone? Audrey? Ari's family? Wes and Dick. I don't know what the proper etiquette is for this situation. My heart thumps in my chest. I glance at the gears wall clock as I climb into the living room. I have seven hours to buy a bunch of gifts. Maybe I could buy something that works as one big gift for everyone and label it, *to all*. A gift basket? That will work. I grab my bag of clothes and pull on my leggings.

"Where are you going?" Wes asks.

"Shopping."

He stands from the table and licks cream cheese from his fingers. "I'll come with you."

"No!" I shout inadvertently "I can shop alone. I know how to stay invisible."

Wes curls a lock of hair around my ear and turns me towards the floor-length mirror. "I know you can, beautiful; just not in that outfit."

Fuck. He's right. I look like a homeless person who stole a bunch of decorations from the dollar store and glued them to my sweater.

"Come here." He gestures for me to follow him to his bedroom. "I got you these for Christmas, but the way I figure it, you could use them now."

I sit on the bed as he passes me two gift boxes with snowmen on the front of them. "You bought me gifts?"

Now, I feel even worse.

I tear the thin cardboard and pull the tissue paper away. Inside the box is an oversized ivory cashmere crew neck tunic sweater. I stroke the soft material with my fingertips. Beneath it, there are thick velvet camel-colored jean leggings. The outfit is more appropriate for where I live in the mountains of Roanoke, but a cold front will dip the temperatures into the forties to low fifties today, so I can wear it now.

"Wes, you didn't have—"

"Oh, shit I forgot a box." He digs into the back of his closet on the floor and pulls out a shoebox. "Here."

The box is unwrapped. I flip the top off and a pair of leather snakeskin heel booties sit in a pile of tissue paper. They're perfect. The entire outfit is perfect. He passes me the other clothing box.

"Don't forget this. You need an entire outfit." He smiles proudly.

I rip the top off and a set of satin and lacy nude underwear and bra sit elegantly inside. These three gifts alone had to have cost him over a grand.

"I figured instead of a colored set I'd get you something you could wear under anything." He scratches his head nervously.

I place the boxes beside me and stand. "This is a very thoughtful gift. I love it."

He slides his hands around my waist and hugs me tightly. "Thank God. Dick thought I should have gotten you something sexier, but I thought maybe something more casual."

More like *domesticated* is what I'm thinking. But I have to admit, he has great taste.

"So, let me guess, Dick got me something sexy." I grin.

He sighs heavily. "More like slutty."

I chuckle and step away from him. "That makes sense. Is there any hot water left?"

"I took like a two-minute shower and have an on-demand system so, yes." He follows me as I enter the bathroom.

I place my hand against his chest. "I know how to work a shower."

"Can we talk about what comes after?" He takes my hand off his chest and kisses the back of it.

"No. I'm in a good mood right now. Don't push your luck." I pull off my ugly sweater and pass it to him. "Now, if you don't mind, I'd like a little privacy."

He puts his head down and closes the door slowly.

When the water falls and starts steaming, I let the warmth cascade over my neck, relaxing my tense muscles. The tea tree shampoo sputters from its container and tingles as I massage it into my scalp. It doesn't smell great, but it will get my hair clean. His bathroom may be tidy, but the color palette is something I wouldn't have chosen. The dark green walls with gold accented fixtures remind me of something from the seventies. At least the shower walls have white subway tiles so it's not too dark.

I glance at the only window. If only I could squeeze through it and scale the building like Spiderman.

The door rattles.

"What?" Jesus, it's like living with toddlers who can't leave mommy alone for two fucking seconds.

I move the curtain aside and Ari pops her head in. "I have to go."

Of course, she does. "Why don't you use Dick's bathroom?"

She enters the room fully. "Dicks taking a shower."

I roll my eyes and close the curtain. "Fine."

The toilet seat slaps against the tank and after only a few seconds of silence, a loud airy fart echoes inside the toilet. Foul air fills the small, steamy space, making me gag.

"Ari?"

"Yyyyeeees." Another fart and the sound of something solid splattering in water follows her straining response.

"Are you fucking taking a shit while I'm in the shower?" I hiss through clenched teeth.

Liquid and solid strike the toilet water simultaneously as her ass flood gates open and contaminate the bathroom with putrid air.

"Maybe," she says softly.

"Maybe?" I slap the curtain aside, and the stench is stronger now. I cover my nose. "Maybe? Are you fucking serious?"

"I'm sorry. Alcohol runs through me like a freight train." She grips the sides of the toilet seat and frowns. "Oh, God, here comes another round."

I turn off the water and snatch the towel from the bar beside her. "Jesus Christ, Ari."

"Odie, will you hold my hand? It hurts. My butt feels like I'm passing lava." A tear races down her cheek, and her eyes plead with mine for mercy as she rocks back and forth.

I slap her hand as she reaches for me, bumping her legs with mine on my way to the door. "Odie, wait. You still have bubbles in your hair." She grabs my slippery arm and squeezes. "Stay and talk to me while you rinse it out."

I yank my arm away and pull the door open. "I'd rather stab myself in the eye with a needle."

"Can I watch?" she yells as I slam the door behind me.

Chapter Twenty-Five
Alone at Last

After rinsing my hair in the kitchen sink and blow-drying it, I dress in Dick's room. He's still in the shower. I've never known any other man who took so long to get ready in the bathroom. Wes and Dick are opposite in that way—Wes prefers a quick and efficient use of water and keeps his showers under five minutes, but not Dick. He prefers to clean his two thousand body parts like he's auditioning for the Lever 2000 body wash commercial.

I release my towel, allowing it to fall silently to the floor. My eyes drift to the bathroom door, debating whether to join Dick.

No. Just go, before it's too late.

I quickly dress, pull on my new sweater, and stop. It's so soft. My hands glide down my abdomen and back up. I could do this all day. Even the pants feel like silk against my skin. They are stretchy and flexible just the way I like them. My sister always had everything posh and plush in her room. Her comforter was faux fur and her sheets were satin and slippery. It was like being comforted by a warm teddy bear with her cashmere sweaters and soft flannel shirts whenever she hugged me. I shake my head, clearing it of distractions.

The snakeskin heels fit perfectly. I step into the living room and turn sideways in front of the floor-length mirror. Wow. I look like someone's hot teacher. All I need now is a pair of fake glasses.

Wes wraps his arms around me from behind. "Oh, beautiful, I'm hot for teacher."

Great, now Van Halen is repeatedly singing '*Hot for Teacher*' in my head.

I've got it bad, so bad… I'm hot for teacher.

Fuck.

He turns me around and crushes me against his chest, his stiff cock grinding into my leg. "How about we swing by the corner store and get you some fake glasses, and we role-play when we're done shopping?"

We. There it is again.

"I'm going shopping alone." I remove his hands from my waist and head for the door.

"Hey, beautiful…" He grins broadly when I turn around. "…with what money?"

Shit. He's right. Everything I had with me is still at the beach house or in the bank.

He slowly walks towards me; the front of his khakis still bulging with an unrelenting hard-on and opens his closed fist. Inside his hand are wedding rings.

"Oh, fuck no." I cross my arms.

The diamond glimmers beneath the ceiling lights. It's not a big one. He purchased it for us to pose as tourists during an operation overseas.

"Come on, Mrs. Charleston. Be my wife for one more operation. Operation Santa."

It's just role play for him, but to me, there's an uncomfortable permanency about wearing a diamond on my left finger.

My body turns rigid as he grabs my left hand and pushes the diamond onto my finger. "We need to get you something nicer—bigger."

I gasp, and my breath sticks in my lungs. Images of the diamond Femi presented to me flash into my head—beautiful, large, and flawless. Unlike this one. This one has hints of yellow and visible black flecks strewn throughout.

Wes presents the crook of his elbow to me. "Come on wife; let's go shopping."

It's just another operation, Odeya. Get your head in the game. I exhale the air trapped inside me through my nose and relax my body. I know what he's trying to do. By role-playing as husband and wife, I have to change my persona and adjust my personality to fit the role. And I take my role as a wife seriously.

Normally.

This isn't for a mission. We are just shopping. He wants me relaxed and pliable. Perhaps he has an ulterior motive for his desperate desire to shop with me.

"Can I go?" Ari stumbles into the room with dripping wet hair, wearing only a towel.

"No," Wes and I say in unison like a truly married couple scolding their child.

We both smile at her frowning face.

Wes opens the door and gestures to the opening. "After you, Mrs. Charleston."

The crowded sidewalk catches me off-guard, and I stop walking as a family with four young children split and go around us. Wes pulls me close to him and guides me forward.

"Why are there so many people?" I ask him.

"It's Christmas Eve. Everyone's trying to hurry up and buy last-minute gifts."

As we approach the Bayside Marketplace, a massive Ferris wheel comes into view. A photographer takes a picture of a family in front of it.

Wes pulls my arm towards them. "Come on. Let's get our picture done."

"No, I'm good." I dig my heels into the pavement scuffing them. "You know I don't like pictures."

"Come on, Mrs. Charleston. The only photo I have with us in it has a decapitated corpse in the foreground. Please? It's all I want for Christmas. A nice portrait of you and I to hang across from my bed to beat off to when you're not around."

I slap him hard across the chest, making him grunt. "I'll do it under two conditions."

"Anything."

"One, you stop calling me Mrs. Charleston. And two, you stop asking me what comes after. No more of this lovey-dovey talk."

Wes frowns and keeps his eyes fixed on mine, debating whether the portrait of us is worth his sacrifice.

"Fuck it," he says after several seconds of silence. "Come on."

He takes my hand, interlocking our fingers, and swings our arms between us.

The photographer sees us coming and grins. "Is that a newlywed couple approaching?"

"No, I'm a serial killer and this portrait is my trophy. I'm going to take it home and stick it in a shoebox under my bed," I say with a straight face.

The photographer's face pales.

Wes shakes his head and chuckles. "She's kidding."

"Am I though? You do have nice legs." I scan his chest and stare at his thighs with a sinister smile.

The photographer swallows hard and points to a place near the pier with the ocean as a backdrop. "Let's have you stand over here. The light will show off those green eyes of yours."

We stand on a pre-painted circle on the pavement. Wes pulls me close to him and the photographer adjusts his tripod. He steps toward us, turns my body, takes my left hand, and rests it on Wes's chest. "Perfect. Don't move."

He steps quickly away from us and looks through the camera lens. "Smile."

I force an insincere smirk, and the camera clicks and flashes, lighting up our faces. My eyes drift to Wes's, and I raise my brows. "Happy now?"

He smiles back at me and says, "Ecstatic."

A second flash makes us both turn our heads.

The photographer nods. "That was perfect. Much better than the first one. Way more sincere." He waves us over to him. "Here, come check it out."

Wes and I squint at the small screen as the man scrolls between both photos. "See the difference. In the first photo, it's ingenuine, forced. But this second one perfectly captures your true feelings. It's authentic."

He's right. Selling our relationship would no longer be an issue once people get a look at this picture.

"It will be ready in an hour." The man says walking towards his booth. "How many would you like?" He passes Wes a laminated price sheet.

"One ten by thirteen, three five by sevens, and three wallets"

I furrow my brow. "Why three five by sevens?

"I'm going to have one framed and give it to Dick for Christmas."

I shake my head. "That's a dick move."

"It sure is." He places his arm around my waist. "Come on, let's get some shopping done."

We browse through several shops, picking up random items for the party. I spot a massive gift basket filled with games, snacks, and movie tickets and an ultimate spa package basket.

"Do you deliver?" I ask the woman behind the counter.

She smiles and pulls out a notepad. "We do up until five."

"Perfect." I fill out the form with Ari's mom's address. The baskets will satisfy everyone.

In a shop window across from us, a twisted sister t-shirt dangles from a hanger suction cupped to the glass. The image on the front is of their band initials in bone. It's perfect for Ari. She's twisted and kind of like a sister whether I want to admit it or not.

I push through the shop door opening and point to the shirt. "For Ari."

"Agree." Wes nods to the salesperson who's playing a video game on his phone.

The young man pauses his game and slides off his stool. "What can I get you?"

"That shirt in a medium." I point to it.

The nerdy man raises his brow. "Weird. I just sold the same shirt in a small like five minutes ago." He takes the shirt off the hanger and stuffs it in a bag.

I glare at him, remove the shirt, neatly fold it, and slide it back into the bag as Wes passes him twenty dollars cash. This dude is probably still a virgin, I think to myself. I've never fucked a virgin before. All my men are well-rounded and experienced. I'll have to try it sometime. A face appears in the window to my left, then quickly disappears before I can see who it is.

When we step onto the sidewalk, I walk away from Wes and peer down the alley by the building. There's nothing there.

"What?" Wes asks, looking over my shoulder down the empty alley.

I shake my head. "I thought I saw someone watching us."

He puts his arm across my chest and moves me behind him. "Stay here." His boots echo with every step as he moves cautiously down the alley and peers behind a dumpster. "Nothing."

Such a gentleman, protecting me from some unseen or imaginary foe. As he strolls back to me, one hand in his pocket with a smoldering look in his eyes, I want nothing more than for him to shove his tongue inside me and fuck me against the brick wall to my left.

The moment he's in my airspace, it's like he senses my mood. I don't know if my body gives off a scent only he can smell like an Eau de Toilette perfume or what, but the minute his hands wrap around my biceps and grip them tight, I know we are about to embark on a fucking adventure like Bilbo motherfucking Baggins.

He shoves me against the wall and props his knee between my legs, resting it against my pussy. "Alone at last." His tongue enters my mouth violently, splitting my lips apart and forcing them open. My hands slap against the brick above my head as he holds them with one hand and gropes my breast with the other. "Fuck, I need you," he says in a breathy voice.

A child stops and gawks at us. I push Wes away as the child's mother grimaces and pulls him down the sidewalk. "Not here."

My pussy twitches as we search quickly for a private space to release the pressure building inside us. "The shop we were just in has a dressing room."

Wes's eyes gloss over, and he grins broadly. "Fuck yeah. Let's go."

The nerd doesn't look up when we enter and walk straight to the dressing room. As soon as the door clicks closed, Wes spins me around, yanks my pants and underwear down, and pushes my upper body forward, folding it in half. I rest my hands on the bench, and he shoves his cock inside me. He thrusts into me hard, then relaxes, hard and relaxes.

I push him back against the door, making it rattle. "Sit down," I order pointing at the bench.

He sits down with a smile, and I back myself onto his cock. His palms wrap around my hips and grip them tight. I grab his knees, grind my pussy into him and let my body glide up and down his shaft with a steady, bouncing rhythm. He kisses my back and lifts my body, helping me go faster. His breath warms my spine as he pants. The air stales with the scent of our sweat and combines juices, arousing me further. I close my eyes and moan. "Oh, Wesley, you make me so wet," I whisper.

The dressing room door rattles as someone knocks, making us pause for a brief second and quiet our labored breathing.

"Hey, you can't do that in here. I'm going to call the cops if you don't go."

Wes and I giggle, and he hands me a hundred-dollar bill from his wallet. I fold it and flick it under the door.

The nerd's hand appears, picks it up, and says, "Just keep it down."

I grind my pussy back and forth, forcing Wes deeper inside of me, needing all of him. He groans softly, his mouth vibrating against the flesh of my spine as his juices spill inside me.

"Oh, fuck," he huffs in a winded voice. "That was good." He lifts me from his lap. "We should fuck in dressing rooms more often."

I turn to him and wipe sweat from his brow. "We're not finished. I didn't get mine; you greedy fucker." I sit on the bench.

Wes removes my heels, takes my pants and underwear off all the way, and smiles. "I'm sorry, beautiful. Let me fix that for you."

He shoves my legs apart, and his mouth disappears inside of me. This is what I'm talking about. His willingness to consume both our fluids without a second thought ignites the fire inside me every fucking time. I grab his hair and press his mouth further into me. His tongue slides out of my pussy runs laps around my clitoris and enters my anus, catching me off guard. I slap my hand over my mouth, stifling a scream, and grab the bar meant to hang clothes on. His tongue leaves my ass. He drags it up my abdomen and puts his fingers inside me, keeping his eyes on mine. I close my eyes, feeling the orgasm racing to the surface. There's another knock on the door, and Wes stops eating my pussy and sits beside me. I grab his hand, ignoring the salesman's pleas for us to go and brush his fingers over my clitoris.

He flickers his fingers rapidly over my pussy lips. "Come on baby. Squirt for me."

The door rattles and swings open. The clerk's eyes widen as my cum sprays from my body and lands on his shirt. He backs against the wall, staring down at the shiny cream moistening his top, and then gawks at my pussy.

I slide off the bench and stroll half-naked to him. "What's your name?"

"Adam," he answers in a shaking voice. "But my friends call me Ace."

Wes squeezes around us. "Where's the bathroom boss?"

Ace doesn't take his eyes off me when he answers Wes. "Down the hallway on your left by the front entrance."

I smear my fluids across his chest and wrap my lips around my finger, sucking it off. "Do you want to taste me?"

The clerk shakes his head rapidly, his eyes darting to the front of the store where Wes went.

"Don't worry about him," I whisper in his ear. "He won't mind."

He swallows hard. "You should go."

I nod my head and back away from him slowly. "You don't know what you're missing." I grab my underwear and pants, shimmy them on, and put on my shoes. "Is there a back way out of here?"

"Yes, but why not just go out the front?" He pushes his glasses up the bridge of his nose and points to the door at the back of the shop.

"Because I want to do some shopping for him alone, and I can't do that if he's with me." I lean close, grazing his neck with my lips, nuzzling him. "Can you help me…" I breathe his name into his ear. "…Ace."

His bottom lip quivers as he fumbles with the keys from his pocket. "Leave the key on the windowsill beside the door once you go out." He holds the keys between us. I run my fingers down his abdomen, wrap my fingers around them, and pluck the keys from his grasp. "Thank you, Ace."

I swing my hips as I strut down the hallway heading for the emergency exit.

"Hey, what's your name," he asks as I insert the key into the door lock.

"Jane." I push the door open and smile broadly. "Jane Doe." His disappointed face disappears as the door slowly closes, and I stroll down the alley, alone with a smile.

I turn the corner, straightening my sweater with both hands and stop abruptly as someone blocks the sidewalk. The shiny alligator shoes at my feet are familiar and unexpected. I look up and see Femi standing in front of me, smirking. His eyes are cold and angry, but he approaches me and strokes my arms gently. "Don't you look lovely today?" he says, his eyes glinting with anger and a hint of lust.

"Femi, I have nothing more to say to you. I've made myself perfectly clear. So, leave me alone." I shrug off his touch, turn around, and walk back towards the alley I just came from. He scurries around me and places his left hand on my chest. In his right hand, he rocks the black velvet box in my face. "You know, I carry this everywhere with me. I keep it here…" He pats the left breast pocket of his jacket. "…right next to my heart. Take it."

I curl my lip up. "No."

His eyes darken. "I said, take it."

He shoves it into my right hand, and I let it fall to the ground. "I said, no. Now fuck off. I have things to do."

I step around him.

My sweater tightens around my throat as he grabs its fabric from behind and swings me into the brick wall, holding me flat against it. His chin rests on my shoulder as he whispers in my ear, "I heard what *things* you were doing. Do you think he could ever take my place?"

I try and push back against his chest, but I can't move an inch. I play dumb and ask, "He, who?"

Femi rubs his unshaven face against mine as he growls, "Don't play stupid with me, my love. I entered the shop when you were engaging in inappropriate behavior inside the dressing room." He reaches in front of me and grabs my pussy tightly, crushing it in his palm. "You may share this with others, but it will always be mine. No one can take that from me. No one."

See? This is why I don't like serious relationships. All I want is someone to ravish me when I'm around and let me go when I want to bolt. End of story. But noooo…someone wants to go and catch deep feelings and shit. Why can't he just accept that I'm like a wild animal, unable to be domesticated and confined to a single person or place? These are the strings I'm talking about. He wants me on a short leash, by his side, and at his disposal. Well, I got news for you, Femi, I'm not a bitch. You will never put me on a leash. I am the alpha, and I will never settle into a domesticated life.

I thrust my ass backward, as hard as I can, knocking him back far enough for me to move away from the wall. "I'm done with you. Walk away, Femi, before one of us gets hurt."

He peers down the alley and back around the corner where his car and bodyguard wait by the curb. "Why can't you just accept we are the same person? There is no one else like you in the world and there is no one like me. We are soul mates—destined to be together till death do us part." He swipes the black box from the ground and opens it. "Now, please. Just put on the fucking ring."

I rub my temples in exhaustion. He's not getting it. I don't know how much clearer I can be. "Femi, I am never…" I smack my palms together several times. "…ever coming back to you. What do you not understand about this?"

He sighs heavily and clenches his jaw. Anger and frustration morph his handsome facial features into something of nightmares. "Why, Odie?" he shouts.

"Do you want me to say it slower?" I growl, growing frustrated with his lack of comprehension. "I. Don't. Want. You. Femi."

Pain lashes across his face as each word hits him. "Odie, I fucking need you. You are everything to me, and I refuse to continue living my life with the scraps you give me." He grabs my arms, his face flushing with mounting anger. "Please say yes." His voice is desperate and pleading, yet I feel only disgust for the man that once upon a time set my soul on fire.

I glare at his fingers, tightening around my forearms. I'll likely have bruises in the shape of his fingers later. "Let go Femi. I don't want to hurt you."

He pulls me against his chest, the anger radiating off him turning into something more potent and dangerous. "The only one getting hurt will be you if you don't accept my proposal."

I roll my neck at him, my body tense in anticipation of a fight. "Are you threatening me?"

Femi's face softens slightly as he purrs, "I don't make threats, my love. I make promises." He strokes the side of my face, then grabs the back of my neck, violently yanking me closer to him—my face inches from his. "Can't you see what you're doing to us? What you're doing to me?" His jaw clenches, and his eyes gloss over before determination takes over his features. "Leaving me is not an option." He grabs my left arm popping the shoulder at the joint and pulls me to his car. "Now, get in."

His bodyguard opens the door.

"Fine." I raise my hands, making Femi think I'm being compliant. He releases my arm and gestures for me to get into the backseat. I bend my knees slightly preparing to duck inside the vehicle. "Wait." I turn and face Femi. "I have something for you."

He steps closer to me and rests his arm on the open door frame. "What?"

I take a step back with my right foot and swing my knee forward, nailing him in the cock. He folds over at once and hits the sidewalk, holding his balls and groans in agony.

I stand over him, pissed that he honestly had the audacity to try and force me to go with him. "If you ever put hands on me like that again, I will cut your balls off and roast them like chestnuts over an open fire." I glare down at him, my face prickling with rage. "I told you one of us would get hurt; you just wouldn't listen, like always."

His bodyguard reaches for me, and Femi raises his hand from the ground. "Leave her," he grunts.

I still hear him coughing like a bitch as I turn on my heels and stride away, my feet barely feeling the pavement, as rage settles into my bones, making them numb. How dare he? Does he think he's some kind of mob boss who can force me into an unwanted marriage like some weak, naive little girl? Ha, the joke is on you, asshole. Even the mob wouldn't fuck with someone like me.

A reflection bobs and weaves in my peripheral vision—ducking inside storefronts and alleys. I can't tell whether it's a man or a woman, but by the way they are moving, clumsily, my bet would be it's Ari. She was supposed to stay at the apartment with Dick.

Across the street, a man pulls his hat down low and crosses in front of a car that honks their horn. I roll my eyes. It's Dick. They are converging on me from both sides, trapping me in the middle.

Relentless fuckers.

I enter a coffee shop, walk straight through, and exit the back into an alley. Let's see how long they can keep up this cat-and-mouse game. I enter an open kitchen door and stroll through a restaurant. It smells heavenly. The charred scent of grilled food and onions floats into my nostrils. I hold my growling stomach and snag a French fry as I pass a table on my way out the front door and walk right into Wes.

"Hello, Sarge." He holds my biceps firmly and glances behind me. "Nice teamwork."

Ari and Dick stand on either side of Wes with their arms crossed. They both have frowns on their faces, a single brow raised, and an accusatory look in their eyes.

I feel like a child whose parents are standing before them waiting for a confession. Only I didn't do a fucking thing.

I drop my head back and gawk at the sky. "Oh, come on. I wasn't leaving. Do you think I'd miss dinner?" I say to Ari. "I gave you my word."

"Maybe so, but you didn't say which Christmas dinner. For all I know you gave me your word and wouldn't show up until three years from now."

She's right. My constant ability to skirt around the truth or say things that could be interpreted in more than one way is no secret to them. It's my way of covering myself if I don't show up or change my mind about being social.

Ari scrunches her nose at me. "Why do you look so ornery?"

"Because I just ran into Femi."

Dick takes my hand gently. "Are you okay?"

I pull my hand away from him. "Yes, I'm fine. Now, let go."

A hand grabs mine as I try and walk away and brings me back to them. "What happened?" Ari asks, refusing to release me.

"Femi tried to make me come with him, so I nailed him in the cock and left. The end. Can we go now?" I peel her tight gripping fingers off mine.

Ari's eyes widen. "He did what? That fucking asshole. Does he think he can just make you be with him? I'm going to have to kill him. That's all there is to it."

I shrug my shoulders. "I handled it. So, let's just head back and get ready for dinner."

"You're right. Maybe, I'll kill him after dinner. My mom will be pissed if I don't show up to dinner on time, especially since I've missed the past three family Christmas's."

Dick and Ari start walking, but Wes hangs back, staring at me with an expressionless look on his face. "Are you sure you're, okay? Because you know that Dick and I have your back."

"I'm fine," I say louder than I intended. "I just wish everyone would fuck the hell off and leave me alone."

Ari and Dick stop walking and watch us from a few storefronts down the street.

Wes raises his hands. "Fine. Come on." He takes my hand, with the intent of walking down the sidewalk as a couple. I remove his hand from mine, twist the ring off my left finger, and curl his fingers around it. "Go pick up the photos. Playtime is over."

Chapter Twenty-Six
Christmas Eve

An older woman answers the door wearing a red and white striped jumpsuit with elf slippers, the bells on the toe tips jingling every time she moves. Her long, thick fake lashes weigh down her lids, making her brown eyes appear darker. At a glance, I see very little physical similarities between her and Ari.

She smiles at us and says, "Ari, I'm glad you're here! These must be the dinner guests you mentioned." She eyes Dick, Wes and me a bit wearily, but moves aside and ushers us in.

"Dinner's about done, but please, make yourselves at home." She grabs our bags with tan, sun-kissed hands, and we follow her into a large living room, decorated elaborately in the holiday spirit. She slides the bags under a brightly lit tree and points to a massive beige sectional with red glittering manicured fingernails—diamond snowflakes shimmering on their tips. "Feel free to have a seat and get comfy," she says, striding out of the room without a backward glance.

National Lampoon's Christmas plays on a large flat-screen television mounted above a wood-burning fireplace. Wrapped presents litter a wide circle under the tree, and garland weaves between half a dozen small Santa statues on a glass coffee table. Cozy for the average person, but obnoxiously overwhelming for me. In the next room, Tyson and Bryce are busy setting a large table, looking ridiculous in bright green and red Christmas sweatshirts. The chairs around it have green and white striped covers with red bows hanging off their backs. Like the living room, the dining room is a little tacky and overdone, but maybe that's what's in style for the Holidays.

Ari stops next to me and rests her hands on her hips. "Where the fuck is everyone?"

"Ari Jane, language," her mom yells from the kitchen in a gritty smoker's voice.

I smile at Ari. "*Jane*?"

Ari rolls her eyes and scoffs. "Oh, I don't want to hear it, *Willamina*."

I cringe hearing that name. My mother gave me my grandmother's name as my middle name to remember her by, and I hated her. She always looked down on us, not caring for my mother's choice of a husband. My dad worked in a factory making half as much as she did, and my grandmother believed she married down. She snubbed us for most of our lives until she developed early Alzheimer's. Oh, what fun that was. When she went into a nursing home, I'd frequently steal her candy bars. She would scream and cry when she realized her candy was missing. Her caretakers didn't believe her, assuming she ate them herself and simply didn't remember. Serves her right.

Bitch.

Bryce shakes his head, chuckling at Ari's vocality. "They went to the airport to pick up Marcy. Her flight was delayed."

"Of course it was." Ari pulls me towards the couch, and we both flop down. "Marcy's my oldest sister," she says to me. "She's always late. To everything. And they say I do everything for attention. I swear she spends hours getting ready, never bothering to look at the time, just so she can be one hundred percent perfect looking at every event. If only people got a look at the huge birthmark she has on her abdomen. It looks like a giant dick. That's why when she's at the beach she won't wear a bikini. She's been self-conscious of it since she was a kid."

Ari and I giggle.

"Ari, are you going to introduce us to your friends?" Ari's mom asks, resting a cheese tray on the glass coffee table and pointedly changing the subject.

I scrutinize her face more closely before glancing at Ari. There is zero resemblance, and I can tell the differences go beyond just physical characteristics. I'm unsure what Ari's father looks like, but she must have taken after him.

"Oh, yeah, sorry." Ari grabs cheese, pepperoni, and a cracker and shoves them in her mouth. "This is Dick and Wes, Odie's boyfriends." She says as she gestures towards the guys. Ari's mom's face goes slack with surprise before recomposing herself.

I drop my head in my hands. "They are not my boyfriends. We served together in the military and remain close friends."

Eyeballing me with new suspicion, Ari's mom says, "That's nice dear" before leaving the room.

"Yeah, friends with benefits," Ari chuckles and takes a swig of punch. Her face twists and her lips pucker. "Who added the vodka to the punch?"

Tyson smiles over his red Solo from the accent chair across from us. "Guilty."

Ari coughs. "Jesus. Are you trying to get us all drunk before dinner?"

"I'm going to do my best.," Tysons says with a smirk.

The front door swings open, and a young woman dressed in a designer trench coat and fur hat floats into the room. Her fire-red hair rests over her right shoulder and stops at her breast. "Is that the punch? Fuck, I need like ten glasses." She takes the cup from Bryce's hand as he enters the room and chugs it down. "Tyson made this didn't he?" She shakes her head and stomps her feet. "Good God that's strong."

I watch her carefully as she removes her jacket and walks towards the coat rack, glancing over her shoulder as she locks eyes with Wes. Her movements are slow and deliberate—from the calculated way she removes her jacket, to the sway of her hips, all for attention. Saying to everyone in the room, look at me, how beautiful am I? Vanity can make even the most beautiful people ugly, and Marcy is no different.

A frumpy, frizzy-haired woman enters a few minutes later wearing a Santa sweatshirt and plaid pants. She extends her hand to me. "Hi, I'm Jeanie, Ari's oldest sister. You must be Odie."

Okay, not everyone in the family got the good-looking gene as initially thought. Jeanie could be pretty if she put on a lot of makeup and dressed differently. But judging by the way she rolls her eyes at Marcy's attire, I think she prefers to live a plain, fuss-free life.

I shake her clammy hand and smile. "Yes."

Her hand lingers on mine and her eyes stare hard at me.

And I thought I was creepy.

Ari yanks her arm down. "Don't gawk, Jeanie, it's weird."

"Sorry. You're just so pretty, and your eyes are so freaking green." She turns to Wes and Dick standing against the wall watching television. "And you are?"

"Odie's friends," Bryce yells from the table.

Ari's other two smoking hot brothers enter wearing Christmas short sets. One has Santa stripping on the North Pole and the other has Elf on the Shelf shitting out

Hershey kisses. But I can't keep my eyes off the most important and entertaining part of their attire.

Their golden thighs.

My mouth waters. Nom, nom.

They both resemble Ari's mom. If they weren't a year apart, you'd think they were twins. When they stand beside Ari's mom, there is no height difference, and they have the same naturally long eyelashes fluttering over their brown eyes. When I saw them on the beach with Tyson and Bryce, all I wanted was for all four of them to drop me into the center of a round bed and surround me like they were preparing to communicate with the dead. Except instead of a séance, we'd have a sexance, and they'd be conjuring some serious orgasms out of me.

Exercise my mother fucking demons, you sexy mother fuckers.

I clamp my thighs together and shift uncomfortably on the cushion.

Ari slaps my leg, giving me a knowing look. "Remember the piss in the ocean?"

Fuck. Nausea rises in my throat and suddenly I feel like a bucket of cold water has been thrown on me. The memory of my leg warming beside Ari in the ocean as she relieves herself comes flooding back. I pull my collar and stand. "Where's the bathroom?" I ask Ari.

I don't need to go; I just need to get the fuck out of this room for a few minutes. The desire to shove her brothers into a closet, strip them of their holiday clothing, and take a bite out of them overwhelms me. Perhaps if I stay in there long enough, the brothers will sit down at the table where they will hopefully conceal their exposed limbs.

Jeanie waves to me. "Down the hall, last door on the right."

As I head towards the bathroom, I try to think about something else, anything else. I sit on the toilet and rest my face in my hands, ignoring the second wave of repulsion at the overly-decorated bathroom. Don't think about them, Odie. Try as I might, visions of thighs and Ari's gorgeous brothers continue flooding my mind. Why can't I stop? Is it the weather? Am I preparing to hibernate for the winter season like a predator needing to stock up for the season? This is another reason why I prefer to be alone. At least I can walk away from situations such as this. I need an addiction counselor or someone to restrain me. Perhaps both.

Maybe an addiction counselor who restrains me and...

No, Odie. Stop it.

The door vibrates as someone approaches the bathroom with heavy footsteps. "Hey, Odie. Are you almost done?" Ari's voice calls from the other side of the door.

Seriously, Ari? I just fucking got in here. "Just a minute," I say as I roll my eyes.

I wipe, flush, wash my hands, and whip the door open. "What, Ari?"

She rubs her hands together and looks at everything but me, her face growing paler by the second. "Umm, so this may be a little awkward."

"What?" I try and step around her.

She blocks the hallway with her body. "Don't go out there yet. I need you to promise me you'll stay civil and not kill anyone. Or threaten to filet anyone. Or promise severe harm on anyone."

"Stay civil?" I move her aside and walk quickly back to the living room. My stomach drops when I see the other guests that are dining with us.

Femi stands-in the entryway, removing his scarf. Two other men stand alongside him, also dressed in holiday attire. To anyone else, they look like perfectly normal dinner guests ready to celebrate Christmas. But because they are with Femi, I can tell they are his bodyguards. He smiles at me, his grin wide and hungry like the Cheshire cat. "Hello, my love," he purrs.

This man just won't quit.

Although his single-breasted maroon suit and jacket set are well-pressed and lint-free, his hair appears as though he's raked his hands through it multiple times.

Ari's mom takes a bottle of wine with a red ribbon wrapped around the top from him. "Thank you, Mr.?"

"Femi. You can call me Femi." He extends his hand to her.

She glances at her two hands still clutched to the wine bottle. "Well, Femi, if we are being informal, you can call me Ari's mom, or mom for short." She turns on her heels and waltzes away from him.

Good for her.

"You're welcome," he murmurs to himself as he rescinds his greeting hand, before turning to Ari. "Thank you for inviting me, Ari."

I turn and glare at Ari. She looks just as surprised as me. She gives me a finger wave and I follow her backward back into the hallway.

"Ari, what the fuck?"

"I'm sorry. I invited him when we were all getting along and not having all these issues. I didn't think he'd show up."

"I can't believe he's here. I made it perfectly clear that it was over," I exhale a long windy breath at the ceiling. "Fuck."

"I'm surprised too. I can have my brothers toss him and his goons out if you want."

I relax my neck and drop my head, staring at the brown high-pile carpet. "No, I don't want any trouble. We'll get through this."

Ari's mom enters the hallway. "Dinner's ready girls. Let's sit down." She folds a hand towel in front of her and disappears around the corner.

I raise my hands and lean my palms on the wall.

Breathe, Odie. Deep breath in, relax, and breathe out. You can do this. It's just dinner. It's just one day. It's just fucking awkward. Argh.

"Come on, let's get this nightmare over with." Ari starts walking away, stops, and gives me a shit-eating grin. "What's the worst that could happen?" She continues walking, leaving me alone in the hall.

Seriously? I could think of a hundred things.

By the time I made it to the table, there was only one seat available to sit in. Across from Femi and wedged between the two brothers in shorts. Garland with mistletoe weaves between ribbons and wraps around a candelabra holding flaming candles that smell like wild cherries in the center of the table. Our plates rest on gold chargers and red and green striped bows secure our silverware beside our Christmas tree napkins. The only thing missing is a tablecloth to cover the transparent glass surface. I have front-row seats to thigh nation.

Oh, sweet fuck. This is the thing of nightmares. Wes and Dick sit by Ari's mom and Marcy. Ari sits beside Femi and won't look at me—a smirk lurking on her face. She shakes her napkin across her lap as her mom says grace. The brother to my right bounces his knee, jiggling the table. Ari did this on purpose. Pushing the limits of my self-control. It's a test, and I'm going to fucking fail. I stare at her brother's cock, tumbling between his bouncing knees. The thin material of his holiday shorts does little to hide the shape and size of it.

Something strikes my shin. I peer through the glass at Femi's snakeskin shoe retreating to his side of the table. He caught me cock gazing and corrected me.

Ari swallows hard beside him. "After dinner, I have to get Henry." Her eyes flick to mine for the first time.

I glare at her. "After dinner, I need to go check out that safe." I furrow my brow at her. "Alone," I say before she can demand to join.

She pouts her lip, giving her best impression of a sad puppy. I know she wants to do everything with me, but after testing my ability to restrain myself at the table, I need some time to decompress.

"What safe?" Femi asks, dabbing his mouth with a napkin.

"None of your business," Ari and I say simultaneously in snotty voices.

He side-eyes Ari, then turns his attention to me. "A secret mission. Didn't we learn from the last one that keeping secrets is a mistake?" While his voice is friendly, there's an underlying threat to his tone meant just for me.

The tension in the room rises. The brother beside me stops bouncing his leg. He grips the knife still in his right hand from cutting his turkey.

What's this? Does he have a temper? Is he preparing to reach across the table and stab Femi with his utensil?

"Do we have a problem?" the brother asks.

Oh, my knight in shining armor.

Marcy slaps the table, making our glasses bounce. "Can't we just have a normal holiday dinner without all the drama and fighting?"

Speaking of drama.

Everyone stares at her. She breathes heavily through her nose, grabs her wine glass, and gulps down the last of it. "Now, if you boys are done measuring, mom would like to make a toast."

Ari's mom stands and raises her glass. "Thank you all for coming. Although I don't know you, I welcome you all into my home and at my table where we are going to enjoy a nice, drama free…" She peers down the bridge of her nose at Femi. "…and trouble-free meal, followed by my famous apple pie. Cheers."

She clanks glasses with Wes and Dick and nods at me. I nod back and glance at Femi. He purses his lips and dips his chin in my direction, the promise of *later* written all over his face. We will keep things civil for her sake.

We eat and are mostly silent, each enjoying a juicy thin slice of an oversized turkey, homemade whipped potatoes, asparagus, and a freshly tossed salad.

Femi eyes me from across the table. "How's your dinner, my love?"

I rest my fork on my nearly empty plate before excusing myself from the table, walking away without answering and taking my dishes to the kitchen sink. Wes tosses his napkin on the table and follows me to the kitchen.

He leans against the counter beside the sink and sighs. "You want us to get rid of him?"

I scrub the excess food from my plate and flip on the garbage disposal. "I'd like to cut off Femi's cock, shove it in the disposal with my table scraps, and grind it up with the rest."

"It can be arranged." Wes turns around and bumps me with his hip. "Just say the word, Sarge."

A throaty laugh escapes me. "It's Christmas. Let's try to be nice."

"Fine." He kisses my cheek.

I walk away from him and Dick passes me on the way to the kitchen. "You good?" he asks, giving me a concerned look that a lover would give.

I give him a thumbs up and keep walking. When I sit back down, Femi's fork scrapes across his plate, giving me goosebumps. He rests his elbows on the table and his hands against his cheek, a tiny smile tugging at the corner of his mouth as he stares at me.

Ari glances at him and me and back again. She raises her eyebrows and flubs her lips, "Awkward."

No, shit, Ari.

Her mom drops a pie at each end of the table, breaking up the staring contest between Femi and me.

The brother to my right nudges my thigh with his. "Be prepared for the best pie you'll ever eat."

I'd like a slice of your thigh pie, you tasty mother fucker.

Ari told me the twin-like brother's names are Michael and Mitch, but they look so similar, I don't know which one the cock tumbler to my right is. The one on my left hasn't said a word to me. Perhaps, he's intimidated.

A plate with a small slice of pie drops in front of me. "Thank you," I say up to Jeanie. Her eyes linger on mine before moving on to deliver a slice to Dick.

The best pie ever is an understatement. The crust is flaky with hints of butter and cinnamon. The sweet apples inside retain their shape and are full of delicious flavor. I have seconds. Ari has thirds.

I unbutton the top button of my pants, giving myself a little extra room. "That was delicious," I say to Ari's mom.

"Yes, it was," Femi pipes up, staring at the flesh peeking out of my unbuttoned pants.

He nods to his bodyguard, rubs his knee with his palm, and leans towards me. "I have something for you." His bodyguard passes him an insulated red Yeti travel mug.

A travel mug, how exciting.

Not.

"I didn't get you anything…" I cross my arms and send him a death stare. "…because you're not supposed to be here."

Everyone at the table stops moving, talking, and eating, their breaths held captive in their throats. The temperature in the room suddenly grows cold as the tension rises and my demeanor sours.

"Ari invited me." Femi glances at Ari's mom's paling face.

I lean towards him, interlocking my fingers and resting them in the center of the table, the insulated cup brushing against my knuckle. "That was before today."

Femi slides the cup away from me and rotates it in his grasp. "But this gift is priceless—something you've wanted since the day we met. It cost me a lot of blood, sweat and even a few tears."

"It's a Yeti," Ari points out rolling her eyes. "Just because they're expensive doesn't make them priceless."

I clench my butt cheeks, suddenly, realizing the present isn't the Yeti but what's inside.

A piece of him.

"Pie?" Jeanie asks, holding a slice in my peripheral vision.

I don't look at her, my eyes unable to unlock from the exterior of the Yeti.

Ari shakes her head from across the table, dismissing Jeanie.

He's right. It is all I've ever wanted from him—a little slice of heaven. A piece of his thigh.

Femi tilts his head and grimaces at Ari. "What's inside is priceless to her."

Her eyes widen as she realizes what he has offered me in exchange for my loyalty, my love, and my freedom. "No way!" She pries the Yeti from his grasp and untwists the top, tipping its contents onto her palm. A Ziplock bag containing something that resembles thinly sliced meat rolls around the plastic. Her jaw drops. "Wow, you must be desperate."

Ari's mom clears her throat. "What's in it?" she asks Ari.

The meat disappears back inside the Yeti. "It's a slice of Femi's gourmet meat." Ari stutters, not knowing how else to say it without blurting out what it actually is.

I take the cup from her. "Not exactly the pound of flesh I had hoped for, but it's an acceptable sample..." My fingertips tighten around its lid as I slide it back across the table to Femi. "...one that I won't be accepting." I release it and it clanks against the glass table.

Nothing is free with Femi. Accepting a piece of him, no matter how badly I want it, will let him win, giving him what he wants.

Me.

Femi frowns at me. "We are meant to be together, and you know it. You feel it when we are together and even when we are apart."

I cross my arms and stare at the wall behind him. "I told you, I can't."

He balls his fist and pounds the table. "Why?"

The cock bouncing brother sitting beside me stands, towering over the table and glaring at Femi, his knuckles resting on the glass. Jeanie stands and places her hand on her brother's chest. "Mitch, don't."

Femi's bodyguards move closer, but Femi raises his hand.

Wes stops behind Femi and Ari and slides the framed photo of him and me between them, dropping it onto Femi's empty pie plate. "It's time for you and your friends to go."

Ari's mom stands and wipes her lips, smearing red across her napkin. "I agree."

Femi nods with a set jaw and a defeated smirk as the rest of the table stands, signaling for him to go. He drops his head, his eyes scanning the framed photo for the first time, the lingering smile on his lips slowly fading away as his face pales.

He sees it. His pointer finger stroking my left hand in the image. When his eyes break free from the photo to look at me, my stomach tenses. There's nothing left inside them, just black orbs of rage and hatred. He grips the edges of the frame with both hands, tilting it slightly upward. I thought he might launch it across the room, but instead, he pushes it across the table to me with glossy and solemn eyes, nods, and walks away without a word. He removes his scarf from the hook by the door, wraps it around his throat two times, and feeds his arm into his jacket as his bodyguard holds it for him. His hand lingers on the front door handle. He glances over his shoulder at me with fire in his eyes. "You don't know what you've done." His eyes drift to Ari's mom. "Thank you for dinner."

The door closes softly behind him, and everyone gawks at me.

I scan the empty spot on the table where I last saw the Yeti mug. Selfish bastard. He could have at least left it for me as a going-away present. I excuse myself from the table and head to the living room.

A red gift bag smacks me in the chest. "I bought you this," Ari says, plunging into the couch cushion beside me making my body tilt sideways.

I scoot over so she's not sitting partially on my leg. "You didn't have to get me anything." I push the bag away from me.

She grabs my hand and shoves the handles into my palm. "Trust me. You'll love this."

I crumple the tissue paper in my hand and grin at her as I realize what she got me. It's a punch biopsy tool. I'm not taking it out of the bag, it will only raise more questions. Her family will assume it was meant for Ari's mom, but the fact is, I've always wanted one. I've always wanted to take multiple samples from someone and boil them like rice with chicken stock and vegetables.

"I can't wait to try it." I look at the wall clock. "Where are Gina and Audrey? Weren't they supposed to be here by dessert?"

Ari glances at her phone. "Yeah, that's weird. I'll call them."

Tyson walks in, carrying a massive box. "Call them later, Ari. Let's do presents."

The rest of the family follows closely behind him and finds seats on the couch, accent chairs, and on the floor. Tyson sets the box down in front of their mom before stepping back to give her room to open it.

Her eyes widen and she covers her mouth. "Is this what I think it is?"

Bryce puts his hand on her shoulder and smiles. "Open it and find out."

While they all have their eyes on Ari's mom, I examine the punch biopsy tool. The box indicates it's ready to use. How convenient. I slip it into my pocket and put the empty red gift bag beside the couch.

Ari's mom tears at the wrapper, revealing a large leather trunk. "Oh my gosh, I love it!"

Ari leans over to me. "My mom is a travel nurse and has all these totes in the back of her station wagon that slide all over the place and look unprofessional. She wanted this trunk to sort and organize everything and be able to lock it. We all chipped in to have it custom-made for her."

"Oh, it even has three compartments so I can sort by category." A tear shimmers in the corner of her mom's eye. "Thank you, guys," she says to her sons.

Quietly, Ari swings a second gift bag in front of me. "Another gift for you."

"Thank you, Ari." I pull the first item out of the bag.

Fuck. I can't help but chuckle.

It's the same shirt I bought her. I guess great minds do think alike. "Umm, Ari…" I reach into the bag I have for her and pass her the same shirt she got me. "…we bought each other the same shirt."

She smiles broadly and immediately strips her Christmas sweater off. Protests arise from the family as Ari's exposed bra-covered breasts are momentarily on display before she slips her new t-shirt on. "I can't believe it. Wow, we must have been communicating telepathically." She tugs at my shirt. "Change yours too so we can match and have Jeanie take our picture."

"Alright," I say as I stand and head for the bathroom. "I'll be back."

The shirt fits perfectly. I smooth it over my stomach and turn sideways, examining myself in the full-length mirror. My hair looks dull and my eyes sag with fatigue. I splash cold water on them and dry my face.

"We waited for you," Jeanie says, passing Ari's third gift to me when I enter the living room.

The doorbell rings and Marcy strolls across the room before whipping the door open. A delivery guy stands in the doorway, holding the gift basket I ordered. Marcy curls her lip at its disappointing contents. "Who sent this?" She tugs it out of the delivery guy's grasp.

I take the basket from her and hand it to Tyson. "I did. It's for the boys."

Tyson smiles at me and carries the basket to the living room so all the brothers can see it. "Thank you, Odie," they say in unison.

"What about me?" Marcy says as she pouts and closes the door in the delivery guy's face, tapping her foot in frustration.

Wow. She's very entitled. Does she think I'm buying something specific for her? She needs to chill out or the only thing she'll get from me is a fucking attitude adjustment.

"Marcy, don't be a-greedy bitch," Ari scoffs, crossing her arms.

A hollow knocking comes from the front door, and Jeanie answers this time. It's the same delivery guy with an annoyed look on his face. I'd be annoyed too if Marcy shut the door in my face before I finished doing my job.

"It's another basket," Jeanie announces.

Marcy snatches it from Jeanie's hands. "This must be for me."

Ari crosses the room and yanks it from Marcy's clutches. "It's not for you, Marcy, you damn narcissist. It's for mom." Ari carries it to her mom and sets it in front of her. "Here, Mom. This is from Odie."

Her mom unties the red ribbon and slides the basket from its cellophane wrapper. Inside is a scented candle, a hundred-dollar gift certificate for a massage, a gift card for a full manicure and pedicure treatment, bath bombs, fancy chocolates, aloe-infused socks, and a bottle of wine.

Ari's mom jumps off the couch and hugs me. "This is great. Thank you, Odie. You've done too much."

Her embrace is a little uncomfortable but not enough to make me recoil. Maybe it's because she smells so good—like a home-cooked meal and floral perfume with hints of cotton candy.

I pass Ari her next gift. She rips it open so fast that the box goes flying and lands on the floor between Jeanie and Marcy.

Marcy picks it up and opens it. "Well, that's just tacky."

I squeeze my knee tightly turning my knuckles white. If Marcy wasn't Ari's sister, I would fly across the living room and bitch slap her.

Ari snatches it from her. "Don't open my gift." Her eyes gloss over as she looks at me. "I love it." She works frantically to remove the gold necklace with the bomb charm from its box and turns her back to Jeanie to have her hook the lobster clasp. "This is the best present ever."

Bryce claps his hands together. "Oh, I get it. A bomb because you like to blow shit up."

Marcy rolls her eyes. "Yeah, like the bathroom. You should've gotten her a toilet charm."

The audacity of this woman is really grinding my gears. "Bitch," I whisper under my breath before dropping Ari's next gift on her lap.

Jeanie chokes on her water and nudges my leg. "You aren't wrong."

Ari unzips the leather backpack I bought her and smiles at its contents. "I can't wait to set these puppies off."

"What are they?" Marcy asks, peeking over Ari's shoulder to look inside the bag.

Ari closes the bag quickly. "They're just fireworks."

Yeah, fireworks that could blow up a car. I couldn't just build a bomb and set it in her bag, so I put some pipes, fuses, and an explosive mixture in a glass jar. The leather backpack is large enough to hold all the makings for her bomb but is also stylish enough that she can wear it without the intention of harming someone or something.

"We once again kind of had the same idea." She hands me a wrapped long and skinny box.

I unwrap it with a smile and slide a stainless steel, engraved, filet knife from inside. My weapon of choice, like bombs are hers. We truly are too close. I stare at the sharp edge and take a quick glance at Marcy.

So, tempting.

Wes takes the blade from me and reads the engraving. "*Let me see those thighs.*" He grins broadly. "You can cut up some serious meat with this." He rubs his thumb over the sharp edge and hands it back to me.

I glance at Ari's brothers wearing shorts. "I sure can."

Ari slaps the side of my leg. "Behave." She grabs a smaller box and hands it to me. "I made this one for you."

I pull the tissue paper out of the box and remove a black lava bracelet with a custom wood coin message that reads '*Nom, nom*' and has an etched skull and crossbones. I slide it onto my wrist. "I love it, Ari. Thank you."

She whips a nearly matching bracelet from her pocket and stretches it over her wrist. "Mine has onyx stones." Her hand disappears inside a snowman gift bag by her feet and reappears holding a hat. "For the cold days." She tosses it at me, and it lands on my lap.

I pull the black knit hat over my head and smile. It has a custom message as well.

Abso-fucking-lutely.

"Here, look inside." She slides the gift bag to me. "Don't take it out."

I peer inside and gasp. Ari took the Yeti, not Femi. Sneaky girl. I will have a piece of him after all. I place my hand around her shoulders and give her a sideways hug. "Best gift of the evening."

"Can we see?" Marcy asks, cranking her neck over the bag.

"No!" Ari and I each take a hand and slap the bag closed.

I shift the giftbag behind my legs, protecting it from prying eyes. "Thank you, Ari. These are unique and thoughtful gifts."

"More like cheap," Marcy says, frowning at the bracelet Ari made her. She drops it in its gift bag and yawns at her subpar pile of presents. "I have to pee. Maybe when I come back something worthy of excitement will manifest into my pile."

She stomps away and disappears down the hallway. I peer at Ari across the room. She holds Marcy's next gift in her hand, no doubt worried about what cruel words Marcy will have for her. I'm not fucking allowing this for another minute. I excuse myself and wait outside the bathroom for the door to open.

The moment it does, I shove Marcy back inside and lock the door. She opens her mouth to scream, and I cover it, holding the filet knife to her throat. "Shut your fucking mouth."

Her head bobbles up and down. I keep my hand over her mouth and glide the blade slowly across her throat and down to her collarbone. "I don't appreciate the way you are treating Ari. She's trying to be a good sister. She didn't have to get you a fucking thing. I know I didn't. So, you will go out there and show her the respect and love she deserves. Whatever the gift she's about to give you, you better be excited and thankful. If you do or say anything to upset her for the rest of the evening, I will not hesitate to cut out your tongue and shove it up that tight ass of yours. Do you understand?" I take my hand away from her tremoring lips.

"Who are you?" She wipes tears from her cheeks.

I stroke her jawline with my finger. "I'm the monster from your dreams, the shadow following you in the dark, and the creature hiding under your bed. And Ari is more family to me than you are to her. And family takes care of family. Something you need to learn."

I turn away from her, unlock the door, and join the others back in the living room. Marcy doesn't come back from the bathroom for several minutes. When she does appear, her face is ashen, and her eyes are glossy. She stops in front of Ari and apologizes.

Jeanie, Ari, Wes, and Dick glance at me. I ignore their accusatory eyes and gulp down my third cup of punch.

"I should get going," I say to everyone and grab my gift bags.

Ari stands and takes the bags. "No, you aren't going anywhere without me."

"Can't you get a ride with Tyson to pick up Henry?" I ask, pulling the bags back from her and pressing them against my body.

"Doc is on her way with Gina and Audrey. I'll have her take me to the general's safe while you go to the house and get Henry, and we can meet back here in an hour. Deal?"

"Ari, what is going on? What safe? What are you girls up to?" Ari's mom stands with her hands on her hips, her brows furrowed in concern and suspicion in her eyes.

"Odie likes to be alone, especially around the holidays, and pretty much any other time. But I won't let her leave me." She looks at her brothers and sisters. "Not the way you guys ditched me."

"Now, Ari that's not entirely true." Jeanie wags her finger at Ari. "You didn't want anything to do with us, remember?"

"That's because you guys let Dad lock me in the basement and wouldn't help me. You guys acted like everything I said was a lie and for attention. Anytime I told the truth, you didn't believe me. You avoided me and even didn't invite me to family dinners." She glances back at me. "Don't leave me like they did. I just want a constant in my life and right now it's you. You're my real sister. I'm probably adopted, and that's why they treat me differently."

Ari's mom rolls her eyes. "Ari, come on. You're not adopted, just insecure and a bit of a storyteller."

"This is ridiculous. She's just trying to be the center of attention as usual." Marcy huffs from her place on the couch.

I glare at Marcy and her face pales. "Ari deserves a little attention sometimes since by the time she was born no one had time for her." I look at Ari's mom. "No offense." I turn to Ari. "I will get Henry from the house. You go with Doc to pick up the safe contents, and we will meet back here."

"I'll come with you," Wes announces.

"No. You two go back to the house, and I'll meet you there later. We won't be long."

"But we want to give you the portrait from above the fireplace. Dick and I want you to have it. Here's what we'll do. Dick and I will run to our apartment and grab the portrait, then we will meet you at your beach house to put it in your trunk. If you want us to stay the night we will, or you can come back to our place. It's up to you."

Good grief. Everyone's doing what they can to keep their eyes on me as much as possible. "Fine." I roll my eyes and wave my hands at them. "Whatever."

Ari's mom winces. "Ari, I don't know about you bringing a lizard into the house."

"Oh, Mom, it's only for a day. I told Tyson I'd bring him; he even bought Henry a mini-Santa hat to take pictures under the tree for Christmas morning."

I picture Henry whipping his tail at them as they try to secure a hat on his head tomorrow morning. I know she'd like for me to be here, but they are doing the bulk of their family gifts tomorrow on Christmas Day and other family will be swinging by, so I decided to spend the morning with Wes and Dick before I leave to go back to Virginia. I wink at Ari and wave from the front door. She winks back, still arguing with her mom and Marcy about keeping Henry in his cage for hygienic reasons.

That's one thing I don't miss about Christmas, the arguing. No matter how much you plan and no matter how well everyone gets along, there's always that one person who mentions politics, religion, or God forbid, what football team is better. Or in this case, family drama and childhood trauma.

I guess it's a good thing I don't care about any of those things.

Ari peers out the window with her arms crossed, her face pinched in suspicion. She doesn't trust me. If she had her way, she would chain us together for life, literally. I don't want that. I don't want any of this. But there is something about Ari that intrigues me—keeps me here, makes me want to stick around and see what she does next. I know she's tired of me running every mission and not letting her do any of them solo. I just worry that without me, she may make a mistake and get herself caught or killed. She's eager to spread her wings and take flight, itching to bombard our enemies with whatever shit comes from her mind, or her ass for that matter.

Who am I to hold her back?

I told myself I'd never get this close to anyone ever again after what happened to my sister, but I find myself worrying about her often, and therein lies the problem. I'm torn between leaving and staying. Either way, I need to let her go—let her be free to make her own choices and live her life. I can't keep her in a cage, but I can't set her free into the world alone either.

I crank the shifter into drive as Ari and her mom argue in the window.

Fuck it. Letting her go doesn't have to mean cutting her out of my life for good. It just means I have to trust that, whether I am with her or not, she will make the right decision.

Ari's bare ass cheeks press up against the front window. She smiles over her shoulder at me as she smushes them back and forth over the glass.

I shake my head and laugh aloud. I'm going to regret setting her free, but it will be entertaining to watch.

Fly little bird. I wave goodbye as I drive off still shaking my head with a smile.

Fly.

Chapter Twenty-Seven
A Slice of Heaven

Agreeing to let Ari and Doc retrieve the contents of the general's safe was the only way to ensure I wouldn't take off on them. I would never take Henry from Ari, not after the bond they have formed in the little amount of time they've been together. Plus, I want to know who else participated in Luisa's operation, and I know Ari will keep that information from me if I don't return to her moms' with Henry.

Femi left without saying anything, which is fine with me. I'm just glad he finally got the hint before one of us got hurt.

Well, before he got hurt.

After I drop Henry off to Ari, I plan to leave. The heat from so many deaths will eventually catch up to us, so it's in our best interest to lead separate lives, at least for a little while. Ari will understand once I explain to her that it's not forever.

I pull underneath the beach house and put the car in park. All the lights are off. A palm tree in the front yard sparkles with red and green Christmas lights. I haven't celebrated Christmas for years, not since my sister passed. We tried the first year after her death, but it just made everyone sad.

Ari gave me something back. Something I haven't been a part of for some time. Celebrating with her, from dinner, to the presents, and her mom's homemade apple pie, brought back that joy I lost so long ago. Even though

Femi put a damper on dinner, it didn't deplete its significance or impact on how it made me feel.

Normal.

And that is the only gift I would ever need from her. Sure, the punch biopsy tool and homemade bead bracelet were adorable and thoughtful. I even loved the stainless-steel razor-sharp filet knife. But that feeling, that comfortability, isn't something you can give back or ever return. It's priceless.

I glance at the insulated cup beside me. Femi finally gave me a piece of him after all this time. I'm glad he didn't take it back when I turned down his proposal. What shall I make? My fingers curl around the cup in excitement. I didn't eat much at dinner. I'm not a big fan of turkey but the way her mom made it, gave it a delicious flavor. What better time than now to enjoy Filet-of-Femi? I step out of the car and pause before entering the beach house. The air smells like rain, and I see suspiciously dark clouds moving closer in the distance. There's one hell of a storm heading this way. I unlock the door, and the scent of Femi hits me. I'm going to miss that smell, but I can always buy his cologne and spray it on a corpse. If I close my eyes and focus on the scent in the air, it's practically the same thing.

He and I had a good run. Our flaming-hot relationship just fizzled out, and he has no one to blame but himself. He shouldn't have pushed me—proposed to me, clung to me. Distance was what held us together and the more he tried to pull me in, the more I wanted to run in the opposite direction.

The kitchen light flickers when I turn it on. I hear Henry coming before I see him. His claws scratch across the tile before he scurries around the corner and licks my ankle.

"Hello, Henry. Give me a minute, and I'll feed you before we leave."

Ari sure has rubbed off on me. I'm talking to a lizard.

I twist off the top of the cup and remove the thin strip of meat. It isn't much, but beggars can't be choosers. I just have to cook it carefully. Perhaps like a single strip of candied bacon slathered in real maple syrup and brown sugar. I pull out a small cookie sheet. It clanks against the corner of the counter startling Henry. I line it with foil, rub the end of a stick of butter in its center, and unroll the meat over it. I sniff it gingerly. "My, my, how lovely your leg meat smells." I stare down at Henry. "Want to have a little meat with your salad today?"

After cutting up spring mix and mango, I take a knife, trim a tiny piece off, and drop it on top like a single crumb of a bacon bit. My knees pop when I kneel and set the bowl on the floor in front of him. He bites down on the uncooked bit of thigh and chews it with his salad. He likes it; won't Ari be pleased?

I coat the slice evenly with a small amount of syrup and sprinkle it with brown sugar. A whole pound of bacon takes twenty minutes or more, but this isn't bacon, and it's only one slice, so I'll have to watch it carefully. I slide it into the preheated oven and sit on the floor beside Henry, watching the thigh meat cook—waiting for the edges to brown.

It doesn't take long for it to start sizzling. Oh, the sweet sound of cooking flesh. The smell fills my nostrils, intoxicating me. I glance at the wall clock. Dick and Wes should be here any minute. I don't know why they insist on giving me the portrait above their fireplace. I painted it for them and that moment is ingrained permanently in my memory for life.

I open the oven door and smile at the browned strip, slightly blackened around the edges. My mouth waters.

The house still smells like Femi, but now it's paired with the inside of him. I turn off the oven, peel the thigh strip off the pan with my fingers, and set it on a white, floral-patterned dessert plate. The tips of my thumb and pointer fingers are red with anger, burnt by the heat. Steam rises from the plate. I watch it float into the air and dissipate.

This is it. The moment of truth. I sit at the counter, pour myself a glass of red wine, and tear off the end of the candied Filet-of-Femi with my teeth. It has the consistency of tough beef jerky with the flavor of sweetened pork chops. I had hoped he'd be more tender so that's a bit disappointing, but I guess I shouldn't have expected anything less from such a small sample.

The clock ticks loudly on the wall. I finish off my wine and shove the remaining filet into my yap. They're taking too long. I grab Henry's travel cage and set it on the counter. He thrashes his tail at me when I pick him up, pissed that I took him away from his dinner.

"They got five minutes. Then I'm taking you to your mother." He stomps around the soil, licking random faux décor in his cage.

A fresh scent of Femi filters into my nostrils. I turn but not fast enough before Femi wraps his arms around me, pinning my ribs against the granite counter and holding me in my seat. "Hello, my love." His left hand glides up my stomach, circles my breast, and stops on my throat, caressing it softly as he sniffs my cheek. "You smell like candy."

"That's because I just had candied Filet--of--Femi." I push back against him, and he leans his body weight into me, making it hard to breathe.

"And how did I taste?" He strokes my cheek with his thumb.

I slap his hand away. "Sweet but tougher than I had hoped."

He grabs my slapping hand, rolling my finger bones together as he crushes my hand in his grasp. "You hurt me, Odie. I wanted this to work between us. I wanted you to be my wife. And you chose them." His chin digs into the space between my neck and shoulder, and the arm around my waist tightens, creating pressure. "I couldn't let them take you from me."

"I didn't choose anyone." I rock my body back and forth trying to release myself. "Let me go. Dick and Wes will be here any minute," I grunt through a clenched jaw and struggle in his tight grasp.

He relaxes his hold. "You aren't listening to me. They're not coming, my love. Don't you hear the sirens?"

My stomach drops, and I feel the blood drain from my face. In the background, the sound of sirens blaring filters into my ears. "What did you do?" I scream as I thrash in front of him.

His arm moves up and tightens around my throat, cutting off my airway. I push off the kitchen island with my foot, throwing us both backward onto the tile floor behind us. I scramble to my feet and dash towards the balcony door. As I'm struggling to get the lock open, Femi slams into me, crushing me against the glass.

My hair pulls away from my scalp as he grabs a handful of it and forces my face against the transparent partition, giving me a direct line of sight to a large cloud of black smoke in the distance.

Femi's hot breath hits my cheek as he growls, "I followed your boyfriend's home from Ari's mom's house. They didn't see me hiding around the corner when they went inside the building. I caught that heavy metal door leading to the stairwell with a piece of broken pallet—wedged it before it could close. Your boys were so busy talking about you that they didn't notice the door never shut behind them. And when they opened the door upstairs, I shot the short one first, dropping him like the pile of woman-thieving trash he is. The big one didn't have much time to react. He charged at me, and despite the two bullets lodged in his shoulder and abdomen, he still managed to tackle me down a flight of stairs. After I shoved his large ass off me, I went up to their apartment and stared at the painting above the fireplace for some time. I see why you felt such a strong connection to your brothers-in-arms—duty above all else, loyal to a fault, and committed to each other long after you left the Army. So, I did the logical thing and put the painting in my trunk before I set their home on fire." He smiles at me and strokes my cheek. "Can you feel the pain of their loss? Can you sense that they are gone high up in the sky, reduced to nothing but ash?"

"No!" I scream and throw my head backward, trying to strike his face but miss.

He twists my hair in his fist and bounces my forehead off the balcony glass, creating an impact crack smeared with blood.

My blood. I'm bleeding. Femi made me bleed. What the actual fuck?

I drop to my knees, and my eyes blur. Blood drips from the torn skin on my forehead, splattering on the floor beneath me. I sit up and crawl towards the front door, but dizziness and my weak shoulder slow me down.

Femi's heavy footsteps echo through the house as he slowly strolls in front of me. He crouches and puts his palm on my face, stopping my forward advancement. Looking up at him, I see nothing of the Femi I've grown familiar with in his eyes. Instead of the annoying love and adoration I'm used to seeing, there is only hatred.

"You and I could have been happy—could have found a way to make this work despite everything."

He strikes me, my spine bowing with the weight of his blow, forcing the air from my lungs and flattening my body against the floor.

Femi lays on top of me, grinding his cock against my ass. His breath warms my neck—the heavy scent of cologne invading my nostrils. "You're like a ravenous creature, drooling over my flesh and waiting for the perfect opportunity to pounce. I gave you a piece of me, something you've always wanted, and you still rejected me."

I chuckle, blood leaking into my mouth. "You gave me a scrap, Femi. And to be honest, it wasn't the gourmet tenderloin I thought it would be. Now if you don't mind, I'd like to grab Ari's lizard and bring him back to her so I can go home." I push up with my hands but can't move him.

"Go, home? Oh, my love, you're not going anywhere." He shifts into a sitting position, relieving the pressure on my upper torso.

I slip my hand into my pocket and tighten my grip on the biopsy tool. It's the only weapon I have, so it will have to do. I swing the tool behind me, aiming for his leg.

Femi grabs my wrist and shakes it from my hand before I have the chance to depress the trigger and stab him with it. "What do we have here? Is this a punch biopsy tool? How nice. I guess you aren't the only one taking samples of flesh today." He presses the tool against my forearm and depresses the button. A spring-loaded cutting cannula removes a quick skin specimen, leaving a bleeding hole. Femi drops back onto my upper back and holds the biopsy sample in front of my eyes. "Now I have a trophy of my own to cherish once I put you down for good."

Put me down? Who does he think he—

He suddenly drops the tool with a small sample dangling from its tip and warm liquid pools beneath me. My eyes widen. I gasp for air but can't take a deep breath as pressure builds in my lungs. Something's inside me. I can feel it pushing its way from the back of me to the front, tearing through my insides.

Femi leans his forehead against my spine. "I love you. I will always love you. But you took everything from me and there must be repercussions, otherwise I look weak. Luisa would have made a wonderful sister-in-law. She would have taken care of you and given you anything your heart desires."

"What?" I murmur, trying to understand what I missed. My head feels cloudy and I'm struggling to stay conscious. What the hell did he do to me?

He swipes his finger through the growing puddle of blood underneath me and draws what feels like a heart shape on my face. "I tried to tell you to stay home, tried to convince you to let me handle this. Don't you understand? I was trying to save you, but your stubbornness and constant need to be in control kept you from seeing that. You are your own worst enemy, Odeya. You say you have no weaknesses, but that's not true. I was your weakness. You trusted me, despite saying all the time you trust no one. Time and time again you allowed me to come with you on these missions to save these tortured and trafficked women and girls. You handed them over to me on a silver platter. And I fed them right to my sister, taking them from one traumatic situation to the next. You did nothing. You changed nothing. You are nothing."

Femi leans forward twisting the blade deeper into my back. I cough blood onto the floor in front of me as breathing grows impossibly harder. "Femi," I whisper as another violent cough rattles my body.

He leans down, putting his ear by my lips. "Yes, my love?"

"Fuck you," I whisper and lunge at him, grabbing his lobe between my teeth and tearing it away from his head.

He slaps his palm against his ear and stumbles away from me, blood draining between his fingers. "Fucking bitch." He kicks my face, dislodging his lobe from my mouth and breaking my front teeth.

I spit out bits of broken enamel and blood and cackle at him for the last time as fluid fills my lungs, slowly suffocating me. He places his heel on my neck, and raises it, preparing to deliver one final blow.

A car horn beeps multiple times outside, stopping him. "Shit."

I can't move.

Femi's snakeskin shoes stop in front of my face. "You always said you'd prefer to be alone. Now's your chance." He leans over me and rips the knife from my spine. "You can't get any more alone than being dropped into a coffin and buried underground." He yanks the balcony door leading to the ocean open. "Goodbye, my love."

The horn beeps again. I force myself onto my elbows and use my legs to creep forward, smearing the pool of blood beneath me. I stare at my red-coated, paling hands, weakening rapidly. I barely make it more than a few inches before my arms give out. My head drops to the floor, and I roll onto my back, struggling to breathe and stare blankly at the ceiling fan. The blade swooshes rapidly at first, multiple blades merged into one, then starts slowing down. I can see each blade now, their stains, and varying degrees of dust. Lightning flashes outside, lighting up the room. I tilt my head and stare through the balcony window. The rain pelts the cracked glass door, and the porch lights suddenly blink out. The storm has taken out the power.

An apparition of a young woman floats onto the balcony and peers through the window. I smile at my sister, and she smiles back. "Take me with you," I whisper.

The floor shakes as the door slams in the distance. "Odie!" Ari's terrified scream echoes through the house as her face comes into view, blocking my sisters.

"Don't die, don't die, don't die," she repeats, tears streaming down her face. She kneels beside me, slipping on the massive puddle of blood. "Who did this?"

I open my mouth but can't find my words. Ari pushes me onto my stomach and presses her hand over the hole in my spine. "I'm calling for help. You're going to be ok, Odie."

She flips her phone open and barks orders. "I don't care about mom's fucking pie, get to my beach rental, now."

My eyes cross and staying awake becomes impossible, so I close them for what may be the last time. All the hard work I've tried to accomplish in saving other women has brought me to this point. And if what Femi said is true, then it all amounted to nothing. Flashes of all the girl's faces race across my vision, one after the other, so fast I can barely tell them apart. I wish I had more time to make things right and take Femi down with me.

"Odie?" Ari shakes me hard. "Who did this?" She grabs my shoulders and jolts me awake. "Odie?"

I can barely see her now—a hazy silhouette in the dark, only lit when the intermittent lightning flashes. The thick blood coating my mouth causes my lips to stick together. They peel apart as I open my mouth and murmur his name with the last air in my lungs, "Femi." Ari's figure, the ground underneath me, and the house fade as I float in the space above us. I look back one last time and stare at the back of Ari's head and my ghost-like face as she pumps my chest, screaming and crying for me to stay with her. My sister appears beside me and takes my hand as we both take one last look at a broken Ari.

"Odie!" Ari screams at me. "Don't leave me. Fight, God dammit!"

* * *

Oh, this bitch thinks she's going to leave me. Does she think dying will keep me from staying with her forever? Think again, Odie. I won't let you die. You are not allowed to leave me. You are not going anywhere. We have work to do. "Wake up, Odie. Stop fucking around. You're not dying. Get up. Open your fucking eyes."

A vehicle comes to a screeching halt out front and multiple feet stomp up the stairs. I can't look away from her. Her eyes are open. She's looking at me. There's even a little smile on her face. She's still alive. "Come on, Odie, fucking say something. Tell me to fuck off. Say you're going to leave, so I can tell you no." I plead.

"Ari, let her go." Tyson places his hand on my shoulder.

I shrug him off. Let her go? Fuck that. I will pump her chest all day if I have to. "She needs blood. Where's mom?"

"Ari, she called for an ambulance. This is beyond mom's capabilities."

My jaw clenches, and the pain in my arms becomes unbearable. Who knew trying to save someone's life could hurt so much? Even my back is screaming in pain.

But I won't stop. I can't. I have to save her.

My body moves up and down rhythmically. I breathe into Odie's metallic-tasting mouth. "Come on, sister. I need you. Don't leave me alone."

Tears blur my vision, distorting her face. Her eyes stare into mine. "I see you. I know you are still there. Fucking breathe!" I scream at her.

Mom sobs in Tyson's arms. "Ari, honey, you have to stop."

"No," I holler at her. "Where's the fucking paramedics? She needs blood. She needs to get to the hospital."

I'm so tired, but I keep pumping and breathing for my friend, adrenaline pushing my body past its normal capacity. A lump in my throat makes it impossible to swallow. My tears drip on her torso. "Come on, please. Please," I shriek and thrust my hands hard into her diaphragm.

Something cracks beneath my palms. I jerk my hands away and another set of hands take their place.

I look up and a paramedic locks eyes with me. "It's okay. You cracked a rib. It happens."

Another paramedic pulls me out of the way. "Let me in there."

Paddles charge and squeal before shocking Odie's chest. I kneel beside them as they raise the charge and hit her again. The machine bleeps a glimmer of hope. They quickly pack her wound, strap her to a board, rush her out the door, and load her into the back of an ambulance.

"Ari, are you riding in the ambulance?" My mom asks from somewhere far away.

My brain goes blank as I slowly stand up, blood soaked through my clothes and coating my hands before I wander away from them and walk mindlessly back to the car. I don't remember opening the door. I don't remember sitting down. I don't remember the last five fucking minutes; I stare at my blood-stained hands as my mom knocks on the car window. I ignore her. Instead, I put the car in reverse and pull away without a second glance. I don't know where I'm going. I'm stuck on autopilot. Femi tried to kill her—tried to murder my best friend.

Ice fills my body, so violently it dries the tears in my eyes and stops the sobs wrecking my body. It takes all of my being to focus on the road. I am beyond screaming and raging. I am beyond despair and heartbreak. I feel numb to the pain. The floodgates in my head open and ideas pour in. When I go blank and my eyes fall empty, this is where I go to wander in the pitch-black nothing inside my mind, wishing others could see what I see— hear what I hear. The voices hiding in the dark, fill my head with a hundred different ways to kill him, drowning out all sense of reason—all sense of what's right and wrong.

Kill them.

Where am I going? I blink back into my consciousness and stare at a flashing vacancy sign in front of a small motel by the pier. Next door is a boat rental company. My phone rings beside me and I glance at Doc's number flashing across the screen.

Kill her.

She's a part of this, part of it all, making her an accomplice. I scan the parking lot I mindlessly pulled into. Where the fuck am I? The last couple of minutes are completely blank.

I put the car in park and place my hands on the steering wheel. "Focus, Ari, for fuck sake." I smack the side of my head several times trying to clear the clutter.

Breathe.

What would Odie say? What would she do if she were here?

Don't do anything rash. Plan it out. Don't let them see you coming.

The phone rings again beside me. It's Doc again. After handing off the flash drive in the general's safe, I knew I had to get to Odie right away to tell her what else I found. But Doc was like a tick latching onto my skin and pumping her diseased nonsense inside my head. She kept distracting me and changing the subject when I tried to get her to take me to Odie. When we stopped for gas, I told her I was going to use the bathroom and never came back.

Kill them all.

"Be quiet," I say to the voice in my head.

I stare at my whitening knuckles on the steering wheel, and glance at my reflection in the rearview mirror. I don't recognize who stares back at me. "You're an efficient and cunning killer. You can do this all on your own. You don't need any help. Make and execute a plan."

The phone rings again. I take a deep breath and answer. "What?"

Doc blubbers on the other end of the line about what happened to Odie and asks if Femi knows and blah, blah, blah.

Fucking fake cunt. You know what he did.

I fight the fresh wave of frustration that threatens to wash away the ice in my veins at the audacity Doc has to play dumb. I run my hands through my hair, grabbing a fistful and tugging hard, desperately needing the pain to bring back the calm rage that I need to keep me sharp. I turn off the engine and calmly say to Doc, "I'll handle the funeral." She starts to say something else, but I hang up on her.

For a second, I allow the anger to take over. My fist strikes the center console and I grip the steering wheel in both hands, screaming with all the rage in my soul. "Fucking cunt!"

The wind blows the boat rental sign back and forth. Heavy droplets of rain strike the windshield noisily. I lean my head against the driver's side door and sob. "They killed my best friend—my only friend. My sister."

The phone rings again and when I look, I see it's Tyson. "Leave me alone," I yell into the receiver when I answer.

"Ari, wait. Odie's—."

I close the phone and throw it in the passenger seat. I don't want to hear the words they want to tell me. I roll my window down, allowing the rain to pelt me in the face. "She's not dead," I say to the howling wind.

She's not.

"She's not dead!" I scream at the thunder crashing above me.

Not to me.

For the next several minutes, or hours, I allow myself to rage and scream and sob. My chest tightens to the point of barely being able to breathe as a panic attack threatens to take over. Sobs wrack my body so violently, I throw open my door, fall to my knees in the parking lot, and vomit. I lay there in the rain for what feels like forever, letting the pain wash over me.

After some time, the cold from the rain sets in and brings me back to reality. My breathing slows down as air is finally able to fill my lungs and I no longer feel like I'm suffocating. The tears in my eyes dry as the icy rage creeps back into my body. My mind goes quiet as my thoughts slow to only Odie's words.

Plan and execute.

I wipe the tears and rain from my cheeks, stand up and climb back into the car. I grab my phone, take a few deep breaths as Odie's voice echoes in my head. *Plan and execute.*

The phone rings twice, and Femi answers.

Chapter Twenty-Eight
Executor Ari

Arranging Odie's funeral was one of the hardest things I have ever done. There were so many steps, so many choices to make—which coffin, lined, or unlined, burial vault or not. Femi and Doc wanted to be involved, but I wouldn't allow it. This was my responsibility as her best friend and sister.

I skipped the viewings and shit and had the funeral home transport the coffin straight to the cemetery. I don't believe in open caskets. No one should see someone they love lying in a box after their death—stiff, pale, and quiet. You need to hold onto the memory of them while they were still alive.

When I found Odie bleeding, surrounded by a pool of blood, she murmured one word to me.

Femi.

How cowardly do you have to be to stab someone in the back? Did he think if he saw her face, he would lose his nerve? I wanted to kill him that day, like immediately. But that would void all the things Odie taught me about learning to be patient and waiting for the right time to strike.

Being in the same room as him made bile fill my palate. Doc tried to offer me anti-anxiety medicine yesterday to ease the shaking in my hands, but I refused.

The shaking didn't come from a place of sadness, or panic. It came from the rage flooding my veins and slamming the valves of my heart open and closed like beating drums around a fire before a tribal war.

Odie's greatest advice to me, one that I plan to tattoo on myself one day, is to never let them see you coming.

Just killing Femi won't be enough. All his employees knew he was deceiving us and were involved in Odie's death, regardless of whether directly or indirectly. Therefore, they all must die. It will take time to get them all, but thanks to the flash drive that was in the general safe, I have a list, and I'm eager to check off their names like grocery items.

At the gravesite, Femi glances around, taking in the sparse crowd attending Odie's funeral. Most of the attendees are his employees. He places his arm around my shoulder, pulls me gently closer to him, and whispers, "Where's Doc?"

The clergy reads a verse from the Bible. I dab my eyes, purse my red lips, and gaze up into Femi's glossy eyes. He looks like shit. His eyes are crusty, red, and puffy, and his hair is rumpled. Dark circles that were evident at Christmas dinner now appear more prominent and while he is well dressed, his clothes are wrinkled. "She's a bloody mess," I say to him.

His face drops, and he tilts his head. "She's that upset?"

I place my palm on the back of his hand that's on my shoulder, give it a gentle squeeze, and nod, "In pieces; the poor thing." I sniff snot high in my nose and tip my black broad-brimmed hat down, concealing my eyes from the staring agent standing opposite from me. The investigators and their little minions litter the cemetery, scattered about like a bunch of flâneurs, waiting for snippets of information to flow from the lips of mourners.

No one is talking. Most of the people here are Femi's people. They're not mine or Odie's. We didn't have any people, not really. Sure, the girls were a part of what we did and our mission, but they didn't have a ride-or-die relationship like Odie and I. My mom and siblings wanted to come and support me in my time of grief, but I said no. All my life there were so many of us, but I always felt so lonely. They had to have seen it. The sadness in my eyes when I talked, and no one would listen. The only time they ever truly were there for me was when I was sick, and that's only because they had to be. I'd get accused of faking most of the time to try and get out of school.

Okay yeah, most of the time I was full of shit and just wanted attention. But the one time I complained I had lung pain when I breathed, my mom rolled her eyes and laughed it off. I didn't have a fever and feeling exhausted wasn't a good enough excuse to stay home, so she sent me to school anyway. I complained to my teacher, and she sent me to the nurse who didn't believe me either but called my mom home from work anyway. Turns out, I had pneumonia. By the time my mom got around to taking me to an urgent care clinic, I had already started throwing up.

There's nothing like the guilt of ignoring your child's cries for help to make a parent more attentive. But time fades and so do memories. Eventually, things went back to the way they always were, and the loneliness returned. In my opinion, their offer to come to the funeral was superficial and an empty gesture of support. They didn't want to come; they were just trying to satisfy the expectations of society and family. Gina and Audrey have strict instructions to stay away. Odie's loss made Gina want to go back home and return to her family anyway, so that's what she did.

Odie was like the glue that held us all together, bonded by trauma, tragedy, and the desire for blood and revenge. Audrey plans to meet up with me later, but I think I'm going to leave her behind. That's what Odie would have done. Anger bubbles under my skin, threatening to unleash and kill Femi right now. But I rein it in with a tight leash, until only the cold, icy rage takes over once more, and my head grows quiet. *Plan and execute*, I think over and over again.

My eyes get stuck on a bee dipping in and out of a partially open peony someone set on Odie's coffin. A tear flickers off my lashes as I blink repeatedly and shift uncomfortably under Femi's embrace.

He pulls me closer as intermittent people touch the coffin, say their goodbyes, and walk solemnly to their vehicles.

"You know, Ari, you will always have a place with us. We can work together—continue what Odie started," Femi says without looking at me. "I should call Doc. She needs to be here, or she'll regret not saying goodbye."

He thinks I don't know what they did—what they have been hiding from us all along.

I step away from Femi and head towards the casket. I rest a single red rose on Odie's coffin, offer a silent prayer, and promise to avenge her. I take a deep breath and remember my plan. With a final glance, I turn away from the casket, a small smile playing on my lips, and let loose a warm, airy fart, releasing my ass essence as I walk away from them for the last time.

Smell you later, bitches.

Someone gags and coughs, but I keep walking. You can't stop moving with these kinds of farts or those fuckers will catch up to you. You have to stay casual, so no one knows it was you. I peek over my shoulder, and

Femi's holding the guy who was standing behind us by the collar, whispering angrily.

As I head back to my car, I think about the games of chess Odie and I used to play. The thing about chess is that you have to think way ahead, plan your moves strategically, and execute them in a manner so cunning that your opponent never sees it coming.

When I dumped the file on the desk in the general's office, I wasn't surprised to see Femi's photo. I had my suspicions when I saw Luisa close a manilla envelope filled with information about us on the yacht. She bent the prongs the same way as him. It could have been a coincidence, but Odie always taught me there are no coincidences, only signs.

Clues.

At the time, I didn't have enough evidence to prove anything. But the picture I found in the general's safe of teenage Femi and Luisa standing between an older couple with pearly white smiles was damning, as was the familial resemblance between the four. And when I saw the photo of Doc sitting on Femi's lap on Luisa's yacht, my stomach dropped and my blood boiled. She not only worked for Femi, but she was Luisa's doctor as well. Everything that happened was a lie—the alleged gang rape, the beatings, the trauma, all staged by them to trick us. The man who Odie killed in the abandoned restaurant freezer was just collateral damage. As for the girls Femi allegedly let go, he handed them over to Luisa and she resold them. Nothing we have been doing has made a single fucking difference. The only ones who made it out for sure were Amelia and the kids trapped in Wallace's cabin in the woods.

It's all fucking bullshit.

My only regret is not getting to Odie before he stabbed her. I should have called to warn her, but Doc brought me to the general's house to remove the contents from the safe, and I didn't want her to know that I knew their secret. So, I stuffed everything back into the safe, except for the flash drive, and lied—telling her the drive was the only thing I found.

They used Odie—used us all to take out Luisa's competition. The Bunker Boys were messing with Luisa's revenue stream. Their operation, Benny and Griffins, as well as the others, gave buyers bargaining power because Luisa wasn't an exclusive provider of broken women. Benny and Griffin took their business a step further by kidnapping women according to what the buyer desired. Luisa snatched whoever, regardless of background, education, age, or artistic ability.

Femi took advantage of Odie's grief. I honestly believe he loved her despite his secrets, but family complicates things. So, when Luisa's number came up, and she was our next job, he had to choose.

And he chose family.

But there is one thing I've learned from all this; family and blood, don't necessarily equal loyalty. If I had to choose between Odie and someone from my family, I would choose Odie every single time. Some people say family is family, and you shouldn't choose anyone over them.

To those people I say, fuck you. Our definitions of *family* differ. Do you think I would choose my aunt I haven't spoken to since I was ten over Odie? Hell no. My aunt wouldn't die for me, save me, or kill for me.

That's why Eve sent two separate files, the one she wanted us to see that didn't include Femi and the one she sent to Audrey and Gina's that had damning evidence against him. Knowing the truth got her killed; protecting her *family* got her killed.

I climb into the driver's seat of Dick's Hummer and pat Doc's severed head beside me. "Femi asked about you." Her gaping mouth and horrified eyes stare straight ahead. "I told him you weren't coming."

Dried blood stains her hair. I move it away from her colorless face and tuck it behind her ear.

She shook violently when I stood over her with my brother's reciprocating saw. I didn't even gag her. There was no need. No one could hear us in the middle of the ocean—no one around for miles. As it turns out, stealing a boat was just as easy to steal as a car.

She was suspicious when I asked her to meet me at the boat launch. I told her I wanted to take a cruise out into the ocean before the funeral and watch the sunrise, but I didn't want to do it alone.

Foolish woman.

I injected her with the same substance we used to fill the lipsticks she helped me create to subdue our enemies and put her down like the fucking bitch she is. When she woke up, thrashing about as I tied her stupid ass down, she screamed, called me names and threatened to have Femi kill me.

Kill me?

That's fucking hysterical. I sat on her face with my bare-naked ass and farted. Have some pink eye, you fucking cunt. But fun and games aside, the moment I put a tourniquet around her left bicep, high up against her armpit, and pulled it tight, she changed her tune and started pleading for her life. She told me everything, from where Femi kept a briefcase full of cash, to where Femi and Luisa's parents still lived.

It didn't matter. The moment those glasses went over my eyes, and the saw roared to a start, I was in work mode. Her body bounced around the table as the blade made its way through flesh and muscle like butter. The bone required a little more elbow grease, but nothing I couldn't manage. Next time I'll have to remember to wear nose plugs because man, when that saw blade started heating up, the smell in the air quickly soured.

I've never heard someone scream so loud. She stayed conscious and alive longer than I thought she would. After removing her right arm, she started drifting off, so I slapped her across the face with her own hand. It's what Odie would have done and seemed fitting at the time. They opened for a brief second before she passed out. It was for the best.

After cutting off her legs, I opened my oversized storage bin on wheels and tossed her limbs inside. Then, I placed my hand on her head and rested the blade against her throat. I was just about to squeeze the saw trigger when her eyes sprung open without warning.

I peed a little; I'm not going to lie. Who wouldn't? I thought she was dead. I combed her hair with my fingers, kissed her forehead, and held eye contact with her as my blade sawed through her neck. Her head fit perfectly in the leather backpack Odie bought me for Christmas. After a quick dip in the ocean to wash off, I changed into the spare set of clothes I packed and headed back to shore. When I made it back to the beach, I called an Uber to pick me up and went to Mom's to shower and get ready for the funeral.

Henry peeks his head out from behind the box Doc's head rests in and cocks his head at me.

"No, you can't keep her. But I did save her arms and legs. They're in the trunk. I'll bleach the bones when we get home and build you a big cage."

I stare through the windshield. Femi's guard is passing him the phone he left in the car.

Odie once told me sometimes it's better to do things alone, then no one knows your secrets—be an army of one. Surprisingly, it was easier to do a job solo than I thought it would be. I guess I understand Odie's desire to always run off a bit better now.

A confused murmur ripples through the crowd still gathered for her funeral. Everyone moves closer to the casket, and I roll down the window. The sound is faint, but I can still hear it. The casket is ringing.

The phone slowly moves away from Femi's ear. It slides from his hand and bounces off the ground. The clergy rests his head against the shiny black and gold death box, confusion scrunching his facial features.

Femi's eyes widen and his head snaps in my direction. He shields his eyes from the sun and squints at me. I hold the trigger in front of my face, ensuring he gets a good look at it, and smile broadly. The clergy's head is still on the casket when I rest my finger gently against the button.

"Forgive me father for this is definitely a sin." I make the sign of the cross on my chest and press the button, blowing up Odie's coffin in an apocalyptic explosion. Multiple people launch backward, landing harshly on the ground; some are on fire—Femi's on fire, his men are on fire.

They're all on fire.

The clergy who had his head on the casket listening to the phone ring inside dies instantly. Doc's scorched torso lands on the gravel drive leading into the cemetery in front of me. People scream and run away from the area while others race closer and throw their blazers onto burning mourners, trying to extinguish the flames. I smile at their fruitless efforts to stop the shrills and wailing of my victims. The wonderful thing about my flammable chemicals is that even if you put the fire out quickly, they absorb into your skin and continue scorching through the epidermis, into the subcutaneous tissue, muscle, and finally bone.

Burn, baby burn. I slap the steering wheel and bob my head.

Burn, baby burn.

I chuckle to myself and shift the SUV in reverse before pulling out of the cemetery. A second explosion vibrates the windshield and rocks the SUV back and forth as I turn onto Main Street. I slam on the brakes, stopping myself from hitting a squirrel running across the road carrying a whole donut with pink frosting in its mouth. The box holding Doc's head tips over, dropping the severed remains onto the floor of the passenger seat. I watch the squirrel scurry up the tree, run across a thick branch, and leap onto a roof.

"Huh," I glance down at Doc's open mouth. "You don't see that every day." I take the gum from my mouth, roll it between two fingers, and toss it in Docs open yap. "Basket." I raise my arms congratulating myself.

A car horn beeps behind me, and I flip them off with my middle finger. "Fuck you, I'm squirrel watching here," I yell out my open window as the car drives around me. I scrunch my shoulders, remembering the rule I just broke. "I know, Odie. I know. Don't draw unwanted attention. I fucking forgot."

Henry leaps on my lap and licks my leg. "Hungry, Buddy?" I pat his head.

He cocks his head at me and licks me several more times. A police vehicle with lights and sirens blares past us heading towards the cemetery. I glance in the rearview mirror at my reflection and smile at the green eyes staring back at me.

The end, bitches...

Or is it?

I suck at sequels. So, if you hate this
one, don't leave a review, lol.
But if you loved it just as much or almost
as much as book one, please leave your
review.

P.S.

Of course, there's going to be a sequel
to the sequel.

Coming late Summer 2025
You Should've Stayed Dead...

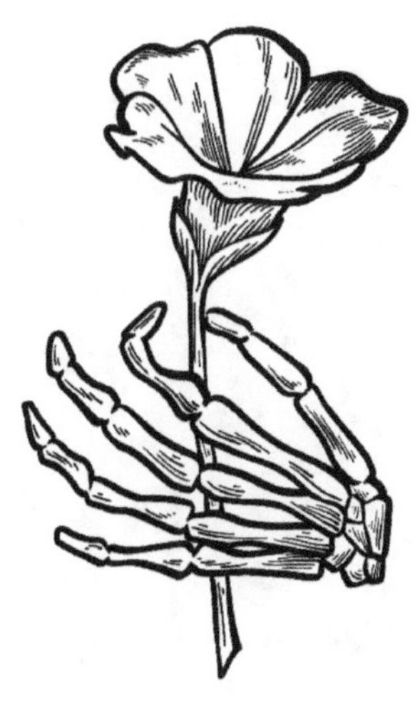